THE PRISONER OF SECRETS

THE PRISONER OF SECRETS

JOHN LOCKTON

Waterside Productions

ISBN-13: 978-1-960583-62-8 print edition
ISBN-13: 978-1-960583-63-5 e-book edition

Waterside Productions
2055 Oxford Ave
Cardiff, CA 92007
www.waterside.com

For Jayne, whose support made the book possible.

TABLE OF CONTENTS

Chapter One

The curse of Ham. That's what it was. Justin remembered old Noah and Ham from his days as an acolyte at St. Barts. Looked it up after what turned out to be the worst day of his life. His father's Bible was brand new. Never read.

"And Noah awoke from his drunken stupor and found his youngest son, Ham, had spied on him in his nakedness, and he cursed Ham's son Canaan even unto his descendants."

How much worse was the curse when you saw your father naked and spied on him "F"ing a woman not your mother?

Manhattan 1954. Labor Day weekend, blazing New York hot. Well over ninety degrees when the bus from camp dropped him off in front of his Fifth Avenue co-op. He smiled happily as he looked around, the late afternoon heat embracing him, welcoming him as though it missed him. He breathed deeply, pushing out stale bus air, taking in the acrid and sweet smells of New York, a well-remembered mixture of automobile exhaust, the scent of food preparation by every imaginable culture, beer, garbage, all with an overlay of what he always took to be the living smell of millions of sweaty people, the smell rising from subways, released by panting people on crammed buses, spewing out open windows of non-air-conditioned apartments crammed with unwashed bodies, a unique New York summer smell that brought him home. He tasted the air, savored the air. Pure joy.

He looked up. A yellowish cast to the Manhattan sky, New York spewing up its dirty air, baking its pollution in the heat. To him the sky was golden, not yellow. No sky like it, the golden aura of a magical place. He loved it. He loved everything about the city.

It sure was hot, hot, hot. The sun blazed the sky, a giant heat lamp. The hotter the better. It would drive the damn tourists inside and leave the city for the real New Yorkers like him. He could almost see the heat. Radiating from streets and sidewalks, reflecting back and forth between walls of glass, street and sidewalk the burners of an oven, buildings the reflecting sides, temperature pushed higher and higher by an absence of wind, blinding light exploding off every glass surface, car windshields, store fronts, stifling air at street level. Down Fifth Avenue people shimmered in the distance, ghostly mirages brought in from the Sahara, moving slowly, trying to manage perspiration in near one-hundred-percent humidity. And everything hung limp, flags, people's clothes, trees struggling to grow on the concrete plain, everything.

Boy, was he glad to be back1 For the last three months he'd been locked away at Camp Passumpsic. Before that almost nine months at Hudson Military Academy. One prison after another.

He took everything in as a starving man takes food. A new paint job on the building, lighter in color not because of use of a different shade of paint but because it involved painting over the true color of New York, the black of grime. On either side of the front door the substantial blue spruce in Romanesque containers looked like they'd grown. He always admired them but hadn't noticed the few almost hidden ornaments from the past Christmas, a promise of something beyond the season of heat. Now here was a New York scene! A very sophisticated-looking couple in fine attire was strutting down Fifth Avenue, the woman puffing away on a cigarette in an ebony-handled holder, balancing it delicately in a long-fingered left hand, displaying a large diamond ring and trailing the scent of what must have been a very generous application of perfume to offset the smell of her melting body, and pulling along a small dog that looked all fur, fluffy fur on four legs. Trailing slightly was a rotund man, much older looking (an expression on his face of what was probably much practiced resignation), his business suit an homily to fine tailoring, huffing and puffing along with a face so red Justin felt that he might keel over at any second. Only in New York would one dress up and strut down the avenue in ninety-plus degree heat. To set it off, in the gutter in front of the building two beer cans and a condom, rich kids in the building thumbing their noses at their parents. Nothing new.

George O'Scanlon was his favorite doorman, a great guy and friend. He finally appeared and came rushing out to the bus with his arms open in greeting. George was supposed to be standing outside the front door but cheated on hot days. Everybody loved him and forgave him.

"Glad you're back, me boy. You're just in time for another Irish drink-em-up." George's face was split ear to ear by a broad grin, the Irish showing in his reddish hair, now grey at the temples, and in his square open-gaze face. Justin had brought George a piece of cake from one of his three birthday cakes from yesterday's birthday party. (One cake for each five years of his now fifteen years). It was George who had given him his first beer, taking him to a party of Irish immigrants where everyone doted on him like he was a son of the old sod. How great was that?

And then there was Pedro, working the elevator. *"Buenos dias, Pedro. Como esta?"*

"Bien, Señor Whitthorne. *Estoy mui bien. Mucho feliz le ve."*

Pedro was always trying to teach him Spanish.

Not only did he have the best address in New York, Fifth Avenue and 69th street, but also the best co-op in the building, northeast corner, tenth floor, five bedrooms plus servants quarters, and stupendous views of Central Park. He paused at the door to the co-op, gnawing on a much chewed fingernail, dreading seeing his father and the woman. Entering he walked quietly as he always did. The co-op was so formal he always felt if he didn't walk quietly and talk quietly he'd get into some kind of trouble, he didn't know what kind, but trouble. So silently he marched across the large front hall, and silently he marched into the impressive living room decorated with Queen Anne and Chippendale antiques, impressionist

3

paintings on the walls, a Renoir over the fireplace. Light flooded the living room. Draperies wide open.

He froze. Not breathing. My God! They were doing it on the living room floor. How *could* they? There were plenty of luxurious bedrooms. He couldn't turn away. His eyes riveted on the scene.

His father lay naked on his back with the top of his head toward him, letting out low moans. The woman was on top facing him, moving backward and forward vigorously, screwing his father energetically, making panting sounds as she moved. His father had his hands on her large breasts, stroking, pulling, rising up to kiss and suck. Next to them an empty champagne bottle and strewn clothing. The woman's movements quickened as he watched. After a few minutes his father groaned loudly, almost a scream. The woman let out a definite scream and collapsed on his father. It was better than the porno movie he'd talked his way into over on Broadway.

The woman looked up. Her eyes went wide, mouth gaped open as she stared at him in shock, then her brows furrowed and mouth compressed. He saw pure hate.

He turned around as fast as he could, dropped his bag with a loud bang, and dashed for the door. From what happened later, he should have kept on going, going forever, and never stopped.

"What are you doing here!" the woman yelled. "Don't try and run away, you little son-of-a-bitch. Sneaking around and spying on us. The worst kind of shitty peeping Tom. Spying on your own father. I always knew there was something wrong with you. You're sick, sick like your crazy mother." Her anger was so great that she didn't bother to cover herself. He was sure he would remember the erect pink nipples for a long time. "You are never, ever going to spy on me again. Damn you. I promise you. I'm going to put you away permanently this time. Perverts get put away." She picked up the champagne bottle and threw it at him, missing as she was still rising naked off his father.

The putting away threat wasn't a surprise. The woman had been trying to put him away since she first came into his life when he was eleven.

4

His father eventually disentangled himself. Justin stood against a wall with his back turned. His father stood behind him, screaming into his ear, so close the spittle hit the back of his head. "My own son spying on me. What the hell is wrong with you? I didn't raise you to be a degenerate." His father spun him around with a hard pull on his arm. "I want to look at you." He looked him slowly up and down as though seeing him for the first time. "You're not my son. No son of mine would do that."

Justin heard his voice high and shaky. "I wasn't spying on you. They let us out early. They were supposed to have told you. There was polio in the girls' camp across the lake."

"Don't make excuses. What you did was inexcusable. I've tried to bring you up a gentleman. What I get is a perverted lout. Get the hell away from me." This was punctuated by a ringing slap across the face. There was muscle behind it.

As he turned to leave the woman stepped in front of him. Holding his eyes with a gaze full of malice. She spoke to him with the slow, momentous delivery of a sentence of death. "You're going to pay for this as long as you live." Then she turned her eyes to his father, drawing him in. "You'll never escape me. Your life will be cursed. *I promise you*. Wherever you are I'll find you. You'll be punished for as long as you live." She said the last with such strength of voice that he recoiled against the wall as though knocked against it. She tried to claw his face. He ducked away and dashed to his bedroom.

He entered his bedroom in real fear and with some pain to his face, hardly glancing at the sexy posters of Marylyn Monroe, Elizabeth Taylor, and Grace Kelly mounted on his bedroom wall, posters his father disliked, which was one reason he put them up. He flopped on his bed feeling no embarrassment for what he saw. He hated the woman so much he couldn't feel embarrassment about anything to do with her, no matter what. Same went for his father. His hatred for his father wasn't as great as for the woman but the hatred was there. What he did feel was anger at himself for letting it happen. Why hadn't he knocked? Of course, he never did. It was his home, or it used to be before the woman arrived.

What miserable thing did the woman intend for him this time? He always thought of her as "the woman." A woman that terrible didn't deserve a name. If she said she would put him away permanently and punish him forever she would. She had done many bad things to him in the past and always did what she said she would. He bit his fingernails ferociously and felt himself grow cold with dread despite the heat that blasted in through the windows of his South facing room. No more his beloved New York. No more seeing Jenny in her apartment downstairs. He was on the verge of crying, fought it, fifteen-year-olds don't cry. But he knew that everything dear to him was about to be lost.

CHAPTER TWO

His thoughts turned to his mother as they always did when he was troubled. He wasn't sure when his mother started being committed to mental institutions. From his first memories she was away for long periods. A tremendous loss. She was the person who gave him love, spending all her time with him when she was home, listening with apparent great interest to everything he said, teaching him to read before he was four, and telling him over and over again how much she loved him. He remembered times in the past when his mother and father seemed to get along fine despite her trips to the institution. It changed midway through his tenth year. Night after night his mother stood outside his parents bedroom door and cried before entering, and often he heard loud voices from their bedroom at night, his mother protesting something, and one night he was awakened by screams to see his father dragging his mother into their bedroom, dragging her by her arms on her back, his mother hysterical.

The diary he found when he was almost eleven answered the mystery of what was going on. His Aunt Gertrude in Greenwich was full of advice. She once said to him, "Life is a series of secrets that need to be uncovered." He was sure it was true, and he liked secrets. But he hoped they wouldn't be as terrible as this one.

The diary was seared word for word into his memory. Whenever he looked at his father the diary pages appeared as though emblazoned on his father's forehead, a criminal indictment drawn up by his mother from her mental distress.

At the time he found the diary his mother had been home from the institution for awhile. He'd done something he'd never done, went into his parents' bedroom when they were out. He didn't avoid their room because he'd been told to stay away. Rather he didn't have reason to go in. Somehow it didn't seem right.

That particular day he'd gone into their bedroom looking for a book his mother said she'd gotten for him. He couldn't find the book in any of the obvious places, and opened the drawer to his mother's beside table. Something odd, the drawer seemed to have a false bottom. He could see down through a crack at the front of the drawer to what appeared to be another level. How different things might have been if he hadn't been curious. His poking found a hidden latch at the back of the drawer and the bottom slid away to reveal a three-ring spiral notebook lying with a pen on top. It looked just like the notebooks he used at school but much thicker.

Very uncharacteristic of him to open the notebook. As a "good" boy he had a strong desire not to do anything wrong. Thinking about it now in his bedroom he puzzled for the umpteenth time what possessed him to open it. Open it he did.

The front page was an instruction to his mother from her doctors about how to keep the diary. Apparently it was part of her therapy. She was required to report what was happening to her at home and how she was reacting to what was happening.

He remembered only reading a few pages before bawling. Each daily entry was a description of things that happened that made her fearful, of her agony in trying to do the day-in-day-out tasks of life and not being able to cope, and worse, what she felt were her failures in not being able to take care of him. The most horrible passages were those dealing with his father. He was described as unsympathetic to her plight, critical of her illness-caused failures, and demanding of frequent sex that she found abhorrent. The entries were a story of her valiant struggle to remain at home as long as possible, trying to stay with him, fighting against the onslaught of the anxieties caused by her illness, anxieties that were being magnified by his father. He could see her courage and loved her more for it.

One long passage haunted him. It burned his mind every time he thought about it and he thought about it all the time. The passage started with the date and time, then:

He wanted to make love with me again last night, or at least he calls it love. This will be the fourth time this week. As you know I always have bad anxiety attacks when he approaches me to make love. You say my sexual difficulties with my husband are a cause of my illness. They probably are. But God knows I try. I try to be a good wife to him, to satisfy his desire. Once in awhile he is very tender to me, telling me how much he loves me. But usually it was like last night. He just came out of the bathroom with an erection. I tried to relax as you instructed. I tried not to protest or avoid him. Tried to think of the techniques you taught me to start to enjoy sex. But I couldn't help myself. I found myself jumping from the bed against my will as he approached. I cowered in a corner crying, giving him every reason I could think of why we shouldn't make love this night. He said nothing, grabbed me by the wrist and threw me on the bed. Then forced himself on me. It's always the same. Even if I follow your instruction, lying there quietly and trying to relax, trying to enjoy it, I always feel he is forcing me to make love. I hate it. I am panicked now at the thought that this will happen over and over again until I return to the hospital. I am desperate to stay with Justin but don't know how much longer I can stand it.

He couldn't bear to read more, and had run from his parents' bedroom to his own bedroom to hide under the bedcovers, crying for hours before having to appear at dinner. The bottom had dropped out of his life. And he had to pretend nothing happened. He shook at the table, not eating, his face tight with the effort of holding back his tears, being asked if he had a fever.

When he read it the first time he didn't fully understand the sexual abuse that was going on. But he could understand that his father had been attacking his mother. Now at fifteen his knowledge of sex had expanded and he understood the awfulness of what the diary described.

Waiting in his room for the verdict he went over to his dartboard, thinking about the woman. At first he threw for accuracy. Then the outrage filled him. Harder and harder. Soon he was throwing with his full strength, grunting with each throw, the point of the dart burying in the board. A dart flew wide, striking the wall, a small chip. Hitting the wall became the objective. He'd be punished but who cared. He pictured the woman impaled against the wall, darts hitting her like the arrows hitting San Sebastian, only worse, crying out for help. She deserved none.

CHAPTER THREE

No dinner that night, despite the fact he'd had little to eat on the bus trip back from Camp Passumpsic. Next morning Elizabeth, their wonderful black cook, his second mother, gave him breakfast, but nobody would talk to him all morning. About 10:00 AM they brought him into the living room, put him on a hard, straight-backed chair, and told him not to move. Living room purgatory!

He called across to his father, "How could I have realized you were in the living room. You know I always go quietly into the living room like that when I get home. I just wanted to say hello to you and Elizabeth. It was an accident. Please forgive me." His voice was still shaky.

His father's reply was to run his hand through his blond hair, a characteristic gesture, and sit silently staring at him, like his son was an alien creature or something.

Maybe his father would have said something if the woman hadn't been there all morning. But she was there, and they were making telephone call after telephone call. A little before noon the woman motioned his father into the study. He could hear them talking behind the closed door.

His father emerged, his mouth twisted down in a sour frown, and announced matter-of-factly, as though it was a common, every day occurrence, and with a good-riddance shrug of his shoulders, "We have a new school for you, Pomford Academy in Massachusetts." It now became clear why he'd seen his father and the woman on the phone all morning. He'd heard of Pomford. Boys he knew said it was the strictest prep school around, a penal colony in Central Massachusetts. Holy bejesus. Locked away for good this time.

He stared at the woman, trying to focus his hate in the strength of his stare. She didn't flinch, stared back just as forcefully. Then from her a small smile, a larger smile, a smile of triumph.

He'd first become aware of the woman shortly after his eleventh birthday, not too long after he'd found the diary. Toby of all people was his informant.

Toby was far from being his best friend. He was just always around. Justin would come downstairs from his co-op in the morning and there would be Toby, waiting for him. Did Toby have any other friends? Toby would latch on to him for the day, follow him around, talk at him constantly as though the more he talked the more Justin would like him. One stupid joke after another, and he would retell them, forgetting he'd already told them.

"What's the difference between eating roast beef and pea soup? Anybody can eat roast beef. Nobody can pea soup."

Toby would laugh as though his jokes were the funniest ever. Justin could rarely muster a smile.

Justin tolerated him because he had one special talent. Toby was different looking—small with a pudgy body and short neck, head too large for the body, oddly shaped, eyes slit-like in a fat face, hair thin of no color, his body usually standing hunched. Toby parlayed this into a Broadway-quality ability to mimic a Mongolian Idiot boy. Justin didn't know where Toby picked it up though was happy to accept its benefits. At the movies, Justin would be let in free as the caretaker of the horribly afflicted Mongolian Idiot, the ticket taker saying something like, "You are doing such a wonderful thing taking care of this boy." At the Central Park Zoo there was one ticket taker who always let them in. "My brother has a Mongolian Idiot." They made sure they knew the days he was taking tickets.

One game Toby played Justin didn't much like. Toby loved riding in elevators and seeing what was on various floors and who was there. They took their act to most office buildings and many hotels in Manhattan. Toby would enter the elevator with his full theatrics on display, often overdoing it with an active drool, push every button on the elevator to unfriendly looks and the obvious dismay of riders who put a high value on their time. At various floors Toby would hold the elevator door open for significant periods so he could look around. Sometimes he would wander off of the elevator and explore an office with Justin in tow. The impact seemed to be greatest in legal offices. Toby would stand in front of the receptionist, drool and stare, causing looks of horror, not sympathy from those used to dealing with well-tailored suits. Toby started seeking out legal offices.

A friend of Tony's father busted them. "Toby, my God. What are you doing? You're holding up the elevator for all these busy people. A stupid-ass trick. I've a good mind to thrash you here and now.' He balled his fists menacingly and took a half-step toward Toby who had flatten himself against the elevator wall. "Your father is sure as hell going to hear about this."

Outside the building, Toby said, "That guy never liked me. My father is going to ban me from ever doing another imitation." He said this sadly, head hanging down, tears in his voice. "Guess this means we won't be hanging out together much any more."

"Sure we will," Justin said, knowing it was a lie.

Toby probably suspected this, and that is what caused him to blurt out. "Your father's seeing another woman."

"What?"

"It's true. I was in the Waldorf riding the elevators, not playing my game, just looking around. Your father and a blond woman got on the elevator separately as though they didn't know each other. They got off together. I held the elevator door open and watched them go into a big suite on the top floor. Your father didn't recognize me. Too busy staring at the woman. Then I started going a lot to the Waldorf. It's one of my favorite places to ride elevators, all the different people from all over the world. They were pretty regular. Middle of the afternoon. One would get on the elevator then ten minutes later the other would appear and get on the elevator. "

"Why didn't you tell me before?"

Toby burst into tears. "I was afraid you'd be mad at me for spying on your father. You wouldn't be my friend any more."

"When was this going on?"

"It started last Spring, I remember the Waldorf was full of Spring flowers."

Not long after Toby's revelation the woman herself came waltzing into Justin's life. It happened at a big deal of a party of his father gave, his father inviting the cream of New York society. The feeling was of a coming-out party for his father. His mother had recently been moved to a mental institution for the more seriously afflicted and was scheduled to be there for four to six months before returning home. His father seemed to be celebrating. Terrible. Justin later believed he'd been invited because his father knew he wouldn't see him much any more. Worst thing he'd ever attended. Everyone seemed to know about his mother's semipermanent institutionalization. Most of the guests came up to them with direct or indirect expressions of sympathy and talked to him a little. A blond woman distinguished herself by failing to say anything to him, ignoring him completely, all her conversation directed to his father and about upcoming parties. She had an upper crust almost English accent like his father. He knew immediately she was the woman.

He didn't believe he'd met her before. Thereafter he met her all the time. She was in the co-op regularly with his mother away. The state of play became clear one weekend. He was sitting in the living room reading a magazine. A key turned in the lock and the woman swept in as though she owned the place. She seemed confident she did.

It didn't take long for her to oust him from the co-op. Who sends a boy away to a military academy at the age of eleven? The woman does when she wants to move her liaisons with the boy's father to the father's co-op. She must have gotten tired of going to the Waldorf to screw. He could hear her saying to his father,

"You have a beautiful co-op. Why don't we use it rather than playing hide and seek at the Waldorf. We'll send Justin away to school so he doesn't disturb us."

His expulsion was announced by the woman barging in one day and handing him a brochure on Hudson Military Academy. Simple as that. No previous discussion. She cut off escape to his bedroom so he had to take the brochure. Just like the hot potato game he'd played when young where the kid who holds the potato at "stop" gets eliminated, the woman's elimination game. She motioned his father aside. After a short talk the woman, not his father, said to him, "Next week you'll be starting Hudson Military Academy up the Hudson in Poughkeepsie. It's an excellent school. It'll teach you discipline, something all boys your age need. I've noticed you're spending too much time in your room. You seem to go there every time I'm here, and that sullen attitude you have when I talk to you. You need to learn respect. Hudson will drill that into you."

"I don't want to go. I like it here at St. Bernards. I'm doing really well. Father, can't I stay? And what happens when mother is home? How can I see her? Please don't send me." The woman shook her head at his father and his father said nothing. Tears trickled down Justin's cheeks and he ran to his room so they wouldn't see his anguished crying.

His father doted on the woman. He made moon eyes at her like some of his teenage friends did with their girlfriends. He'd lean down from his tall frame to hang onto her every word. And when she was away he was always quoting things she said or telling him how wonderful she was, all this with no seeming embarrassment in the fact that he was still married with a wife in a mental institution, and no acknowledgement that his only child might resent another woman taking over the home of the child's much-loved mother.

He could see how his father became entrapped by the woman. She was truly beautiful. He had seen her beauty at eleven. She was

the epitome of a New York society beauty—small boned, fine featured, not the pretty, soft look of some Hollywood stars but more
chiseled, the wide-eyed, high cheek-boned look of an aristocrat,
very Anglo-Saxon blond, and with a figure and bearing that commanded attention. She walked down the street as though she was
better than everyone else. She looked like she thought she was, and
he was sure many seeing her thought the same. Men half her age
turned around and stared.

His father was easy prey for the woman. He was a weak man.
No secret. He'd known it for a long time. He'd been at his Aunt
Gertrude's house in Greenwich, the best aunt anyone ever had. His
father's younger sister, who had four houses, each spectacular, and
she and her husband, Uncle Ben, doted on him. No children of
their own, they always treated him as a son.

That day he'd been practicing billiards in the game room
of her grand colonial house, went out the back door and quietly
approached the manicured garden where his father and Aunt
Gertrude were seated, not sneaky, just quiet. Aunt Gertrude had
established herself as the self-proclaimed guardian of all things
related to family. She readily admitted to family members that protecting the family name and reputation was a life goal. And she was
always reciting family stories of accomplishment and talking about
their position in society.

"You're wasting your life." Aunt Gertrude seemed very upset
with his father, her voice far louder than the calm, cultured one
she normally used. "All you do is go to parties and sit in your
clubs. No real job ever. You may think that time your uncle George
brought you into his brokerage firm was a job. It wasn't. He was just
being nice. Living on your good looks and your position in society
isn't living. It's lazy. And you always take the easy way out, avoid
anything that might ruffle your privileged life. I can name twenty
examples where you just ducked. Frankly, your whole life has been
weak and worthless. It's a disgrace to the family. I'd been hoping
you'd change with your wife ill and the responsibility of the boy.
Nothing. Don't you ever want to do something with your life as an

example for Justin? Justin's a great youngster. He deserves a better father."

His father jumped up with his face scrunched in anger, grabbed him by the arm and hurried him to the car and driver and proceeded back to New York, missing the luncheon Aunt Gertrude had planned, always the best. He didn't talk to his father the whole way in.

The woman was increasingly taking advantage of his father's weakness, controlling everything in his life, manipulating him to her whim and will. She loved to travel so they travelled extensively, the haunts of the idle rich, this despite the fact that his father told him not once but many times that all travel was overrated. Justin would be in the living room with them and she would pull out some papers and say something like, "There's a fabulous new resort hotel opening in Bellagio. I've gotten us invited to the opening. We're booked for Tuesday evening on Pan Am. Then I've gotten us in that suite I like at the Gritti," and so on. If the woman wanted to go, they went. His father was home very little except for the occasional periods when his mother was home. Then the woman would cease to exists for the duration to reappear the day after his mother went back to the institution. And when his father was home and his mother away the woman dragged him into the mad dash of New York society. "Here's the agenda for the week," she would say, handing his father a printed schedule. "The only night free is next Wednesday, and I've decided to invite the Carlisles, Farnsworths, Bullards, and Mc Calls over here for dinner," inviting people for dinner as though the co-op was hers. He never heard his father say no to anything.

He told his mother what was going on. She must have known because she didn't react with surprise. Her face grew sad, he thought she might cry, and in a quiet, serious tone she said, "I love you very much. You're all I care about. As long as I have you what your father does is unimportant to me."

After that, whenever he tried to bring up the woman and his father she brushed it off and turned to another subject. He concluded much later that she didn't go to lawyers because she feared that with her mental illness custody would be given his father.

He didn't know much about the woman. His father never talked about her background and none of his friends knew anything about her. Only by chance did he discover she was still married. Aunt Gertrude had come unannounced into the co-op. Very unusual. She'd stopped visiting when the woman appeared in his father's life. Somehow she knew the woman was attending a charity event that day and wouldn't be around. He couldn't help hearing what transpired. Most of what was said was said at very high decibels.

Aunt Gertrude started in on her father as soon as she got into the living room, not even bothering to sit down. "You've brought scandal to the family. No Whitthorne in history has ever paraded a married woman through society as you have. How can you get publicly involved with a married woman? And making it worse, your wife is in an institution and her husband is bedridden with a stroke. Shame. Shame on you. It's a sin against God. You're betraying your wife. You're destroying the family name. Don't you care about the family? Everyone in the family is being hurt by your behavior. I hear their complaints and they're growing. You're always the one talking about protecting the family name. You can protect our name by dropping her."

His father said, "It's okay. Her husband has the best medical advice. Before he became Under Secretary of State he headed a law firm that did a lot of work with the medical community. He knows exactly his prognosis. He'll be bedridden the rest of his life. So he released his wife. Told her to go out and enjoy herself. A fine gesture. There's nothing wrong."

From his aunt, "Who told you the husband had released her? The woman, right? Have you talked to the husband? No. She gave the same story to a few other people and they doubt her. Her

18

husband is apparently the jealous type. The scandal isn't going to go away. People tolerate it because of the social positions you both have. But the gossip is fierce. For your son's sake, and the sake of the family, do the honorable thing. End it."

His father replied, his voice now even louder and angrier than Aunt Gertrude's, "I'll ask you to stay out of it. I need her. I'm not going to let her go no matter what you or anyone else says, and that's that."

Aunt Gertrude stormed out and his father punched a pillow on the couch.

Whatever the truth to the story of the husband's by-your-leave Justin could see that the woman was indeed enjoying life to the fullest, enjoying life to the fullest at his expense and the expense of his mother.

As the week and months passed, he locked away at Hudson Military, the woman triumphant in his co-op, his resentment grew, fueled each time he saw her sashaying through the co-op in place of his mother and the increasing manipulation of his father. How many times did he say to his father, "Does she have to be here so much?" It got him nowhere. His father's response was, "She's a wonderful woman. With you mother away you should be happy she's here to help."

Help. She was making his life miserable! The only one good thing in his terrible life was that when his mother was home, and it was getting less and less frequent, the school released him for most of her stay and let him do his school work from home. He'd had to fight for that.

It was only at thirteen that he learned the full enormity of what was going on. His mother had been home for the previous ten days and had just returned to the institution. He'd been allowed down from Hudson Military for part of her stay and was still at home. Curled up in the high-backed Queen Ann chair by the fireplace in the library he'd been nursing his sadness and reading a book. The phone rang. His father came in and answered it not realizing he was there. From his father's voice he could tell he was happy to find who was on the call. At first the conversation was about his mother's condition and the fact she was getting worse. Justin thought his father was talking to one of her psychiatrists. Then his father said. "It's working just as you suggested. I came on strong almost every night. She's back in the institution, hopefully permanently this time." This was followed by discussion of upcoming events on the New York social calendar. His father put down the phone and started whistling to himself. The call was with the woman!

The horror tale he read in the diary was a report of the success of his father and the woman in plotting to institutionalize his mother.

He went cold, and when his father left went into his room and cried off and on for hours, a combination of rage and fear about what would happen to him if he confronted them. The woman would do something terrible if she found out that he knew. Definitely lock him away and maybe worse. Night after night the plot was all he could think about. Sometimes it would wake him up. The secret festered inside him. He couldn't stand holding it any longer. He had to stop the hurting of his mother. He had to be brave whatever the consequences. For weeks he thought about what he'd say to them, practiced it, building up his courage, ready to tell them that he knew everything.

He picked a Saturday afternoon when his father and the woman were seated in the living room, unusual as they were often out and about on Saturdays. He seated himself facing them, then stood in front of them only a few feet away. His fear had him shaking slightly. "I have something to say to you," this said in a nervous thin voice that he later wondered if they even heard. They didn't look at him and continued talking about some upcoming party. He sat back down, courage failing.

After that the only revenge he took, a small revenge, was to refuse to answer the woman's questions and to leave the room whenever she entered, hiding out in his room or joining friends elsewhere as much as possible. Driven out of his own co-op by God! When he had to be in the same room with her he watched her with looks of enragement, looks he was sure she understood.

Several months into this he was down from Hudson Military for a weekend at home and in the living room with both of them. The woman asked him something. As usual he gave no reply. When she asked again he turned away and mumbled a partial answer. His father jumped from his chair. "I've had enough of this! Go to your room. And no dinner."

A little while later his father banged into his room, his face in a grim scowl. He grabbed him by the shoulders and shook him hard. "What the hell is wrong with you? I will not have you treating her that way. You're being a real jerk. Where's your breeding? Go out and apologize. Promise her you'll never act this way again. She's tolerated it to date. She's a fine lady. She understands it's difficult for you to see her replacing your mother. But enough is enough. If she sees any more surliness, all weekends from Hudson Military will be canceled. She'll call them and have them hold you there on weekends. You understand?" He nodded. "You've got to get over this nonsense of resenting her because she's replacing your mother."

The nonsense was what his father was saying. He almost blurted out what he knew. As before he didn't have the courage and ended up making the required apology. With every word of his apology he felt a betrayal of his mother. He went back to his room and pounded his fist against a bedpost until his knuckles were raw.

He'd almost let it out several times later. Time and time again he didn't have the courage. He berated himself repeatedly, talked to himself, even swore at himself. "You miserable 'F' ing coward." He said it over and over again as though he could swear himself into action. No action. He couldn't get over the certainty that if he confronted them he'd cut himself off entirely from his father and bring awful retribution from the woman. He would have to carry the terrible secret alone, probably for as long as he lived.

One day not long after that he was walking with Chauncy Johnson, a former St. Barnards schoolmate, going out for ice cream in Central Park. Halfway Chauncy stopped, looked him up and down, and said, "You've changed. You used to talk to me about everything. You don't anymore. I do most of the talking. Where's the fun? What gives?"

He'd responded, "Just some things with my family. I don't want to get into it, okay?"

Gradually Chauncy drifted away, as did a number of his other friends. With what was going on it was difficult to talk to friends about the normal subjects— girls, school, sports, movies. It all seemed frivolous in comparison to his secret. He was sure that the boys at Hudson Military sensed his insecurity. Why else had some of them started ribbing him, making him the butt of jokes, a prime target in snowball fights and for general hazing?

An unhappy existence. Caught between Hudson Military which he'd grown to detest and a home that'd been taken away from him.

CHAPTER FOUR

Aunt Gertrude had told Justin, "Life is a series of strings. How they tie together makes your life." For Justin, one string threaded through a doctor's office in Pomona, California, in the year 1933.

The plaque on the door of the doctor's office said "Henry J. Benson, M.D." Sometimes this brought a knock on the door from the sick or the injured. The office was only a short walk from the main street of Pomona in an attractive white building, a one-time residence of a leading citizen. He always greeted people who came to his door as politely as possible, trying to show genuine concern, telling them he was not the kind of doctor they were looking for, and recommending someone who was.

That day, October 2, 1933, the one knocking was Dodi Hicks, an overweight, meddling senior employee of the California Department of Public Health, his principal contact with the department.

He never knew what "Dodi" was a nickname for. He never cared to find out. Dodi was noxiously bureaucratic and full-of-himself. Whatever Dodi was up to was the most important thing in the world. He was important so the task he did was important. Today the most important thing in Dodi's world was the Nazi delegation.

Dr. Benson would have been happier to have met the Nazis in his office. Photographs of California adorned the walls, pictures of landscapes and mountains that he'd taken on various hikes around the state, some being twins of his work for sale in local galleries. Directly across from his desk, smiling at him throughout the day, was a photograph of his darling wife, Helen, the love of his life and defender against the demons that haunted him. Next to her picture was a picture of a fourteen-year-old girl in the dress of the 1920s. He fingered a livid four-inch scar on the right side of his head as he looked at it. On a side wall was a picture of the members of the California Eugenics Foundation, seated front center David Starr Jordan, first President of Stanford. On either side Charles Goethe, first Chairman of the Board of California State University, Ulysses Sigel Webb, Attorney General of California for thirty-seven years and throughout an ardent supporter of eugenics, Robert Andrews Milliken, Head of the Department of Physics at Cal Tech and a winner of the Nobel Prize, Lewis Terman, developer of the I.Q. Test, and a number of other Californians of similar eminence.

The office was set up with comfortable chairs and couches so positioned that one could have a meaningful conversation in relaxed surroundings. He'd held many meetings there with senior state officials, leading citizens of California, and representatives from important eugenics foundations and government organizations from around the U.S. Once the governor of California, James Rolph, had visited. But it wasn't good enough for Dodi. He wanted pomp. He argued with Dodi about this, believing the German delegation wanted its visit to be without publicity. He'd lost.

They walked over to the Town Hall for the 11:00 AM meeting (Dodi waddled) and arrived at the same time as the four-man German delegation who had driven from Los Angeles. Dodi had festooned the room with alternating Swastikas and American flags. How stupid. The Germans were obviously surprised, confirming his view they didn't want their presence widely known. Dr. Benson entered the room with a mixture of nervousness and excitement, his stomach was roiling. Would his life-long stammer rage to the point of blocking speech?

He'd been planning the meeting for a month. Over the years he'd made many presentations to the high and mighty of government and industry, all without problem. This was different. For the first time he memorized everything he was going to say. First writing it out. Then going over and over it in his office, trying it out, practicing not only words but tone. He wanted to get across the importance of eugenics to civilization and make it seem easy, not revealing the difficulties they'd had getting it launched in the U.S. and the growing back-lash against forced sterilizations.

The previous evening after dinner Helen had asked him about it with concern in her voice. She knew him so well. He was sitting on the Mexican rebozo-covered couch in the living room. At first he talked seated then got up and paced around the living room.

"I know I've been all tensed up and distant these last few weeks. I'm sorry. This meeting tomorrow has got me bugged. It's the most important thing I've ever done, far and away the most important. It's got to go right. If it succeeds it'll be the culmination of everything I've worked for. If it fails, I honestly believe my dream will die with it. I've not said this to you before, but I have serious doubt California is ever going to get where it needs to be in eugenics, and other states are even further behind. God knows I've worked hard. We've a long way to go to sterilize all defective women in California."

Helen said, "You've done what you can do. It takes time."

He shook his head, his stutter appearing. "There's too much b-bureaucracy, too much disorganization, too much sentimental clap-trap about s-sterilization being wrong. The only way we'll get there is if someone shows the way. That could be Germany. My hope is to persuade the Nazis to take our eu-eugenics laws and approaches and run with them. Maybe we can get them to put in a really strong, national eu-eugenics program. They're a highly organized country, an order driven country. They can get away with much more than the bureaucrats have allowed us to do here. If we can get Germany to apply the laws and approaches of California full bore it will produce a robust national eu-eugenics program. Then we can turn the German experience back on the U.S., confront the n-nay sayers with proven success. To me it's the only way. I've thought about all the possibilities. Not trying to be overly dramatic and w-worry you but I truly believe how this meeting goes will determine whether American eugenics lives or dies a slow, painful death."

A loud. "Damn it." He'd felt the memories grouping, opening the doors to his conscious mind, the demons advancing in full array. *God help him.* Something he hadn't experienced in a long time. He stopped the conversation and dropped back down on the couch, body hunched forward from the waist. He started trembling, covering his eyes with his hands as though the world was too frightening to glimpse. The memories pushed everything else from his mind, yanking him from the present, no more of this world. He was usually able to block them out. Not this time. Too many worries about the future of eugenics and all the tensions of these last few weeks.

One psychiatrist among many he'd consulted said he was suffering from constant trauma from his memories, a circle of memories producing trauma that in turn brought more memories producing more trauma. Whatever it was once he started thinking about his sister the horror film reeled through everything. No escape. Every detail had to be visited. Over and over again he had to live her death as though he was standing there watching her die.

His memories always started the same way, 1910, a beautiful fall Baltimore day. He raced into Patterson Park behind his sister. Leaves of autumn kicked along as he charged down the dirt path. Not many people around in the early morning. The two of them had gobbled their breakfasts and raced from the house in the hope of being the first youngsters to the swings and other apparatus on the far side of the park. He thought his sister was the prettiest girl around, shining blond hair almost down to her waist. She'd just turned fourteen. He was almost twelve. His sister was hurrying him along with gestures and encouragement, "Come on Henry," almost as though she were his mother, and he did think of her that way. His mother was cold and demanding. His father was away most of the time on sales trips. It was his sister who gave him most of his love.

The path took them through a section of dense woods, trees close together and brush on either side of the path grown thick in the humid Baltimore air. Suddenly, a man blocked the path. Going quickly along they almost ran into him. Large, mortuary white of complexion, almost albino despite dirt on hands and face, hair matted and sticking out as though he'd been sleeping in the woods, filthy clothes, face twisted in an odd way, one eye higher than the other, nose not on straight, one side of the mouth bent upward, looking as though someone had squashed his head in the birthing, the most frightening looking thing the boy had ever seen. He froze in panic.

The man grabbed his sister's arm. He started to run away. The man's voice followed him, thin and high. "You run away I'm goin to hurt your sister something terrible. You want that?"

He returned.

"I've been waiting for you two. You come by here every morning to play. We can play together. I have some great games to show you."

He said this with a large, lopsided grin, perhaps the only grin he could make with his twisted mouth.

His sister started screaming, and he ran at the man punching and kicking for all he was worth. The man threw his head back and laughed, then reached back to his rucksack and pulled out a white cloth which he put over his sister's face. She slumped to the ground. Then it was his turn. The cloth smelled of some chemical. He fought it, felt himself losing consciousness.

He awoke in a small shack, dirty burlap bags on the floor and old board siding, warped to allow cracks of light into the dusty interior. They were somewhere near a railroad track as he could hear the movement of trains.

His sister's arm had been tied, but not her legs. Both his arms and legs were tied. The man was undressing his sister. And when he had her undressed he started running his hand over her body, her breasts and between her legs, making mewing sounds as he did this, and sometimes looking over at him with a crazy grin on his face as though one man to another he thought he would enjoy watching. Then the man pulled down his pants and lay on top of his sister, moving vigorously and panting loudly. His sister had been crying and now started screaming and kicking out with her legs as much as she could, which wasn't much. Finally the man groaned and rolled off her. The boy could see blood between her legs.

All the time he'd been yelling help as loud as he could, but with little hope it would be heard over the noise of the trains.

The man turned to him and said scowling, "You do that any more and you're dead."

The man tied his sisters legs. She was still moaning. Later she asked, her voice shaking, "What are you going to do with us?"

"I ain't decided. May kill you. May not. I have these voices inside me that tell me what to do. I'll know."

He pulled a sandwich from his rucksack and ate it, not offering them any. But did give them a little water. As the day wore on the man twice again mounted his sister. By now there was a copious blood flow, and his sister was lying staring vacantly at nothing as though life had been driven out of her.

The man pulled out another sandwich for dinner. Then took out a flashlight and started examining him, stoking his legs and buttocks. "Used to do it with a fellow in the asylum. You're sister's not much good anymore. Maybe I'll do it with you in the morning."

The man lurched over to a corner and fell asleep, some burlap bags cushioning his head. Henry was awake all night, the dread growing as morning approached, remembering the asylum remark.

When the man awoke he was a different person, furtive, peeking repeatedly out the door in obvious worry. The boy heard him say repeatedly to himself, "Can't let them get me. What to do." Then shake his head as though willing it to tell him.

After what seemed like an hour of this the man straightened and looked around in a new way. A broad smile on his face he stared first at his sister and then at him, and started whistling softly. Cold fear grabbed the boy. The man pulled a small knife out his rucksack, sat down next to his sister still lying on her back, and while looking at the boy as though thirsty to see his reaction, cut her throat. He screamed.

The man leapt up. "Told you not to do that." The man grabbed a heavy board, and the last thing Henry remembered was the board coming down on his head with the man still smiling.

That he was alive was due to a railroad policeman checking for hoboes. When he woke up in the hospital, swaddled in bandages, the policeman visited, apparently asking to be called if he recovered. (A matter he later learned was in some doubt). Charlie Williams was his name, a big rough looking fellow whose kindly eyes looked ready to tear in telling how he heard his moans and carried him a mile to his car, all the while trying to hold his head steady to prevent further injury to what he thought was a fatal head wound.

He'd started wailing in pain as the memories overwhelmed him and Helen had come hurrying over, putting her arms around him, cradling him like a baby, what she always did when he had these attacks. He'd looked up at her. "My sister's death can't be in vain. We must prevent people like that madman from being born. I have to succeed with the Germans." He'd stood up and spoke strongly. "I've just got to Helen. If I can just convince them tomorrow how much better the w-world would be. Germany a model for the elimination of defective people."

Helen had said, "You *will* succeed. I'm sure of it. And if it gets tough remember I love you," then a big smile, a warm kiss as they got to bed, and a restless night for Henry worrying about the day that meant everything.

CHAPTER FIVE

D r. Benson and the Germans met in the early afternoon around the long Pomona Council Chamber table. He sat at the head, Dodi at the other end, and the Germans on either side. Dodi started the meeting with introductions, first an introduction of him, a glowing description of his role both as principal spokesman for the eugenics program in California and as the lead surgeon among the many surgeons conducting sterilization operations. Then the Germans introduced themselves. All were well dressed, business suites much better tailored than what Dr. Benson could afford. All spoke excellent English. And all were young. The leader of the delegation, Dr. Gerhard Mulder, looked to be about his age, thirty-four. Dr. Mulder introduced himself as a surgeon, as was the other doctor in the group, Dr. Dieter Hauptmann. The remaining two were Nazi party functionaries.

He liked Dr. Mulder immediately— an open, honest face and as the meeting went on none of the imperious, bombastic, overbearing nature he'd imagined to be characteristic of Nazis. Quite the contrary, Dr. Mulder talked in a quiet unassuming voice, smiled in what was almost a shy way about certain things, sometimes said self-deprecating things about himself and projected humility rather than Nazi arrogance. Dr. Mulder and Dr. Hauptmann could have been twins. They looked exactly alike. Same blond, blued-eyed Aryan look, same height, five eleven. The only difference he could detect was that Dr. Hauptmann bore a scar on his chin that he assumed was a university dueling scar. He must have flinched. The brave ones held their head still and displayed their courage by a scar on their cheek. He realized he, himself, looked a lot like them, though they didn't have his large English nose, the source of occasional jokes from Helen. The two Nazi functionaries also had the Aryan look, one very blond and the other sandy haired.

Dr. Benson took a deep breath and delivered a brief welcome to the Germans, inquiring whether they were happy with their accommodations. Getting a host of "*Jas.*" To his relief his stutter was largely absent.

Dr. Mulder responded by thanking them lengthily and in rather flowery English for their hospitality and saying how beautiful he found California, a place he always wanted to visit. Then Dr. Mulder read from a prepared statement.

"When Chancellor Hitler was chosen to lead Germany a few months ago, one of his goals was to bring in modern methods to create a better state. He believes strongly that the German race has certain strengths which must be preserved and enhanced. One way he believes this might be accomplished is through eugenics. We are part of a commission that has been set up to explore introducing wide-scale eugenics to Germany. Our role within the commission is to study what is being accomplished in the U.S. Along the way we've already visited New York and several Southern states. California has been chosen as our base as we and Hitler view it as the epicenter for eugenics in the U.S. And we particularly wanted to meet with you as your work is recognized in Germany."

Good start. Dr. Benson felt a small burst of pride, unusual for him as he considered himself a humble man. He knew he had reason to be proud. His methodology for patient interaction and sterilization surgery was now followed by most other states. A little international recognition was fine so long as it advanced the cause.

Dr. Benson replied to the comment about California being the epicenter, "Well you're right there. Thirty-two other states are sterilizing unfit people, but we've done approximately 80% of the combined total of eu-eugenic sterilizations in the U.S., and by the way, call me Henry. I don't want today to be taken up with presentations. If you're agreeable we'll make it more of an informal discussion. I think we'll get more out of it if everyone can jump in at any time with questions and c-comments."

Dr. Mulder said, "*Ja*. Sounds good. Please call me Gerhard. We Germans tend to be too formal." He paused. "Germany is still in the early stages of developing eugenics programs, far behind England and America. For several years America has been pressing us to bring eugenics to Germany. Your Rockefeller Foundation has been in the forefront, giving us almost two million dollars to found two eugenics research institutes, the Kaiser Wilhelm Institute for Anthropology, Human Heredity and Eugenics in Berlin, and the Institute of Brain Research, another part of Kaiser Wilhelm Institute. They've also been funding Otman von Vershuer, our leading geneticist and his brilliant assistant, Josef Mengele. Their work, particularly on twins, has been groundbreaking. Much support is coming from your Carnegie Institution eugenics laboratory at Cold Springs Harbor, New York. They've started sending us results of their work. And they entered into an open-ended contract with Germany to help introduce a national eugenics program. Many Germans are scheduled to visit their laboratory to learn eugenic science. On the way back we're going to stop to thank them.

"Despite all your help Germany hasn't gotten very far. It's been a lot of talk and a lot of study in the institutions. I'm sorry to say very little action. Under the previous Weimar regime there just wasn't the will to sterilize a lot of people. We haven't even passed the first eugenics laws in Germany to allow us to start sterilizing. When did you pass your first laws authorizing compulsory sterilizations?"

"1907 in Indiana."

"We're so far behind."

Henry interrupted, stuttering slightly, " If y-you're going to Carnegie Cold Spring Harbor for help you're going to the right place. They're the intellectual center of eugenics in the U.S. The eugenics laws in California and other states are the re-result of their work. One interesting thing you should look at when you're visiting. They've amassed a vast data base on people and families, been working on it since 1904, people's genealogy, hospitalizations, welfare office records, criminal records, and m-much more. They're studying how society can be improved by eliminating certain types of individuals, families, bloodlines, even whole p-peoples. How to improve the gene stock."

The blonder of the two Nazis turned to his compatriots and said something in German, his voice animated. A ten minute discussion in German ensued.

At the end Gerhard turned to Henry and Dodi and said, "The problem for us with a data base like Carnegie's is we don't have thirty years to build it up as Carnegie had. Our commission is suppose to come up with recommendations that Chancellor Hitler can put in place quickly if he wants to. But one advantage we have in Germany. I think you call it a 'leg-up.' Interesting term 'leg-up.' I picture a man not advancing at all but teetering on one leg." He gave a small laugh.

"In Germany most people keep careful record of their ancestry. We could introduce laws requiring people to disclose their ancestry to get a marriage license, or as a condition to government employment, and for many other things. Germans are used to getting government approval for a host of activities, I believe far more than in America. And municipal records are extensive and go back generations so we will be able to check the accuracy of information received. We should be able to build a national data base very quickly. It will be up to Chancellor Hitler to decide whether to do it." Henry felt some hope that marrying by ancestry was to happen, a great step forward.

Gerhard leaned forward toward Henry, enthusiasm in his voice. "Have you read *Mein Kampf*?"

Damn. He should have read *Mein Kampf* before the meeting. He admitted he'd not and got angry looks from the two Nazis as he expected he would. Had he lost them? He tried to look as apologetic as he could, "I know Hitler's a great man. I've wanted to read *Mein Kampf* for some time. After having the chance to meet you, an example of the new Germany, I'm going to read Mein Kampf as my highest priority." Friendliness returned to the discussion.

Gerhard said, "When you read *Mein Kampf* you'll see Chancellor Hitler studied American eugenics law. Some of his views are based on American eugenics." Gerhard turned again to his prepared statement, "In one passage, for example, he says, 'There is one state in which at least weak beginnings toward a better conception of improving progeny are noticeable. Of course, it is not our model German Republic, but the United States.' Recently he said at a Nazi party meeting. 'I have studied with great interest the laws of several American states concerning prevention of reproduction by people whose progeny would, in all probability, be of no value or be injurious to the racial stock.' He is particularly interested in the laws and approaches of California and suggested we might copy them."

Henry felt a surge of optimism. He leaned forward in his seat and paused, looking each German in turn in the eye, his voice rising, "We are flattered. I have de-devoted my life to eugenics and think eugenics is as important to creating a civilized world as is ending starvation and combatting disease. Not all political leaders in America see it that way, even in California, and we are only one of forty eight states. What is needed is for someone to establish a national program under a strong leader. Your Chancellor could be that leader. You have an opportunity going fo-forward that California doesn't have. I'm hoping you'll take what we have in California, expand it, put substantial resources behind it, organize it with your entire government behind it from top down. Your program would be a model for the rest of the world. California would thank you and fo-follow. Other states, and I think other countries, would thank you and follow."

A woman brought coffee and donuts to a side table and the meeting took a break. Henry rather wished there hadn't been the interruption. He'd seen from the German's glances at each other he was making progress. Several of them held up their donut and looked at it as though they hadn't seen one before.

Henry said, "These are donuts from April's Donut Shop here in town, the best donuts anywhere. Don't you have donuts in Germany?"

Gerhard said, "There are sweet rolls like this in Germany but without a hole. They're called Berliners. We Germans love our sweets. If you put a hole like this in baked goods in Germany people would feel cheated. Probably riot. We've rioted about many things in recent years." He said this with a wry smile. Was Gerhard thinking about the infamous riots that brought in the National Socialists? Dodi had quickly consumed three donuts and was reaching for a fourth when Henry glanced at Dodi's protruding belly and commented, "It's said the healthiest part of the donut is the middle."

That got a smile from the Germans and an angry look from Dodi.

Henry sat back in his chair and said in a more reflective tone, reciting some of what he'd memorized in preceding weeks, "I've been involved in eugenics for fi-fifteen years going back to college. The dream I've followed is of a world purified from what I call defective people. Our list in California includes those with de-degenerative physical illnesses, mental incompetence, de-degenerate personal behavior, that's homosexuality and lesbianism, multiple children that society has to foster, public immoral behavior, that's prostitution, and repetitive criminality, particularly when drugs are involved. You will want to put together your own list based upon your needs. Don't just take ours." The two Nazis had pulled out pads and were taking notes.

"In California we estimate that between one and two percent of people of child-bearing age are what we classify as defective. California has a population of six million. Somewhat less than four million are of child- bearing age, so that would be up to 75,000 de-defectives. Applying the same analysis to Germany, with your population of seventy million you will probably find a defective population of up to 800,000. Think how much better Germany would be if none of these defectives had p-progeny."

A few smiles and nods from the Germans.

There's another consideration. The future cost to Germany of maintaining defective p-progeny. I understand Germany is suffering even more than the U.S. in this terrible global depression. Think of the money Germany could save in the cost of asylums, prisons, doctors, nurses, wardens and guards, and much more, money that could be spent on improving the lot of worthwhile citizens."

Gerhard asked, "Have you quantified that?"

"No, but it would be many millions of dollars."

So he'd given them elimination of defectives and saving money. It was time to bring up positive eugenics. "Positive eu-eugenics are just as important as negative eugenics. The brightest and the best should only marry the brightest and the best, and their children should again marry the brightest and the best. Selective breeding can create a highly intelligent group or class to lead the world of tomorrow. As you may know this thinking is behind the English upper class. In the 1880's an Englishman name Galton, a cousin of Darwin, developed the idea that Darwin's principles of evolution could be applied to the breeding of people. Some call it "applied evolution." The English upper class bought into it lock, stock, and barrel. If people of the upper class married others of the same class, never diluted their g-genes by marrying below their station, the intellect and capabilities of the upper class would grow with their offspring and they would dominate England forever. Lower-class people would be kept in their place. The English snob is eugenics in action. Their eu-eugenics is great but the English snob is to be avoided." Henry chuckled and found several of the Germans joining him, probably having experienced the English snob.

Gerhard said, "I read some of Galton's analysis on intelligence of the upper class being passed through the generations. Thought it was weak."

"I agree. But I think in general he was right. We just don't have the necessary analytic tools yet. I'm sure some day we'll have them. What we'll find is that characteristics like intelligence, em-empathy, cultural adaptation, creativity, and maybe even character, are inherited just like physical appearance. My belief is that the mind is still evolving and natural selection, or man-made selection, works for the mind as well as the b-body.

"In the U.S. we have been promoting positive eugenics in many ways. One example is we have positive eugenic contests at county fairs across the country. We call them 'Best Family' contests. Competing families are judge on the intelligence, appearance, genetic history, health, and other qualities of family members. Quite large cash prizes are awarded."

As Henry spoke he could feel his enthusiasm building, his voice growing louder, the stutter almost disappearing. The full German delegation was now responding with nods of agreement and wide smiles. Excellent. They seemed to be eating it up. Time to feed them the big picture argument.

Henry leaned forward, smiled at each of them individually, focusing intently for a few seconds on each German's eyes as before. "When people ask about eugenics, what you need to say is all we are talking about is good birth. A noble concept indeed. As you probably know, the word 'eugenics' comes from Greek roots of 'good' and 'birth.' And it's really very simple. If parents are encouraged to provide the be-best environment for their children, good nutrition, health care, a loving family situation, why not encourage them to have children with good genes. This is a moral imperative. Promoting good birth secures the well-being of future generations. It should be a national goal of every country."

Now a dose of how to do it. "You'll need an extensive public-education program on eugenics. In the U.S., our initial focus was on convincing people what we were doing wasn't new, that civilizations throughout history have seen the need to keep themselves genetically strong, an intellectual argument. We cited the established programs of England, and the ancients did their part." Henry smiled. "We dragged Plato out of his grave and re-referred to the *The Republic* where he espoused selective mating to create a 'guardian class,' and denial of mating to those of inferior capability. Then Sparta where they set up a eugenics commission, smothering all children the commission decided would be unfit as warriors or mothers of future warriors. Rome where by law physically and mentally defective children had to be killed by their parents. Also examples in China, India, and many other lands. A lot of people had never heard of Plato and had only limited knowledge of Sparta and Rome. We eventually learned to drop the intellectual arguments. Concentrate instead on specific horrible examples of murder, rape and the like by named people who should never have been born, and describe their brutal story with as much detail as the public could stomach."

Henry paused, reached below his seat, and held up with almost reference the big gun in his pitch, a framed quote from Oliver Wendell Homes. "I keep this on the wall of my office right across from my desk. This is all you have to know about where eugenics stands in the U.S." He passed it around.

"It is better for all the world, if instead of waiting to execute degenerate offspring for crime, or to let them starve for imbecility, society can prevent those who are manifestly unfit from continuing their kind. The principal that sustains compulsory vaccination is broad enough to cover cutting of Fallopian tubes."

Henry gave them all his broadest smile. "This is from Oliver Wendell Holmes's 1927 United States Supreme Court opinion in Buck v. Bell, a decision legalizing eugenics in the U.S."

The Nazis were obviously impressed. One commented, "This may be an American decision, but Holmes is revered throughout the world. A very strong precedent. With Holmes involved, Germany will have little problem embracing eugenics."

Henry said, "Exactly. As I mentioned, when we introduced eugenics in the US we could cite England and a number of countries and thinkers of antiquity. It'll be so much easier for you with the Holmes's opinion."

Singing from the street interrupted the conversation, something in German. Henry got up and went to a window followed by the Germans, and eventually Dodi raised his bloated body to stand with them peering out. About thirty men were gathered before the front steps of the Town Hall building dressed in mismatched tan clothing, somebody's idea of a uniform, and on the steps stood an individual dressed in tan with a red Nazi armband. On either side of him were Nazi and American flags. The blonder of Henry's two Nazis guests said they were singing a German anthem, "Das Liedder Deutschen," The Song of the Germans. The singing stopped and the man on the steps addressed the group. They couldn't make out what was being said. Every once in awhile the man on the steps raise his arm in the Nazi salute and was saluted back by the assembled men.

Henry could see that the Germans were very unhappy with what was occurring, irritated expressions on their faces. It could jeopardize what he was trying to accomplish. Putting on his best smile as though it was nothing he said, "We've had a productive meeting. Let's end it here. After listening to me this long you deserve an evening exploring Los Angeles. Dodi can guide you. I'm sure he knows all the hot spots." Unhappy German looks changed into smiles and Dodi blossomed, talking animatedly to the two Nazis about what beckoned. "We'll continue tomorrow morning and meet in my office. It's only a few blocks away. I promise you no anthems there."

Henry whistle softly to himself as he drove home from the meeting, excited to report success to Helen. Yes, it had gone very well. A good day for his sister.

CHAPTER SIX

September 9, 1952. Justin had one day free before being hustled to Pomford for pre-admission, enough time to see the love of his life. Jenny lived in a much smaller co-op below them on the second floor— willowy, almost as tall as he, shining dark hair, wide dark blue eyes, and sort of buxom. He thought a lot about that. When he was down from his lock-away at Hudson Military he would watch out his window for the departure of her mother and father. Her older brother was usually out all day. He was a three sport jock at St. Barnards with regular practice sessions and games. With everyone out, he would give his signature knock at her door, one beat, then two, then one. She was usually standing by the door waiting for him, though she never said she missed him despite all his absence at school. Then it was slow dancing to her records, some kissing. She didn't allow much. When he tried he heard, "Spence girls don't let boys take liberties."

A lot of talk, often about their dreams. How many times he'd said to her, "I'm not going to be like my father. I'm doing something with my life." Maybe it would be medicine. There'd been many successful businessmen in his ancestry, a few lawyers, no doctors. It'd be great to break new ground, get out from under the confining hand of the family.

When Jenny spoke her dreams it was children, a luxurious townhouse in the Upper East Side, and to be near the top of the social ladder in New York, the last thing he wanted though he didn't tell her that. He wouldn't as long as there was slow dancing and kissing.

This visit he made sure at the outset she understood it was her last chance for a long time to show him how much she cared for him. She kissed him with more passion than she'd ever shown and led him to the couch in the living room, a first. He caressed her body pressed tight against his as he experimented with French kisses, again a first. He had moved his hand to stroke her breast. She wasn't fighting it, making little happy sounds.

With a bang the front door slammed open and in marched Mc Murray, the older brother, all six feet two of muscle. He was gonna get the hell beaten out of him.

Instead Mc Murray addressed Jenny with a sardonic smile. "You ought to let him do it." Mc Murray laughed. "You'll love it. All the girls I do it with love it. With your looks you're made for it. You know you're going to give in sometime. You might as well get started early so you can enjoy it longer." He laughed again. Mc Murray turned to him. "What do you say, Justin, wouldn't you like to see her naked. Get a little nooky?"

He felt himself blush pink, then couldn't help himself, smiled happily, thinking of Jenny naked.

Jenny gave him a swinging slap on the face and dashed to her room.

He wasn't astonished by Mc Murray baiting his sister. They hated each other. What concerned him was that Jenny might not like him anymore, thinking all he was interested in was sex. Some truth to that. Why did he have to smile? He may have lost her.

CHAPTER SEVEN

Right on schedule the next day Justin was in the big Cadillac, his father at the wheel, headed to Pomford to tie down admission. The drive up from New York City started out with both of them relatively silent, though his father did point out West Point and lecture on the Revolutionary War and Benedict Arnold's treason. "A lack of good breeding." Any questions his father asked Justin met with short replies. Why should the prisoner make nice with the captor? Justin sat with his arms crossed and shoulders slumped, not looking at his father, staring at the road ahead.

Finally the apology came. Justin could see his father had been brooding over it. At one point his father even started quietly talking to himself, running a hand through his hair, forgetful of Justin's silent presence. What his father delivered was, "I didn't want to send you away like this. The woman (he used her name) said that unless I sent you to a school that will keep you away she'll leave me. I didn't want to do it. I argued with her about it. She originally wanted to send you to her cousins in England and put you in Stowe, a very strict English school. At least you'll be in the U.S. You have to understand I love her very much. I don't want to lose her."

As usual, no expression of love for him. Justin couldn't remember when if ever his father said he loved him, and what about love for the woman still his wife?

His father continued. "This will be good for you. It's supposed to be a great school. And when I work some things out with her we'll be able to spend more time together."

He said the last without conviction, evidently he was as doubtful as he was about being able to sway the woman on anything.

Justin picked up immediately on the "send you away" language. "Won't Pomford let me come home some weekends like Hudson Military Academy did? And what if my mother comes home?"

His father kept his eyes straight ahead, not glancing at him. "No. Pomford allows only one weekend a year if the parents want the boy to take it. And they will even keep the boy over Thanksgiving and Christmas. Obviously there's a break in the summer. We're already working on where you will go next summer. Maybe England or maybe to your aunt Gertrude's in Greenwich."

This was total banishment. Not a surprise. Any other boy would be screaming bloody murder. However, Justin found himself sitting silently, unmoving, containing the bile rising in his throat, holding back the anger. What was the use of yelling about it. His father had no control over anything.

New York, all its bustle, all the things he loved to do, how could he stand to lose New York? New York pulled at his mind, not wanting to let him go, trying to reel him back. Behind were doormen who had coddled him since he was a child, his bedroom window view of Central Park, the Zoo and the Wolman rink, place of memorable skating parties, Avery Fisher Hall where he occasionally heard something he liked, most of the music interminable, and museums and art galleries which he always found interesting. Everything he knew was vanishing —elevators and Checker Cabs, Walk and Don't Walk Signs, F. A. O. Schwartz, the hum of traffic and shrill of sirens through the night, proper punishment for tourists unaccustomed to the noise. And loss of friends. He hadn't made many being excluded from New York much of the time, but there were a few, some very close ones. He managed to talk to only a few before he left.

Fred Staley had said, "What? Pomford? You've got to be kidding. That's a prison. My cousin was sent there. He tried to run away twice. Never got very far. They have the whole countryside organized to catch Pomford runaways. Just like a Nazis concentration camp in World War II."

The Nazi concentration camp reference had been particularly disconcerting.

He spent the next few hours staring out the window, trying to hold it together. What he was facing, he would have to face alone. And what he was facing sounded bad.

All along the drive he'd been thinking about his mother as his misery deepened. Now he focus on her. She would cry for him if she knew about Pomford as he always cried for her. Thank God she didn't know what was happening. Her love for him was a long way off. It was all he had. And the man sitting next to him was responsible for it all.

About half-way his father started trying to convince him that Pomford was a good school. "It's supposed to be a bastion of good breeding. Boys at Pomford are selected for their good families. The school is at the forefront of creating well-bred leaders for America. It's a school for gentlemen."

Same old story, breeding. He remembered standing before the portraits of Grant and Lee in the upstairs corridor of the Union Club, thirteen years old then. Among the many clubs to which his father belonged the Union Club was the most prestigious. It had the distinction of being the oldest club in New York City, housed in an architectural gem of a building on the corner of 69th and Park. According to his father it was the home away from home of every male of prominence in the City, the place everyone with a desire for social success wanted to be. The descriptions below the portraits said Grant had been a member of the Union Club after his presidency and Lee had been earlier when he was Commandant of West Point, before he joined the Confederacy. Strange that the club displayed their portraits next to each other as though best friends. Or maybe it was that when Grant joined the club subsequent to Lee, Grant instructed his portrait be placed next to Lee so that anyone looking at Lee's portrait would remember Grant defeated him.

His father had furrowed his brow and looked hard at him, making sure he had his full attention, unusual for his father as normally he was in a light mood at the Union Club. "Look at Lee. You can see the Southern breeding. He was a gentleman." His father ran a hand through his hair and smiled at the portrait of Lee as though Lee was an old friend. Now look at the picture of Grant. No gentleman. He was a thug. The North should never have won the war. There were just too many thugs in the North for the gentlemen of the South to handle."

His father was still fighting the Civil War. He often bragged about the prominent Southern families from which he and his mother were descended, and his family's leading role in founding R J Reynolds Tobacco Company, the source of his father's fortune.

"You were bred a gentleman like Lee. They say breeding counts. It does. Never forget it. When you get older you'll run into many thugs like Grant. Not gentlemen. Don't associate with them. Ignore them if they try to be your friend. Choose only gentlemen of good breeding like you. Seek them out and befriend them. People with your background should only associate with people of similar background."

He'd asked, "How do I know if people I meet are thugs or gentlemen?"

His father had smiled broadly, seemingly pleased to be asked the question, "They will show you what they are made of by how they treat you. A thug will disrespect you, try to belittle you before others, treat you unfairly. A gentleman may disagree with you, even show he doesn't like you, but never disrespect you."

It was at the Union Club that his father would play what Justin thought of as the "suck up" game. They would be sitting at a table in the main, second-floor dining room, and his father would pop up and hurry over to greet someone of social importance entering the room. Or if people of social importance were seated when they entered his father would go over to their tables to talk. And correspondingly people at many other tables would come over to talk to his father. Those of higher social status and wealth were being

being sucked up to by those of lesser status, a public display of the hierarchy of New York society, with his father having to do little table-hopping and receiving much table-hopping because of his estimable social status. His father treated those coming to his table with little respect, often continuing to eat as they talked, and he assumed his father got the same reaction when he played the suck-up game at other tables. Justin hated it, thinking it demeaning, and more than once said to his father, "Can't you stay at our table. It's like you're begging, going to those other tables."

To which his father replied, his mouth pursed in irritation, "That's a stupid thing to say. People of breeding greet other people of breeding. I'm trying to befriend people who can help me and help you. That's what people of breeding do."

He hadn't responded. What Justin got out of it was that good breeding involved sucking up.

Justin could see why his father kept talking about breeding. He fit the bill. Very English looking, a full head of pale blond hair, prominent English nose, light blue-gray intelligent eyes, somewhat weak chin usually thrust out to hide its weakness, erect posture, tall athletic looking frame, a man who commanded attention. He'd seen his father's face in some of the portraits of English lords at the Metropolitan Museum. But him? He hated to look at himself in the mirror. Pimples on his cheeks and starting to appear on chest and back, scrawny, narrow shoulders and small bones on a thin frame. Not short, five feet eleven and growing, but when compared to the burley boys who played football at Hudson Military Academy he looked like a pimpled, flat-chested girl. He'd been given his father's name, Justin Montgomery Whitthorne II, a name that brought derision at Hudson Military. The name was about the only way he was similar to his father.

The further they got toward Pomford, the more he bit his fingernails, ignoring repeated admonitions from his father to "stop that." A few years back his father had experimented with painting a bitter substance, purple in color, on his finger tips. He bit them anyway, spitting out the bitterness and had to hide his hands behind his back when friends approached. Having purple fingers meant you were still a baby. Eventually his father had given up on the fingernails as he gave up about everything else he tried in life except, of course, the woman.

When they got into Western Massachusetts, Justin did start to get a little interested. Rolling hills defined the horizon, the advance guard of the Berkshires. What impressed him was the orderliness of everything, regular green ridges looking like a refined lady had folded her neat green napkin on the earth, the orderliness of the white New England towns matching the orderliness of the horizon. He'd exchanged the chaotic life of New York for an environment where everything was carefully controlled. A quite different rural setting from Camp Passumpsic in Northern Vermont. There nature was in charge in her undisciplined ways. In Western Massachusetts, man had tamed nature.

They entered the Pomford Valley shortly after 4:00 PM for their 5:00 PM appointment. Cresting the steepening green hills they saw below a broad sunless valley split by a river doing lazy coils through meadows shaping extensive Pomford Academy playing fields, flowing darkly, lifelessly, the sky increasingly overcast, perhaps signaling a thunder storm. Everything looked gray and bleak despite the early September date. Whatever summer the valley had experienced seemed to be leaving early. Justin had a distinct feeling of disquiet.

His father felt it too, commenting, "It looks pretty somber."

They drove down the main street of town, actually about the only street, squarish, white, colonial houses arrayed on each side, impressive, but unwelcoming in their formality and stark whiteness, the houses set off by towering elm trees that increased the formality of the scene. This wasn't a town that reached out to visitors. And no people. No people walking the sidewalks. No people on porches or looking out the imposing front windows of their houses. Only one or two parked cars on the entire street. Eerie, a foreign country after New York.

After some scouting they found a colonial building bearing the sign, "Administration Building." They were twenty minutes early and got out of the car to stretch their legs. Total silence. Not even a bird chirping a salute to the end of a summer day.

Then in the far distance, C*lip clop, clip clop.*

A horse-drawn carriage was approaching though the gloom from the far end of the street, the horse black, the carriage black, the sky behind the advancing carriage black, the carriage looking like a black creature of the storm. A chill ran down Justin's spine and he shiver slightly in the warm air. As the carriage drew nearer Justin could make out the driver, a smallish gentleman, made smaller by being hunched forward in the middle of the high carriage seat while talking to the horse, reins held casually in one hand, not being used much as the horse seemed to know the way. Despite the hot afternoon, the man was dressed formally— dark blue almost black worsted suit, old-fashioned straight collared white shirt, dark maroon necktie, again almost black, a strange outfit to be wearing driving a carriage on a hot summer day. As the carriage drew nearer Justin could make out more blackness, jet black eyes behind thick-lensed metal-rimmed glasses, heavy black eyebrows, and steel gray hair parted in the middle like photographs of his nineteenth-century ancestors hanging on the walls of his co-op apartment library. But it was the contrasting whiteness that struck Justin most. The man's face and hands were almost as white as the shirt he wore, white as the marble grave markers in the small Pomford cemetery they passed, a face that seemed not of flesh. Was the man's blood red? Spectral like the vampires. If there was ever a vampire face his was it.

The whole thing reminded him of a scene in a Western movie, the body of the villain being transported in a black carriage to boot hill, the only difference being that the carriage approaching didn't have a casket strapped to the rear. But the man sure looked like an undertaker.

The horse drew the carriage up to the door of the admission's building and stopped without command. Stepping down from the carriage, the man didn't shake his father's hand, inquire who they we were, or introduce himself. No questions about the drive up or anything else. He just silently ushered them into the administration building. He was much smaller than he appeared when driving the carriage, at least six or seven inches shorter than his own five foot eleven height. The man didn't look at him.

They proceeded to a quite large office, furnished with what appeared to be Early American antiques, like many in the co-op. On the walls were pictures of numerous black horses, black carriages with the man at the reins, and diplomas for degrees, Yale, Amherst, Columbia, and two others he couldn't make out. Behind the man's desk a lot of signed pictures, including Eisenhower and Truman, as though he was marshaling his importance against whomever sat opposite him. The man moved behind his immense desk and sat, looking much taller than when he'd been standing because his chair was positioned on a raised platform.

They stood before the desk for a minute, then another minute, then another minute while the man read something. Finally his father asked if they could sit down, scowling in irritation. The man looked at them coldly, nodded yes, and motioned them to low chairs set before his desk. He loomed over them from his high seat, probably a well-thought-out position, his face illuminated by a single desk lamp, emphasizing its whiteness and severity. The rest of the room was quite dark, both from the heavy overcast outside and partial draw of the curtains. The lit face of the man hung over them, dominant. gaunt, scary. This was what the poor sailors on the Pequod might have seen, Captain Ahab standing above them with his peg leg planted in the deck. Not good. Ahab took all on a deadly pursuit.

When the man finally spoke his voice had a strong New England accent and was as dried out and emotionless as his body appeared to be.

"I am Doctor Jeremiah Cranch, Headmaster of Pomford. I have been Headmaster since 1902." He said this not with pride but seemingly to establish his authority.

Grimacing at them as though they'd done something wrong in their being before him, he said, "This is all highly irregular. It's much too late to join the sophomore class. Class starts in a week. Admissions for this year closed months ago. Why don't you wait and apply next year?"

His father leaned forward with a puzzled frown on his face. "I thought it was all arranged."

The Headmaster replied, "John Chandler called me. We do listen to John's opinions. He's been a great supporter of the school and restored many of the colonial buildings you saw along Main Street, and he does know boys. I didn't give John a yes or no answer on your son. Only agreed to meet you."

He then turned his hard black eyes on Justin and said. "How did you come to know John?"

In a scared voice Justin replied,"I've never met him," though now he knew where the woman's calls had been going.

The Headmaster then addressed both of them, his voice raised and glowering down at them, "I don't understand. Why are you taking my time?"

His father said. "I talked at length to John. The woman did, too." (He gave her name.) John said it was all arranged."

Something appeared on the Headmaster's face that looked like he was struggling with a private smile. "She and John used to be very close friends and came here often together."

Justin father's eyes widen and he went rigid for a few moments.

The Headmaster made no further objection to his admission and Justin took that as an acceptance, the last thing he wanted. However, the Headmaster continued. Justin felt this was not because he was interested in him. Rather because it was his routine in all admissions. He always did his admissions routine so he was going to do it with him.

"Tell me about yourself."

He told him he led his class scholastically at Hudson Military Academy, and then started to tell him about the subjects he liked. The Headmaster cut him off as though not interested in scholastic achievement and asked, "What sports do you play?"

"Well, I swam a little on the third team at Hudson, the back stoke, not much good, and played a little soccer, not much good at that either. I don't like sports much."

This produced the hardest look from the headmaster that they'd experienced. "At Pomford everybody plays sports. However inept, you will be assigned to a team. We practice every afternoon without fail. No lallygagging."

This was not encouraging.

The Headmaster turned to his father. "Any disciplinary problems."

"No. The teachers say he's among the best balanced boys at the school, always trying to succeed and trying to please. The only problem I have with him is sometimes he doesn't stand up enough for himself, gets bullied by thugs at school."

He wished his father hadn't said that about bullying. Again a slight smile on the Headmaster's face that indicated it had registered.

The Headmaster never asked more about him. Instead he turned to his father with his admissions spiel.

"Only a small percentage of boys who apply to Pomford are admitted. Going to Pomford is a great privilege. We look for boys of good breeding who can be the future leaders of America. We intend that they carry on their good breeding to produce further generations of leaders.

"A boy is malleable during his adolescent years. Our approach is to use moral instruction, discipline. and athletics."

This wasn't good. He didn't need discipline or moral instruction, and he certainly didn't need athletics.

"We model ourselves the English public school system. They've had generations of study and experimentation with teenage boys. They've concluded that boys need to be segregated from society in their teenage years, sent away for three or four years under constant direction and conditions of strict regimentation and tight control. Without segregation and control teenaged boys are disruptive to polite society. They develop habits which lead them astray in later life.

"Eton, Stowe and the other English preparatory schools are serving the needs of the English upper class with segregation and control. We serve the American upper class in the same way. Discipline is the key.

"What the English have found, and we've found, is that teenage boys actually want discipline and control. They're looking for direction and don't mind the control as it gives them direction. We're proud we have the tightest discipline of any preparatory school in New England. Throughout the day our boys are checked in and out of every class, study hall, meal, athletic period, and everything else, and they are locked in at night. The boys only have about four hours of free time during the entire week. That's Sunday afternoon after lunch. If we gave them more time they'd just get into trouble. We know where they are and what they're doing every second. Other prep schools take a looser approach. They end up expelling a lot of boys for unsatisfactory behavior. We don't. Through our approach we bring almost every boy who enters Pomford through to graduation. We never expel anyone."

Great. His father and the woman had found a school where no matter what he did he would continue to be locked up. And four free hours a week? The prison movies he'd seen gave prisoners more weekly free time in the exercise yard. He shuddered.

"Because we feel the need to apply constant attention to our boys you will find we allow few weekends away from school."

His father said, "I heard it was only one weekend a year?" The Headmaster glared at his father, pursed his lips, and shook his head as though irritated his father had intruded in his spiel, "Seniors get one weekend. They need to be in good stead."

More confirmation of bad news.

There was more,

"Athletics is a very important part of our program. Through athletics we develop leadership and teamwork just as at Eton. Boys need to be kept active through athletics or they'll stray. You need to wear them out." A small sound from him like a chuckle swallowed. Could he chuckle?

"We expect our boys to pitch into tasks like waiting table and kitchen duty. It's part of being a family, a tight-knit family. Pomford and all the teachers here become like fathers to the boys. We expect them to behave toward us with the respect due a father."

He had to be kidding. No normal family would exercise the control Pomford exercised.

The Headmaster continued with the first enthusiasm they'd heard from him, and a smile, or maybe a grimace trying to be a smile. With the deep frown lines on each side of the man's mouth Justin thought one smile a day might be the quota.

"The boys we graduate are very special. They populate the secret societies at Yale, the clubs at Harvard and Princeton and have leading student roles at other colleges and universities. Later they are bringing moral direction to government, business, and particularly education. Our graduates head many secondary schools and colleges across America, carrying our objectives everywhere."

The Headmaster stopped there, perhaps because he realized it was unnecessary to promote Pomford to someone he'd decided to accept.

He then asked his father a very odd question. "Tell me about your ancestry. Normally we do a genealogy study on all boys seeking admission. We haven't had time to complete one on your son."

His father stiffen. What was that about? Then his father opened up and started talking happily, his breeding a subject he loved to talk about— a description of the English aristocrats in his pedigree and that of Justin's mother, of vast plantations in the South, and of the founding of R J Reynolds Tobacco. But then he aired all the family dirty linen, albeit in an amusing way, an aunt who wanted to do nothing but play marbles, a great uncle who mixed rum with the milk on his cornflakes, and went on from there, his mother's grandfather who in his imbecility insisted on stabling his horse in the living room and had if fed off fine china, like one of the roman emperors he'd read about. Several more.

It embarrassed Justin. Why give this cold fish such information? To ingratiate himself with him? Or maybe trying to make the genealogy study unnecessary. While his father told all the stories, laughing as he told them, the Headmaster never laughed. Instead his mouth turned increasingly downward as his father talked.

"Doesn't the boy's mother also have mental problems?"

His father gave the Headmaster a look that caused Justin to feel his father was going to tell the Headmaster to go to hell. Instead he said, "Yes. It's very sad. She's a wonderful woman."

Obviously the story was out.

The Headmaster then turned to Justin. "As I said, we have a reputation for never dismissing any boy no matter what the boy does. We've kept as students thieves, cheats, boys who refused to study. These are boys that any other school would automatically kick out. If a boy is a miscreant we use athletics and discipline to bring him to a moral life. But we never keep boys here who do not want to be here. If at any time, Justin, you don't want to be here just let us or your father know and you can leave immediately." Turning to his father he said, "We even refund all tuition paid for the semester so there is no financial penalty in leaving." Turning back to Justin he added, "We don't want any boy here that doesn't like it here."

It sounded like he was encouraging him to leave when he hadn't even arrived. Was this departure speech given just to him or to all entering boys?

"Ordinarily I don't admit boys who have a lot of mental problems in their families." He shook his head. "This is a major exception. I'll probably come to regret it."

Justin sure hoped so.

"With your inexcusably late application all the dormitory rooms are taken. You're going to have to sleep in a master's house off campus."

Justin didn't know the significance of an off-campus house, worrisome as the Headmaster thought it was second rate goods.

They stood, and he followed his father's lead in reaching across the desk to shake the Headmaster's hand goodbye. (A dry, thin, lifeless hand it was.) The Headmaster didn't rise to their hand-shake. His father then sat back down (causing the Headmaster to look up with eyes widened in surprise).

His father paused for a moment, ran a hand through his hair, then said, "I'd like to pay the tuition now." He pulled out his check book, wrote a check, and handed it to the Headmaster. "I may be going to Europe and want to make sure the acceptance is set and tuition paid before I leave."

The Headmaster sat motionless starring at them, obviously debating it, said nothing and put the check in a drawer, then turned back to his reading, not looking up when they left.

In the car Justin said, "That was strange. He never asked about my grades. Maybe he already had them."

His father said, "I doubt it. We didn't send Pomford your grades and the military academy wouldn't have sent them without our permission."

His father tilted his head up to the ceiling of the car for a few moments, obviously thinking, then said in a contemplative voice. "That sure was a strange interview. He's a very different man. Not at all what I expected. I've never had anyone question me about my genealogy, particularly when he doesn't even know me. A gentleman wouldn't do that. I didn't trust him with his talk about a genealogy study. That's why I gave him the check. It cements your admission with no chance for him to wiggle out."

For Justin another nail in the coffin.

They stayed that night at the Pomford Inn, a traveller's rest going back to colonial times. They were the only people staying at the inn and suffered an execrable dinner and for Justin a sleepless night of worry. The next day dawned still gloomy and this matched Justin's morose mood at breakfast. His father seemed gloomy, too. Maybe kicking him out created some second thoughts. He hoped so but doubted it.

It was no better on the drive down to New York. The trip was largely silent. His father and the woman had managed things very well. From what the Headmaster said he couldn't escape from

Pomford by behaving badly, no matter how badly he behaved. And while the Headmaster offered, maybe encouraged, the option of voluntary departure this option was unavailable with his father and the woman barring him from home. He was stuck at Pomford for three years. Prison for three years with no possibility of parole.

As they approached New York his father said. "We're going off to Europe tomorrow so I won't see you before you go to school. You'll be fine. You have breeding. Don't forget it. Breeding will see you through."

His father nodded as if to himself. "You've always gotten good marks. I'm proud of what you achieved academically at Hudson Military Academy. Now you need to keep up the grades at Pomford. Work hard at the books. You can be admitted to Harvard, Yale or Princeton like the other boys the Headmaster mentioned. That's where men of breeding go and you should go."

Of course, his father had gone to College of William and Mary in Williamsburg. He always explained it as a choice to be close to his Southern roots, though Justin suspected it was because he didn't have the grades. His father continued to stare straight ahead at the road, not seeming to understand what he was doing to him.

Justin turned toward him in his seat. "How can you be sending me to Pomford? We both know Pomford is a lousy school for me. Discipline and athletics. I hate athletics. Can't you resist the woman? Please don't send me there."

His father reached over and put a hand on his shoulder in what Justin took as an an attempt to express sympathy though looking at his father's cold blue eyes he saw no genuine concern.

"I know you hate this, and the interview was terrible. But there's some good news. (The woman) tells me it's just as the Headmaster said. The sons of the best families in the U.S. attend Pomford. These are boys whose fathers are leaders in the country. It has a far better bred group of parents and students than in any other prep school in America."

Justin twisted in his seat and stared out the window. How many times did he have to hear this breeding crap?

His father continued, ignoring his lack of attention, "You're going to meet well-bred boys of good family who can help you throughout your life. They'll help you financially and help you socially. Seek these boys out and make them your friends. They're probably the leaders of your class. With your family wealth and social standing you should join them as a leader of your class. I've found that building a network of well-bred friends is one of the most important things I've done in my life and you'll find it, too. And whatever you do, don't pal around with any thugs. It is an old adage but true that you are the company you keep. Understand?"

Justin did not reply. His father evidently hadn't considered what it meant about him to be in the company of a woman criminally plotting against his mother.

CHAPTER EIGHT

His father leaned over toward him and delivered what he must have felt was the clincher, "Your mother would be proud of you going to Pomford."

That did it. His father bringing his mother into it after what he'd done to her. Justin looked his father up and down. Cold determination gripped him. He couldn't hold it back any longer. The dam was bursting. Disgust was too great. Hate was too great. The secret was out. He started, his voice shakier than he would have liked. He'd never challenged his father before. Always the dutiful child, his parents' "good boy," trying to do nothing to upset the apple cart with his mother ill. Now was different.

"How can you talk about my mother after what you and that horrible woman did to her?" The car swerved and his father looked over as though he'd not heard him, or heard him wrong, his face frozen in disbelief.

"Don't pretend you don't know what I'm talking about." His voice stronger now. "Mother laid it all out in a diary. You probably never saw it but the hospital had her keep a diary of everything you did to her. I think some of the things would put you in jail." The surprise on his father's face turned to fury, white knuckles on the steering wheel, voice in rising decibels, lips drawn back and teeth exposed as though he wanted to take a piece of his flesh.

"Your mother is ill. She imagines things."

"No. I overheard a telephone conversation where the woman was directing you to do just like the diary said, sexually attack my mother. I was in the big chair in the library reading. You didn't know I was there because I was snuggled down behind the back. You got a call. I remember it exactly, word for word. The two of you were plotting to keep my mother in the institution. And you laughed about it. Laughed."

His father grimaced as though remembering. He made no denial.

"The woman is evil. You've let her manipulate you. She wants to put my mother away so she can have you all to herself. Same with me. Put me away. How could you get involved with someone so evil?" He was talking loudly now. "You talk about breeding and thugs. You're a thug, the worst kind of thug. Preying on my mother. Plotting with an evil woman."

His father had gone pale under his expensively maintained tan, his shoulders hunched forward. He looked smaller, a defensive posture, "You don't understand." He spoke in a high, uncertain voice, unlike him. The car was abruptly braked and his father reached over to hit him. That he missed was due to the blasting horn of a truck barreling down on them from behind.

With his father again focused on the road Justin took several deep breaths, trying to be calm, wanting to deliver what he had to say with seriousness and effect. "Yes I do understand. You're in cahoots with a criminal. The woman is a criminal. Plotting to institutionalize and maybe kill another person is criminal. I looked it up. Twenty years or more in prison. When I heard your telephone call I thought to go to the police. Probably should have. It's been like living with two murderers. You're murdering my mother. And the worst of it is you're laughing about it. Maybe you noticed how nervous I've been." He bit a nail. "With what you're doing to my mother, I didn't know what you'd do to me. Now I know, Pomford. The police wouldn't have done anything. That's why I didn't go to them. No proof. You'd have told them I was just upset because the woman was replacing my mother. But you and I don't need proof. We know what's been going on."

Justin's feeling was one of exultation. He wasn't a wimp. He'd stood up to his father, done the right thing. He thought of his mother. Some small revenge on how she was treated.

His father said nothing and sped up to more than eighty miles per hour, his lips compressed to the point where the flesh above and below ballooned out, his face rigid, the car weaving dangerously through traffic, jerking the wheel in anger. He started chain smoking, normally a few cigarettes a day, his long fingers tapping one cigarette after another from the pack, not even glancing at Justin, his existence rejected. Arriving at the co-op bags were stacked in the front hall, all set for an early morning departure of his father and the woman to London. Their mission was accomplished and they could leave. They'd successfully locked him away in prison, and with him and his mother both removed the world was now a play-pen for them both.

He started talking to himself in his bedroom. "Well, you've really done it this time, cut yourself off completely." Aunt Gertrude was virtually unreachable and connection with his mother was non-existent. He was on his own. And when the woman found out he knew of their plot her anger at him would be even greater.

An "F" ing disaster. All the "what ifs" scrolled through his mind. What if polio hadn't struck across the lake? What if the bus driver hadn't raced to New York to beat the rush? What if his father waited to get to a bedroom before jumping on the woman, or maybe it was the woman who jumped on his father? Ham's curse. Couldn't get it out of his mind. The woman had said, "You'll be punished for this as long as you live." No hope. Only dread. What more did the woman have in store for him?

CHAPTER NINE

Henry Benson's meeting with the Germans convened again the next day, October 3, 1933. He'd observed the Germans buying into everything he said and was determined to close the deal. The meeting was delayed by Dodi until late morning. He could understand the reason when he saw the hungover condition of Dodi and the two Nazis. Finally he got everyone settled in the comfortable chairs of his office.

One of the Germans asked about the picture on the wall of the members of the California Eugenics Foundation. He named them getting the comment, "Impressive, very important people."

"Yes. David Starr Jordan, the first President of St-Stanford was particularly important to eugenics. He's seated in the middle. You may be familiar with his widely read book, *Blood of a Nation*. It declared human qualities and c-conditions such as talent and poverty were passed on through birth. This originated the notion of 'racial purity,' something you hear about all the time now." He turned to Gerhard. "Do you know whether this was one of the books Hitler read in writing *Mein Kampf*?"

Gerhard didn't nor did the Nazis.

Henry said, "I'd be interested to find out. It'd be fascinating if Hitler's racial ideas came in part from St-Stanford. In addition to Jordan, there have been many other distinguished Americans that have been leaders in eugenics, for example, Alexander Graham Bell, Luther Burbank, and Margaret Sanger."

The blonder of the Nazis, apparently the less hungover of the two, asked, "Why do you focus on eugenics. Wouldn't euthanasia be a better solution for getting rid of the unfit? Eugenic sterilization seems so slow. It only takes effect in the next generation."

His fellow Nazi nodded.

"Great question. In the early days the U.S. looked at euthanasia to deal with the de-defective, not eugenics."

The two Nazis leaned forward.

"We were going to follow Sparta and Rome. Carnegie Institute published a seminal p-paper espousing euthanasia. Quite a bit of support developed from certain parts of the intellectual community and many U.S leaders believed in it. The most commonly suggested approach was the so called 'lethal chamber,' local publicly operated g-gas chambers. A gas or diesel engine would be hooked up to the chamber and the exhaust fed in, poisonous carbon monoxide. One of the leading supporters was the head doctor for all the U.S. armed services during first World War, Dr. Popenoe. He wrote a widely read textbook, *Applied Eugenics,* that advocated euthanasia.

"I agree with you that euthanasia would be much faster. And it would make sense for people with incurable c-conditions. I would include feeble mindedness, schizophrenia, cerebral palsy, epilepsy, muscular dystrophy, Huntington's disease, and physiological abnormalities such as dwarfism. We haven't been able to implement it. The problem is the American p-public. Eugenicist have felt American society is not ready to implement a lethal solution. I don't approve of it but many institutions and doctors have been quietly improvising lethal solutions on their own. I happen to know that one of the largest mental institutions in Illinois has for years been f-feeding all of its inmates milk from tubercular cows. The death rate each year is between thirty and forty percent. And many doctors in mental institutions and prisons make it a practice to deny medical help to de-defectives who become ill. All of these efforts are necessarily very small in contrast to the size of the problem. At least in America it's much more effective to have wide-scale eugenic sterilization. You may be able to do more euthanasia in Germany. And the eventual result is the same, defective genes are prevented from passing to the next generation." Henry thought about it for a moment. Germany introducing euthanasia, that would be something. Could Hitler really get away with it? He decided to give them a warning.

"Many Californians don't like Mexicans and Chinese. They find little objection to sterilizing Mexican women with too many welfare children and sterilizing Chinese prostitutes. That's not the way to go. You end up with racial targeting rather than targeting of de-defectives."

The two Nazis glanced at each other.

The second German surgeon, Dr. Hauptmann, said, "How do you determine who's unfit and undesirable? Do you have a commission of some sort doing evaluations? And please call me Dieter."

"In California there's no commission. It's up to the wardens of prisons, directors of m-mental hospitals, and various state welfare agencies. They identify those they feel qualify as unfit. Then they call on me to perform sterilization surgeries. I believe it's much the same in other states. It's all government. In America we've given government, not doctors, the decision on who's unfit."

Furious writing of notes by the Nazis.

Again from Dieter, "Well, if the head of a state institution wants you to sterilize someone do you have any leeway to decide against the operation? What if after you examine the individual she doesn't seem to be defective?"

Henry nodded, "I have s-sometimes called off an operation when I f-feel it might endanger a p-patient's life. But the law is the l-law. And if the head of an institution d-decides to sterilize someone my job is to perform the st-sterilization."

He said this for Dodi's benefit and realized he had stuttered quite a bit saying it. The reality was that to protect women he found deserving he would sometimes insist that their health was too poor to tolerate surgery. But he wished the question hadn't been asked and that he didn't have to answer it as he did.

The two German surgeons frowned, obviously unhappy with a system that took the decision on sterilization out of their hands.

Gerhard said, "What about male sterilizations?"

"We're doing some, but not n-nearly as many as for women. I understand you're going to meet with Doctor Leo Stanley at San Quentin prison. He has an interesting technique where he's t-trying to reverse the criminality of inmates by removing their testicles and replacing them with the testicles of dead men who have good traits. I understand he's performed about 500 of these surgeries but I don't know the result."

Another question from the blonder Nazi? "Does this mean that the California sterilization law authorizes not only sterilization but also medical experimentation on those deemed defective?"

Henry hesitated, not wanting to provide any support for medical experimentation on people, however defective.

Dodi stepped in with no appreciation for the significance of the question. "Sure. If people are defective they're good subjects for medical experiments. It will benefit all society."

Again the Nazis were writing. Henry glared at Dodi and said, "Whatever Dr. Stanley is doing, I feel experimentation on de-defective people is totally immoral."

The sandy haired Nazi shook his head in obvious disagreement.

Henry then explained his surgical methods, tubal ligation and hysterectomy. "Usually I do a tubal ligation, cutting the fallopian tube so that male sperm can't reach the woman's eggs in the ovary. This would be on women who aren't pregnant. In fact, a l-large portion are pregnant. The institution that contacts me wants to ensure that after the current baby is born there'll be no further babies. For these I often do a C Section to deliver the baby coupled with a hysterectomy."

Dodi said. "We call that a Mississippi appendectomy."

This brought a laugh from the Nazis.

Henry frowned at Dodi and shook his head in irritation. "We don't use such terms in the profession. What we're doing, what California is doing, is producing great benefit to society. We don't joke about it." No stutter this time. He stared hard at Dodi and decided it was a good time to break for lunch.

Why Doti had chosen a Mexican restaurant he'd never know. And Dodi had chosen the meal—enchiladas and tortillas slobbered over with piled up beans, cheese, guacamole, and sour cream. Dodi said with the same pride one might display in taking someone to a fine Parisian restaurant, "This is the best Mexican restaurant this side of LA."

The sandy haired Nazis screwed up his face in disgust and Dieter stared at his plate as though he couldn't believe what he was seeing. Henry said, "Have any of you had Mexican food before?"

Strong negative shakes of the head from everyone. The sandy haired Nazi leaned over and said something to the others in German, again making a face. Gerhard looked sharply at the Nazi. Henry didn't know what was said but suspected it was something like, "We feed better looking slop than this to the pigs in Germany."

The delegation didn't eat much but they made up for it in beer consumption, particularly the two Nazis. After several the sandy haired Nazi said, "The German problem is much greater than you imagine. You say we have 800,000 possible candidates for eugenics. We have five times that number we should simply eliminate. They're sucking the blood out of our society."

Gerhard replied with a quiet voice, "Our delegation is charged with examining sterilization practices and procedures, nothing else. I've heard you express that opinion before. As long as I'm involved, euthanasia won't be part of our delegation report."

Conversation then turned to lighter things, what they had seen that impressed them (New York and the Grand Canyon), American women, very much liked with only Gerhard, the one married man, not joining in with ribald stories of escapades across the U.S., and the hospitality they received from complete strangers when it was learned they were German visitors.

Gerhard turned to Henry and and Dodi and said, "If Germany decides to go forward can California continue to provide advice and help? This has all been so very valuable."

Dodi said he would request it of his superiors but was sure it wouldn't be a problem.

Henry rose from the table and addressed them in a strong voice of commitment. "Whatever California decides I can assure you that you will have my personal help. If Germany succeeds California succeeds."

He looked around and continued. "Does anyone have any questions?" There were none. "Thank you for patiently listening to my presentation, a lot of words. I think it would be helpful if you saw what we do. I have a sterilization procedure scheduled in a nearby prison this afternoon. Would you like to accompany me."

Gerhard instantly said, "Yes," and Dieter agreed.

Gerhard turned to the two Nazis. "Do you want to accompany us or go back to Los Angeles?"

The two Nazis conferred for a moment and the blond Nazi said, "I don't think we'll get anything out of seeing a surgery. We'll go back to Los Angeles." In saying this he looked over at Dodi. Henry was sure another night in the watering holes of Los Angeles was planned.

As the luncheon broke up, Gerhard addressed Henry and Dodi. "On behalf of us all I want to thank you for the meeting. You were open with us, gave us the things to avoid, and most important, you gave us instruction on how to accomplish eugenics in Germany." His voice got very serious and he spoke slowly, focusing on Henry. "I want you to understand that if eugenics goes forward in Germany a major responsibility will be yours. I don't think that Germany could get there without what you personally have taught us."

Henry's felt he'd become a comrade in arms with the Germans. The meeting had succeeded far, far beyond what he'd hoped in his most optimistic dreams.

They piled into his old Chevrolet, he thought probably quite different from the limousines they commanded in Germany, though they remained of good cheer as they proceeded to the prison.

Gerhard and Dieter both turned out to be graduates of Heidelberg, the leading medical school in Germany, and perhaps the world, both with degrees in obstetrics and surgery. Gerhard was currently a practicing physician. Gerhard said without bragging that his patients were from the leading families of the new Germany. Dieter said with some bragging that he was a professor at Heidelberg and considered an authority on surgery related to obstetrics.

Henry said, "Like you I graduated with degrees in obstetrics and surgery, Johns Hopkins."

Gerhard said, "We know it well. Fine university."

Henry said, "I completed my residency in 1929 at the start of the depression. Few well paying opportunities existed then. When this position opened, I took it with enthusiasm. I already believed in eugenics from the eugenics course I took at John's Hopkins and a bad personal experience. By the way I failed to mention that our colleges are very much involved in eugenics. Stanford, most of the Ivy League, and many other colleges offer courses on race theory and eugenics. They're oversubscribed. Some 20,000 college students are currently studying eugenics.

They started discussing the upcoming surgery and Gerhard asked, "How do you get the women to submit to the surgeries?"

"Well, the law allows us to use physical force to immobilize the women for surgery. I've never needed to do that. I do everything I can to protect women from the traumatic experience of knowing they're being st-sterilized. My usual subterfuge with non-pregnant women is to tell them I'm doing a routine examination for cancer, then tell them I've found a small cancer that is easily removed, anesthetize them and do the tubal ligation, explaining it as removal of the c-cancer. For pregnant women, when I do the C Section and deliver their baby, they are unaware that at the same time I've done a hysterectomy."

Along the way they passed a stable with a number of corrals and Gerhard commented on it.

Henry said, "There's another approach that is sometimes used but I didn't mention it. Those deemed defective, but not mentally ill, are being segregated in paddocks like that. We call them 'colonies' or 'camps.' Several thousand are already confined to colonies across the U.S., and we hope to expand. Colonies keep the unfit away from society, and by keeping men and women in separate quarters they control the birth of undesirable children."

Gerhard gave him an odd look he couldn't interpret.

At the prison the warden escorted them to the infirmary. It was old fashioned in equipment and set-up. He could see the Germans looking around in apparent surprise, quite different he supposed from the well-equipped hospitals of Germany.

After introductions, the warden, a small officious-looking very bald man said, "The patient is a Mexican woman. She's been arrested repeatedly, vagrancy, prostitution, small thefts. And she seems to have a low I.Q."

Dieter asked, "What do you think her I.Q. is?"

The bald warden shrugged, "Don't know. She hasn't been tested. But she's not very bright."

Henry said to the two German doctors, "Because the woman is pregnant I'll be doing a C section and hysterectomy."

Gerhard said, "Wouldn't it be easier to have a natural birth and later do a tubal ligation, avoid the need for a hysterectomy?"

"Yes, Tubal ligation is always my first choice. As you know, a hysterectomy is a major operation and the operating conditions aren't always the best." He looked around the room when he said this. "If the baby is delivered through natural birth we have to wait some time to do a tubal ligation, and the woman might slip through our fingers and get pregnant again before we can catch up to her. If we do a C Section and continue on to a hysterectomy we get the st-sterilization done while we still have her."

The woman was brought in, pretty little thing, very pregnant. She looked to be in her early 20s if that and very frightened. She had to be pulled into the operating room by a prison guard and said in a pleading voice, crying as she said it, "What you do to me?"

Henry explained in a calm, he hoped reassuring voice, "Doing a little operation so you can have your baby. Sometimes to have a baby you need to have an operation."

"*Porque?* I have two children, no operation. Why this time? I no want one." She struggled in the grip of the guard.

"Well, sometimes after you have had two children the third is more difficult so we operate to help you have the baby."

"*No es correcto.* You're wrong. My friend all have five, six *ninos*. No operation."

"I don't know your friends. I do know you need an operation to have the baby. Do you want your baby to be alive or not."

"Baby die if no operation?"

"Yes. And you may die also."

Henry saw no indication of low I.Q. in these questions. But with the two German doctors in attendance he went ahead and performed the operation with what he thought was speed and efficiency, getting compliments from both doctors. He thanked them and said, "Just one of many. It has become almost easy. I usually do three or four a day, often more, more than 3,000 in the four years I have been at it."

What he didn't tell the Germans were the failures. Just last week he'd operated on another Mexican woman in a similar prison, a prison with an even more primitive infirmary. The operation seemed to go all right, baby delivered, hysterectomy completed, but several hours later he got a call that the woman's blood pressure had dropped precipitously and she was having great pain in her stomach. He hurried back to the prison and found the woman in septic shock. His effort to save her was to no avail. The autopsy showed he had somehow managed to cut into her bowel and the putrid material from the colon had escaped into her body and blood. He'd come home to Helen full of remorse after trying to save the woman over a largely sleepless thirty-six hours.

She asked him what she always asked when he lost a patient, "Did you try your best?"

He said, "Yes."

"Then please put it out of your mind. No doctor would fail to lose some patients operating under the conditions you face."

That was comforting, and it was even more comforting to realize that the woman who died had many problems and would probably have been eliminated by euthanasia had it been approved.

Henry decided to try and cement the relationship with the German doctors even further, all in support of adoption of California eugenics in Germany. He gave both Germans a broad smile. "The day went so well I'd like my wife, Helen, to meet the two of you. She'd enjoy it. We've talked about your visit. Her ancestry is German and she's been following events in Germany. Are you available for dinner? Dinner at our house? I'm sure she'd be delighted. I'd be de-delighted, too."

Gerhard quickly accepted saying, "You're so kind. It'll be wonderful to get a home-cooked meal after all the hotel food."

Dieter said, "My apologies but I already agreed to go with the two others to Los Angeles. I'm a bachelor and Dodi is promising the beautiful girls of California we've heard so much about. And I do want to see Hollywood. We didn't get a chance to see it last night with all Dodi's bar hopping. Is that what you call it, bar hopping?"

Henry and Gerhard both said, "Yes," and wished him well.

Henry called Helen to alert her, told her of the success of the meeting which brought effusive congratulations, dropped Dieter off where he could get back to Los Angeles, and headed to his house.

As they were driving Henry said, "I met Helen when I was doing my residency at John's Hopkins. She was a nurse, the most beautiful woman I'd ever seen, fell in love with her the minute I saw her, and for reasons I've never understood she agreed to marry me after a courtship of only a month. It's been a wonderful marriage. I'm a lucky man. The only thing missing is ch-children. We're thinking of adopting."

"Remarkable," Gerhard said. "That's exactly my story. I met my wife, Brigit, when I was doing my residency at Heidelberg. She was a nurse and very beautiful. I'll show you her picture when we get to your house. It's a love marriage. We have no children and are thinking of adopting as you are. We live in a smaller city like you do, Ulm, Germany.

Henry said, "What do you do in your spare time in Germany? For us it's a lot of hiking. We have a cottage at Mammoth Lakes in the Sierras, mountains almost as high as Switzerland, hard hiking. Also, we love the beach. Beautiful beaches in California. We often go down to Newport Beach for the day. Every Sunday it's the Lutheran Church. And I've somehow gotten myself on various committees of the City of Pomona."

Gerhard replied, "Well, just like you, we love hiking and have a cottage in Murren, Switzerland. Sometimes we drive to the beaches on the North Sea like you do to Newport Beach. And like you we're active in the Lutheran Church and community. How extraordinary."

Henry was beginning to feel a real kinship and thought Gerhard was too.

The meal Helen prepared was excellent. He was pleased to see she didn't try to prepare sauerbraten or some other German dish. Instead it was a plain American meal, meat loaf, mashed potatoes, tomatoes and lettuce from their garden, and artichokes, a vegetable Gerhard didn't know, all accompanied by some good California wine. The wine drew compliments from Gerhard.

Conversation at dinner was homey— what life was like in Ulm, how the Bensons were spending their lives in Pomona, the hikes the two couples had taken, what Gerhard had experienced growing up in Germany during the First World War and living the desperate days afterward, and what the Benson's much easier life had been growing up in Baltimore. Much laughter from many funny stories about medical school, then mutual expression of hopes for the future, for an end to the depression, and please no more wars. Some time was spent by Gerhard telling them in detail about the cottage he and his wife owned in Murren, Switzerland, the beauty of the Jungfrau area, and the Mulders' plans to eventually retire there. He showed them a picture of his wife. She was beautiful as he'd said. And he invited Henry and Helen to visit.

After dinner they adjourned to the living room and Henry dug out his good brandy. The house was of modest size and not impressive from the outside. But he was proud of Helen's decoration of the inside. She'd used Mexican colonial furniture and vibrant colors to expand the rooms and make them far more interesting than neighbors' houses, none of that dull, 1930s style furniture. With Helen's decoration he called the house *"La Hacienda."* Gerhard very much liked it from the way he looked around smiling.

With brandy consumed, and Nazi functionaries no longer looking over his shoulder, Gerhard said, "I strongly support eugenics. We must encourage desirable people to marry each other and have many children, and we must sterilize the defective. Also, I agree with you we must not allow experimentation on the defective as your Dr. Leo Stanley is doing. And the reluctant way you answered the question about allowing government to decide who will be sterilized indicates an agreement. It has to be the doctors.

"Another thing where we agree, if we want a credible eugenics program in Germany we must avoid targeting of racial groups. I tell you, just the three of us, we'll face a lot of pressure on this back in Germany. From what you said you also have pressure, in your case regarding Hispanics and Chinese. And on the way here we learned there's targeting of blacks for sterilization in the American South. The pressure in Germany might be much greater. Jews and the Roma, you call them gypsies, they're hated by many Nazis. If it comes up, I intend to strongly resist."

Henry said, "Good. It can destroy eugenics. And it can sneak up on you. Recently I was called to the woman's wing of Folsom prison. The assistant warden wanted me to do a t-tubal ligation on a woman who was guilty of some petty crimes, crimes that appeared to me to be no more serious than those of most of the other inmates. The jerk took me aside and whispered to me the woman was Jewish as though that was a terrible thing to say out loud about anyone. Then his eyes went sort of crazy and he threw out a lot of rubbish, stuff about the Jews killing Jesus and not allowing any more Jews to be brought into the world. I tried my usual approach that the woman

72

wasn't well enough for surgery. He didn't buy it and made all sorts of threats including denying access to the prison. This would have put a serious crimp in the eugenics program. I am sorry to say I acceded to his wishes. But it still bothers me.

"The whole doctrine of eugenics is a potential breeding ground for discrimination and much worse. It's the thing that worries me most about eugenics. One view of Galton is he was a racist, discriminating against the lower class. So very easy to move that to blacks, Chinese, Hispanics, Jews and Roma."

Helen changed the subject and said to Gerhard in a friendly way, "You're a Nazi right? What's it like to be a Nazi?"

"Yes I'm a member of the party." He said this forthrightly, straightening up as he said it. "But I don't go around bragging about being a Nazi like the two men I'm with. That doesn't get you anywhere. Some people don't like Nazis. They think Hitler will cause trouble in Europe. That notion is wrong. Hitler is basically a good man. He's only interested in bringing Germany back from the effects of the terrible war."

He then swirled his brandy around for a moment and said thoughtfully, "Hitler has many faults. They are small against what he's starting to accomplish for the economy and for the pride of the nation. You may not know how bad it was in Germany until recently, the currency having no value, and people actually starving to death."

Helen said she'd read a lot about it.

"Germany is starting to come back economically with Hitler's industrial policies. You can see it even in the short time he's been in power. What's especially gratifying is that for the first time since defeat in the War Germans are taking some pride in being German. Hitler is lifting both the economic depression and the depression of the German mind. I am a strong supporter of Hitler."

Helen said, "From what I know I approve of Hitler but I don't know enough. There are lots of people in the Los Angeles basin of German ancestry. Many of us are in contact with each other and many believe in Hitler already. I'm not sure where it will go. There is some talk of getting together to help Germany." She paused and looked away for a moment. "I have a question for you. A good friend of mine is married to a man of German ancestry, second generation. His parents immigrated to the US when his parents were first married. The man is a strong supporter of Hitler. He has a good job and wants to quit it and take his family to Germany, a wife and four children. I've been telling her they shouldn't do it. There are too many unknowns about Germany. They should stay here. The U.S. is safe and a good place to raise a family. What do you think about the risks?"

"I didn't initially support Hitler. Some of the tactics the National Socialists used to gain power were abhorrent. But as I said a few minutes ago, he has lifted Germany as I don't believe anyone else could have done. Now Germany is on the march with singularity of purpose. Hitler has given us purpose. And he has given us strong leadership. There is something about Germans, maybe it's genetic, that they need a strong leader with a strong purpose. It was even there back when we were battling the Romans. A strong German leader, Arminius, was followed by the normally feuding German tribes and destroyed the Roman legions in the battle of Teutoburg forest. Give us a strong leader and we will follow with total national commitment. Von Hindenburg, President of the Weimar Republic before Hitler, was not a strong, purposeful leader. With Hitler in the lead there's no stopping us. I applaud your friend's husband for wanting to join us."

Henry had been sitting quiet for some time, listening, and during the conversation over dinner and thereafter there had been very little stutter. Now he stuttered badly. "I t-told everybody at the m-meeting that I went into eugenics because of a c-course I took. But I also said there was a personal reason. I had an older sister, Lillian, Lil for sh-short. Loved her dearly. She took care of me like a mother. She was raped and ki-killed. The killer had been in and out of asylums all his l-life. He forced me to watch him kill my sister. Then gave me this scar trying to k-kill me." He fingered the scar.

He stared off into space, hands gripping the arms of his chair, his voice grew loud and angry, practically yelling. "How could someone like that be alive, his mother a lunatic, his father a criminal. Why? Why wasn't he eliminated? If he were here I'd run my scalpel through his damn throat like he did my sister."

Helen hurried over to him and put her arms around him. "Henry, calm down."

He shook himself. "Sorry. When the memories come over me, I get sort of crazy. After the rape and killing, I couldn't speak for a long time. Ended up stuttering, and you can see I still stutter. Cowered away from everyone other than my parents. They had to home school me for years, and I was so afraid I wouldn't leave the house except clasping the hand of a p-parent. Many years of psychoanalysis. I'm still working through what happened. Helen has been a God-send." He squeezed Helen's hand.

"I decided at fifteen I'd dedicate my life to preventing such things from happening and always thought I'd go into law enforcement, maybe the FBI. They recruited a lot of agents in Baltimore. Then at John's Hopkins I took the eu-eugenics course. That changed everything. I became convinced that rather than being an FBI agent hunting down murderers and rapists after they commit crimes it would be far better to prevent the crime from ever happening. All my work is worthwhile if just a few men like the one that killed my sister are prevented from being born, or maybe even one man. If you question U.S. eugenicists closely, you will find many of them motivated by similar horror stories in their f-families or among their friends."

Gerhard said, "My story is quite different, fortunately no trauma like you suffered. My family in Ulm was lower middle class, my father a baker. He'd been gassed in the War and had trouble breathing. Died young. He was a generous man and gave bread when he could to the many starving during the terrible depression after the War. It was what I observed then that turned me to an interest in eugenics. Some people and families were of noble character, doing the right, moral thing, trying their best, even while starving. The character of others took them to degeneration and thievery, a lot of prostitution and crime. I remember my father giving bread to someone who said he needed it for his starving family. I later saw him selling the bread on the street. And I learned he was also prostituting his thirteen and fifteen-year-old daughters. Another remembrance is of a young boy, clutching tight the bread given by my father to feed his starving family, and seeing him viciously knocked down and the bread stolen. He later died. I have many similar stories of those years. As I grew older I came to feel there had to be some genetic difference that distinguished those with character from those without. Why were some people intrinsically depraved? It couldn't all be environmental factors. About everyone in the depression was facing similar circumstances. We didn't have eugenics classes in our university but I spent a lot of time thinking and reading about genetics. I became convinced as you did that what you call defective people shouldn't be born."

Gerhard looked from Henry to Helen and a smile lit up his face, Henry felt the smile of someone who felt very close to them.

"I've been very fortunate in life, fortunate to find my marvelous Brigit, fortunate to be part of the eugenics movement in Germany. I was a very good student but so were others. Set up my practice in Berlin, and the husband of one of my patients ascended to a top position in the Nazi party. I cured her of a relatively minor aliment. She recommended me to friends, wives of other top Nazis, and when the position on the eugenics commission opened, and I sought it, they vouched for me. Fortune has brought me exactly where I wanted to be just as you are exactly where you want to be, and both of us have been on the same path since our teenage years or before. Sort of brothers in eugenics." He laughed and Henry reached over and gave him a clap on the back.

"Time for me to head back to Los Angeles. We have an early departure tomorrow. Welcoming me into your house like this has been wonderful. And as I said, if Germany moves ahead it will largely be your doing. I think you could see we are all sold on recommending California eugenics to Germany. The real question is whether Germany can afford it. To do eugenics right means new hospital facilities, doctors, and other major expenditures. Germany continues to struggle with the depression. Little wealth exists for new projects. It all depends on how strongly Hitler feels about the racial purity he talks about and writes about."

Henry didn't remember ever getting to like someone and know someone so quickly. He felt they'd known each other for years and thought Gerhard felt the same way. Gerhard made a promise to bring Brigit to the U.S. to visit. Addresses were exchange, with both Henry and Gerhard committing to regular correspondence.

Much shaking of hands and hugs at Gerhard's departure with Helen commenting afterwards, "That's one of the nicest men I've ever met."

Henry said, "I agree. And so many similarities to us."

Henry drove Gerhard to the railroad station and on the way back thought about the similarities. They somewhat bothered him. Whenever he'd related an aspect of his life, how he met Helen, their life together, Gerhard quickly joined in with the same story of his life. And all the things in the eugenics world he opposed— experimentation on defectives, government deciding who gets sterilized, racial targeting—- Gerhard had gone to pains to explain he opposed, too. It was all rather too pat. Did it mean anything? Why would Gerhard want to establish a close friendship with him? He had no answer. But he was suspicious by nature given his past and resolved to retain a small suspicion about Gerhard.

Almost a month later they received an effusive thank you letter from Gerhard. From the letter you would have thought Gerhard had never eaten a good meal before or been in the company of friendly people. They imagined he must have spent a lot of time with his German English dictionary looking up all the flattering words he used. He was "ebullient" about the meeting, the experience was "transcendental," and so on.

The letter went on to apologize for not writing sooner, saying that he'd been in non-stop meetings on eugenics and that Germany had decided to go ahead with a national eugenics program. He described the program, a much more extensive one than in California. Positive eugenics—they would foster breeding of outstanding children by giving marriage loans to desirable couples who marry. Also, they would forbid abortion to women who would birth desirable children and discourage marriage where there was unacceptable ancestry. This would be done by requiring those considering marriage to first examine the blood lines of their prospective partner back to their grandparents and produce those at the Register of Marriages, and many marriages between races would be outright banned.

Negative eugenics—they had finally passed a eugenics law authorizing sterilization, modeled on California law, and had already started a strong sterilization program, calling eugenics "racial hygiene." Under the program, well equipped and well-staffed sterilization units were being placed in mental hospitals and prisons across Germany. These would deal not only with those already resident at the sites but also individuals collected from the society at large for deviant behavior, immoral conduct, criminality, children out of wedlock, too many children in poverty, and many other offenses. The list was longer than in California. Also, the letter said, *We are experimenting with euthanasia, applying it as you said to people with incurable psychiatric and genetic diseases and grave bodily deformity. Our methodology is to put them in buses, tell them they are going on a nice trip, and channel the bus's carbon monoxide exhaust gases back into the bus. At this time it is too small scale to justify the lethal chambers you mentioned. And to your idea of colonies separating defectives from society, we are already experimenting with what we call concentration camps.*

The last part of the letter was a lyric description of a hike he and Brigit had taken near their cottage in Murren, snow-capped peaks, wild flowers. The Bensons felt they were there with them it was so beautifully written, full of nature and love between Gerhard and Brigit.

At the end there was a shy admission, an after-thought, that he had been chosen to head the racial hygiene program and that he was setting up his headquarters in a castle, Hartheim.

Helen gave Henry a big smile and big hug. "You should be very proud of what you accomplished for Germany."

"Your work, too. I think it was at that wonderful dinner that did it. Good food, good conversation, how could he not buy into our California program?" They laughed and gave each other a big celebratory kiss.

CHAPTER TEN

September 20, 1954. No happy send-off to school for Justin. The only one home was Elizabeth, a few tears from her, a loving hug, and a lot of good wishes. It was Detective Sargent Brian O'Reilly who drove him up to Pomford.

Of all the police officers who moonlighted to drive for them, Sargent Brian O'Reilly (call me Brian) was the best. Brian was the one who was usually hired to drive him back and forth to Hudson Military. He looked like what an Irish cop should look, square strong face under bright red hair, an out-thrust jaw, watchful bright blue eyes, broad shoulders, and the kind of body Justin had seen on boxers the one time his father had taken him to a boxing match. He was not as tall as his father but someone he was sure no criminal would want to confront. What he liked most about Brian was that he would tell him real-life police stories. Sometimes kidding around he'd try and scare him. Other times he'd describe a crime and challenge him to ask questions and try to identify who did it.

Half way to Massachusetts, Brian asked him about Pomford. He hadn't been able to confide in anyone about his fears, hadn't told Jenny during their departing tryst as he didn't want to come across as a weak worrier. Brian was probably assuming it was some rich-kids magical Neverland like in Peter Pan. He'd become a friend through many drives together so he told him the truth, a frightening headmaster who talked about control and discipline, check-in and check-out routine all day long, focus on athletics, definitely not his thing, and the absence of escape with no weekends allowed and maybe not even Thanksgiving and Christmas. He got afraid all over again as he went through the litany, biting his nails in a big way.

Brian exclaimed, "Holy Mary Malone, that's awful." He turned his head and stared over at Justin, momentarily taking his hands of the wheel though he quickly recovered. They drove silently for a little while, Brian obviously thinking. He had four boys, one Justin's age. Maybe he was thinking about them. Finally he said in a quiet voice, "Why would your father send you there?" Justin gave him no answer and Brian continued. "I think I told you that when I was a boy I lived in a small town in Ireland, Corrick-on-Shannon. Outside town there was an orphanage and an orphanage school for boys. It was run by some very strict Jesuits, non-stop discipline. The boys had no freedom whatsoever. I would see them in town. There was always a Jesuit right next to them watching everything they did. When we were bad my father threatened my brother and me with being sent to the orphanage. That scared us much more than any threat of a whipping.

"There was a small river near our house. The train to Dublin went over the river on a high trestle. The rumbling of railroad ties sometimes woke us at night. Starting when I was seven, I regularly went down to the river, trying to catch frogs and fish, though at seven I wasn't much good at either. One day just after I turned eight, I was walking along next to the trestle looking down into the water for frogs when a shadow fell on me. I looked up. A boy was dangling from the trestle his feet just two feet above me, a rope around his neck. He was wearing the lousy clothes the orphanage gave its boys. His face was purple, almost black. His mouth was open as though trying to scream and his hanging tongue was black. I couldn't much tell age when I was eight but knew he was much older than I. They later told me he was sixteen. I ran terrified back to the house, running faster than I'd ever run before, screaming all the way. Cried off and on for weeks despite everything my parents did to comfort me. I still get nightmares about the hanging. Get more nightmares from that hanging than from all the horrible things I've seen as a cop.

"Things like that happen when you lock boys together under strict discipline. No freedom. It's not healthy. The worst comes out."

He turned to Justin, tears in the eyes of this gruff Sargent of Detectives. Putting his big hand on his shoulder he said, "I'm very sorry for you. It shouldn't be happening. A good boy like you shouldn't be sent into strict discipline. The school is totally wrong for you. I want you to promise me something. If anything bad happens to you at the school call me. I'm not kidding. Call me."

Brian handed Justin a card. "This has both my number at Headquarters and my home number. I usually don't give out my home number. But I want you to call me day or night if you need help. Whatever you do don't lose it. Promise me."

"I promise."

The gloom inside the car came to be matched by gathering gloom outside. It had been sunny and bright coming up the Hudson Valley and through New York to Western Massachusetts. But as soon as they got near the school low gray clouds appeared, shielding the sun and darkening the landscape.

They drove directly to the admission's office, its location burned in Justin's memory by his last visit. He'd been told that his sophomore class would also include a large group of boys who had been admitted the previous year as freshmen, prior-year boys, and signage divided the milling group of boys and parents into those admitted the previous year and newbies.

At the door was a man who looked like the headmaster— same bleak, unsmiling face, dark suit, dead white skin, only taller than the headmaster. The man dealt with several other boys and they waited. Finally it was their turn. He introduced himself as Edmund Cranch, the admission's officer, confirming Justin's observation, son like father. A scowl appeared when Mr. Cranch heard his name. With grudging slowness he pulled several documents out of a beat-up briefcase.

Turning to Brian he said, "These are the admission papers, responsibility waivers, rules of conduct we expect parents to sign on behalf of their sons. You failed to sign when we mailed them to you. We need your signature before we can admit your son."

The man had to be stupid. Brian was dressed in a nice looking sport coat he'd put on for the occasion, but looked nothing like the aristocratic parents of other boys standing around them.

Brian explained the situation, that his father was in Europe and hadn't been around to sign papers.

Cranch's frown deepened. "We assumed Mr. Whitthorne would be accompanying his son. Father's always want to see their son's entrance to school. Without signed admission papers there's not much we can do. It's a matter of legal liability."

Brian said, "This is easily handled. His father is getting back shortly. I'll take the papers back to him for signature and get them back quickly, even if I have to drive them back myself."

"No. We can't admit him. You'll have to take him back home. Maybe apply next year." Cranch appeared to be one of those bureaucratic types who got power out of rigorous enforcement of rules.

Brian said with a somewhat intimidating look on his face, "I'm a police officer, not a lawyer, but I know a contract when I see one. As I understand it, the Headmaster personally accepted the tuition check from Justin's father. You can't renege on the contract by bringing up some papers that weren't mentioned when the check was accepted."

Cranch said, "The Head has never allowed us to admit a boy without the boy's papers being signed in advance. We haven't even completed the genealogy study, but I'll take it up with him."

From that Justin learned that the Headmaster was called the Head. Cranch disappeared into the administrative building and they were left cooling their heels for a good half hour. Justin turned to Brian. "For a moment there I didn't think I'd have to go to Pomford. But then what? Probably something worse. The woman has talked about sending me to a strict school in England. At least I'm in the U.S. where I can call my aunt Gertrude, or maybe you, if something bad happens."

Cranch finally came out looking quite unhappy, gave them an angry look, and proceeded to admit a number of boys who had arrived after them, from what Justin could hear assigning them room numbers in the various dormitories, giving them class assignments, schedules, an orientation map, and providing a description of the athletics available for later sign up.

Only when everyone else was processed, and looking around finding nothing else to do, did Cranch turn back to them. "All right. We've agreed to admit you." He grimaced as though he had a bad taste in his mouth. "I think it's a mistake without the signed papers. However, the Head says to waive the rules for you. Never happened before. You've some powerful friends." He then gave Justin the materials he'd given the other boys being admitted, going through them in a perfunctory fashion. For his rooming assignment, Cranch gave Justin the name of a house on main street, Claiborne House, with no further direction. Justin got the impression Cranch was hoping he'd get lost trying to find it. This was not a good start to his career at Pomford.

They finally found the house. It proved to be almost a mile away from the classrooms and even further from the dining hall and gym. He anticipated a very unpleasant walk to breakfast and classes in rain or snow, and probably at many other times. Claiborne House was impressive, one of the largest on the street and the only one with a full portico and columns. He noted Ionian.

Parked in front of the house was a Cadillac limousine with a chauffeur in full livery standing formally beside. The front door of the house was partly open, seemingly in invitation. He knocked anyway and a man appeared. Except for one thing, he was an ordinary looking man, receding brown hair, face undistinguished, not memorable, of average height, a small belly giving lie to his athletic body. The exception was his eyes, cold, piecing blue eyes, the strongest eyes Justin had ever seen. Justin felt a mote of fear. The eyes looked him up and down as though trying to force out everything hidden. A power to dominate in the eyes. This wasn't somebody you could joke with. No way, no how.

The man introduced himself with a deep voice as Mr. Brown. He didn't make the same mistake Edmund Cranch had made of assuming Brian was his father, and called his wife, Shirley, to meet him. She was very pretty, bobbed blond hair, big blue eyes, looking to be in her early forties with Mr. Brown much older, maybe in his late fifties. Her welcoming smile contained a note of sympathy.

Mr. Brown said, "I teach sophomore English." He reached out and took Justin's class assignment sheet away from him, no by-your-leave. "You're in an advanced English class. You won't be in my class."

Justin had a small feeling of relief. Not somebody he wanted to teach him.

"I'm the baseball coach. In the spring, come and try out. Now let's go upstairs and meet your roommate."

Roommate? Nobody had said anything about a roommate. He trudged up the broad, beautifully balustraded stairs behind Mr. Brown, the suitcases lugged behind by Brian. The bedroom turned out to be quite spacious with a high ceiling, a bed on each side, two mammoth dressers and two desks, and the art on the walls some of the klutziest he'd ever seen.

Mr. Brown saw him looking at it. "Those were done years ago by our two daughters. They're at Stoneleigh Prospect School for Girls now. Have to keep them out of the clutches of you Pomford boys." He said this with a straight face, dead serious, not joking.

Three people were on the other side of the room. Closest was a very attractive man dressed impeccably in an expensive business suit. He knew expensive clothes when he saw them. Further away a quite beautiful woman was busy unpacking suitcases into a dresser. She was also dressed impeccably and expensively.

Seated on the nearest bed was his erstwhile roommate. At first look he couldn't find any resemblance to his parents. There was an odd pudginess about the boy's body that made him look like he hadn't yet lost his baby fat. His face was also pudgy. He looked like a crib child grown large, a small, pouty mouth, unremarkable gray eyes embedded in flesh, definitely not a handsome fellow. On a closer examination he could see some small resemblance. It was his parents with their bodies stuffed with squiggly jello or something.

The family, the Randolphs, turned out to come from Philadelphia, big muck-de-mucks he assumed because they'd met his father on one occasion and knew a number of his father's more important friends. The roommate was introduced as Gerald.

"Don't call me Gerry. My name is Gerald." His voice was high and squeaky as though it hadn't changed yet. Odd.

Brian helped Justin unpack and the Randolphs and Brian left together. Tears burst from Gerald's eyes at his parents' departure. He seemed about twelve, not fifteen.

Mr. Brown came in and laid down the house rules, the sheriff laying down the law. It was primarily about keeping quiet and not venturing anywhere on the first floor. His eyes flashed when he said that. Something like pain of death to go on the first floor where the girls were housed. Also, they were told they were expected to keep their room clean and make their beds. Really? At Hudson Military they had maids to clean rooms and make beds.

Later Justin walked with Gerald down the long Main Street to the dining hall, a substantial building composed of the dining room itself and a large assembly room. They were required to sit on the floor of the assembly room for what they were told was the first of the weekly assemblies that would be held throughout the year.

The Head stood before the fireplace addressing them. The initial part was a welcome to the new boys and hope that the returnees had a good summer and were ready to buckle down for a productive year. Occasionally he smiled, the same spectral smile that had frightened Justin, but at least he was smiling. He seemed genuinely please to have five hundred boys under his thumb. While the boys didn't look alike they were all the same kind of upper-class boys he met at social gatherings in New York, a wasp-only gathering. And so many were blond-headed, a school of blond-headed blue-eyed boys. Did the Head purposely choose blond-headed boys for Pomford?

The Head said, "You students come from the finest families in America, the best breeding in America. With your family backgrounds, you have the capability to becoming the future leaders of America. That's the goal of Pomford. Turning out leaders. That's what we expect from you. That's what your families expect of you. That's why they sent you here. We will do our best to educate you and direct you to that goal. Then we will pass you on to the leading universities in America. They're working with us to carry on what we start. Gentlemen of breeding leading the country, not just in this generation but in future generations. We expect you to carry on through your families and your breeding to produce future leaders for many generations to come, marry the right women, woman of breeding, raise children who understand the importance of good breeding." In the last part he got quite animated. The Head seemed as obsessed with good breeding as Ahab was with his whale. Same damn stuff as his father spouted. Ahab was a little crazy in his obsession. Maybe the Head was, too. Great news.

"Each of you must make an utmost effort at all times, not just in studies but in moral behavior. Any shirking on studies will not be tolerated. Demerits will be given for failure to study and for any foolishness in class. Missing check-ins without excuse will also result in demerits." The Head's face hardened and his voice rose, "Thievery, drinking, cheating, bringing girls on campus, and particularly degenerative behavior will not be tolerated." He did not explain degenerative behavior but raised his voice further when he said it.

He turned his gaze slowly boy by boy over all the boys in the room. The frown lines around his mouth had deepened. An intimidating look. Making sure each boy got the message. Some new boys drew back.

Then the spectral smile appeared again and his voice dropped. "The symbol of Pomford is the whale, strong and intelligent. You're all Pomford whalers. All together on a voyage. And just as whalers on a ship, you need to help each other. If you see someone struggling with homework help him. If you see someone struggling on the playing field, instruct him. And for all of you, extend particular help to the new boys and welcome them to our family.

"A whaling ship was one of the great enterprises of mankind. Working together, small numbers of whalers captured great creatures many times more powerful than the puny whale boats they were rowing. You too are going to have an impact on the world far greater than your numbers. You are part of a movement taking us through the generations that will produce better men and women for America."

Again the Head had donned his Ahab enthusiasm. Some of the boys glanced at each other and rolled their eyes or grimaced. They'd obviously heard it many times before.

"Now for you new boys, we believe very strongly in athletics. The boy becomes a man through athletics."

That let him out. A boy forever.

"Each of you will be part of an athletic team each season. Football is the Fall sport, the most important game you can play at Pomford. Basketball and swimming in the Winter; Baseball, lacrosse and track in the Spring. You may be on a third-level team, or JV, or varsity. But whatever team you're on play your hardest. You'll be playing other schools and the goal is to win each game, and that's not just JV and varsity games. Third team games, too. Pomford has the best winning record in New England. It's your boys' job to keep it that way."

His frown came back. "For you new boys, we have very strict rules here. Obey them. At first you'll find them hard. But over time you'll find they are meant to protect you."

Again eye rolling from some of the boys.

"The rules guide you to best behavior and keep you out of trouble. They give you direction. Without rules you'd waste your precious Pomford learning time on foolishness and immoral behavior. Unlike other New England prep schools, we don't write down our rules. You'll learn them through living them. We do it that way because it's exactly how you'll learn the rules of life when you become an adult, by living them. All your life you'll face hard rules that you need to follow to become a respected leader. We're teaching you here how to live by the rules."

Justin's mind had been wandering a bit. He'd been looking around at the other boys. The rules brought him back. What a lot of bullshit. From what he'd heard Andover and Exeter were great schools and managed to operate just fine without all these restrictions. And what was all that lecturing about students' future lives, marry the right woman, raise the right children? Made no sense. What was a prep school doing trying to control the future lives of its students?

The Head continued with a lot about the proud history of the school, about alumni who had gone on to be leaders of America, and for the new students some of the ins and outs of daily living. Afterwards he introduced the Pomford staff, starting with coaches, again athletics first before scholastics. Finally it ended. Much too long a spiel. His ass was getting sore on the hard floor. The dinner almost made up for it, excellent roast beef.

A boy at his table, a prior-year boy, said to the table, a lot of new boys present. "Don't be fooled. They always lay out good food at first. Gets you new boys thinking everything will be super. You're being fattened up for the kill."

On the way back he asked Gerald how he came to be off-campus like he was.

Gerald said, "I got admitted in the Spring. Then I got real sick. They never found out what it was. My parents told the school I was sick and the school thought I wasn't coming. But they never returned the deposit. I got better and my father called the school a few weeks ago and told them I'd recovered. They had to take me. I sure wish I hadn't recovered when I did.

"I hate being away. I get scared when I'm away. I never wanted to come. My father attended Pomford, and his father. My father said almost all the boys here are sons or grandsons of prior students. That I had to attend to carry on the family tradition. It's the worst thing that ever happened to me."

Back at the room Gerald cried himself to sleep and then had crying jags throughout the night, making it difficult for Justin to sleep. Lying there he took stock of things.

His feeling was of being in an unknown world, a stranger in some foreign country with everything unsettling. Almost like when he was lost in the woods that one time at Camp Passumpsic. Faced now not with dense underbrush but rules equally confining, rules denying him freedom and which would require him to do things he hated. The head had said welcome the new boys. He'd looked around at the other boys. Would they become friend or foe? None had welcomed him. A cause for concern.

The next day was as gloomy as the day before. Some good news. Not just in English but also in other courses he'd been assigned to advanced classes designed for the most intelligent boys, with the most challenging curriculum and best teachers. They must have gotten his transcript from Hudson Military. And best of all, he was allowed in the biology class, though it was usually restricted to juniors. He'd told Jenny he might want to be a doctor, and he did. As the days progressed he had no complaint about the courses. He found he could handle them with relative ease though many struggled. It was the rules that got him. They were much worse in practice than what the Head had laid out.

The check-in system would have made San Quentin proud. It made no sense. The teachers knew what students were in their classes. But you still had to stand at semi-attention at class entrance, state your name clearly (no mumbling), and get your name formally entered on the sign-in sheet while wasting class time standing there waiting. Same check-in rigamarole at assembly, church, athletics, study hall, and everything else. The dorms were even worse— bed check at lights-out, like they were all six year olds, the only advantage of not being in a dorm. One day he was late to a class because he'd been talking to a teacher in the prior class. This got him a demerit and a warning that three demerits would result in kitchen and garbage duty, whatever that was.

Then there was athletics. He stared at the sign-up board a long time. It wasn't going to go away however much he wished it. There were two choices, cross country and football. Running through the dismal Pomford Valley as fall turned to winter, no thank you.

Football had sign-ups from all the sophomores he wanted as his friends, the most popular boys. He put his name down.

He'd never played football before, and when he checked in to the first practice found that none of the popular boys were on his third team. They were all on the JV and one large fellow was third string on the varsity.

One boy who was on his team was a fellow he'd started to think of as "The Suit," Reginald Montford III (never Reggie), the heir to one of the great Detroit automotive fortunes. He stood out from everyone as he always wore a double-breasted business suit and carefully polished shoes rather than the blue blazer/sport coat, chinos, white buck combination all other boys wore. He seemed nice enough. The Suit was in one his classes. They had some good conversations. One day Justin asked him why he always wore a suit. All he got by way of answer was, "Because." Maybe with his wealth he had stiff-necked parents who required their son to dress as formally away as at home. However, his parents weren't monitoring him at school. Or perhaps it was his way of demonstrating to other boys that he was a cut above. The Suit definitely seemed to feel he was better than everyone else, bragging about his wealth and family. Justin could see trouble coming. If you're different from other boys you were an easy target. He had seen it with two boys at Hudson Military and a boy he knew in New York.

At the assembly the Head had introduced a man named Jenkins as his assistant. The Head said his factotum, a word Justin liked. Jenkins was a square man, muscular, ruddy complected, always appearing upset at something, often looking suspiciously at the boys as though he assumed they were all criminals. The first day of football practice Jenkins came down from the administrative office and opened the lockers holding the football gear. It turned out every time anyone wanted athletic equipment, football, baseball, you name it, Jenkins and his key had to be hunted down. Justin was told it stemmed from boys making unauthorized use of footballs in the past. All this strictness for a few footballs, wow.

Other boys described Jenkins to Justin as the Head's "enforcer." Whenever a boy did something forbidden, it was to Jenkins he was sent. He had a reputation for harshness. It was said that very few boys had a session with Jenkins without coming out with a scared, whipped-dog look about them.

Getting into the football uniform he felt a little like a gladiator preparing for battle, sort of ego boosting. Maybe this would be all right. He pictured myself charging through the line for a touchdown like he'd seen at the one New York Giants football game he'd attended. Yes, a running back or maybe quarterback, he'd accept either.

Instead when he got to where the team was gathering the coach looked him over and said, "You skinny guy, what's your name?"

"Justin."

"We're going to make you a guard."

"And you over there looking stupid what's your name?"

"Reginald Montford the third."

"Well Reggie, from now on you're a tackle."

So much for glory. He and The Suit were grunts, linemen, The Suit a little bigger so a tackle rather than a guard. And he didn't think The Suit had been looking stupid. Perhaps embarrassed for not being in his usual business suit and baffled as to what was going on just as he was. Gerald had told him he'd also signed up for football. Justin looked around and spotted Gerald. He'd been assigned as water boy and minder of the equipment.

They were first taught the three point stance. The Suit fell over, looking like he'd never had to squat before in his life. Maybe he had servants to do the squatting.

The coach said, "Your problem is you've got too much fat in your ass. You're bottom heavy." Then coach practically doubled over with laughter as his own joke. Justin sympathized with The Suit though he found himself laughing along with everyone else. Around campus The Suit became "Lard Ass" to many of the boys. "Crisco in the can."

Then there were drills, pushing a sled type thing he could hardly budge at maximum effort, tackling a dummy stuffed with straw. The first time the dummy swung back at him, knocking him over. Not much better the second time. He got the same derisive laughter as that given The Suit when The Suit fell from his three point stance. Couldn't he just grab onto opponent's clothing and helmet as they ran past him in the line? Not allowed as it made sense.

Every day a repeat of the practice, always worse. Wind sprints. He would try to stretch out on the ground afterward but was always rousted right up for another wind sprint. Contact drills. He was usually paired with Harry. Harry didn't look very big but most times Justin ended up on his back on the ground. Harry would stand over him grinning and say something like, "Loser" or "Weak ass." Play drills. He found sometimes he was a pulling guard and had several runners knock him aside when his slowness got in their way. Worst was practice on rainy days, which seemed to be most days. They did call it off if it was raining heavily. But drizzle, "Pomford boys don't let a little damp stop them," was the mantra. Rain running down his face, he would look over at another boy and be sure the boy was going to try to kill him in the next play. This was the shittiest thing he'd ever had to do. By far the shittiest in his entire life.

His despair increased as the weather worsened. From constant complaining he knew the other boys felt it too. They were being oppressed by the tight restrictions of the school. The weather added to it, oppression from above to match the oppression from below, dreary in a soul constricting way, a place where human existence was constrained and all the bad magnified within a prescribed space. Rain during football practice was only a small part of it. It was always miserable, football or no football. Why? Much speculation from all the boys. Clearly the slow moving Pomford River had something to do with it. Fog tendriled up from the river each morning, wrapping the white houses in dismal gray, so thick it was sometimes difficult to practice football passes, and lasting all day, often days on end. Boys appeared then disappeared ghosting through the fog, talking apparitions. The surrounding hills trapped the fog, and when a wind finally came, and the fog dissipated, gray clouds swept in to take the fog's place as though the clouds had been waiting stage left for a signal from the hills to enter the Pomford theater. If they were lucky one day in four was brighter, often a pale light masquerading as sunshine that gave emphasis to the grayness of the rest of the days.

He said to Gerald, " Isn't this the freakin lousiest weather ever, day-in day-out horrible?" Gerald gave his usual response to about everything, "I want to go home."

He'd been looking forward to the autumn leaves. Sugar maple, beech, birch, elm, sumac, and other normally colorful trees and bushes abounded in the Valley. The weather of the Pomford Valley deprived him of that joy too, obscuring the leaves in fog, robbing them of their vibrant colors by thick overcasts, and finally dashing them to the ground in a violent rain and wind storm. Pomford seem to require even bright Fall leaves to be gray.

Sitting on the football sidelines one day, rain drizzling on their faces, The Suit echoed his thoughts, "I think the school is breeding the bad weather. Maybe you noticed. Bad weather seems to come from miles around to sit on us. Then it doesn't leave. Maybe it likes the darkness here. Right at home in the dark atmosphere. Dark school attracting dark weather. Misery likes company."

Justin wondered about it. Noah in the Bible suffered with constant rain because of the iniquity of the people. Pomford? The worst of it was a prior-year boy told Justin that what they'd been experiencing was good weather for Pomford. "Wait until Winter."

They read *Ethan Fromm* in English class. Pomford was Ethan Fromm country in spades. Ethan Fromm would have felt right at home in the Pomford Valley, a melancholy landscape, an incarnation of frozen woe. Hard to be nice to each other with bad weather all the time. Many swearing matches between boys he thought were friends and a few fist fights, not many. Pomford had a strict prohibition against anything physical backed by the threat of months of onerous kitchen duty for offenders.

He did see the famous Mutt and Jeff fight. Daniel Harrington (nicknamed Gunner, a basketball player who never had the ball without shooting) was about the tallest boy in school. His roommate,

Markham Grainer (Mouse), was about the shortest. They were always together and known around campus as Mutt and Jeff. The fight was apparently because Gunner had taken most of the space on the lower shelves of their closet and Mouse had trouble reaching the top shelf. For best friends to fight over something so petty showed how bad things had gotten, lousy school, lousy weather, lousy on friendship.

Mouse flailed and flailed at Gunner, rapid punches one after another. None landed. Gunner held him away with his long arms, all the while laughing and mocking. "Runts can't fight. Look at you. Arms too short to reach anybody. Just a 'F'ing stupid windmill." Mouse had one advantage in being short. He was close to a vital part of Gunner's body. Mouse planted a beautifully aimed kick to the balls. Gunner writhed to the ground, "You bastard. I'll get you for this."

Mouse danced around him, continuing to throw air punches, then danced some more, clasping his hands above his head in victory. Grinning from ear to ear, "Always my best punch." A rare moment of laughter for Justin. For the two boys months of kitchen duty.

The only half-way decent day was Sunday. A leisurely breakfast with lots of great jelly doughnuts laid out for the taking on long trays in the kitchen. Ten o'clock was church in the red-brick congregational church. He always admired the thin white spire reaching up, maybe trying to get away from Pomford. Rousing church songs, the boys belting it out, and a sermon on some moral subject from one of the faculty, a time to close the eyes for a little rest.

After lunch was free time, boys gathered on the broad lawns, often in fog or rain, chucking a football around, playing touch football and other games, or meeting in protected places to talk. New boys would clump with other new boys, though some would make a try at befriending prior-year boys in their own clumps. This was generally unsuccessful. It was as though the prior-year boys, having gotten through a year at Pomford, felt they were members of a special club, didn't want to share that club with new boys. A survivors' club.

On Sundays, Justin found himself excluded from joining any of the other boys, whether new or prior-year, and the same thing during the week, all Gerald's fault. The boys shunned Gerald. They looked over his doughy body, heard his squeaky child-like voice, and backed away. And when Justin was with Gerald they backed away from him, too. He very much feared they thought he was like Gerald, Gerald and he a pair of losers. Awful. He was saddled with the bad image of Gerald.

He tried to ditch him. Impossible. Gerald latched on to him like he was a beloved older brother, or like Gerald's father had died and he'd become his father. Maybe it was shyness, or maybe a traumatic past experience with boys that made him fearful. Whatever, Gerald didn't seem to like other boys, only him. All conversation was reserved for him. And he couldn't get away from the conversation. Gerald insisted on walking together to the dining hall and classes. Waited for him after class to corral him into walking back together to the room. Then Gerald tried to talk to him after dinner when they were supposed to be studying. It was mostly about his parents and how much he missed them and missed home. Sometimes tears at those times. How different was the sheltered, love-protected life described by Gerald from his own. He never responded with his own stories. Gerald probably wouldn't believe a family life so terrible and different from his own. And if he did believe him he might latch on even more tightly out of sympathy, the last thing Justin wanted.

What could have caused Gerald's parents to send him to Pomford? Made no sense. Justin felt he was missing something. Third generation or not, Gerald needed to be home where his parents could take care of him. He needed constant ministration. Gerald at Pomford spelled disaster.

Sometimes Gerald would launch into a rant, his high voice getting shriller, "I hate Pomford! I hate the teachers. They're mean to me. And the boys are mean to me. You're the only one that's nice. It's the worst place in the world. The worst place I've ever been." Then a few tears would trickle down Gerald's face.

Justin hated Pomford just as much and commiserated with Gerald, comparing notes—lousy food, demeaning check ins, athletics designed to embarrass with public failure, unfriendly fellow students. What had happened to the Head's admonition to help the new boys?

Gerald's emotional balance worsened as the weeks progressed—Increasingly strong rants against the school, tearful entreaties to his parents to come and get him, as though they could hear him, and a substantial fall-off in doing homework. One day in mid October Justin returned from class, unaccompanied by Gerald for a change, came into the room, and found a new Gerald. Gerald stood formally as he entered, looked at him with more purpose than he had seen in him, and in a deeper voice than he'd previously used said, "I'm going to commit suicide. My favorite uncle did it in Pittsburg. I can't stand it anymore. Please don't try and stop me."

Justin, shaken, said, "You can't do that. What about your parents. They love you."

"I found out you can't call home. They only have one outside phone for boys. It's in the administrative office. They don't let new boys use it. I think they don't want us calling home and complaining about the school. I can't reach my parents to ask them to take me home."

"Well, that doesn't make sense. I'm sure if you asked and said it was important they'd let you." Gerald stared at Justin, then Gerald's lips pursed in determination and he slowly shook his head.

The next two days Justin spent a lot of time with Gerald, watched him closely, talked to him about light things. No more suicide talk from Gerald.

On the afternoon of the third day Gerald pulled him aside before lunch and said, "They finally let me talk to someone in the Head's office, his son Edmund Cranch. I begged Cranch to be allowed to call home. He asked me why I wanted to make the call. I was afraid to tell him. I didn't want him to know it was because I hated the school and wanted to go home. They would have punished me for not liking the school and kept me here to silence me. So I left without calling."

Gerald was definitely not thinking clearly.

The next day Gerald said he wasn't feeling well and wouldn't go to breakfast. In the middle of breakfast, Justin had a realization— Gerald hadn't looked sick at all. He dashed from the dining hall, ran the blocks to the house (the wind sprints paid off), up the stairs, burst into the room. Gerald was sitting on the window ledge, his legs dangling out, dressed in his best clothes as if appearances mattered, rocking slowly back and forth as though trying to get up his nerve. With the first floor raised for the portico, and high ceilings throughout the house, Gerald was a good twenty feet over the brick sidewalk below.

Justin stopped short, turned and raced down the stairs into the Brown's forbidden living area. Shirley was there and hurried up the stairs with him.

At the door she said in the calmest and most comforting voice imaginable, "Now, now. What seems to be the trouble? I'm going to personally take care of it whatever it is. Look at me. Stop looking down. I promise you from the bottom of my heart I'm going to make everything all right." She said this with total conviction. "Tell me what the problem is. If you tell me I guarantee I'll fix it. And I am going to get your parents right up here."

Gerald stopped rocking. "You're going to get my parents here?"

"Certainly. They'll come here as fast as they possibly can. By tomorrow if not sooner."

He got off the window sill and started packing.

The relief on Gerald's face when his parents arrived was so great it balanced out the shock of seeing Gerald on the window ledge. Had it all been staged to get release from Pomford? Maybe that pudge head had some smarts after all.

Now he was alone against Pomford. Unprotected. All of the other new boys had roommates, a team to face challenges. Gerald may have been a weak team member, but at least he was there.

CHAPTER ELEVEN

With Gerald gone Justin reached out to other boys. He wanted to be part of things. The new-boy population was trying to find itself. It was like the *Lord of the Flies* book he'd just completed. Boys locked not on a tropical island but in a New England prep school, a school as foreign for many as a tropical island. How should you react to each other? Who would be a leader and who a follower? What clique should one join? It all had to be worked out by the new boys themselves and done in a pressure-cooker competition for athletic achievement, academic success, and popularity. No guidance from the school. The only restraints the school imposed were the check-in system, a prohibition against fighting, and the sleep-through Sunday sermons on morality.

It seemed at first like nobody had an identity, every new boy trying to find himself and gain prestige by whom they palled around with, and many by bullying other boys in an attempt to establish themselves as better than the boys bullied. The earlier bullying intensified. Verbal abuse became common. New boys turned against each other in the frustration of confinement. A hierarchy was being established, but the whole process was brutal to many boys. A few more cruel nicknames appeared. In addition to The Suit being chased around campus by keening calls of "Lard Ass," another boy, large and with a prominent nose, became "Rhino." He did look like a Rhino. Other new boys made grunting sounds when he appeared and moved away as quickly as possible, not wanting their standing in the developing social hierarchy diminished by being seen with a rhino. A thin boy became "Skelty" and tended to be ignored in any group as "too thin to see" or bumped into by boys muttering, "didn't see you." Mostly it was remarks by one boy to another, cruel jibes, belittling comments, meant to be funny to other boys but mean to the recipient. "Well monkey's can talk." That to a boy who did look a little like a monkey. "You're so pretty. Do you have a boyfriend?" and "You'd look good with breasts," the repeated comment to a boy that did look rather girlish. To a boy who failed a number of courses, "Dumbo lives." And "Stop following us. What are you? A dog?" Said to a boy who was trying to hang out with a group on the Sunday playing field.

Most of the boys under attack responded in kind, throwing back, "Stick it up your ass," or, "Eat shit," and like retorts. Eventually when the boy under attack continued to respond with insults, like for like, the boys tended to lay off. Insults traded back and forth became a constant. Never anything physical. The results of the Mutt and Jeff fight were well known. The prohibition against physical confrontation was being rigorously enforced. In October one boy ended up on kitchen duty much of the Fall just for pushing his roommate.

Much of the bullying was more subtle, exclusionary. A comment made by one boy with no response except blank stares at him from other boys. A walk-away when a boy approached. Sunday-afternoon teams chosen with a boy consistently left out. Even unfriendly looks could do it, relegating the boy to reside among the unaccepted, to a place where others looked down on him. Several boys were surviving by scurrying behind other boys, picking up the dribs and drabs of their companionship. The strenuous effort made him embarrassed. Camp followers.

The school didn't interfere no matter how bad the bullying and seemed to support it, or at least condone it. He saw teachers smiling at effective taunting of a devastated boy. And later he heard a long-time teacher talking to a new teacher as they watched some bullying. "At Eton they believe surviving bullying is one of the things that turns boys into strong men. We feel the same."

The world of the prior-year boys was different. Hierarchies had been established. Boys were already locked in the place assigned by their peers. Jockeying for position was finished. No taunting of prior-year boys by other prior-year boys. Not one prior-year boy assigned a cruel bullying nickname. And by his observation none of them joined in the overt or subtle humiliation of The Suit, Rhino, Skelty, or any other first-year boys.

The prior-year boys had organized themselves into three cliques. Erstwhile intellectuals formed one clique. They stayed mainly to themselves, were generally incompetent in athletics and not physically attractive, some even a little feminine. It was an obvious group for him to join. That he didn't was because the boys in that group weren't popular and he very much wanted to be popular. Also they made it very clear they didn't want him, rarely talked to him despite sharing advanced classes. Besides, they were all dull grinds of people. Another clique formed the core of sophomore athletics. They weren't as tightly bound together as the intellectuals, and some greeted him in friendly fashion, but he'd little in common with boys focused on athletics. The third was the one he liked best. A shifting cliche of twenty or so of the most popular boys, all were physically attractive, some athletic but without athletics being the center of their lives, and different from many others in that they behaved like gentlemen—no taunting, nice things said to other boys, congratulations even if not fully deserved, encouragement and support for others. That was probably how they got to be leaders of the class. Their good breeding was obvious.

He'd parted ways with his father but his father's instruction echoed in his mind: "Seek out boys with breeding, popular boys who are leaders. And you will know they are gentlemen not thugs by how they treat you."

He'd do what he could to be part of that clique, more because he liked them than because they were popular or gentlemen. They were great. If he was going to be a student at hated Pomford he deserved to be among them.

He knew two of them slightly from the few New York parties he attended between bouts of being sent away. They had to be aware that his father was at the top of New York society and that his family background was one of the finest in America. With this background he hoped the two boys would bring him into their group.

The two were roommates and usually together. He tried to become their friends, tried to sit next to them in assembly and church and to join them when they were with the popular boy group. He would approach the two of them, enter the conversation of the group, interject witty and intellectual comments that he hoped would gain him acceptance.

"The Head is like a coachman I know in Central Park. His horse and carriage are the most important thing in his life. If the Head's carriage ran over one of us my bet is he'd get out and examine the carriage, not the body." Then Justin would laugh trying to get others to join him.

Or

"The Head keeps talking about us and the whale. The whale is the biggest animal so it carries the most shit." More laugher from Justin..

Or

"The Head chose those Polish women to work the kitchen because they can't cook edible food. Cuts down on the school's food bill if nobody will eat the food." Again more laughter on his part.

Not much laughter in return. The popular boys usually just heard out his comments with a disinterested, unselfconscious watchfulness as though they were doing what they had to do to satisfy the Head's edict to be nice to new boys. Then they would move away, talking among themselves, excluding him.

One Sunday most of the popular boys in the class were grouped together talking on the playing field. As he came up to them, elated he could approach so many at the same time, he overheard a comment about the continuing terrible weather. He marched into the group and said with what he thought was an authoritative voice, "I've been doing a study of the weather here. Back in New York I read a number of books on the weather, got interested, and explored the science of weather forecasting. What we're experiencing is a series of persistent lows. You probably don't know this but the jet steam was discovered by the Japanese during World War II and used to carry fire balloons all the way across the Pacific from Japan. They were starting forest fires in the Western U.S. Well, the jet stream brings the lows and must be right above us from what I've observed. And the effect of the North South positioning of the Berkshires and Pomford's particular situation creates a microclimate—" All the boys turned away as a group and continued their conversation with him excluded.

In hindsight he believed showing off his intelligence was a mistake. Was intelligence ever a source of popularity among boys? He didn't see any of the other scholastic stars in his class being very popular. Maybe those he approached thought he was talking down to them.

The bond that the popular boy forged during the challenges of the first year at Pomford seemed an impenetrable barrier. One of the prior-year boys confirmed it, a jock named Randolph Crimmins (Randy). He was among the most popular boys in the school, tall, good looking, well bronzed from sailing on his family yacht all summer and keeping up his tan at Pomford, face to the sun during the rare sunny intervals. He was surprised Randy talked to him.

Randy took him aside after what had been another rejection as he attempted to join a group of popular boys. He said with a not terribly friendly look, "The head said to be nice to new boys. So I'm doing it. You're my one attempt to be nice to a new boy. I don't want to do it again so listen up. You ever watch war movies?"

"Yes. I watch them a lot."

"Then you remember there's often a group of soldiers who've gone through hell together, a platoon, a company, whatever. They've become brothers in survival. Then the movie will bring in a fresh-faced recruit. You'll watch the recruit being excluded from the group, having to prove himself. In movies he's usually accepted in the end. That's what the audience wants. There's no audience here. I'm not saying it was war last year. But it was tough for everyone. The restrictions were terrible. We grew together trying to deal with the school. Brothers in surviving Pomford. You're the fresh-faced recruit in the movie." Randy turned his back on him and marched away, the new boy requirement satisfied.

Discouraging. Where did that leave him? How was he supposed to prove himself? No one much wanted to even to be with him. He sensed what he had to offer was inadequate and that he had to be on his guard. Then a disconcerting thought. Was he repeating his father's hated behavior at the Union Club, being a suck up? Here he was trying to curry acceptance from the most popular boys just like his father curried acceptance from his social betters? Like father like son. But realizing what he was doing didn't change things. Having friends and becoming popular had become central to his life.

The Head's main focus in the Fall was varsity football. He talked about it at length at each assembly. According to the Head, Pomford had few losing football seasons in all the fifty-three years he'd headed Pomford.

In an early Fall assembly he looked with stony eyes over the assembled students and said, "How could you lose last Saturday to the Trinity freshmen? (Trinity was a college, not a prep school rival). Terrible play in the line. (The Trinity line outweighed the Pomford line by a good number of pounds per player). The whole school loses when we lose. Everyone here should understand something. All of you will lose unless the team plays harder, not just the team." He gave a threatening glance around the room.

Lose what? No food? And what were they supposed to do, beat up the team if it failed to perform? Bunch of crap.

Justin was told the varsity head coach, Mr. Tomlin, had been hired away from one of the top colleges in the Northeast. There he'd been head coach and a winning one for many years. He said to The Suit, "What prep school brings in a top college football coach?"

They looked at each other and said simultaneously, "Pomford does."

"Ringers," were also part of the deal, top high school football players from around the country who would come to Pomford for their senior year, or sometimes an extra year after high school, for these players a stepping stone to a good college in return for being the Head's gladiators. Much grumbling from players on the JV about this. He overheard many complaints.

One JV tackle, still on the JV his senior year when he'd hoped to be playing varsity, said to group that included Justin, "I worked my ass off all summer for the school and the team. Kept on Tomlin's regime. No drinking, no screwing around. Missed half the fun. For what. Shit that's what. I come back here and find that muscle-bound farm boy, Wacker, playing my position. From Iowa. Iowa, by God. The guy's name is stupid. Wacker. Probably wacking off all the time. That's why he's so stupid. Have to give him special tutoring for the easiest classes. Trying to keep him from failing until after the football season."

There was revenge. In a critical play against Andover, Wacker was outwitted, ended up sprawled on his back, and through the gap ran Andover for a touchdown. The Head, who always sat on the team bench, was on Wacker so long and loud that Wacker walked around the campus for days with his head down in seeming shock. And the whole school joined in calling him "Topple Over," "Topple" for short, this despite eking out a three point win in the Andover game. Had the Head, himself, invented the name "Topple" to torment poor Wacker? Was he that vindictive against boys he didn't like? Certainly the Head didn't stop the torment.

The football games were interminable and usually in rain. Varsity football brought rain. Pomford ringers would run through and pass over the likes of Choate, Hotchkiss, Exeter, and Andover. The students were required to stay to the very end no matter how far Pomford went ahead, then made their bedraggled way back to their rooms, changed, and had to appear for assembly.

There was always assembly after a winning varsity football game, which meant after about every game. Players were introduced to compulsory applause, compulsory as the teachers were watching to identify non-participants. Justin got a demerit warning for not clapping. The Head's lecture followed. Every time the same general speech though with differing words. A lot about the winning tradition of Pomford, further teams to be faced, the need to not let down on the strong effort just made, sort of an after-the-fact prep rally. But a reference to breeding always snuck in. The Head would say something like, "You succeeded today because good breeding brings the commitment, hard work, and practical intelligence necessary to win. Breeding shows through and showed through today. With good breeding you win and win in the right way."

The Suit said afterward, rolling his eyes,

"Win in the right way he says. Is using ringers the right way? I've heard other schools have some fifth-year boys but for them it is largely giving boys an academic opportunity, not recruiting athletes. And he talks about breeding. Our star running back, Guadopolo, is Italian. Those two large lineman, Kowalski and Laudanov, they were recruited from the Polish community down the river in Greenfield. How about Lightmoon! From Oklahoma. He's got to be part American Indian. It's lack of breeding that's winning for us."

As October proceeded it was already fully Fall, early in the Pomford Valley, trees brown and autumn-bare, grass dead, the sky white when it wasn't raining. Justin had still not made any friends, except perhaps The Suit, but now he mostly stayed away from The Suit as The Suit was so unpopular. And rarely did other boys converse with him. Even sitting together around a table in the dining hall it was usually he who initiated conversation. Thirty two days had been ticked off on his wall calendar. The ticking went slowly. Would it ever end?

His exclusion from the sophomore dorm to dwell instead at Claiborne House had one benefit. He wasn't sucked into the great turkey caper, a scheme hatched by some boys he knew slightly living in the sophomore dorm. One of them had discovered that there was a turkey farm about two miles out from the school. They thought it would be great if they had their own turkey, sort of a mascot for Thanksgiving. Five boys were deputized for a late-night raid. Justin was standing with some other boys when one of the participants in the raid told what happened. The fellow had been in Jenkins' office and came out looking shell shocked. Kitchen duty the rest of the year.

"Damndest thing. You never want to raid a turkey coop. Even worse at night. You can't see what you're doing. We thought we could sneak up on the coop, quietly open the gate, grab one when they were half asleep. No way. Those turkeys went wild as soon as we opened the gate, and boy are they fierce. Johnson ran after one, tried to grab it, and got pecked so hard he had blood running down his face. Not the friendly turkeys you see on television. You'd think you got one and it would jump away at the last second, peck the hell out of you. Sharp claws, too. And they're fast. Faster than we were. Finally we got one cornered, took all five of us and even then we all got pecked and clawed before we got a sack over its head. The other turkeys made a mass escape. It was like that breakout in the movie about the mass prisoner escape from the Nazi prison. Not a turkey in the enclosure. Scattered all over the landscape, squawking madly, seemed to be happy as hell to be free."

All the Pomford students, every class, was enlisted in a turkey roundup. The farmer had apparently heard the ruckus, peered out his window, and seen the boys high-tailing it with the turkey. Classes were cancelled the next morning by a very angry Head and all were dispatched to chasing turkeys. It became a game as to who could catch the most turkeys, a welcome respite from routine. A lot of hilarity. Some boys from the intellectual cliche tried to pounce on a turkey and collapsed together in a great muddle with the turkey looking on as though amazed at their stupidity. A football player chased after a turkey, cornered it against the side of a pond, and ended up in the water when he lunged for the turkey and missed. So much for a football tackle on a turkey. A somewhat fat boy Justin didn't like struggled up a tree after a turkey, got his hands pecked for his trouble, and fell in a foul smelling heap into a neighboring farmer's pig stye. He came up looking like the creature from the black lagoon. Pig shit in foul lumps festooned every part of his body, slimy locks hung down both sides of his head, a wail of outrage and disgust from his mouth. Justin bent over in laughter.

By the end of the day, Justin's turkey haul was the most of anyone, three turkeys. He got congratulations from boys who wouldn't talk to him before.

"That was really smart what you were doing."

What he'd done was to bring along a lot of sweet rolls from breakfast. He found that by laying pieces of sweet roll on the ground, starting far away and then closer, he could coax some of the less skittish turkeys near enough to grab them, albeit with many a peck.

Later he heard one of the teachers say to another teacher, "Things like this turkey raid wouldn't happen if the Head dismissed boys from school for bad behavior. Every other prep school does it."

He supposed it was true. The boys knew they could do just about anything and not be kicked out. In one way that was good news. He hated the fact he couldn't get himself kicked out. But joyful shenanigans could be organized with no one having to fear being kicked out. The turkey raid was by far the best thing that'd happened at Pomford. Not that it changed things. Same exclusion. No new friends from his turkey-hunt success.

That evening, in the darkness of his room, he sensed the old walls shudder as they steered a Fall gale around the house, and he thought about chance, the accident that had brought him there. How did accidents happen to a person—car crashes, lightning strikes, falling tree limbs, coming in on your father fornicating—were they avoidable or destined? Once they'd decided to occur were they there waiting for you, seeking you out, waiting as patiently as a crocodile on a river bank waits for prey? The crocodile had sure got him.

One boy who would talk to him was a junior, Fred Jamison, his father a senator from New Jersey. Fred was almost painfully thin, brown hair and gray eyes that stared through thick glasses. Despite his thinness he was a star athlete, captain of the cross country team. He turned out to be the lead gossip of the school, talked to everyone who would listen about what was going on. Fred would sometimes sit next to him at dinner and talk and talk, mouth full or mouth empty didn't matter, he talked through it.

Out of the blue Fred asked him, "Do you know about the suicide?"

"No."

"They've tried to hush it up. Horace Youngwood was the fellow's name, sort of a gawky looking guy. He was a senior. Had been bullied non-stop for three years. Called "Ichabod" like Ichabod Crane. I understand his whole class gave him the silent treatment because he complained to the Head about the bullying they were doing. Of course, the Head did nothing. They found him drowned about a mile down the Pomford River by the big bend. Had stones in his pockets."

"I've walked that way."

"Well, I was down by the river that Sunday and got to see the body. It was really amazing. He was real pale. Eyes staring. Maybe he was looking at the fish." Fred chuckled. "And his tongue was out and his mouth open with a little water drooling out." Fred demonstrated. "The most interesting thing was I could see he crapped himself. You should have seen it." All the while Fred was munching away at his food.

That was the pits. Justin started to feel a little queasy. He remembered what Brian had said about repressive confinement of boys and the suicide in Ireland. Brian would have thought the Pomford suicide a natural. With Fred's and Brian's descriptions the one thing he'd never do was commit suicide

Most of the conversation he overheard in the dining hall and elsewhere on campus revolved around the same subjects—athletics, things they did not like about the school, and girls. Jokes that were told were usually stupid, though he laughed along with everyone else. He'd learned it was deemed an act of aggression not to react to something as everyone else was reacting. He even had to laugh one day at a burping contest, something he hadn't seen since a ten-year-old at camp. Never did he hear anyone talk about what they were personally feeling at Pomford, their fears, their hopes for the future. It was as though they were inmates of a prison, couldn't talk about fears because others would take advantage of their fears, and didn't want to talk about hopes as they were so ephemeral that in talking about them they'd go away.

As to girls, everyone had a story. One would tell how far he got with a girl and another would "that's nothing" him. The stories would progress from a feel to fingering to one fellow who claimed his father had taken him to a whore house in Paris, doubtful as he was always bragging about something and couldn't give many of the juicy details the boys wanted to hear. Justin never said anything about Jenny. He hadn't lost her as he feared in the aftermath of the episode with her brother. Writing regular letters to her was about the only happy thing he did. He spent extensive time drafting his letters, trying to convey his passion in poetic language. Her replies were getting shorter and shorter. Unsettling.

On evening after writing her, his gaze was drawn to the darkened window. He hauled himself to his feet and went over. His reflection stared back with an expression he didn't recognize. There may have been a boy somewhere in the world more desolate than he. He doubted it.

CHAPTER TWELVE

Back in California the years passed slowly after the German visit in 1933. Henry felt increasingly discouraged about the progress of eugenics in the US. The fervor seemed to be departing with everything focused on the Depression. Leading citizens of California were gradually withdrawing as directors of the California Eugenics Foundation. Now it was mostly state bureaucrats, and God help him, in early 1935 Dodi had become a director. Fewer and fewer articles appeared in scientific journals about eugenics, and those that did were increasingly negative. Worse the Depression was changing the kind of women referred to him. More and more it was poor women, about ninety-percent Mexican, impoverished women whose additional children might be a burden to the state. Dodi and his ilk seemed to be using eugenics as a way to cut down the overburdened welfare rolls of Depression-era California. Referrals of the mentally defective and criminal had declined. He said to Helen, "I didn't get into eugenics to give hysterectomies to impoverished Mexican women. That's not what it's supposed to be about." Should he even continue?

He and Helen talked it over with Helen urging him to stay with it. "It's your life's work."

"Okay a while longer. I want to see what happens in Germany. If the German program blossoms it may drag California back on track."

And the program in Germany did seem to be blossoming. At the end of 1935, a California colleague visited Germany and wrote him,

You will be interested to know that your work has played a powerful part in shaping the opinions of the group of intellectuals who are behind Hitler in their epoch making eugenics program. Everywhere I sense their opinions have been tremendously stimulated by American thought. I want you, my dear friend, to carry this realization with you the rest of your life, that you have really jolted into action a great government of seventy million people.

Wonderful. After the German delegation left he'd had California publish over one hundred thousand German-language booklets explaining eugenics and promoting it as a national cause for Germany. With his support California paid to have these booklets widely circulated in Germany. The same colleague who visited Germany, and who had written him the laudatory letter, reported from a later visit that the booklets were being widely read and were generating popular enthusiasm for eugenics.

With the encouraging news from Germany Henry soldiered on in his eugenics crusade, bolstered by Helen's optimism that things would get better after the Depression. "Wait until people have a chance to study what happened. They'll have to conclude that supporting defective people through the Depression placed a tremendous burden on society."

He wasn't so sure. Why hadn't the German introduction of eugenics at the end of 1933 immediately reenergized California eugenics as he'd hoped it would?

Two letters a year was the average from Gerhard. They would always start by tracing developments in eugenics in Germany. Gerard was obviously very proud of what was being accomplished. The initial eugenics infirmaries in existing institutions were being replaced by purpose-built separate facilities. The bloodline-tracing project and the loan program to foster desirable marriages were both going well with the goal to produce more blond, blue eyed Aryan children and fewer non-Aryan ones. In a letter in 1937 Gerard was able to state with obvious delight that they had done well over 100,000 sterilizations, far exceeding the number in the US. Always the letters ended with superb descriptions of the natural wonders he and Brigit saw in their hikes, particularly around Murren, and in descriptions of skiing adventures, something the Bensons had never tried.

Henry's letters in return were filled with their life, their hikes, their gratitude for having each other, also his frustration with the eugenics program in California. Gerard wrote back in several letters that he shouldn't worry. *When the world sees what Germany is accomplishing in eugenics the whole world will want to copy it.*

A different kind of letter arrived in 1938, plain white envelope, mailed in Pomona, address letters cut from a newspaper. Henry thought it might be a clumsy advertising circular, opened and read it, and sat down white of face.

Helen came over, "What's wrong. Somebody die."

"I don't think I should let you read this."

"Don't be silly. We share everything."

He handed it to her and had her to sit down before she read it.

The letter was composed of pasted down words, again cut out of newspapers.

Murder justified by doctrine is still murder. You killed my sister. You and Helen will also be killed. The two of you are not worth a day in my sister's life. Look for me. I am next to you. But you no see me. The man beside you on Main Street, Pomona, when you go into the Safeway. Seated across from you in your favorite restaurant, Papa Joe's, watching you eat your artichoke dish favorite. Passing you on your hikes around Lake Arrowhead. You always smile when you see me. Closer and closer, sometimes almost touching you. Closer and closer to killing you. But I no act swiftly. I want you to suffer a long time as I have suffered, knowing all the while you may be killed at any moment. And when it happens it will be when you no expect it, as my sister died no expecting death from your hands.

Helen's was shaking all over when she finished reading. "What should we do?"

"Probably a nut case. I'll call Lieutenant Burns down at headquarters. He'll get to the bottom of it."

Burns arrived promptly, a good friend of theirs from church. He remonstrated with them for all their handling of the letter, saying if they got another not to open or handle it. Then he said, "It is obviously written by someone intelligent, trying to scare you as much as possible. We'll check it out but I wouldn't worry too much if I were you. It's very rare for someone who writes a threatening letter to act on the threat. I can't remember one case in Pomona and I've seen a lot of threatening letters. The writers of these letters accomplish what they want just by making the threat. They don't want to kill. They want to scare. Many doctors get a threatening letter at one time or another."

Henry admitted he'd gotten one a few years back.

But this wasn't one time, a letter a week, regular as clockwork. Following police instruction they didn't open them, but the police said they were all the same, pasted down words cut out from newspapers and magazines. The police tried to trace them with no luck. At one time or another they were being mailed from every postal box in the greater Pomona area.

The effect on Helen was probably just what the writer intended. She wouldn't go on hikes any more or out to dinner. Shopped as little as possible while looking fearfully at those around her. And her sunny disposition disappeared under despondency. Henry wasn't much better, and took to weekly storm-ins to police headquarters, demanding action. Eventually they asked him not to come in any more while assuring him they were doing everything they could, even putting surveillance on some of the postal boxes.

As though somehow tied to the threat letters, a great change came in Gerard's letters in 1938. Everything was stilted and formal, looking like Gerard had carefully studied every word he wrote. The Bensons had heard some disturbing things about what was going on in Germany and concluded Gerard was probably writing as he did for fear of people reading his mail. There were, however, some instances where Gerhard had cleverly gotten around the censors. In one letter of 1938 he wrote,

Agriculture is booming. We have decided to put in large horse paddocks throughout Germany like the ones you described.

Henry read it as large camps for undesirables planned through-out Germany.

A letter in 1939,

Our programs are going well. They are focused on the same type of per-son as in the surgery you described at Folsom prison.

Focus on Jews.

Then in 1940 a letter said,

Remember the book written by the World War I doctor you mentioned. I find it excellent and we intend to follow it on a large scale.

Mass euthanasia.

Putting it all together what Gerhard was telling him was that there were plans for wide-spread incarceration of Jews in camps and the start of a mass euthanasia program. His cohorts in the California and national eugenics movement were ecstatic that what the U.S. had birthed was flowering in Germany. They saw it as the realization of their goals and work. He knew the truth.

He contacted the State Department and gave them his infor-mation. They thanked him but he didn't hear anything further. Probably they knew it already.

The 1940 letter from Gerhard was the last Henry received. After that he was no longer anywhere near Pomona.

The weekly threat letters continued through 1938 and into 1939 with Helen getting increasingly distraught, and in the middle of 1939 a nervous breakdown. One morning when he went out to get the paper a dead pig was spread-eagled on the stoop. A knife was implanted just where he would do a C section and hysterectomy. The note said, *Closer.* He tried to block Helen from seeing it but she heard him gasp and pushed past him. When she saw it she col-lapsed. Perhaps that was what triggered it. Within a month she'd been diagnosed with the severest form of metastatic breast cancer and in two months she was dead.

She was his life, his support against memories of the past, his love eternal. The road ahead led nowhere, a meaningless wilder-ness where life was not worth living. His minister feared he would commit suicide and spent long hours counseling him. And it only got worse when two weeks later he open the door to get the paper and found his next door neighbor's beloved poodle impaled the same way as the pig. The note said, *One down, one to go.* His friend, the lieutenant, said he'd put a guard on the house.

On top of this from bits and pieces picked by colleagues visiting Germany he had corroboration of what Gerhard was revealing in his letters. His worst fears about Germany were being realized. Germany was step by step on a path that could lead to incarcerating and killing many Jews, tens of thousands, maybe hundreds of thousands, maybe more, innocent people who would be killed as a result of his work. He started having terrible nightmares about Helen and about Jews. Many nights the killer of his sister advanced toward Helen, knife in hand, and he too young and small to do anything but scream. And there were Jews, Star of David marking their clothing, being pulled away to their deaths with their arms stretched out toward him in condemnation.

Four AM. Blinking in the dark room he lay unmoving for a long time, his pajama top stuck to his back. Sweating all night, night sweats started at Helen's death, the pillow and sheets so damp they were almost wet. He began talking to Helen, more loudly, almost praying to her.

"How can I live with you gone? This is death already. I'm dying here Helen. I can't stand living without you." He got up and paced back and forth across the small, beautifully Helen-decorated bedroom, every glance reminding him of how much he'd lost. "Helen, I've got to get out of here, get away, disappear where everything isn't you. If I don't I'll die. I'll to die to be with you." He sat and thought about it, still talking to himself. "The eugenics program won't miss me. A dead end. Going nowhere. Nothing lost if I disappear. Ditch that sadistic letter writer." He shook his head and tears came to his eyes. "But I can't disappear from what I did with the Germans. God help me Helen. That's forever. If I'd told the minister he might have wanted me to kill myself, join all the Jews I have helped kill. How could I have been so stupid? I was so full of being a big shot, setting a whole country on eugenics and becoming a world leader in eugenics. I never bothered to think through how they might use it. I can't ever escape from what I did. Can't escape as long as I live. My life's work captured to kill Jews. Captured by Hitler to feed the hate in *Mein Kampf.* I can't stand it." He got down on his knees. "Please help me, Helen. What I did was horrible. I don't even want to practice medicine anymore!"

He agonized over it for more than a week, looked at it from every angle, concerned that his judgement was clouded. Everyone including his minister warned against making major changes right after Helen's death. However, he couldn't get away from despairing about where life had taken him. The choices he'd made, the events of the last few years, everything demanded he throw aside his past life, throw aside a mission pursued since the age of fifteen. He made the decision to move in sorrow, in self-doubt and desolation, and expected to live in misery, Helen and the Germans, double misery. For several weeks after he made the decision he drifted, drinking steadily, not shaving. Twenty-five years of his life wasted. Nothing of value accomplished except finding Helen, which made losing her even worse. He couldn't think where to move or what to do next.

Again it was his minister who came to the rescue. Reverend Sanders said, "If you must change your life, and I advise not doing anything this quickly, but if you must you should consider making a clean break. Your photos are in demand and maybe you could make a living as a photographic artist. I have another suggestion though. I've observed how you relate to the youngsters at church. Your Sunday school class is the most popular. Have you considered teaching? You'd be good at it."

Henry had thanked Reverend Sanders profusely, seeing it might be the answer, a profession he could quietly practice in his sadness and one that would honor Helen who had volunteered as a substitute teacher in Pomona.

He explored the possibilities with several of his friends in the eugenics movement. Several schools were identified. He wrote all of them with a description of his background and expressed that he wanted to enter teaching, get out of the limelight of eugenics, and spoke of the tragic death of his wife as a reason. Only one response, maybe because eugenics was out of fashion and a eugenics background was now suspect, particularly with growing knowledge of what was happening in Germany. The letter he got from Pomford said their biology teacher was retiring and invited him for an interview.

The interview was strange. Who comes to an interview in a horse and buggy and looks like he stepped out of the nineteenth century? Rather than focusing on his medical practice and capability to teach biology, the whole interview was about his experience in eugenics. Finally under questioning he told Dr. Cranch about the horrendous attack in the Baltimore park that propelled him into eugenics.

Dr. Cranch smiled at him, or at least stopped frowning. "I think you're one of us. We would welcome having you join us. Come to Pomford at the end of the Spring term. You'll have the summer to settle in. You can rent the Mason house. It's being vacated by the present biology teacher. He's moving to Florida. I think you'll find it a very comfortable house." Henry reached across the desk and shook Dr. Cranch's dry hand. This would give him two-and-one-half months to do what he had to do. What he kept from Dr. Cranch was his role in bringing Germany to eugenics and much more.

His purpose was to depart California without the threat writer knowing. He enlisted his best friend, a real estate agent, and swore him to secrecy. Papers were signed allowing the agent to sell the house without need for Henry's further involvement. An account was set up out of which the agent would pay any bills that came in after his departure. The agent would send the proceeds of the house sale and any money left after bill paying via secure wire transfer to an account in the East. For the move, the agent found a small firm that for well above normal rate would load the van after midnight, be out by dawn, and destroy all record of the transaction. The moving company would deliver to a warehouse in Boston and another moving company would take it from there to Pomford, without any contact between people of the two moving companies.

At 5:00 AM on a morning in June he left the house and clambered up to a seat in the moving van, and they were off. He didn't look back at the house. No one in town including his minister and his many friends were aware he was even thinking of departure.

The staff and teachers at Pomford, those who were staying over the summer, were very welcoming. Meals were delivered to his door for many days. He assumed they knew of the recent death of his wife. As he got to know the other teachers he found that all of them had backgrounds in eugenics, the sole exception being some coaches who were teaching but had been hired for their coaching abilities. He was the only one who had a background in negative eugenics, sterilizations. All the rest had been involved in promotion of positive eugenics, believers that through breeding those of exemplary racial background and intelligence with others with the same qualities a superior race could be developed. They had written pamphlets, and in some cases books on the subject, or had been involved in studies of racial and genetic superiority echoing those of Francis Galton, the 1880s father of eugenics. He asked one of the teachers about it, a nice guy named Frank MacComber who had gone out of his way to befriend him.

Frank said, "What you're going to find is that Pomford has become a center of positive eugenics. It's the Head's personal project. Pomford is his opportunity to prove out positive eugenics. He uses genealogy studies to hand-pick boys of the best breeding, then schools them to seek mates with similar background. Already he's onto a third generation of students. Children and grandchildren of former students are being nurtured to carry forward superior intellect and genetic stock. It's early on but it seems to be working. You see our boys in leading positions in America."

Henry said, "I don't see how we can make much difference, one small school."

"You're right. A large part of the Head's program is to grow a network. You'll be surprised at how many schools and universities

119

have bought into our program, usually not publicly, but behind the scenes. That includes a number of leading girls' boarding schools and colleges. And even where a school has not bought in we seek out faculty members in sympathy with us who are willing to spend time with worthy students, subtly guiding them."

This wasn't great. He'd intended to leave eugenics and here he was in a hot-spot of positive eugenics, life in a time warp, a throwback to the golden years of positive eugenics in the early part of the century. It felt like Galton was still alive. Didn't the Head know support for positive eugenics had died in America with the Depression? Maybe he was just refusing to acknowledge change, living in 1900 not only in attire and carriage transport but also in belief system.

Henry decided to play along with it, seeing no alternative if he wanted to be a teacher at Pomford, but participate as little as possible. He'd come here for peace, not further involvement in eugenics. And he was consoled by the thought that with positive eugenics at least no one was going to get killed.

CHAPTER THIRTEEN

Fall at its most dreary had settled on the Pomford Valley. White houses on Justin's way to class looked ever more like tombstones, tombstones escorting him to small deaths. Skeletal elm trees strained upward along the way, trying to escape from the unhappy ground of Pomford, their leaves long since burned, small warmth quickly extinguished by the cold Pomford air. Early mornings were around freezing but the clamminess was what he most noticed. Did the humidity in the Valley ever fall below one hundred percent? Mold formed in the back of his closet. Shirley helped him clean it out, saying, "It happens every Fall. The worst climate in New England." She shook her head in disgust. One gray, vanishing day after another escorted the coming of winter.

Many mornings on the way to breakfast he would see the Head out for an early carriage ride on the paths and byways of Pomford, a black presence clopping along, Captain Ahab out searching for … what? Every day dressed for a funeral. He'd been told early on that the Head didn't know how to drive a car. His conveyance around campus was his carriage, and in the rare good weather, a golf cart. When he wanted to go somewhere else Jenkins drove him in a gigantic Cadillac that the boys nicknamed "The Head Mobile." That morning when the Head passed the Head stared at him with an appraising look. Disquieting. Times before when the carriage had passed the Head hadn't bothered a glance.

Just before he got to class he approached a group of new boys. He knew two of them slightly from football. They looked at him and snickered among themselves, exchanging some sort of joke, then

turned their backs to him and walked away. What was that about?
Between classes a similar thing happened with another group of
new boys. Only this time the boy who made comment to other boys
held his nose while looking at Justin. Again they walked away laughing. At dinner that night nobody wanted to sit next to him, the
other boys shunning him, some throwing their hands up in mock
defense or holding their nose.

Walking back from dinner he heard it for the first time, a
long drawn out "DEEETH," starting with one voice, picked up by
another, then many boys. He turned around. That was him they
were looking at. Him they were calling after. Echoing down the
canyon of white buildings, the whole campus hearing it.

My God.

He hurried back to his room and locked the door, shaking. What
the "F" was this? What had he done? The cries indicated something
major. Boys mocking him, maybe hating him. How could this be?
Something incomprehensible. He'd no understanding of what was
going on. Totally numb inside. Could it be a practical joke of some
kind? Not with that many boys involved. No joke but a terrible thing
happening. His mind went round and round. Nothing out of the
ordinary these last few days, same tedious football drills, same conversations with other boys, as usual with him starting the conversation. Could he have said something or done something to offend
someone? He couldn't think of anything, and it had to be more
than offending one boy or a group of boys. He had a restless sleep
of doubt and worry. The next day more of the same, "Deeth" called
at him by a new boy standing with a group of other boys, the boy
looking like he was trying to show off to the group, and later the
same call from someone in a group of boys walking behind him. At
football practice nobody talked to him and he got looks from some
indicating they wished he wasn't there. The whole school seemed
in on it. He was the only one who didn't know what was happening.

He and The Suit walked back together from practice. The
Suit hadn't been one of those who shunned him so he asked him
about it.

The Suit looked at him with sadness in his face and shook his head in disgust. "It's been going around that you have terrible breath, could kill a cat. And they think you've been brown nosing the teachers, hand up all the time, talking to teachers after class. There's a joke that your breath stinks because you've been brown nosing the teachers so much you've been eating their shit. Then somebody invented the name 'death breath.' It's all over the class. Deeth is what they came up with for short. No one knows for sure where name death breath came from. No boy has been bragging about inventing it and usually you hear bragging. Or maybe it came from someone in administration. Whoever invented it must really hate you."

Pretty bad when The Suit takes pity on you because you're liked even less than he is.

Back in his room he sat rocking in pain on his bed, rocking much as Gerald did on the window ledge. Hurt and disbelief, his mind struggling with the realization of what was happening. How could this be? What could he do? A bottomless hopelessness. He'd never thought much of himself and now others were saying they didn't think much of him either. His body ached in consort with the pain of his mind, stomach roiling, nauseated, blood on the ends of his fingers where he'd bitten his nails into the fingers themselves. Deeth was irresistible, incomprehensible. It destroyed who he was.

He cupped his chin and nose with his hands and breathed into them trying to smell anything bad. Nothing. Again. Nothing. He thought of the old joke about a fox smelling his own asshole first. Could a human smell his own bad breath? He sprang up, grabbed his toothbrush, and hurried into the bathroom. A vigorous brushing. Then another. Maybe he hadn't been that good about brushing with everything going on and no mother. Mouthwash unopened since he arrived was swirled around his mouth.

On the way to dinner a group of new boys taunted him with Deeth and another group he approached put up hands in mock horror and held noses. What to do? They stood there looking at him, waiting for his reaction, waiting for him to say something, waiting for him to yell "Eat shit yourself" or "Up Yours," or something similar as he'd heard other bullied boys do, maybe throw a punch. Instead he found himself unable to respond, holding his breath, immobile, frozen in uncertainty. After what seemed like minutes he walked away in shock with the boys staring after him.

His father's admonition had come to his mind. When he'd complained about bullying at Hudson Military his father said, "Ignore them. You're better than they are. You have breeding. Don't let it bother you. Just turn the other cheek as the Bible says. Walk away from those bullying you. Don't give them the satisfaction of thinking what they do has any effect on you."

But what was going on did have an effect on him. It mattered terribly. A poor defense to pretend something doesn't matter when it matters terribly.

Dinner that night brought avoidance by more boys than the night before. He crept back in despair to his room, stretching himself on his unmade bed with limbs so leaden he felt he'd never move again. Tears made their way to his eyes. He finally dozed off—jerked alert with his heart beating too fast and Deeth sharing his bed ... dosed off ... jerked alert ... dozed off ... jerked alert ... all night, fits and starts, riding the horror of it until a final jerk alert at 6:00 AM to face another self-destroying day.

Those throwing Deeth at him were all new boys. And they were a particular group of new boys, mostly boys who like him were trying to gain popularity, trying to move toward the center of things, but unlike him trying to gain attention by being loud and showoffs, definitely thugs by his father's definition. Classifying them as thugs helped a little bit but not much. Did they think he was getting too close to the class leaders? Was that why the attack? A competition? That couldn't be. They must have seen he wasn't being accepted by the popular boys.

His tormenters never called him Deeth face to face, boy to boy. Rather they would be part of a group of boys and call Deeth at him out of the group as though trying to mobilize the whole group against him. From the prior-year boys there were no catcalls of

Deeth. Rather they found ways to avoid him, not sit next to him, shy away from him when he approached.

Weekly assemblies had degenerated into recitations by coaches of sporting accomplishments for the week. "I am happy to report the JV beat Hotchkiss last Saturday thirty-five to seven." Then a tedious laying out of the game nearly play by play, with student athletes involved in big plays being asked to stand for applause. Next the third team, same tediousness, and never any mention of him as sat on the bench the entirety of games, happy to be out of the mud. The next assembly he came in early and sat in the middle of the area where sophomore students usually sat. Other boys came in and sat so that there was an unoccupied space around him, a hole in the gathering, almost like he'd seen in pictures of a Petrie Dish where a deadly bacterium had been dropped in the middle, the most humiliating experience of his life. The name he'd been given foreclosed human contact, placed him in a realm of isolation, like he had a terrible virus to be avoided, the plague or something. If you were The Suit and had Lard Ass keened after you, or were Rhino or Skelty, the nicknames didn't forestall human contact. People would occasionally approach and talk to you. Whoever dreamed up his name didn't want that. They wanted no one to approach him. Everyone was to shy away, put distance between themselves and his bad breath, no socializing with other boys. The bad breath was like the leper's bell that kept people away in medieval Europe. Eventually a teacher came over and motioned everybody in the Petrie Dish together. The boys moved toward him, some with obvious reluctance, making faces. The teacher didn't ask what was going on. He seemed to know. Was the faculty in on it?

He vowed never again to go to assembly early. Instead, go in after most boys were seated so he could sit among them without boys having a opportunity to space away from him, though he was to find at future assemblies some boys did get up and move away. Chapel was better—long white benches set under the high ceiling of the four-square New England church and the sound of the organ reminding him of the happy times attending St. Barts in New York.

No opportunity for bullying in church. He tried to sit wherever the popular boys sat but near the back. Wherever he sat surrounding boys generally ignore him and talked to him only if they had to. Before the last notes of *Jerusalem* sounded, always the final hymn, he was out and away. Boys would taunt him if he got caught in the normal crush of boisterousness at the exit.

One Sunday he sat near the back and slipped out early. Nobody objected to what they probably assumed was a bathroom call. He sat down outside on the church steps. The steps pushed cold through his khaki pants and he pulled his blazer tight around his shoulders, shuddering, more from his situation than the cold. His life had come under the control of the other boys at Pomford, unravelling as they willed, spinning apart, no different from *Lord of the Flies*. The barbarianism of the confined boys in *Lord of the Flies* was the barbarism of the confined boys of Pomford. In *Lord of the Flies* the barbarianism found release by attacking one boy, Piggy. At Pomford he'd become Piggy. The pent-up emotions of five hundred confined boys, their frustrations, their anger at being imprisoned were being focused on him. Pomford barbarianism might be more subtle than *Lord of the Flies* barbarism but what he was experiencing was equally as bad as that experienced by Piggy. He was in a cage and the cage was full of animals. He got off the steps, looked around at the gray day. A Christian anthem was projecting loud-voiced from the church reminding him of happier days in New York when he had attended St. Barts with his mother. He proceeded in slow step to the safety of his room, head down, not glancing around, not wanting to see any more of Pomford. Life was playing with him, playing in the cruelest possible way. First, no mother, then the diary, then the plot, now this. He punched a tree as he passed, hard, grimacing in pain. This damn life. He wasn't alive.

It became a game of avoidance of other boys and pretending that he didn't mind what they said, and when he couldn't avoid them trying to be inconspicuous, all exhausting work. Could he become invisible, no presence, no sound, no existence? Did he still exist? The first times the question popped into his head it was with a note of self-pity. Now it was with panic. Justin Whitthorne—remember him—was evaporating, disintegrating, disappearing—sinking into an abyss where his disappearance was the goal of many. What little life had given him had become death in progress.

He thought about his mother. He always thought about his mother, more now with the bullying. He missed her and her love terribly. His routine was to write her a letter a week, something he'd always done while she was in an institution. He kept it innocuous and cheerful, no letting on what was really happening. In return, he got occasional letters that were getting increasingly disjointed and nonsensical, measuring her decline. He was going the same way. She was committed to an institution where people did things to her she didn't comprehend for reasons unfathomable. How did that differ from the institution in which he'd been committed? Not much. Mother and son in their separate crazy houses.

Every time he thought of his mother he thought of revenge against the woman who had plotted to take her away, revenge for his mother's sake, revenge for his own sake. With the bullying these thoughts intensified. He daydreamed about it, impractical scheme after impractical scheme, all of them depending upon escaping from Pomford and reaching the woman, impossible. Still he couldn't stop dreaming about it. He had to find a way to avenge his mother.

He couldn't last long as things were, not for the three more years of Pomford. His body and brain ached with the weariness of trying to think it through. Every night he went to bed dreading what the morrow would bring. Dread each night. Dread every day. Always new degradation. Rejected at home, rejected at Pomford, punishment for existing, a motherless boy with a hated father and a life of torture. He didn't even feel like masturbating any more.

Only one moment of relief appeared in the whole dreadful period. He was at a dining table that included two boys, both ends on the

Junior Varsity football team. Galworth Jones (Jonesy) was tall and thin as a rail, his long arms regularly snagging passes over defenders. The other boy, Scott Blainesford, (Scotty), was stocky and heavier, almost fat, and specialized in plowing ahead after catching passes with defenders clinging to his back. They were rivals on and off the field and constantly challenging each other. That night it was gray meat again. Many guesses as to what gray meat was, off-putting in color, sometimes with a sheen that looked like it'd been rubbed in motor oil, and a taste that was even worse. One boy who'd spent time in Africa said he thought it was bush meat. Whatever it was it was terrible and Jonesy wasn't having any of it.

He moved it around a little on his plate, and then just stared at it with a look of disgust on his face.

Scotty said, "The reason you don't catch many passes is you're too thin. Getting weak. Here you have this perfectly good food in front of you and you're not eating. If you're ever going to be any good at football like I am you've got to learn to eat like I do. It's easy. You see that thing on the left of your plate. That's a fork. On the right is a knife. You cut up the beautiful brown meat in front of you and put it in your mouth. Then you chew and swallow. Maybe if you do that enough you'll catch some passes."

From Jonesy, "You're full of crap. I can eat as much as you do any day of the week. Just don't like gray meat."

"Ridiculous," a broad smile on Scotty's face as though sensing an opportunity. "I can eat you under the table. I can eat you under this table. Want to try me?"

"Sure."

The rules of the contest were agreed upon. The chosen weapon was gray meat. "Choose you weapon. Gray meat."

Everyone assumed Scotty had a large advantage. Jonesy had been quoted as saying about gray meat, "If I don't know what it is it's probably shit. I don't eat shit."

The boys at the table donated their gray meat to the contest, many plates of gray meat still untouched by gray meat haters. Two boys were dispatched to the kitchen to pick up more, reporting back that the request for more gray meat had created astonishment and excited conversation in Polish. And so it started, one helping at a time, a rhythm building. One, two, three, four, and on.

Between helpings Scotty would make comment. "Eating a lot of food is like anything else. It requires training. You have none. The muscles in your stomach can't handle it. They'll poop out," then he laughed uproariously. "So much poop you're going to stink up the whole dorm."

Later, "I'm told this is partly pressed sheep dung. Hold it in your mouth and run your tongue over it. That's it. Taste it. Let your mouth really taste the shit. Now swallow it and feel how good it is going down." He'd evidently heard Jonesy's comment about shit.

Later still, "What you're feeling in your stomach is a blockage. I had an aunt that had a blockage. It killed her. She was skinny like you are. Skinny people die from blockages. No loss to the team if you let yourself die. I'll catch all those passes you've been missing. Death by gray meat. What a stupid way to die." Scotty laughed which brought on a paroxysm of coughing that Justin thought would bring up vomit. Somehow Scotty held it back.

By nine or ten helpings, Justin had lost track, Scotty had gotten very red of face, was burping regularly, and occasionally holding his stomach, doing so in a nonchalant manner though failing to disguise that his stomach hurt because he grimaced every time he touched his stomach. Jonesy had none of these symptoms and had said nothing throughout. He'd been eating methodically and had chewed each mouthful thoroughly as though he enjoyed what he was eating, and at intervals Jonesy smacked his lips to the evident annoyance of Scotty. With each bite Jonesy stared intently at Scotty, not with anger on his face but with what appeared to be curiosity about what would happen to Scotty, like Scotty was a lab animal in an experiment.

Scotty half rose and leaned forward on the table. "You son-of-a-bitch. If you eat any more you're going to explode." At the word explode a canon of gray meat fired across the table from Scotty's mouth. Jonesy, covered with pieces of gray meat, sat impassibly as though nothing had happened, put down his fork and knife in the orderly fashion one would do at the Queen's banquet, and said quietly, still staring intently at Scotty, "I win."

Scotty rolled to the floor spewing more gray meat and holding his stomach. Then started yelling. "I'm dying. Jesus it hurts. God it hurts so much." He was sniffling, and his eyes were full of tears when two teachers appeared and half carried him to the infirmary. Scotty didn't get back on the football field for ten days. In the meantime, Jonesy starred, grabbing down a game winning touchdown pass in each of the two games Scotty missed.

What Justin got out of it was some vomit on his shoes when he didn't move quickly enough, and a precious moment of hilarity at seeing Jonesy sitting immobile with pieces of gray meat stuck to his face, lodged in his hair, decorating every inch of his clothing, playing with a last piece of meat on his plate as though he might eat it vomit and all, and then turning to the many boys assembled around him, flicking a piece of meat from the lapel of his blue blazer, and saying with a puzzled look on his face, "Is that all there is?"

Justin laughed and laughed, and laughed every time he thought of it, and thereafter many a boy when confronted with gray meat at dinner, would say, "Is that all there is," and burst out laughing.

Another thing Justin got out of it was a friendly acquaintance with Jonesy. Scott Blainesford was a loudmouth. Justin didn't like him, and throughout the match Justin was saluting Jonesy's progress with, "Way to go Jonesy," and other encouragement, getting in return a smile from Jonesy.

A few days afterwards Jonesy sought him out. "Thank you for the support in that stupid-ass eating contest. I want you to know how sorry I am for what's happening to you. You don't deserve it. A lot of mean boys here. They're a miserable bunch. Maybe it makes them feel good to make someone else miserable. When they find somebody they can attack, they attack. It's sick. I knew there was a problem a month ago. You're not among the invited boys, right? Everybody knows about someone who isn't invited."

"Invited, what's that?"

"In the first months new boys get a formal written invitation for Sunday afternoon tea with the Head and his wife, Frieda. Usually it's twenty to thirty boys a Sunday. I've gone to many of them, three or four a year. The Head asks the boys how they think they're doing and what they like at school, but mostly it's the same lecture he gave at the first assembly. If I hear the word breeding again I'll barf. The head is fixated on it. You've got to always honor your breeding by being a gentleman. You've got to seek out a woman of good breeding to marry. You've got to find roles in government, business, and particularly education where your breeding will have maximum impact on the world. Give me a break. I've heard it so many times I can quote it verbatim, and I'm going to hear it almost three more years. By the time I graduate I think my mind is going to be jelly, well-bred jelly. When I was young all I wanted was to be a fireman. Guess that's out. I'm supposed to be doing good-breeding stuff instead." He shook his head ruefully and laughed.

Justin said, "Where does my not being invited come into it."

"Well, I don't really know. Maybe the Head thought you wouldn't be staying and didn't want to waste tea and lectures on you."

Well, this was something. Had he offended the Head in some way? Could breaking the admission rules by his late arrival have done it, together with being a poor athlete? And what about Gerald? Had Gerald been forced out in some subtle way because he also pushed his way in?

After that Jonesy was always friendly to him, making room for him to sit with him at assembly, greeting him, not really a friend but he'd take anything.

Demerits started accumulating. The school gave demerits not only for being late at check-in (as he'd found out), but also for such things as having lights on after curfew, not following instructions and, most importantly, not being adequately prepared for class.

The latter gave teachers great leeway to punish those they didn't like. The teacher got to decide what was and was not adequate preparation.

By reputation by far the greatest misuser of demerits was his German teacher, Hauptmann. The student body, even those who never had him as a teacher, thought him by far the worst teacher in the school. He came to class unprepared, wouldn't answer questions from students, and worse, ran his classroom by fear. Demerits were only a small part of it. Hauptmann used ridicule and intimidation—"Stand up, Jeffries. I want the whole class to see someone so stupid he can't correctly pronounce a single word in that entire sentence," this to a shy fellow who visibly cringed with everyone staring at him—and "If you don't get those verb forms right I'll have the Head take away all your free Sunday afternoons the rest of the semester," this to a large part of the class. (Hauptmann made a lot of threats about what he'd get the Head to do).

Justin had taken German for the same reason he'd taken biology, to prepare for the possibility of becoming a doctor. Big mistake, and the mistake became more obvious with the advent of the bullying. He led the class. But Hauptmann started heaping demerits on him for no reason whatsoever. Was Hauptmann aligned with the bullying?

The class in general hated Hauptmann, even those he favored with no demerits. With all the demerits Justin's hatred of Hauptmann was personal.

His other teachers were the best in the school and yet he started getting lack of preparation demerits even from a few of them. These were unjustified. He was always adequately prepared. One advantage of having no friends was that he wasn't diverted from studies by conversations with friends. The demerits came on the rare occasions he was asked a question in class and didn't give the right answer. He noticed that he was being asked the hardest questions and no demerits were being given to other boys who missed answers. Clearly he was being given "I don't like you" demerits just like Hauptmann was handing out. Why? Were the teachers in cahoots with the boys bullying him to try and become more popular with students? Made no sense as teachers would gain nothing by being popular. He had no answer to his class demerits. Other demerits also kept finding him. Five for having his lights on for five or ten minutes past the 9:30 PM curfew. Mr. Brown had apparently been standing outside his room observing, and didn't do the nice thing of giving him a single demerit as a warning so he could correct. The school didn't like him any better than the Pomford boys did. An attack on all fronts was being directed at him. But why?

The one teacher who didn't give him demerits was his biology teacher, Mr. Benson. Everyone called him Mr. Benson though at one point he acknowledged that he had a medical degree. "I have permanently left the practice of medicine. Please call me Mr. Benson, not Dr. Benson." How different from Hauptmann. Hauptmann required everyone in class to address him as "Professor. "I was a leading professor in Germany and I'd ask you to address me as such."

Mr. Benson was the ideal teacher—inspirational on his subject, articulate, ready to happily answer any question, caring for his students on an individual basis. Justin admired him greatly and tried his hardest in his class, particularly as Mr. Benson was the one teacher who tried to protect him from bullying. It happened at the end of the second week of November. He came out of the school library with Mr. Benson not far behind. A group of boys were gather by the library steps, he never found out why, and included some of his principal tormentors. The combined Deeth cry that went up must have been heard for half a mile.

Mr. Benson yelled at them, furious by the tone of his voice. "Stop it. Only morons bully. What are you, six years old?"

The boys dispersed, looking very surprised. No one had ever told them that bullying was wrong.

Justin turned to Mr. Benson and thanked him, and Mr. Benson said in passing, "Terrible. Shouldn't be allowed to happen."

In his desire to avoid other boys he started using his free time Sunday afternoons to wander the campus. He tried to catalog the birds as he had done in Central Park. There were few smaller birds and he'd seen few the whole time he'd been there, a robin or two early on, some wrens and finches, and migrating ducks by the river. What he did see was vast flocks of crows, thousands of crows. They had driven out the smaller birds. There were cornfields in neighboring farms that may have brought the crows. But they congregated in Pomford itself, roosting in the elms on the campus. For Justin they became a manifestation of Pomford, black birds attracted to the blackness of Pomford, the crow a better symbol for Pomford than the whale, the crow a species that preyed on those they found weak. The designation used in England for a flock of crows was apt for Pomford, a *murder of crows.*

One Sunday in November he ventured down to the stables. He liked horses. One reason he enjoyed Camp Passumsic was that they assigned you a horse for the summer, your horse to care for and maintain, feed and curry, and to ride on overnight trail rides all around Vermont. He'd been inducted into the "Passumsic Rough Riders" for his riding skills, a proud achievement, the only athletic thing in which he'd ever succeeded.

The Pomford stable turned out to be quite large, stalls for twenty or more horses of which fifteen were filled. He peered though the window of a shed next to the stable and spied two one-horse carriages. Someone had told him that one of these carriage had been given to the Head by Eisenhower in a ceremony at the White House. To the right as he entered the stable were four slightly larger stalls that contained black horses he assumed belonged to the Head. A man was currying one.

"What do you want?"

"Nothing. I like horses. Can I curry one of the horses?"

"Go back with the other boys."

"They don't like me."

The man approached him and looked him over. He appeared to be in his late seventies or early eighties. A broad kindly face was topped by a thatch of unruly white hair, sharp blue eyes with wrinkles of humor at the corners, a little bit over-weight and jowly.

He walked slightly bent over and with a small limp, maybe a riding accident. The man handed him the curry brush and pointed to the horse he was working on. Then walked away saying nothing.

Justin finished currying the horse the man was working on, then did two others. Then a fourth. He looked around for the man to give him back the curry brush, didn't see him and left the brush on a table, going back to his room.

The next Sunday he went again to the stable. The man was sitting on a chair before the stalls, his face turned to the pale November sunshine occasionally sneaking around the gray clouds of Pomford, a cigarette in his mouth, a bible sitting on his lap. He said nothing but handed Justin a curry brush. Justin curried all the horses that day except one stallion who looked dangerous and tried to bite him when he neared its stall, a horse named Imperator by the plaque on the door. Again he left the brush on a table when he couldn't find the man.

Thanksgiving was upon them. Much excitement around campus the week before, escape from lockup, the boys trying to ignore how temporary it would be. Maybe because the pressure in the cooker was about to be released he heard little taunting that week. Boys seemed a little friendlier to him. Pomford had already been freezing up. Many were out skating on neighboring ponds. And a week before Thanksgiving the first major snow storm roared in, not the light, pretty snow that decorates branches and lifts one's spirit, rather a sludge of wet snow dropped heavily down to bury the valley as though it no longer deserved to be part of the living world. The day afterward there was a glimpse of sun and then the gray cloud mantle of Pomford returned, the snow dull in the limited short-day light, not glistening like snow in Central Park after a snowstorm, the Pomford snow adding its slushy weight to the general despair weighing down the school. Then another miserable slushy snow the day before Thanksgiving. It looked like Pomford was ordering up snow every few days just like it ordered up rain every few days all Fall, lousy weather in a lousy place.

He went through new snow back to the stable, interested to see the horses in the snow. Again he curried horses, and this time also fed them, but not the one ornery horse. Again no conversation with the stable man who left as soon he came in.

He went to bed that night disconsolate. He was the only boy staying at Pomford over the holiday. No New York. He longed to be looking at the New York skyline, buildings laying claim to half the sky, bright lights to offset the darkness in his life. In his imagination he was in the twirl of brightly clothed skaters admiring the newly-lit Christmas Tree at Rockefeller Center. He walked past the red buckets set out to capture the early generosity of Christmas, bells ringing in white-gloved hands. He smelled roasted chestnuts and the scent of the north woods brought to stands of fir trees waiting to go to happy homes. And he took Jenny to the three parties and two dances of the prior year. Only he wasn't doing any of this, another low point in his life, terrible not to be there. He liked Thanksgiving in New York more than Christmas. Thanksgiving was anticipation, a magic time coming. Christmas, the magic was already there, nothing to look forward to, and usually not as good as you'd hoped. .

The one saving grace was that the Brown's had invited him to Thanksgiving dinner, turkey and all the trimmings, very much to be looked forward to after the Pomford food. The daughters were home. He'd seen them in the distance, Fawn and Melissa, both lovely, long blond hair, nice smiles like their mother, Fawn his age and Melissa two years younger. They were the first good thing that'd come into his life in a long time, though when he sat down at the table he saw Mr. Brown's strong gaze on him delivering a caution.

Mr. Brown's grace was interminable. Justin focused on Fawn and she returned his glances with a slight rolling of her eyes. This was good. Contact established. Conversation at dinner was banal—weather, events in the Pomford Valley over Christmas the girls might enjoy, the doings of relatives he had never heard of, and a recitation of past events he hadn't been part of. No one asked him about himself or how he liked school, and Mr. Brown never gave the girls an opportunity to talk about themselves. Mr. Brown was trying to get through the meal with him knowing as little as possible about the girls, and they him.

Whenever he looked at Fawn, and he did so often, he would find her looking at him then quickly gazing away. She had lovely eyes, deep blue, almond shaped. He could get lost in them. It became a game with both of them giving small smiles to the other between glances in a way unnoticeable to the rest of the table. She had a way of lowering her eyelids when she smiled and tossing her head when she talked. He was captivated, and her face was beautiful, far more beautiful than Jenny's. Could one fall in love across a Thanksgiving dinner table with someone one hadn't met before? When he left the table he was sure of it.

He went to bed that night feeling much happier.

The next morning he went out to get breakfast at the dining hall. (They were providing simple meals during his stay). As he stepped through the front door Fawn appeared from the interior of the house and walked out with him.

"I heard you coming down the stairs. They're right over my room. I told them I'd get the newspaper so I can only stay a moment. Meet me behind the market at 2:00 PM."

She hurried back inside with the paper before he could tell her how great that was.

With a morning to kill he went back to the stable, a raw feeling in the air. The man was mucking manure out of the stalls. "You still here? Why aren't you home?" He had a pronounced New England accent.

"My father doesn't want me home."

The man handed him a shovel and he joined, the two of them completing the mucking in about an hour. Then the man pitchforked in clean straw and again he joined him. As they finished the man turned to him and said, "Not good to be kept from home."

Justin explained that a woman had attached herself to his father, didn't want him at home, that she knew John Chandler and had him locked away at Pomford precisely to prevent him from being home.

"I know Mr. Chandler. What's the woman's name?"

He gave him the name, about the first time he'd said it.

"I've met her. She used to ride here a lot with Mr. Chandler. Real uppity. A society dame. Treated me like a servant. Wanted me to help her on her horse and kowtow to her, expected me to be like the grooms in Central Park or wherever fancy place she rides. I can see what you're up against."

Nothing more was said. Justin hurried off to grab a quick lunch and find Fawn. He arrived early at the market, walked behind and into a sheltered area where the high shrubs on either side gave protection against being seen. Fawn had also arrived early. It had started snowing lightly, an announcement of more snow to come, and snow flakes glistened on her hair, lovely.

"I can't stay long. I'm supposed to be shopping. My father's very strict. He won't let us meet any boys."

"Why not?"

"My father is always talking about good breeding. He's afraid we're going to meet the wrong kind of boy. He keeps lecturing us about how we have to marry gentlemen, men of good breeding. Stupid."

"Same thing for me. I get the same lecture on breeding all the time. The worst is the Head. He can't open his mouth without talking about good breeding."

"Well, I'm not going to let my father decide who I'll marry. They want to breed us like dogs. I'm not going to marry some pureblood jerk just because they want me to." She gave an angry frown and stamped her foot. Again endearing.

"You won't believe this but you're the first boy I've been alone with for just forever. And I have to sneak out to see you. I hate it." She shook her head sadly. " All the other girls at school have boyfriends. Seeing you I decided to do something bold, try and meet you. You probably think I'm very forward, maybe one of those naughty girls. I'm not. I've never done anything like this before. Usually I'm the one that tells all the other girls not to do things that might get them into trouble." She smiled as though remembering, a magical smile. "I decided some time ago that the only way I can meet an attractive boy like you is move quickly and take a big chance. Normally I guess a boy and girl would get to know each other through a lot of dating, sort of gradually decide if they wanted to be boyfriend and girlfriend. That's impossible for me. When you came to dinner and I saw how attractive you were, and I think intelligent, too, I decided maybe you could be my boyfriend. All last night I was working up my courage to approach you. You're my chance, probably my one chance for a long time. I'm hoping if you like me we could jump over all that dating stuff. If you don't like me all I've done in meeting you is embarrass myself a little bit."

She stepped back and put her hand to her mouth, shaking her head in a coquettish way so lovely he could hardly stand it. "Here, I've not asked you the most important thing. Do you already have a girlfriend?"

"There's a girl I'm writing to in New York but she doesn't seem to like me much anymore. Look. You don't have to talk about being embarrassed. You've been bold so I'll be bold." He went still and looked her full in the face, feeling himself committing to a new world. "You're the most beautiful thing I've ever seen. I love you. I knew it when I saw you at dinner. And regarding that girl in New York, I'm never going to write her again."

They stood staring at each other, Fawn's eyes gradually tearing. "That's wonderful. Oh so wonderful." She started sniffling and pulled out a hanky, blowing her nose.

She told him a little about herself, the tight control by her father, the strictures of Stoneleigh Prospect that she hated, and he learned she led her class academically, and he was able to tell her he did just about the same, but before he could say much about himself she looked at her watch. "I've stayed too long," and hurried away saying over her shoulder, "I'll try and be here the same time tomorrow."

What a great thing. He skipped back to his room and whistled his way to the dining hall and back, the first time he'd whistled at Pomford.

The next day he went to the stable early. Two men were saddling up, Mr. Benson, his biology teacher, and another teacher who he thought taught history. Benson gave him a broad smile, saying, "Glad to see my students examining biology on a larger scale. Much better than my lab frogs." Then he laughed. He really liked Mr. Benson.

The man running the stable came out and talked to the two men a bit about the horses. These were boarded horses. Apparently the owners welcomed their horses being exercised by the teachers. The stable man was called Joe by the two teachers, so part of his name had surfaced.

When the men rode off Justin said, "Joe. I don't know your last name. Can I help with the horses today?"

"My last name is Henderson. You can call me *Mr.* Henderson." He seemed a little grumpy that he'd called him Joe, handed him a curry brush and pointed to the horses. No further word from Mr. Henderson, no thank you when he finished. He'd never gotten a thank you.

Again Fawn was waiting for him behind the store when he arrived. Both of them were very bundled up on a freezing black afternoon, Fawn with a wool hat like a beret set at a sassy angle. He started telling her more about Pomford, controls stricter even than Stoneleigh Prospect, how he hated it, and then he started on New York.

She interrupted, "We don't have time for that." She came close to him, took his head in her hands, and gave him a long kiss, pressing her body against his. "I've never had a chance to do that before," her hands still cupping his head and her gaze roaming over his face. Then she kissed him again even longer.

He pulled her closer, feeling the curves of her body melting into his through the clothing, kissing her exquisite eyes, her soft lips, more passionately than he'd ever kissed anyone. Time stopped. He was lost as they continued to kiss.

She pulled away abruptly looking at her watch. "I've got to go, and my ogre of a father is taking me back to school Sunday. We won't be able to get together again. There's something I want to do before I leave. I'm scared about it because I don't know how you'll react. You may think badly of me. I hope not. It means I love you and never want you to forget me. It's a present for you, the only present I have to give. One of my girlfriends told me she did it with her boyfriend. I think about it all the time. Can you sneak out at night?"

"I don't know. Your father keeps the front door locked." He thought for a moment. "There's a shed under my bathroom window. And I think there's a trellis for roses or something on the side of the house. I'll have a look at it. Maybe I can get down that way. How can I reach you to let you know?"

"There's no way. If you can do it come to my window after everybody is asleep, say 11:00 PM. My room is in the south east corner of the house. There'll be a light on. Gotta go now. Whatever happens remember I love you."

The trellis was where he remembered and looked sturdy enough. He could probably get down alright, though maybe with a few rose bush scratches. Getting up, he didn't know, but it was probably worth it even if he had to stay out in the cold all night waiting for the dining hall to open.

What did she plan? Possibilities swirled around in his head. The snow had continued, now fairly deep, so he doubted she intended an outside tryst. An invitation into her room? She would be too afraid of her father. What then? He hurried through dinner, his excitement mounting. In his room he checked his watch ever ten minutes or so. Fortunately the snow had stopped and a little moonlight was filtering through racing clouds. Off in the distance the open country rolled away lonely and forbidding. He had a little trouble finding the trellis with his feet when he hung down from the window. Finally on the ground he made a circle through the untrodden snow and gradually approached her window. The night was so still he could hear the snow crackle under his feet. Pale light reflected from banks of snow and the rising moon outlined buildings with faint white lines. Breathing quickly he looked up and down the street, seeing no one. Avoiding the light steaming from her window, and hugging the shadows, he edged cautiously forward, holding back his body and craning around a corner of her window until he could glimpse inside. He did not see her, and after some debate with himself about the wisdom gave a soft rap on the window. For a moment nothing, then a door cracked opened at the back of the room, maybe the bathroom, and she emerged, walking toward him, graceful, soft and flowing in her movement, wearing brightly colored pajamas. Her hair was down to her shoulders, shining, and she stepped into the full light with a marvelous smile. Their eyes met as he pressed against the window and she smiled more broadly. Slowly her hand went to the top button of her pajama top and she undid it, then again slowly the next and the next, until the top fell away. Small high breasts, erect pink nipples. His erection was so strong it hurt. Was she going to go further?

She reached down and stepped out of the bottom, showing no embarrassment, proud of how she looked, showing him how she looked, her going-away present to remember her by. She was the most exquisite thing he'd ever seen. She slowly turned around so he could see everything, her tight behind, her long legs, the golden fuzz between her legs, then facing him again she smiled one more time and turned off the light.

He had no memory of climbing back up the trellis, though he had the scratches to prove he did it. He masturbated. Then again. Then a third time toward morning, his whole night full of imaginings and hopes.

He did not go to the stable the next day but stayed in his room listening. Around noon a commotion, the girls were leaving. He hurried down the stairs, trying to look like he was going on an errand of some kind. Perfect timing, the girls emerged from the back of the house with their suitcases just as he got to the bottom of the stairs. He said, "Let me carry those," hoping for a goodbye moment with Fawn.

Her father shooed him away. "We'll handle it."

As they went out the door Fawn looked at him hungrily as though she wanted to leap in his arms and not go back. Her father didn't see the look. Her mother, Shirley, may have.

He was afraid to even wave when the car left the curb, and he walked away down the street as though he was, indeed, on an errand. When he looked back after some time Shirley was frowning after him. He shook his head in disbelief. He'd not even gotten Fawn's address.

Things were better for a while when the boys came back from Thanksgiving break. Maybe the vacation had released some of the frustration that'd been focused on tormenting him. Or maybe he didn't notice it that much after meeting Fawn.

The first thing he did was to go to the library and look up the address of Stoneleigh Prospect School. He sent a letter to her simply saying "Hi," and giving his post office box address in the school post office, not knowing whether it would get to her or somebody else might open it. A response came back almost immediately saying how wonderful it was that they met, how she was thinking of him all the time, how she loved him, and how, "If Simonetta Cattaneo Vespuci, the Genoese noblewoman, could display herself all over Italy and down through the generations as the model for Botticelli's *Venus* then my own unveiling to a single viewer was perhaps not too sinful."

He looked up Botticelli's *Venus* in the library and decided there was a marked resemblance, but he thought Fawn lovelier. She was finer boned, her breasts more beautiful, and her face unmatched by any girl he'd ever seen.

In his response letter he wrote,

The Venus in the painting is supposed to be both an earthly goddess who inspired physical love and a heavenly goddess who inspired intellectual love.

Your present brought both to me, intellectual love because I realize what intellectual bravery you had to do what you did. And you are the most beautiful thing I've ever seen. The Homeric hymn on which the picture was based salutes you, 'The gold-wreathed and beautiful Aphrodite.' But you are not, 'Carried over the waves of the resounding sea on soft foam' as the poem says. You're already seated in my heart.

Her response did not contain poetry but lyric description of the Stoneleigh Prospect campus in winter, and ribald and cutting descriptions of fellow students and teachers.

One of the girls had a gym teacher fondle her in showing her a basketball move. He is sort of a cute guy so she confronted him and tried to get him to date her and thought she'd made a catch. She's been following him around the campus ever since. The girls are desperate around here. It's wonderful I have you to love.

Always her intelligence, and she obviously had a literary bent. Most important, she said one more time she loved him.

The first week of December he was assigned to kitchen and garbage duty to work off his demerits, unearned demerits. This involved getting up at 5:30 AM and going to the kitchen to help set up for breakfast, then dashing from class, and later from study hall, to do the same thing before lunch and dinner. The kitchen was populated by middle-aged Polish women, many of them stout, recruits from the large Polish community in Greenfield, probably neighbors of the two Polish linemen. They treated him as a servant, "Take this pot over there, this stack of dishes over here." Then in dishwashing he was always given the dirtiest pans to scrub clean. He'd never before had to wash even a dinner plate.

Garbage was the worst. The garbage truck pickup was from a paved area about one hundred yards from the back of the dining hall. Who had designed it that way? He was supposed to manhandle the garbage cans over there, usually about ten a day. They were too heavy for him to pick up, as he was later to see some other stronger boys do. Rather he would tramp down the snow and slide the cans over, pulling mightily and having to rest often. The only good thing about kitchen duty was he was away from the other boys so opportunities to taunt were few.

He had to find a private place for them to meet over Christmas. Behind the administration building he found an empty shed and was able to force the door, somewhat dirty inside but it would do if she could get away long enough for something serious. Or maybe he could crawl in her window. Could she lock her door? He could hardly stand the wait for Christmas vacation. And he would be at Pomford part of the vacation. Yippee! His father had called, hadn't talked to him, but left word with the school that except for Christmas, itself, he was to stay at school through Christmas vacation. For Christmas he was not to go home but to his aunt's house in Greenwich.

Two weeks before Christmas all his hopes were dashed. Fawn wrote that her father had decided they would all go to her uncle's house in North Carolina, and worse, that somehow her parents had picked up on them together and had warned her to stay away from him. Had someone seen them together? Or had her mother noticed the look she gave him going out the door at the end of Thanksgiving weekend? Stupid, stupid, stupid to have gone down to the front hall to get one more glimpse of her. Fawn was the only thing he had. He couldn't stand not being able to see her.

Immediately after that bad news came the worst day of his life, life not being satisfied with punishing him once in forty-eight hours it had to punish him a second time. The glee club concert was a pre-Christmas event each year. Earlier in the Fall, a rag-tag rock and roll band had been put together, composed entirely of sophomores, not much professionalism but a lot of enthusiasm. Somehow they'd persuaded the Head to be allowed to play as a follow-on to the glee club concert. He entered the auditorium late as usual, trying to avoid the petri-dish effect of boys not sitting next to him.

As he came in two classmates pointed to an unoccupied seat in the front row where the popular boys sat. "Why don't you sit down there. You can hear much better."

"You've got to be kidding. They don't want me there."

"Try it. What've you got to lose."

He decided he didn't in fact have anything to lose and walked down with the two boys. They spoke to the front-row boys.

"Is this seat vacant? Whitthorne here always sits at the back. We thought for a change he deserves a front row-seat."

Strange. Nobody called him Whitthorne anymore. He turned and looked back to where he would have been sitting. Many of the boys were looking at him, some whispering back and forth. Again strange. What was up? The concert was uneventful through the glee club part. Then a sing along with the glee club. With his poor voice he mouthed the words. Next came the band. The band started out all right, playing current well-known pop songs. He could sense anticipation of some sort building. The band stared at him from the stage before starting the last song, laughing with each other. Out it came, a play on a popular LaVern Baker song that'd just been released.

"Tweedlee Tweedlee Tweedlee DEETH

I'm as happy as I can be

Jimminy cricket jimminy jack

you make my heart go clickety-clack

Tweedlee Tweedlee Tweedlee DEETH."

Four more versus all ending in a loud DEETH joined in by all the assembled boys, freshman, juniors, seniors as well as sophomores, the Head looking out from his perch at the side smiling as broadly as he'd ever seen him.

Then the last versus ending,

"Ow Tweedlee Tweedlee DEETH

Ow Tweedlee Tweedlee DUMB

Ow Tweedlee Tweedlee DEETH

Ow Tweedlee Tweedlee DUMB."

The boys were now yelling out DEETH and DUMB so loudly that they were almost screaming, five hundred boys in full voice joining together to mock him. Not individual attacks as before, rather the concentrated dislike of the whole school.

He ran from the auditorium to hide in his room at Claiborne House, pushing aside boys laughing at him, calling Deeth at him. After only a short time in his room, the chorus gathered outside the house. "Tweedlee Tweedlee Tweedlee DEETH." This went on for some time until Shirley went out and put an end to it. He found blood on his left leg. He'd squeezed his leg so hard in pain that his few remaining nails had cut his leg through his khakis.

In succeeding days the School didn't let up. Now the silent treatment. Nobody wanted to be seen talking to him after what happened at the Christmas concert. He hid in his room, waiting until class or dining hall was to start then dashing in at the last second. He skipped athletics entirely, to hell with the demerits, and skipped dinner one night after having the table sing his song to him the previous night while a teacher, seated at the table, did nothing. All the doubts about himself that had dissipated because of Fawn came back.

The boys of Pomford didn't need the spear used to kill Piggy in *Lord of the Flies*. They had focused mockery, as sharp as any spear.

There was a solution. He thought about it all the time now. It would come into his head and he would try and force it out. It wouldn't go. He dwelled on it more and more as the days passed. Sometimes it would wake him up at night with a specific plan or greet him first thing in the morning. His mind was pulled along, squirming to avoid the unavoidable. There was no way out. Worst was when he was alone just before bed and remembering how his mother also found no way out.

December 17th. That was the day, his father's birthday, a birthday present for his father. He dressed methodically in warm clothes, wondering why he bothered— red wool socks his aunt said she'd knitted, though difficult to conceive of her doing such a plebeian thing as knitting, matching wool hat and scarf from a cousin, put on because they were so garish, what happened would be easily visible. For out wear he chose his almost new Brooks Brothers clothes, if you're going to go you should go in style. He exited down the trellis early in the morning, barely light, too early for the front door to be unlocked, another sorrowful Pomford day. He felt the damp more than the cold though it was a cold day. Why was it that at Pomford one felt the damp no matter how cold it was? He would be happy to escape the weather.

He looked around intently, seeing things he didn't remember seeing before. A few yellow leaves dangled from limbs, memories of summer, and under the trees lay windfall branches from fall storms. One branch lying atop another was pointing directly at him, signaling what? The snowy meadows tiered down to the river, each tier almost exactly the same size as the one below it, orderly steps to the water. With levies they could be the hillside rice paddies he'd seen in pictures of Asia. He noticed that the tall grasses sticking up through the snow were all bent toward the south, something he hadn't registered before. He studied it. The grass was hiding from the roaring north wind, soft-looking in the distance, like you could stroke it. He remembered the friendly neighbor's cat at the co-op, brown as grass, his hand running through its fur. He hated to give up animals. A flurry of snow. He opened his mouth to catch it, to taste it. Why hadn't he paid attention to the taste of snow before? Overhead the clouds streamed by in their usual sad gray attire, swirling as he'd not previously observed, Pomford bouncing the wind off its hills, arrogantly putting its mark on the very clouds. His ears heard everything. He thought he could hear individual water drops falling from trees where the snow was melting and could distinguish differing notes played by the wind as it scooted around variously shaped bushes. His pace slowed as he approached the river. Lots of animal tracks were in the snow. He examined them, small animals "field mice"? Then he continued to the bend where Fred Jamison said it'd happened, ever more slowly, step by step, being dragged toward the river, dragged toward the place of welcome. The Pomford was flowing pitch black, oily swirls of current ready to carry him below, ice rimming the edges that would break under his feet. He thought about the water temperature, probably around thirty. Would the cold ease the pain of his drowning, shock him so much he wouldn't feel the water filling his lungs? Unlikely. It would be horrible.

He bent down and picked up the rocks waiting for him along the bank, filling his pockets. Standing without moving he stared at the river for some time, feeling it. The river pulled at him. The sinking darkness pulled at him. Head down, unseeing, the cold wind growing in strength and throwing snow down the back of his neck, a shove toward the river. What Brian and Fred told him didn't scare him anymore.

His mother. It would be terrible for her if they let her know. He doubted they would, and from what he understood of her condition she might not comprehend if they did tell her. Fawn. She might grieve. But if he'd lived she would eventually find out the truth about him, how worthless he was. That would be the end of that. His father? His father would probably care but mostly because suicide would be a blotch on the family name. The woman. Ah, the woman. He could see her laughing delightedly when she heard, a bottle of champagne opened. Perhaps she'd drag his father back to the floor of the living room to celebrate her victory and a call to the Head to thank him.

The Head. "Damn." He started talking to himself. "The Head was smiling. Evil bastard. Yes smiling. He knew. Could have stopped it but didn't."

He went motionless for a moment, thinking, then raised clenched fists to the heavens, threw his head back and screamed as loud as he could yell, "Aaaaaagh," a cry of anger at himself.

"God. You stupid shit." Too busy reacting to see it. It was all an F'ing plan. Knock Piggy on his ass with the concert. Give him the same silent treatment they gave that poor Horace Randall. Let him die in the river like Horace.

Again he yelled with fists clenched to heaven,

I'll be damned if I'll give them the satisfaction, screw the whole damn school!

Justin turned around and found himself walking briskly back from the river. What was he feeling? Shaken. A wave of nausea gripped him as he realized the nearness of his own death, a sensation not unlike crippling vertigo. Ham's curse has almost got him. His hands were trembling as he tossed away the rocks. But there existed a feeling of something accomplished. He'd stepped through a barrier of some kind, entered new territory. They had thrown their worst at him. He'd survived. He realized something and said it to himself, almost a prayer of thanksgiving.

"By God I'm going to get through it."

In the days before the terrible glee club concert Justin had stopped again down at the stable. A man who introduced himself as Mr. Henderson's son was there instead of Mr. Henderson. Said his name was Daryl. "Pa has a cold." Nothing more said. As taciturn as his father. Daryl didn't ask him to help so he left.

The first day of Christmas vacation he went again to the stable. Mr. Henderson was back, shoveling snow from the entrance to the stable. A heavy snow had fallen the night before. He looked weary. "You stuck here for Christmas vacation like Thanksgiving?"

"Most of it." Without a word Justin reached for the shovel, which was willingly given, and completed the work.

"You don't look very happy," Mr. Henderson said.

Justin told him he'd hoped to see his girlfriend over Christmas and that hope had been dashed. "That's on top of everything else awful around here. The worst things in my life." He spat that out angrily. He had reason to be angry.

"I take it you don't like Pomford."

"I hate it."

Mr. Henderson rolled his eyes up in exasperation as though wanting to throw his hands in the air but too tired. He said in an irritated voice, "You're making a *mistake*. It's one of the best prep schools around. The Head is world famous for what he's accomplishing. You ought to be thankful you're here. All you spoiled rich boys are alike. You complain about it when you get a little discipline, criticize the school when you ought to be shaping up." Mr. Henderson started to walk away.

Justin yelled, "It's not like that at all! The boys call me a terrible name, Death Breath, and call it around the school after me wherever I go, and the teachers don't stop them, even seemed to be in on it. Nobody will talk to me. Everybody excludes me. At the Christmas glee club concert the whole school attacked me, yelled Deeth at me. They all wanted me to die. And I keep being given demerits I don't deserve." It felt good to get it out. Finally tell someone, even a stable guy.

Mr. Henderson turned back and looked him up and down. "You don't look it but do you have any Jewish blood, an ancestor?"

"No. All English."

"Well, there must be something. Nothing happens here without the Head being part of it."

That fit with what happened at the glee club concert.

Mr. Henderson said, "Do you ride."

"Yes, lots at summer camp."

Mr. Henderson brought out a brown mare for him and a bay gelding for himself, and as he was mounting said, "Call me Joe. What's your name?"

He laid out Justin Montgomery Whitthorne II.

Joe whistled. "Pretty fancy. I'm going to call you Monty. Good riding name. And your horse's name is Matilda. She's a good ride." Matilda was stalled next to Imperator. Joe said, "Don't get anywhere near that horse. Beautiful but vicious. Even the owner, Mr. Robinson, has trouble riding him, and he's a very experienced horseman. I have to saddle Imperator for him. No one else in this area will touch him. They shouldn't. You have to spend a lot of time with him, as I have, to do anything with him."

They set off on the snowy trails. He'd never ridden in snow before. Matilda was sure-footed and picked her way without a slip. The branches of passing trees were coated with snow, each branch a different bright design, winter decoration against the bright blue sky. Joe said nothing for awhile, maybe thinking. "I've known the

Head for seventy years. I'm eighty two and he's in his late seventies. Knew him and his family when he was a boy. We grew up together in a town near Pittsfield, an interesting and sad story.

"The Cranchs were fairly prosperous. Owned a small iron foundry. They were from fine stock. Both his mother and father traced their ancestry back to the Mayflower. Can't say the same for me. A lot of wild Irish slipped in." He laughed.

"The Cranchs were prominent in all cultural and charitable activities of the community, Pittsfield, too. They seemed to feel that with their ancestry they were entitled to take a leading role. They took it. Paraded their ancestry all the time, sort of lording it over others. In the late 1890's a gentleman opened a large foundry on the other side of Pittsfield. It had more modern equipment, less costly to run than Cranch's foundry. The new foundry hired away one of Cranch's key employees, I understand doubled his salary. The man hired away knew Cranch's customers, cost structure and pricing approach. With that knowledge the new foundry undercut Cranch at every turn, even when Cranch was selling at below cost to stay afloat. Finally, all the Cranch's resources were gone, their beautiful home mortgaged to the hilt, his wife's jewelry sold along with valuable memorabilia going back to the Massachusetts Bay Colony. The foundry was forced into bankruptcy. It was bought for virtually nothing by the owner of the new foundry.

"It turned out that the behind-the-scenes owner of the new foundry was a Jewish gentleman from Boston. He'd made a business of setting up modern foundries around New England, often close to old established foundries.

"The Cranchs had to move into a small apartment in town. Old man Cranch couldn't take it. Mad as a hatter. I remember him scaring the hell out of me in the local hardware store, coming in and ranting in a loud voice against Jews, talking crazy to everyone and no one. He got so bad he would wander down the main street of town yelling at the sky about Jews to all who passed. I know there was talk of putting him away but he made that unnecessary. He hung himself on a beam at the door to his old foundry, now owned by the Jew. The sign he left next to him said, 'Killed by Jews.' That's why the Head hates Jews.

"I don't disagree with the Head on many things. On this one he's wrong. The reason his family foundry failed is that his father was too full of himself, too focused on his ancestry and position. He failed to see times were changing. He had to modernize. It had nothing to do with the guy being Jewish. Same thing would have happened with a non-Jew. All over New England entrepreneurs were bringing in new methods, not just for foundries, but for textiles, ship building, agriculture, everything. Very few of them were Jewish. Those family businesses which realized that modernization was necessary survived. Old man Cranch had his head in the sand."

Joe said nothing further until they had almost returned. "You ride well."

"Thank you. And thank you for the ride."

"These old bones don't like riding much anymore but it's wonderful to ride in the winter. I might do it again."

"I'll come back after Christmas. Merry Christmas to you."

"And Merry Christmas to you."

The policeman who shuttled him from Pomford to Greenwich was one he'd not met before. Justin asked about Sargent O'Reilly and learned he was fine. He'd been promoted to lieutenant, great news. Conversation was limited, a little about the officer's police work, a little about Pomford, a little about the weather (mixed rain and snow) and what they were observing. Justin revealed nothing of what was going on at school. Same with his aunt Gertrude and her husband, Ben.

He knew if he told Aunt Gertrude she would tell his father and it would get to the woman. She would have a field day, a failure at one of the best schools in the country, a weakling, couldn't take a little boyish hazing, and he was sure she'd tell his father that the whole experience was positive, a toughening experience, great for him. She would insist he stay there. And while she wouldn't say it to her father, she'd be filled with joy on hearing of his terrible life, a pleasure he didn't want to give her.

His stay in Greenwich was uneventful though a wonderful respite. He was a great fan of Aunt Gertrude, a woman of monumental exuberance who threw love at him in great bundles, lots of hugging and kissing, joyful sharing of the merriment of Christmas. Her husband, Ben, was also the best, full of stories of hunting and fishing, about the only thing Ben had ever done having worked few days in his life. Justin hated to lie to them when they asked about Pomford as they were such loving people. But he did. Two days after Christmas he was headed back to Pomford. Aunt Gertrude would have welcomed him longer but she and Ben were headed down to their house in Palm Beach for a New Years party. They had their chauffeur drive him back to Pomford, the only good thing about the return.

The first full day back at Pomford he returned to the stable, a day of snow showers with once in awhile some glints of sun throwing light on the gray rim of the fields, gaunt leafless trees black and brittle on the hills. Joe was there and ready for a ride. Through the early part of the ride he was silent, his usual state. They stopped at the top of a hill, hemlocks casting blueish shadows on the snow around them, looking down on the campus.

Joe said, " I may have given you a wrong impression of the Head when last we talked. He's a remarkable man, a friend of presidents. I'm fortunate to know him. He put himself through Yale after his father's suicide and has taken Pomford from being an also-ran to being one of the foremost schools in America. I don't mind telling you he saved my life. I was so sick from drinking I was dying. He spent a lot of time with me, straightened me out, and financed me to buy the stable."

So Joe was the owner as he'd surmised. It figured with the careful way he took care of the stable and horses.

"Now I admit he's not always easy to deal with. He's a driven man and pushes aside anything that gets in the way of his objectives."

"What are his objectives?"

"I'm not sure I know them and you'll never find out. But I do think he's gotten more rigid as he's aged, become more driven, trying to accomplish things before he dies."

Justin said, "Well, I can tell you one of the things he's accomplishing is absolutely destroying me. Don't you think he's behind the bullying?"

Joe said in a serious and slow voice, looking into Justin's eyes to gain his total attention, "He's not destroying you. You're letting it destroy you. You're destroying yourself."

Joe looked around the beautiful snow covered hillsides and said, his mouth pursed in thought, "I said before he probably knows about the bullying. He knows about everything that happens at Pomford. But your situation is very odd. He's not mean spirited. He loves his boys. Very proud of them."

"Well he certainly doesn't love me. He hates me. He smiled at the glee club concert when everyone yelled Deeth at me. He was in on it."

Joe looked over at Justin on Matilda and gave a long sigh, Do you ever read the Bible?"

"No."

"You should. It helped save me from death. Read Isaiah 50:6 and follow it. Also, you should read the 39th Psalm." He paused for a minute or two. Then said in a contemplative manner, "My family comes from Nantucket way back as did Dr. Cranch's family. That's how we know each other. And that's why the whale is the symbol for Pomford."

So Ahab was in fact from Nantucket. It figured.

"I thought of something from Nantucket that may help you better accept what's happening. When I was young my sister and I occasionally found ambergris on the beaches. As you probably know, ambergris is vomited out by whales. I miss the beaches and I miss my sister. She died a few years back. What's going on reminds me of the whales and ambergris. I don't know why it's happening. Pomford seems to be trying to vomit you out like its symbol the whale. But don't be thinking it's the end of the world. When amber-gris comes out of the whale it's tremendously valuable. It doesn't look like much. And it stinks to high heaven, just like the boys say you stink. But it's an important ingredient for perfumes and many other expensive products. You are tremendously valuable, too. Whether you stay here in the whale or go elsewhere you are tremendously valuable, an intelligent, healthy human being with the whole world before you. You can do anything. They're trying to make you feel worthless, a piece of trash on the beach. Don't buy it. You can't see your value, how special you are. You're too close to it all. I can see it. I can clearly see your value. You're going to have an outstanding life. I guarantee it. When the bullying comes say to yourself, 'This nothing to me. I'm a valuable human being. They can't touch my value." As your life develops you'll start to see your value more and more. Just hang in there. Anyone who survives what you've been through has got to be very special. You'll come through it fine. You're a brave boy to have survived it this long. I admire your courage."

Justin didn't like being compared to stinky ambergris and thought the analogy was a bit far-fetched, but it sure was great having someone on his side.

One more thing from Joe on the way back. "I've had several sons. When they were teenagers they all thought that how things were when they were teenagers was how it'd be the rest of their lives. Not so. Teenagers don't seem to be able to anticipate that things will change. In a few years you're going to be quite a different person. And the world will change. What appear to be problems now will disappear. Just have patience." This talking brought Joe to a coughing fit which doubled him over in the saddle, and he had several more coughing fits on the way back.

When they got down from their horses Joe grabbed his attention again. "Patience. Patience is the greatest virtue. I learned patience from my grandfather. He'd sit fishing for hours, rod in hand, me by his side, no bites. I asked him about it one time. How could he spend so much time with nothing happening? He said,

'Life is about waiting. If you hurry what God plans it won't happen. Every man that has a good life has a waiting life.'" He put a hand on Justin's shoulder. "Learn patience as I have. If you wait all this bad will disappear. Something very good will happen. I promise."

Back in his room Justin opened the Bible next to his bed, still in its cellophane wrapper, never opened, bibles in all the rooms of Pomford. Isaiah 50:6 read:

To those who pulled out my beard, I did not hide my face from mocking and spitting. Because my Sovereign Lord helps me I will not be disgraced. Therefore, I have set my face like flint, and I know I will not be put to shame.

Great thought. Set his face like flint. Very inspirational, though he'd heard that by some accounts Isaiah ended up being sawed in half by the king.

The next day he read the 39th Psalm. It said in part:

I have become a reproach to all my enemies and even to my neighbors, a dismay to those of my acquaintance; when they see me in the street they avoid me. I am forgotten like a dead man, out of mind; I am as useless as a broken pot. For I have heard the whispering of the crowd; fear is all around; they put their heads together.

That was him all right. At least the Psalm ended hopefully, asking the Lord to shine his face on him and save him. There was some comfort in knowing people in the Bible had been treated as he'd been, but though he'd been praying it didn't seem to do much good.

Several days later he went over to the stable and found Joe's son, Daryl, and was told Joe was sick.

"How long do think he'll be sick?"

"Don't know. He smokes a lot."

Daryl started to retreat into the stable. Then turned and said, "I can't back-stop him very long. I'm an auto mechanic. Don't have time to do this."

"Can I help? I've been helping Joe on Sundays when I have free time, currying and mucking out."

Daryl looked him up and down as though doubting a boy in a blue blazer could shovel horse shit.

"Sure," and came over with a smile and a handshake.

In the period before the other students returned, Justin determined he would focus on preparation for the January mid-term exams. He intended to crush the exams with all the time he had to study, some small revenge for what the school was doing to him. He also determined to use the time to think through what was happening to him. In the Fall every time he attempted to reason it out he'd been blocked by some new bad thing occurring. Now he was going to find out what was happening once and for all. He'd been singled out for the worst punishment the school could inflict. Why him? He planted himself at his desk the next morning, early thinking the best. Everything that had happened came clear in his mind, reliving the pain week by week through the Fall.

Was he targeted because he'd been trying to join the popular boys, other boys competing for popularity and trying to drive him off? He'd already rejected that idea. Anyone could see he was never going to be popular, no threat to anyone trying to be. And other boys seeking popularity hadn't come under attack.

For some time he'd been thinking that the Head was behind it. Made no sense. Joe Henderson had said the Head knew about it. He had to. That didn't mean he started it. If the Head wanted him out he was out. The Head didn't have to invent names to bully him out. And he thought it would be beneath the Head, friend of Presidents, to invent a demeaning name for one of his students.

The best possibility seemed to be everyone saw him as an erstwhile Piggy, defenseless.

"Let's target Justin. He's a weak one. No resistance. Blood in the water."

Well, there was a lot to that. No resistance was part of his nature, ingrained. He'd rarely stood up for himself. Here he was fifteen and never had a fist fight. How stupid was that? Not even many verbal confrontations. He was a good boy in a world that seemed to give popularity to cut-ups who challenged authority and did things that led other boys to break the rules. How badly he'd handled the boys when they first started calling Deeth at him, walking away, not challenging them, the worst course he could have taken. He still couldn't understand what possessed him. Why hadn't he punched someone or issued an angry retort. The boys had looked at him in surprise when he just accepted it. There seemed almost regret on their faces that they hadn't stirred up the usual combative response. That was what was supposed to happen at Pomford, response in kind. The taunting might not have built up steam through the Fall if he'd shown resistance. No resistance, keep taunting. And it was no excuse that his father had advised to turn the other cheek to bullying. Everything his father said was a piece of crap.

Why was it so difficult for him to stand up for himself? Was it because he was too afraid of not being liked, too afraid if he stood up to others he wouldn't be liked? In the isolation ward of Pomford being liked was desperately important. There was little else. He thought about Piggy always trying to please, always trying to talk his way into friendships. That got Piggy killed.

Wanting to be liked wasn't new. As far back as he could remember he always tried to be a good boy, to be liked, to gain approval. His mother had schooled him that way, constantly reinforcing it with reward and love. How many times he'd heard his mother introduce him to friends with, "This is Justin. He's a very good boy." Hard not to try and be a good boy when you're told over and over again you are one. Good boy, Rover. Good boy, Justin.

A lot had to do with his mother's illness. He remembered early on developing a strong fear that if he wasn't a good boy his mother's stays at the mental institutions would become more frequent. She would stay away if he wasn't good. He could keep her home with him only by being good.

A searing memory came to mind, Camp Chingachgook.

It still pained him to think about Camp Chingachgook. He'd gone there with his best friend, both ten years old, an exclusive boys' camp on Lake George. The camp had a chef recruited from a leading New York restaurant, that kind of place. His friend and he were the youngest.

When he arrived other campers had gathered around him. "Are you going to try for the Darby Hicks award? It's the award given each year to the camper who does the most to help other campers. It's a really big deal with a special award ceremony. Darby Hicks saved another boy from drowning and in doing so drowned himself. The camp goes all out to honor him." He'd happily eaten up the lies, said, "Yes," and embarked on a quest for the Darby Hicks award with total commitment, helping others in every way he could, cleaning up not only his cabin but neighboring cabins, taking cabin mates' laundry to be washed, eventually becoming almost a servant to his cabin mates including his best friend. (Who was not slow to use his services.) Every waking hour at camp he tried to help others. Awards were given at the end of camp but no Darby Hicks award. He was devastated and cried. Everyone laughed at him.

Finally one older boy, maybe fifteen, nicer than the rest, explained it all. "Each year a boy is picked and fooled into seeking the Darby Hicks award. It's become sort of a camp tradition. A lot of these jerks are too lazy to clean up after themselves and they think it's funny to get someone else to do it. You were the camp choice for this year."

"Why me?"

"You were such a goody-goody boy, always trying to please, an obvious patsy. The jerks knew they could trick you."

That was when he started biting his nails.

He got up from his desk and walked around for some time talking to himself, "Could being a good boy and wanting to be liked produce this monstrous bullying? Maybe if you were a good boy and didn't go along with some of the stuff you'd get a little kidding and a little taunting. I happened to him at Hudson Military. But this, no way. This kind of bullying doesn't come from being a good boy and wanting to be liked. And what about all the other boys here wanting to be liked? Some real mommy boys. Goodie-two-shoes if I ever saw any."

If it wasn't competition to be popular, a vendetta from the Head, or good boy personality, what was it? There was no answer. All he'd done was to get himself all worked up reliving the painful memories.

It'd been snowing heavily all day. The snow subsided by dinner. Walking back to his room, he kicked the new snow ahead of him, watching it float glittering in the light of the full moon, trying to get his mind off his futile attempt to find the cause of the bullying. He looked ahead and stopped dead. That looked like his father's Cadillac parked in front of the Head's house. He didn't have to approach too closely to see it was. What? All the lights in the Head's house were on. He knew for reasons that he couldn't explain it was essential he find out what was going on. The Head's house was unusual on Main Street as it was set back from the road. Also, there were very few bushes around the house like at other houses. It was a gaunt, isolated pile set in open fields, very difficult for a stealth approach, particularly with a full moon. He did a reconnoiter. The back, with fewer lit windows and hidden from the car where he'd noted a chauffeur sitting inside, presented the best opportunity. Should he run up to the back of the house at full speed, hoping to cross the moonlit fields when no one was looking out? Or approach more slowly?

He chose the latter, step by step, watching for any movement in a window indicating someone might be looking, ready to dash away. He'd gotten fairly close, so close that if someone saw him he could be easily identified for whatever punishment Jenkins might concoct.

A door flew open, he assumed the kitchen. Light flooded the landscape and out came a Polish looking woman with a tray, much prettier and younger than the Polish women in the school kitchen though he assumed from the same community. No place to hide. He hit the deck like a Nazi sniper had just whistled a bullet past his ear, didn't even use his arms to brace, fell full length flat face down from his toes in the deep snow, seeking disappearance, hoping the grey color of his wool jacket would give him some protection. The woman's head swiveled toward him. He saw her stare, then shake her head as though not believing what she glimpsed. Off she went to the car with her tray. Justin didn't dare move. Snow had gotten down the front of his jacket and was coldly melting on his chest. His hands were growing numb. Fifteen minutes passed. Half an hour. More. The chauffeur must be sweet talking the cook. He was ready to get up and make a dash for it when she appeared around the corner, moving briskly in the cold. The temperature was about zero and the usual Pomford north wind was blowing strongly. He had light mittens. His fingers were numb. His hands were losing feeling.

He got up and moved around the house keeping below the window ledges and looking in by taking quick glances at the corners of windows. Pay dirt at one larger window, he figured it was the dining room. Three people sat around the table eating and conversing, the Head, his German teacher, Hauptmann, and surprise, the woman, not his father who he'd expected to see. Seeing the three of them together he felt a chill run through him, and it wasn't from the cold. A coven of witches.

He couldn't hear what they were saying but it was obvious they knew each other well, a very amiable conversation. The Head was smiling at the woman more than he'd ever seen him smile and the woman was talking in animated fashion back to him like they were long time best friends. And several times the woman reached out to Hauptmann's sleeve in talking to him, looking at him with more regard than she showed his father. He couldn't take the cold any longer. Now no feeling in his feet to match no feeling in his hands. Can you get frostbite on you feet wearing light boots in two hours of below zero wind-chill? He hurried back to his room as fast as his cold feet would allow, filling his tub with hot water and soaking hands and feet for some time.

He couldn't believe it. Only hours ago he'd asked himself who caused the bullying. Now here was the answer clear as day.

It was the God damn woman out to punish him.

He never figured the woman to be that close to the Head or he would have known earlier. There was no other answer. With her hatred she'd not only cursed him into Pomford but cajoled the Head into making sure the school gave him the hardest possible time. Maybe she didn't pick the death breath name, though it was a clever enough name to be her. However, when the name appeared she somehow got the Head to subtly encourage it. He could see her celebrating every time she talked to the Head and heard from the Head what was going on.

And that horrible glee club concert. Now he was sure she was behind that, too. A opportunity for her to drive him to suicide. She didn't need to get involved in what song the band played. The band found him a juicy enough target to come up with that humiliating song on their own. All the woman had to do was to get the Head to make sure everyone on campus knew about it and then not intervene. He could hear them discussing it, the woman saying, "Please just let it happen. He has done very bad things to his father and to me, accused us of some terrible things. He needs to be punished." She must have been very surprised and unhappy that no suicide occurred.

The real mystery was what had brought the Head, the woman and Hauptmann to meet like that. One more secret on top of many. It felt like his life was bound in secrets. The meeting had to be about something more important than bullying Justin. Whatever it was it was bad. With that group it had to be bad. He vowed to find out. A personal mission. His face would be set as flint. Patience his watchword. Maybe he could do something proud to avenge his mother.

And with what he learned about the woman and the bullying he set himself to fight back against the bullying. No more Piggy around school. From here on out those who bullied him would get a strong response.

He looked down at his badly chewed fingernails. "That stops now." Chewed fingernails are for losers. I'm no loser anymore."

CHAPTER FOURTEEN

While Justin was going to Greenwich for Christmas Henry
Benson was stuck alone at Pomford, rattling around his
house and feeling sorry for himself. Shirley had disappeared, a family visit to North Carolina with her husband, George Brown, and
their two girls. She'd told him she'd tried everything to keep them
in Pomford for Christmas. George ruled the roost and off they
went. He missed Shirley so much. Christmas vacation had been one
empty day after another.

Now New Year's Day, January 1, 1955, snow blowing wildly
around the house, the temperature near zero and falling. Henry
had gotten up slowly that morning. Why bother? After wandering
around the house aimlessly for some time he poured himself a large
cup of coffee, five teaspoons of sugar, one of his few indulgences,
then built a roaring fire in the fireplace of the simply furnished living room and pulled over an immense wing chair to sit by the fire.
The walls were decorated with the many photos of Pomford Valley
he'd taken over the years. He studied them intently one by one, the
memories flooding in, taking stock, New Years a time for taking
stock. There were a lot of bad memories though some good, hard
to believe he'd been at Pomford fifteen years.

At first he'd found his choice of Pomford ideal. The initial
summer, the summer of 1940, was spent exploring his new geography, photographing every aspect of nature in the Pomford Valley,
learning fly fishing from some of the Pomford teachers who were
experts, and riding, something he'd not done in years. He found
the times of quiet he sought. Healing came in the gentle rippling

of water along the banks of trout streams, chirping of waterside birds, stillness maintained to photograph a moment of nature, the clopping of horses hoofs carrying him along green paths of the verdant hills. He also became active in the Congregational Church of the neighboring town of Greenfield and took up bridge again, something Helen and he had often played early in their marriage. He thought he'd found the ideal peaceful place.

The Fall term dashed some of his hopes regarding Pomford. It wasn't the teaching. With his medical background he found that teaching biology required little preparation, and he got tremendous satisfaction in bringing boys along to knowledge. But he was appalled by the extreme control Pomford exercised over its boys, far greater than what he'd had himself in school and far greater than what he'd heard any other prep school was using. And the faculty meetings were insufferable. They focused on positive eugenics rather than course materials and student achievement—a recitation of the names of other schools and individual professors recently persuaded to the eugenics cause, happenings at conferences, usually private affairs, and goings on in Germany so far as they could understand them from leaked reports. The comment from many was along the lines of, "How can Germany stray so far. What they're doing is endangering eugenics as a moral imperative." Never any concern expressed for the people subject to the German program, an omission Henry found highly reprehensible. Henry noticed that the Head sat stoically through these discussions.

Worse was what he observed at Sunday teas. The Head and his wife, Frieda, held the teas most Sunday afternoons for rotating groups of boys. Very intense. Always the same. The Head would start with something like, "You boys should never forget you're better than most. Your bloodlines are superior. And if you don't dilute them by marrying beneath you, your children's bloodlines will be even more superior, and your children's children after that, on through the generations. Your family will be in the forefront of America for all time. Think of what's possible if you do as we instruct." At that point the Head normally leaned forward toward each boy in a circle around him, looked him individually in the eyes, and fervor had come into his voice.

After that each boy was taken off for an individual discussion of his family and genealogy. They had each boy's genealogy going way back. The Head, and particularly his wife, had them practically memorized. "Your uncle George has been very successful after leaving Yale. What traits did he have that made him successful? And whom did he marry? Wasn't she a Smith graduate from a prominent family? Don't you think it was the combination of the two of them together that made him successful? Isn't he an example of how having the right character and intellect, and then marrying an intelligent, well-bred woman, leads to success in life?"

At other sessions other relatives of a boy were discussed, always at some point including the father and grandfather and always emphasizing the boy's responsibility to carry his family's intellect and other capabilities to future generations by marrying an intelligent woman of good breeding.

From the Head's wife. "You carry your parents' blood, their good birth. You must carry it forward. You're here for the future." A constant refrain. "You're here for the future."

The boys were buying into it. It sounded at little like what was going on in Germany with the Hitler Youth. And with all the extolling of families he could understand why fathers would want to send their sons to Pomford.

Tea with seniors was different. They were being launched on a mission. The Head would say, "You boys need to bring to others what you have learned here about the importance of preserving and enhancing your bloodlines. Each of you at some point in your career must commit to teaching. Maybe you take three or four years after college and before graduate school to act as a student advisor in a college, or perhaps an assistant teaching position in a prep or boarding school. Or maybe after your first career you turn to teaching. But best if you make teaching your life work."

It seemed like the Mormon church sending out youths to seek converts, the religion of Cranch and Pomford seeking adherents.

He found it vaguely sinful and wrong despite his previous support of positive eugenics and stopped going to the teas.

Henry poured himself another cup of coffee, glanced outside, concluded that no way would he shovel the walk in this weather and settled back down in his chair by the fire. He chuckled to himself, then laughed. He was thinking about the "pie ladies" that had appeared with the advent of World War II. Being single, quite attractive, and with many men away fighting the war, he was a target. He'd talked about it to Frank MacComber, a fellow bachelor.

"It's amazing. I'd meet a lady at church, or maybe playing bridge. A couple of days later a pie, or maybe some brownies would show up, something small. If I accepted the gift graciously, and I always did, more pies and other goodies appear, followed by delivery of something for dinner. I could predict from when the first pie arrived the date when the dinner will arrive. Then a series of conversations after church or bridge. Then an invitation to have dinner at her house, to see, 'How he liked her cooking.' That invitation always came ten days to two weeks after the post-church or bridge conversations started. The old adage is that the way to a man's heart is through his stomach. I've had some great meals and some meals that it was all I could do to not run to a bathroom. Then after five dinners in her home, always five, if I don't bail out an opportunity to stay overnight. These gals around here were all on the same dating timetable, regular as the New York Central. It was the damndest thing."

He smiled to himself thinking about his success in avoiding the traps set. Some of the ladies were quite lovely but no one close to his Helen in beauty or brains. He didn't share a bed with any though several offered.

Henry frowned. His memories had taken him to his role in the Holocaust. They always did. Several times a day.

Throughout the war he gobbled up every piece of Germany eugenics news that came into Pomford. It wasn't much and often contradictory, but always very disturbing. He started having more nightmares, one in particular that came often. He was in an auditorium delivering a lecture on eugenics. He knew he was in Germany though he'd never been there. Nazi faces turned up to him at the podium, each face in adulation of the doctrine he was preaching. The back of the auditorium would open up, revealing a train. All its windows were dark. He knew it contained something terrible.

As allied troops entered Germany in 1945 he started to see newspaper reports of the liberation of concentration camps and the atrocities discovered. This was usually buried in the back pages, stories of the progress of the war dominating the headlines. He dreaded to open a paper. Any hope he had that it might not be real ended on April 12, 1945. The Sixth Armored Division had just liberated Buchenwald. He was in the faculty lounge when Frank MacComber came charging in waving the *Boston Globe*. He put it on a table in front of Henry and the other teachers and opened it up to the center section, a spread of pictures of Buchenwald. Prisoners lay on the ground, one so thin his thighbone seemed to puncture the skin. Another picture was of a vast open pit filled to overflowing with naked dead bodies the heads shaved. The enormity of what he'd done came to him as never before. He reached out to the paper and held it up so he could see more clearly, his hands shaking. Skeletons with no flesh reached out for him through a wire fence, their eyes set not in faces but in bones, accusing him, reflecting the terror they'd seen, staring at him, staring personally at him, blaming him. My God! How could he have been part of this? This was a direct result of his presentation in California. A direct result of all the booklets he circulated in Germany. His fingerprints were all over the Holocaust. His doing.

He remembered sitting there for some time, his mind going over everything he'd said in his presentation and in subsequent contacts with Germany. Then going over it again, then again, his mind struggling for an outlet. There was none. Under his breath he'd said, "Does the fact I wasn't there absolve me?" No. A criminal who plots a murder is guilty along with the murderer. He was as responsible as the man who pulled the lever at the gas chamber.

How could he live? How could he continue to lecture students? Pretend he was a moral person?" He looked at the pictures again and started crying in front of the other teachers. Then wailing, "No, no, no," hitting the sides of his head with his hands, nausea creeping up in his stomach. He ran out and threw up on the sidewalk, then again when he reached home. All night he lay on his back in self-loathing, then half asleep he would moan as the faces appeared.

Henry's memory of that horrible day of the Buchenwald pictures was as clear as if the prisoners had just marched into his January living room and sat down opposite him, haunted eyes damning him to hell.

The day after the *Boston Globe* revelation, he'd gone to the Head's office in his disheveled clothing, unshaven, his eyes red from grieving and tendered his resignation. When he explained his reasons the reaction was not what he expected.

"We knew all about your history before we hired you. You were merely a messenger to the Germans. You didn't invent eugenics. You didn't invent the U.S. eugenics program. You didn't invent the California program. You just told people about them. The programs were in existence already, invented before you got there. As for the Jews, people won't say it but many sympathize with the German hatred of Jews. Jews can be unscrupulous and hold themselves out from the rest of society, think they're more intelligent, claim persecution to gain advantage. Here we understand what you accomplished for Germany and respect it. You're better off staying with us, your friends. Elsewhere people would reject what you've done, not understanding. Why don't you take a few days off and think about it. I'll get a substitute for your classes."

He was still amazed at the Head's lack of sympathy for the Jews. How could he have not seen the Buchenwald photos? He had to have.

After a week during which the great tempter suicide frequently appeared, he returned to the Head's office and withdrew his resignation. From his knees he'd been speaking to Helen. She wanted him to continue to live, and if he resigned where would he go and what would he do? But the Head had it wrong about him being only a messenger. He'd done everything in his power to get Germany to adopt the California program, on his own initiative sent more than one hundred thousand eugenics circulars into Germany to condition the country to accept programs to eliminate undesirables. Everything he'd done led directly to the "Final Solution" to the Jewish problem, the Holocaust. The nightmares had gotten worse with the eyes of Buchenwald staring at him.

As 1945 wound down he'd started worrying about the Nuremberg trial. A large number of defendants argued that what they did was legal and acceptable, Germany was emulating the laws of the U.S., specifically the laws of California. Until the trial ended in October, 1946, each day Henry checked the mail and listened for a knock on the door, a summons to testify at the Nuremberg trial. And when it was over he felt relief, but also that he should have been forced to testify, to publicly admit his guilt, to be punished for what he did.

Thinking back on it from the vantage of the new year 1955, he berated himself for not leaving Pomford when the Buchenwald pictures appeared. He would have avoided his role with Gerard but also, of course, no Shirley.

In March 1946 he'd received a letter from Switzerland with a return address for Dieter Hauptmann. He remembered him from the German delegation visit to California. It was the first letter other than advertising material he'd gotten from outside the immediate area since he left California. When opened the letter was not from Dieter but Gerhard Mulder.

I wrote you several times before the war and had the letters returned saying you were no longer in Pomona and had left no forwarding address. What I was writing you was that I had escaped to Switzerland in 1940. My opposition to the concentration camps and treatment of Jews put me in mortal danger. I barely got out with my life. And Brigit had died of breast cancer. There was nothing to hold me to Germany.

You will note the letter is nominally from my best friend, Dieter Hauptmann, who has passed away. You may remember him from your presentation in California. Throughout the war he continued to teach at Heidelberg, a lot of excellent work on eugenics. He is no longer alive. Recently I was able to obtain a Swiss passport and with the war over came out of hiding. I've been casting around for a career as far away from eugenics and Germany as possible. Teaching was an obvious choice. I taught classes at Heidelberg. Among the people I contacted was a professor at Princeton I knew from eugenics. They didn't have anything there, I expect as negative eugenics has gone out of favor because of Germany. However, he wrote that he understood Pomford had hired someone involved in negative eugenics and mentioned your name. It would be wonderful to work alongside you at Pomford.

The final part of the letter was a summary of his qualifications, most of which Henry knew, and a request for help in obtaining admission to the US and a position at Pomford or elsewhere.

Henry read it twice and had the inclination to immediately refer it to the Head with a strong recommendation. My God. Breast cancer just like Helen. He decided instead to be cautious, first get some more information. He hadn't communicated with Gerhard in a long time and a lot of terrible things had occurred in Germany. He wanted to make sure he knew what Gerhard had been up to. What was he doing in Switzerland from 1940 until now? How was it that he had a Swiss passport, something he knew was very difficult to obtain? How was it that when Dieter died he was able to take his identity? Why was he still using Dieter's identity now that the war was over? And most important, what was his involvement in moving the German eugenics program to euthanasia of Jews, the "Final Solution"?

The answer From Gerhard came back fairly quickly.

Henry,

You are right to ask your questions. What happened in Germany with the Holocaust defies the notion that people are human. I am ashamed of my country and the allegedly civilized people who allowed this to happen. Every German owes an apology to the entire world. Those of us who had any involvement with it are consumed by guilt and shame.

At least I fought it as I could, not by publicly defying Hitler, which would have been futile and have resulted in my death, but by quietly introducing various processes and procedures which required the determination of eligibility for sterilization and euthanasia to be made on a case-by-case basis. No mass determinations regarding an entire racial group, like the Jews. What I did held back the evil for about a year, saving a lot of lives of Jews who managed to get out of the country. Mass transport of Jews and high-volume gas chambers were held back until 1942 and 1943.

During the war I worked as a hospital orderly in a small hospital in a remote corner of Switzerland. I got the Swiss passport through a government official of my acquaintance, a classmate and friend from Heidelberg. He knew I had escaped from Germany and sympathized with the reasons. Dieter had been worried about the increasing danger I faced in Germany. On his death bed, dying of kidney disease, Dieter insisted I take his identification to allow me to cross into Switzerland. We still looked almost exactly alike. If I tried it under my own identification I would have been stopped at the border and probably killed. I've kept his identity rather than going back to mine to avoid the big and time-consuming legal hassle of trying to undo my current identity. The Swiss do not look kindly on those using a false name on their passports to enter their country or residing in their country under a false name.

Please let me know if there is any further information I can provide. My conscience isn't clear but I have some solace in getting out when I did.

Henry had studied the letter against Gerhard's letters to him in California, letters he'd kept despite discarding about everything else related to eugenics. He had noted that in one of his 1939 letters Gerhard had indicated his eugenics program had already turned to sterilization of Jews. And everything he read said the attack on Jews had started long before 1940. If Gerard opposed persecution of Jews so strongly why didn't this force him to leave much earlier? He did some research in the Nuremberg Trial records to see if Gerhard was being sought as a war criminal but could find nothing. The records covered those convicted and those arrested and awaiting trial but not those still being sought. Finally he decided to give Gerhard the benefit of the doubt. Gerhard may have gotten out late but at least he got out. And supporting someone who had opposed German treatment of Jews made him feel a little better about himself, a small propitiation for his role in creating the German horror. But most of all, he felt sympathy for Gerhard, Brigit dying of breast cancer as Helen had.

When he made the recommendation to the Head he was surprised to find it immediately accepted. The German teacher was retiring. This was strange. He was only fifty-five and never told him of an interest in retiring despite them being fishing buddies. When Henry asked the German teacher about it all he would say was that it was time. He didn't seem very happy.

When Henry had called the State Department to find what he needed to do he discovered it was very little. All the work on submission for the visa had to be done by Gerhard at the US Embassy in Switzerland. Henry's own role was to be that of sponsor. He wrote a sponsoring letter saying that Dieter Hauptmann had been a distinguished professor at Heidelberg, had opposed the Nazis and escaped to Switzerland in fear for his life, had a job waiting for him at Pomford, and that he, Henry, stood behind him financially.

Two weeks after he submitted the Head appeared in his office. "With your background in eugenics, and what happened in Germany, there's concern you might not be a good sponsor. A second sponsor has stepped in. You might hear something about it from the State Department."

So he wasn't even needed, but who could Gerard have known not involved in eugenics? He noticed the Head didn't give a name. Something was going on that he didn't understand. Something else he didn't understand. Gerhard's visa application was processed quickly, not what he expected. He'd understood visas for Germans were being processed slowly and carefully by the State Department in the wake of the war, screening for former Nazis.

The Gerhard who arrived at Pomford for the start of the Fall term, 1946, wasn't the same Gerhard he remembered, not the same quiet of voice, somewhat self-effacing, gentlemanly person who had visited California. The new Gerhard spoke more loudly, and there was a hard look about him, particularly in the eyes, eyes that Henry felt had seen many bad things. And Henry saw arrogance in the curve of the lips and the way he walked as though he owned the world, a Nazi strut. Still Gerhard greeted him warmly and seemed to want to take up where they left off.

Over the next two weeks Gerhard told him at length about his life in Switzerland and earlier adventures with Brigit in Germany and Switzerland. He had him over one night to his house for dinner, (Gerhard said repayment for the dinner in Pomona), and they went on a horseback ride together. Henry continued to think of Gerhard as Gerhard, and addressed him as Gerhard in private, though did a good job in always calling him Dieter in public.

Sitting by the fire Henry wondered anew why he hadn't been suspicious right from the first. It had taken him two full weeks to get really concerned that Gerhard hadn't talked about his role in Germany. He invited him over to the faculty lounge late one day when no one else was around.

"Gerhard, I'd like to know in much more detail what happened in Germany and your role. I'm sorry to bother you about this but I feel a great responsibility. Germany took my presentation in California as a basis for the worst things man ever did to man. I need to know what role my presentation played in the Holocaust. I need to understand what role you played."

Gerhard leaned back in his chair and stared at him with his cold eyes. "Your presentation had no effect. Hitler had already decided on eugenics."

"Then why did you come to California?"

"Hitler asked us to do it."

"Well, what about all the circulars I had distributed in Germany extolling eugenics?"

A little crossness in Gerhard's voice, "I already told you. Hitler had already decided."

"What you're saying isn't correct. I've had reports from knowledgeable people in the eugenics field who were in Germany at the time who said that the presentation and circulars had a large impact. The California laws I covered with you in the presentation were what you copied and what the defendants quoted in the Nuremberg trial."

Gerhard gave no answer, just sat impassively staring at him. The friendliness Gerhard had shown him to date seemed to have departed.

"Well, what was your personal role? I sponsored you largely on trust. I went out on a limb. I didn't know much about what you did in Germany. I was happy to sponsor you. Still am. We had an excellent relationship in Pomona. But now I'd like to get comfortable I did the right thing. Please fill me in on what you were doing. "

Gerhard was definitely angry now, his face a grim mask.

"You weren't responsible for the Holocaust. I wasn't. I don't talk about things of the past. They're behind me. I'm not going to dredge up the past to make you feel better. You have all you need in my letters from Switzerland."

"Gerhard, I confess to being suspicious. Forgive me. With what's happened to me in my life I'm a suspicious man. I compared your letters from Switzerland with your letters to me in California. In your letters from Switzerland you say mass transport of Jews and high-volume gas chambers started in 1942 and 1943. I've checked that and they're accurate dates. However, in your letters of 1939 and 1940 you were already secretly letting me know of planning for mass executions of Jews. How could you have known in 1939 and 1940 of the planning unless you were part of the planning? As I understand, planning for these things was done by Hitler's inner circle. I'm frankly having great difficulty believing that the head of eugenics in Germany wasn't part of that inner circle, very involved in planning and managing the whole Holocaust. I need a lot more than what you said in your letters from Switzerland."

Gerhard did not reply and got up with a dismissive gesture of his hands and an arrogant smile as though nothing Henry thought or did could affect him, then walked away in his brisk Nazi strut.

Henry remembered that his principle feeling was not that of anger but of consternation. He'd let someone into the country who might be really bad. Should he contact the State Department? If he did so he'd probably find himself in a lot of trouble for bringing in someone under an assumed name. And there'd probably be limited sympathy with his background in eugenics and work with Germany. Being courageous wasn't appealing.

Thereafter he and Gerhard rarely talked, stayed away from each other where possible. Occasionally he would pick up papers for a faculty meeting from Gerhard's house and he from his, but studious avoidance where possible. Though no new evidence had surfaced since their confrontation in 1946, his suspicion had grown.

Henry got up and deposited his empty coffee cup in the kitchen. Looking out the widow the blowing snow, and particularly the wind, had become worse. How different from lovely Pomona. The only thing good about Pomford was finding Shirley.

Shirley entered his life in 1950. Her husband, George Brown, an older man than Henry, had been recruited to Pomford to teach English. Henry found him hard-head, humorless, dogmatic in his opinions, though he did have a distinguished career in eugenics. Shirley looked fifteen or twenty years younger and was beautiful, blue-eyed, and blond-haired like Helen.

He got to know her over bridge, her love for bridge equaling his, often a warm smile for him, and as time passed the smiles increased. He smiled back, smiling both outside and inside. Escorting her home was next, a walk from the house hosting the bridge that particular evening to the Brown's house on Main Street. He learned quite a lot about her in these walks, and she heard his life story in return. She spoke of growing up in a small upstate New York town. Her father owned a pharmacy and was an avid supporter of eugenics. She'd met George at an eugenics conference where he'd been the featured speaker. Her father had been impressed with him and urged her to marry him when he came courting. She'd just turned twenty, had lived a sheltered life, and was totally naive.

George was often away from Pomford. He was the point man in outreach to other institutions in promoting eugenics and was the Pomford representative at conferences around the country. One evening she invited Henry in. He tingled with hope. She dismissed the baby sitter, checked on the girls in the back bedroom and came calmly to face him. Her beautiful blue eyes gleamed in the pale light and the smile he adored came on her face. Still calmly she said, "I love you. Make love to me."

In an instant the calm became an explosion. He responded in kind. It was the most passionate lovemaking he'd ever experienced. Never before this hunger. It was as though he'd been saving himself all the years since Helen died. The same for Shirley. George had not made love to her for a year and she never enjoyed lovemaking with him anyway. It was she that asked the practical question, "What do we do now?"

"I don't know. I love you. Are you willing to divorce George?"

"It's too soon to think about that. The children are my life. I need to protect them."

"Will you see me again?"

"Certainly. I couldn't stand not seeing you."

So that became the routine—bridge, walks home, and the many nights George wasn't there, passionate love. Several times he raised the divorce issue, saying he wanted to marry her and be a father to her children. She ducked him every time but finally said, "I want to marry you. I want it nothing more in the world. But I've had two divorces in my family where young children were involved. The effect on the children was devastating. Let's wait until the children are older and can handle it a little better."

He was unhappy in not being with her but believed her. They would eventually be together.

He smiled as he sat in the warm living room thinking about it, glanced outside and noted that the wind had blown much of the snow off the front walk to drift against the house, done the clearing for him. He congratulated himself for not venturing out.

CHAPTER FIFTEEN

January 3rd, 1955. A new term. Boys arrived back in a glow from time with families and laid off him for awhile, he knew a very temporary reprieve. The Pomford weather punished him instead. Perhaps in retribution for the boys temerity in leaving the valley, Pomford turned its dank weather bitterly cold, colder than over Christmas, below zero many days in a row. Shirley told him it was fifteen below one night, the cold magnified by the constant damp. One or two boys proclaimed, "Cold as a witch's teat." Soon everyone in class was echoing it back and forth. He could tell how cold it was by how loudly the snow crunched beneath his boots and the crunch sound grew as January progressed. To breakfast, back from breakfast to his room, to class, back from class, to lunch, to athletics, and so on. He was the only one subject to the full impact of the cold. Boys in dormitories needn't go far to do anything. Added to the cold was the north wind, gusts so strong he sometimes had to huddle against a building with his back turned against whiteouts of blowing snow. Arrival at destination necessitated a vigorous and lengthy rubbing of ears and nose and stamping of feet to bring back circulation. One time he couldn't feel his nose for such a long period that he assumed frostbite and was ready to dash to the infirmary. Did anyone see his situation? Did any student or teacher inquire about his welfare? Would anyone care if he froze to death along the way? No. The school would probably give less importance to his freezing death than to reading about the freezing death of one of Jack London's characters in the Klondike.

The winter sign-up board for athletics gave three options— basketball, no way as he'd never been able to shoot baskets, hockey, he didn't like skating despite skating some in Central Park, and swimming. Because he'd done a little swimming at Hudson Military, he decided on swimming. It turned out he didn't like it any better than football. The stroke he chose was backstroke. At least he could breath. Endless laps, time trials with the coach yelling at him because he didn't try hard enough, snapping towels in the locker room after practice, he on the receiving end of more than his share. Worst were the long Main Street walks back to the house after practice, his hair still wet, ice forming on cold days, a dismal walk in a dismal season.

Things weren't helped by the fact he only had one letter from Fawn over the Christmas vacation. She complained that she was having great difficulty getting to a mailbox, her father watching her like a hawk, that her cousins were stupid, that she was bored stiff and miserable and was close to crying sometimes about not being able to see him.

When the Browns returned to the house after Christmas vacation he tried to avoid them. The times he did run into Mr. Brown in the front hall he would get a hard look of appraisal. This wasn't good. He considered stopping all correspondence with Fawn but couldn't bear doing that. Regular correspondence resumed. No longer did they write about possibilities together, the likelihood seemed too distant, mostly rather banal comparisons of what was going on at their schools and recitations of their past lives. Justin did spend some time composing a poem about the life in New York they might have together though the poem never came off.

In mid-January Justin's frustration got the better of him. He researched some Greek mythology and turned from a New York poem to a love poem,

Across the room she walks, a present
Carries all his hopes and dreams
The light plays on her, she's the light
Love she brings him to his sight.
Softly, gently shows her lover

apples more precious than Hesperides
pink the tips, flowers of Chloris
and curve of body, such loveliness.
Aphrodite weeps at such a rival
I who see you am atremble
A gift more marvelous than all before
My love to you whom I adore.

He was sure with her intelligence she'd look up the references and feel his passion.

About a week later Mr. Brown came charging into his room, the angriest-looking man he'd ever seen, waving the love letter he wrote to Fawn. Now he knew they had Stoneleigh Prospect checking her mail. How could he have been so stupid, putting his return address on envelopes?

"Stand up. Look at me."

Justin looked into his intimidating eyes.

"What have you been doing with my daughter?"

"I only talked to her twice for a few minutes when she went to the store." His voice shook.

"Don't lie to me!" He held up the letter. "There was much more. What's this about her breasts?"

His eyes bore in, focused rays of hate.

"Well I did see her through her bedroom window." He squirmed and tried to look away.

"Look at me. Was she undressed?"

"Just the top."

Mr. Brown slugged him hard on the side of his head, knocking him to the floor, his ear ringing. He towered over him, spittle flying from his mouth, raging. "I can be a violent man. And I take revenge. If you have anything more to do with my daughter I will beat you to an inch of your life, probably kill you. I'd love to kill you. When I get violent I have trouble stopping myself. Do you understand? Do you understand that you miserable fucking shit? You're going to die if you see her again. Die, you hear me?" He was yelling at the end.

Justin feared he'd be killed right then and there. In panic he said, "Yes. I understand," and cowered on the floor, his voice weak, barely audible.

"You should be expelled. Perverts who peek in windows have no place at Pomford. The Head probably won't expel you. He never does. But I'll tell him about it. The whole campus will be watching you. Evil boys like you get watched." He clumped out.

The only good news was he hadn't put anything in the letter about her beautiful bottom. And Mr. Brown's supposition that he was a Peeping Tom at least gave some protection to Fawn. But despair, ability to correspond with her had been snatched away.

The watching Mr. Brown threatened didn't seem to occur. If the teachers were watching him with special attention he didn't notice it. Just more of the same. The taunting that had diminished after the Christmas vacation came back in spades. Reality sunk in for everyone, confined winter days stretching forever. He noticed something that he hadn't noticed before. It was really only fifteen or so boys that were making the long drawn-out calls of Deeth. They were all in the classes for less-intelligent students, thugs indeed.

Most of their calls of Deeth came from behind him, never directly to his face. With his new found resolve when one of the thugs called Deeth from behind he took to quickly turning around, fists clenched, and confronting the boy.

"You asshole. Grow up. Stupid boy in stupid boy classes."

Or,

"That's stupid. That's why you're in stupid-boy classes."

Or,

"You dumbass. Can't remember my name. That's why you're in stupid-boy classes."

But mostly.

"You stupid shit. Grow up."

And always the finger and something else. He would run full speed up to boy who was taunting him, and getting very close, would blow his breath on his face as strongly as he could. The reactions of dismay always set him laughing.

The effect of his confrontations wasn't to stop catcalls of Deeth. The thugs continued though from within groups of boys and at greater distance so he couldn't identify who was taunting. Deeth calls already had major effect. Deeth had become his monicker. Justin had been lost. Everyone in the school now addressed him as Deeth. When the opportunity presented itself he would correct them. "It's Justin, not Deeth." Some used Justin for a few minutes after that, only a few minutes. Most ignored his comment. In his new resolve he still hated being called Deeth. However, he found that what had terribly wounded before now merely irritated. With his belief that the bullying originated with the woman he came to view the taunting boys as mere conduits of the woman's punishment, not totally responsible for their actions.

While he couldn't leave Pomford he found a way to escape within Pomford, the infirmary. A wonderful thing was the infirmary—food brought to him so no need to go to the dining hall, lessons delivered so no need to go to class, no long cold walks from swimming. He would go over to the infirmary with a pretend cold or other minor respiratory problem. The admitting nurse was lazy. She'd pop a thermometer in his mouth and go back to reading her trashy magazines, giving him time to place the thermometer next to a lightbulb for a boost to an admission level temperature.

One time he screwed up, held the thermometer by the lightbulb too long, ran it up to almost 104 degrees. A doctor rushed over from the Greenfield Hospital, was mystified his temperature had descended to normal so quickly, and he was ejected to his sad daily life. Other times he did better, stringing it out, playing the same lightbulb game once admitted as he played at admission, a stay of a week or more with an inexplicable low-grade fever.

The only thing bad about the infirmary is it gave him time to think. All the awful memories roared through his mind, then roared again and again, his mother, his father, the woman, the Head, the bullying, thoughts chasing each other with no relief. He tried shaking his head to throw them out. Couldn't. It was as though he had a disease inside eating at him only this disease didn't seem to have a cure.

It all came to an end when the nurse came in unexpectedly and found him with the thermometer pressed against a lightbulb. No more escape from Pomford that way. In a way he was glad. Out and about he didn't have so much time for the black thoughts that seemed to be taking over his mind.

In the new term Justin finally started making friends. Maybe other boys could see that with his confrontations with taunters he'd become worthy of knowing. All the new friends were loners. Justin came to think of them as "lone-wolves." None was very popular, and all of them ignored the Deeth stuff, maybe because the taunting made him a lone-wolf himself. And why seek popularity anyway in such an asshole school? The first who befriended him was John Bienville. He came from New Orleans, strong Southern accent. He proudly stated at every opportunity that he was named after the last French governor of the Louisiana territory, a direct ancestor. At the same table with Bienville one night Bienville collected scraps from everybody, saying it was to feed his alligators.

"Feed your alligators?" Justin asked.

"Sure. I keep two in my dorm room. They're not real big yet. Maybe a foot and a half each, but growing fast."

"How come the school allows you to keep them?"

"Well, my father and grandfather kept them while they were at Pomford and it's sort of a family tradition."

Justin felt it was probably something else. The family was a major benefactor. Justin swam daily in the Bienville pool.

Bienville said, "Anyone here want to feed them? You can feed them by hand."

Everyone quickly declined, shaking their heads, looking like they knew something. With little interaction with other boys, Justin rarely knew anything that was going on and accepted the challenge, feeling it might elevate his status to show he was brave. Bienville beamed at him. The alligators were quick, and he barely avoided being badly bitten, just a small nip. Another patsy, a freshman Bienville had somehow waylaid to the sophomore dorm, was not quick and ended up with a pretty good mashing of fingers. That happened when Justin was there. He helped Bienville convince the boy not to take it to the infirmary. That would have been the end of the alligators. From then on Bienville was nice to him, telling him wild stories about catching alligators that he always doubted but never questioned. Bienville seemed to consider him a good friend.

His next friend, Alexander Peabody from Boston, came as a result of a major scandal that took everyone's mind off the endless winter, at least momentarily. A teacher, his own English teacher Mr. Fitzgibbons, was fired, and Dudley Johnson, a senior, expelled, first student anybody had ever heard of being expelled.

Mr. Fitzgibbons being let go was terrible. He was Justin's favorite teacher after Mr. Benson, kindly, giving him high marks. Why was he dismissed? Nobody knew. Wild rumors swept the campus.

Justin tracked down Fred Jamison, the font of all gossip, determined to understand the reason for the dismissal. Fred said he was trying to find out what happened and promised to tell him if he did. Several days later Fred saw him across the dining hall and motioned him to a corner where they could talk. "I tracked down a janitor who'd seen it all. Gave him twenty bucks and he spilled the beans. Fitzgibbons was fucking Johnson in the ass in one of the shower stalls."

Justin drew back. "That's possible?"

"Sure. But it must be awfully messy."

Well now he knew what was meant by degenerative behavior, and soon, thanks to Fred, everyone in school had the story. At least it took attention off him for awhile.

Fred had said to him, "If that's what makes them happy in this miserable place why not," and Justin sort of agreed.

Alexander Peabody was in his class with Mr. Fitzgibbons, as he was in most of his classes, a very smart fellow, just as devastated as Justin about losing Mr. Fitzgibbons. Alex wanted to be a poet and Mr. Fitzgibbons was helping him. Fitzgibbons was apparently a published poet. One of the oddities about Alex (all the lone-wolves were a little odd) was that when you talked to him he was prone to branch off with references from poetry, "As Wordsworth said," and then quote more than you wanted to hear. He'd memorized long passages from poets he liked. Over time mutual commiseration about the loss of Fitzgibbons progressed into the exchange of views on Boston and New York, and dissertations on art from Alex. Alex's father owned the leading gallery in Boston, and Alex had spent a lot to time in art museums. Justin had often visited the Metropolitan Museum, but mostly he listened when Alex talked about art, many good conversations.

Then there was Humphrey Bishop, far from a bishop, a large, heavy square of a boy, more dirty jokes than anyone else in the class. Everyone called him by the name "Horney," a nickname he seemed to cherish. The Fall before Horney had been positioned in the center of the JV football line. He couldn't run and didn't tackle much, but nobody could move him, so he often got mention by the Head during post-game assemblies. His claim to fame was masturbation. He kept a daily diary of his masturbation, sometimes getting up to seven times a day.

One snowy Sunday afternoon Justin's wanderings took him past the shed where he'd intended the tryst with Fawn. He often walked that way thinking about her, and there was Horney, fiddling with some boards at the back of the shed, an out-of-the-way place for Horney during a snowstorm. Curious, Justin approached, the sound of his footsteps deadened in the snow.

Horney finished with what he was doing, turned, and recoiled at seeing him. A magazine with a half naked girl on the cover fell to the snow, the snow holding the magazine toward him in arresting presentation. Justin had found Horney's cache of porno magazines, rumored to number over fifty. The whole class was looking for it. Humphrey entreated him not to tell, promising to share the magazines. Justin agreed, more because it was an opportunity to join with another boy than because he wanted to see the magazines. The result was that Horney brought him into his group of porno-obsessed boys, a friend of sorts, but definitely not the gentlemanly type boy his father said he should befriend. Horney's teeth were greenish and Justin doubted he ever brushed them judging from Horney's foul breath, an awful grayish reek that smelled like something really bad had died in his mouth. Justin mused some about only his own bad breath being counted on the ledger of capital crimes. Horney was given to exclaiming "fuck this" and "fuck that" at regular intervals, and farting in public followed by excessive laughter seemed to be what delighted him most after masturbation. Horney considered himself master of this occupation and was given to wise statements about farting like, "If you really have to force it it's probably shit," and "There's no more nerve-racking moment than attempting your first fart after diarrhea." Justin could only stand to be with him short periods of time, only marginally better than having no friend at all.

Mid-years came and went. He thought he'd done very well. The procedure was that grades were given out by the Head himself. By accounts it could be an unpleasant experience. He lined up alphabetically with other sophomores in front of the administration building. No calls of Deeth, everyone was focused on survival. His turn came. The Head delivered Justin's grades to him as though he was reading an accounting ledger, no enthusiasm for his accomplishments whatsoever. The Head was picking at a thumb nail and seemed to think that more important than his good grades.

After reciting his grades the Head looked up and leaned forward, his mouth a disapproving line, black eyes narrowed, boring into him, projecting dominance, Ahab looking down at him from his high desk as he had the day he and his father gained admission. Justin sat up straight in his chair and looked the Head square in the face, no domination of Justin. "Too bad your athletics consist of peeking in girls' windows. I still have to tell your father about that. And I understand you're not happy here. I told you when you were admitted you could leave at any time. These midterms are an excellent time to make that decision."

Justin had been preparing for this moment. He said in a strong voice, "I can't go home. The woman won't let me. (He gave her name.) She'd rather have me here at school with the terrible bullying she arranged. Wish I knew who was helping her."

He was proud that he said this looking unflinching into the Head's eyes.

It was the Head who turned away, his lips compressed in a straight line. Then with an angry scowl, "Leave."

If Justin had doubts about the source of the bullying before, he had none now.

CHAPTER SIXTEEN

The next day after Mr. Benson's biology course Mr. Benson took him aside. "I want to congratulate you on your exam and thank you. When a student turns in an examine as strong as yours it makes a teacher feel his teaching is worthwhile. Some boys make a teacher feel he needn't have bothered." He rolled his eyes and chuckled. "You turned in one of the best exams I've received in fifteen years of teaching, remarkable from the youngest st-student in my class."

Justin smiled happily and stood straighter with his chest puffed out a bit.

Mr. Benson addressed him more seriously, eyes focused on his and his voice slow and filled with sympathy. "I don't understand how you were able to do so well with all the bullying."

"Everybody hates me so much I have plenty of time to study."

"You have to get to your next class. I'd like to understand what's going on. Do you want to come over to my house for tea next Sunday, four o'clock?"

"Sure."

After class that day he went down to the stable, or really snuck down as he was supposed to be in study hall. Daryle was there in the watery sunshine, red eyed, looking like he'd been crying, a forlorn weary appearance.

"Pa died last night. God, it was awful. He couldn't breath. He had a hell of a hard life trying to take care of us and to die that way. He was a great man." Daryle was blubbering with tears running down his face. "Now I have to manage this." Daryle glanced around the stable. "Ma needs the money. We can't give up on the stable. It was Ma's and Pa's only source of income, about the only thing they owned." He blew his nose and shook his head. "I've got to find someone. I can't manage it long term. I've got my garage job to worry about."

Justin said, "I'll help."

"You've got your school work to look after. I'll put an ad in the paper. It's going to be difficult finding someone willing to take low-enough pay. Ma needs to get a reasonable profit."

Justin said, "He was very good to me. I'd like to go to the funeral." Daryle gave him the details.

He approached Pomford with a request for release to attend the funeral, and Edmund Cranch, who handled such requests, turn him down flat.

"I'm not going to bend the rules for a Peeping Tom like you. Boys are only allowed off campus for funerals of near relatives."

He felt closer to Joe than any of his relatives, except perhaps Aunt Gertrude, but didn't bother arguing the point because he knew he'd not succeed.

The next Sunday Mr. Brown had Justin sit for tea in one of the largest wing chairs he'd ever seen. He sunk almost a foot into the soft cushion. Mr. Benson laughed. "That's my favorite chair. Couldn't resist buying it. The old lady in Greenfield I bought it from was so small that you could hardly see her in the chair. I always like to see the startled expression on people's faces when I seat them there." Another laugh from Mr. Benson and Justin gave a small chuckle.

Mr. Benson sat across from Justin, his eyes darkened with concern. He leaned forward. "What's going on with all this bullying? The glee club concert was about the worst thing I've ever s-seen. Maybe I can help. I hate bullying."

Justin hesitated in answering. He liked Mr. Benson but if he told him everything would it get back to the Head, and then the woman? All he needed was for the woman to find out he was talking to a teacher about her criminal role in the institutionalization of his mother.

"I don't think I can tell you. You might tell the Head what I tell you. That would get me into a whole lot of really, really bad trouble."

Mr. Benson's face registered surprise. He looked away for a moment. "I think what I'm hearing is that this is more than some boys doing some very bad bullying."

"That sure is right."

"Well. I don't much like the Head for many r-reasons. I'm not going to talk to him about anything. I can absolutely guarantee that. I won't talk to him whatever you tell me. I hope you've at least told your father or mother what's going on."

"No. My father and I aren't talking and my mother is in an insane asylum. I haven't told anyone."

A deep frown appeared on Mr. Benson's face. "Bottling stuff up inside isn't good. I did it once, when my dear wife, Helen, died. It nearly caused me to kill myself. Some people like to keep secrets to themselves, but a bad secret can eat you up inside. It can hurt you much worse than if you let go the s-secret."

Justin thought for a moment. "I had something like that last Fall. I'd been holding a really bad secret for years. Holding the secret made other boys say I had changed and wasn't any fun anymore. And I had changed. I was afraid to let it out because of what it would do to my life and that of several others. Finally, I got up my courage last Fall and confronted someone. It did make my life much worse. But I felt good doing it."

"Exactly. You've got to confide in someone. Why don't you give me a shot. Just tell me what you can. And one more time, I'm definitely not going to tell the Head."

Justin looked off for a few moments and thought about how much he could reveal. It might be good to have someone with information in case something happened to him. The woman was capable of anything. "Yes. I think someone should know a little in case something happens to me. Death breath, Deeth for short, what you hear them calling me, was carefully chosen. They wanted to totally ostracize me in school and cause me maximum grief. When you're Deeth, unlike other bullying names, nobody wants to get close to you. Boys fear if they get close to me they'll get all stinked up. It was designed to prevent me from making friends, which it has." Justin took a deep breath and exhaled with a sigh. "The person behind the bullying isn't here at school. It's a woman who has become my father's mistress. She hates me because of something I did to her. I didn't do it intentionally. She insists I did. I'm not going to tell you the details. You might tell the Head. She has done some really bad things. I know about them and she knows I know about them. I'm her target."

Mr. Benson looked at him in disbelief. "You've got to be kidding."

"No. That's only the half of it."

"I think we should go to the Head."

Justin said plaintively. "No Head. You promised."

"Yes. I promised. No Head."

Mr Benson leaned back in his chair. "Before I came to Pomford I was involved in California in activities that helped bring about the Holocaust. The Nazis called it the "Final Solution" for the Jews in Europe. Exterminate them. You know about the Holocaust, right?"

"Yes. Terrible."

"After I learned what happened in the Holocaust I realized I could have done a number of things that might have h-helped prevent it, maybe not, but I didn't really try. I had advanced notice of the planning for the Holocaust and didn't try very hard to tell people about it. I could have but didn't." He leaned back further in his chair and said in a contemplative tone. "Humans have a history of disguising the presence of evil from others, even from themselves. They make light of it, convince each other that evil is to be tolerated, that it should be treated with understanding, or stupidly they think evil can be negotiated with. What they don't do is forcibly confront evil. That was Neville Chamberlain appeasing Hitler before World War II. That's everybody like me who knew something of the Holocaust and did n-nothing."

He leaned forward again toward Justin. "What you're dealing with sounds to me like real evil. Are you fighting it?"

"I'm trying to. I made a vow to get to the bottom of it all. It's very difficult."

"If you'd like I'll help. After the Holocaust I have a low tolerance for evil. Come back next Sunday."

"I want to think about it. I'll let you know. Thank you."

He was afraid he might be trusting Mr. Benson because he liked him. Better to give it a little time, see if anything changed in his treatment on campus over the next weeks. If nothing did, it would probably mean the Head hadn't been told. He could go back to Mr. Benson.

Later that day he had the blackness settle in as it had at the infirmary and now a number of other recent times. The bullying, the plot, the hate of the woman, his mother's situation, all came at him like a flight of the black crows of Pomford, attacking him with hopelessness and a doubt that he could cope with life anymore. Maybe he shouldn't have been so happy to avoid that suicide.

For three weeks Henry Benson heard nothing from Justin about getting back together. Then after Friday class in the third week Justin asked, "Are you around if I come over this Sunday?" Justin appeared very tense, as though he'd had to buck up his courage.

Henry said, "Sure. Four o'clock."

Justin appeared to be just as tense when he arrived on Sunday. He kept his hands clenched before him as though ready to ward off attack, and when seated in the big wing chair spilled some tea in his saucer, his attention elsewhere.

Henry gave him a warm smile of welcome and said, "Relax. You're all tensed up. Remember, I'm here to help you."

Justin didn't relax but burst out his story, a soldier trapped behind enemy lines talking to the first person who would listen. In rapid fire Henry heard about the naked living room incident, Justin's mother's diary, his discovery that the woman had gotten his father to abuse his mother and put her in the institution, and the jovial meeting of the woman, Hauptmann, and the Head.

Henry was horrified by the story. He looked down. His tea cup was still in his hand, tea untouched, his fingers white from how hard he'd been grasping the saucer. How could this have happened to such a nice young kid? It was almost as bad to murder a boy psychologically as to murder his sister with a knife.

He went over and put his hand on Justin's shoulder, hoping he would feel his sorrow and support. "That's the worst story I've ever heard. Most boys would have fallen apart. You didn't. Remarkable. Very b-brave."

Story told. He could see Justin visibly relax.

Henry said, "I'd like to ask a question I didn't ask last time."

Justin nodded.

"How do know the bullying is the woman."

"I looked at all the possibilities. It's the only one that makes sense. I'm told that when a bullying name gets invented the boy who invented it will brag. No bragging for death breath, and you've got to admit it's a very clever name. Then I thought for a while it might be the Head who started it. He certainly knows about it. But for a friend of presidents to organize bullying of a boy, no way. I think, though, that the Head is a willing enabler of the bullying. I confronted him in January about it. He was giving me my mid-term grades. I complained about the bullying and blamed the woman for it. He didn't deny it and kicked me out of his office."

Henry said, "I think Hauptmann is a bad apple. I haven't been able to pin down how bad."

"Well, he's a terrible teacher, that's for sure. By far the worst in the school."

"I've heard that."

"Why does the Head keep him on?"

"Good question."

Justin shook his head, "Wish I could have heard something from the window. The woman acted as though she had very high regard for Hauptmann, and the Head as though he was his best friend. I've never seen the Head smile and laugh so much as he did with Hauptmann and the woman."

"Hauptmann may be the key. I'm sorry to say I helped him get to the US under an assumed name." Henry smiled. "Now you have something on me if I spill the beans on what you told me."

"Hauptmann's real name is Gerhard Mulder. In Germany he was a Nazi and involved in some of the steps that led up to the H-Holocaust." Henry then explained that he knew Gerhard and Dieter from California, that they looked exactly alike, that Gerhard claimed Dieter had given him his passport on his deathbed, and that with their resemblance Gerhard was able to use Dieter's passport to escape to Switzerland and somehow get a Swiss passport to come to the US.

"I was suspicious and checked him out on the German list of Nazis being sought for war crimes. Nothing. So I wrote a letter supporting his application. With what you've told me I think I need to check f-further, probably the Israelis. They've been compiling information on all the Nazi bad guys."

Justin's eyes had grown wide. "A Nazi. It figures. I should have known he was a Nazi by how he behaves in class."

"He may be a reformed Nazi and have opposed the Holocaust as he claimed to me. So don't go telling any of your friends about this. You asked me not to talk about our conversations and I'm asking you, okay."

"Okay."

In parting Henry promised he would contact the Israelis promptly. He watched Justin leave with a lilt to his step and a whistle on his lips.

The next day Henry called the Israeli Embassy in Washington, D.C. and was referred to a woman who identified herself as Sasha

Cohen. When he said he wanted to check on a possible Nazi living in the US she interrupted, saying in a very friendly voice, "We get ten or more calls a week from people who think a Nazi has moved in next to them or into their neighborhood."

Henry explained that this was something more, an individual who had headed eugenics in Germany, had been involved in the groundwork for the Holocaust, and who had come into the US under an assumed name."

There were a few moments of silence on the other end of the line. Now the voice very serious. "What's this person's name?

"Gerhard Mulder, Doctor Gerhard Mulder."

"Where is he now?"

"I'm not going to tell you that quite yet. If this is a false alarm, it'll stir up a lot of unnecessary trouble."

"I suppose you won't give your name either."

"You can call me Henry."

A sigh from the other end of the line. " All right Henry, I'll check in Israel. We have so many wild-goose-chases. But once in a while it's worth it."

While he was waiting for Mr. Benson to get back to him on the Israelis, Justin got a single letter from Fawn. She told him they were watching her carefully at school, but would ask her best friend to mail this one. Her father had come up to school and slapped her so hard on the side of the head that her ears rang for hours, not the first slap but the hardest, and called him a pervert and a Peeping Tom. She thanked Justin for not revealing her role in the disrobing. Her letter was full of love but also sorrow, doubting there was any way for them to ever see each other again and concerned that in the lack of communication he'd find someone else. She said she considered having him send his letters to one of her friends but had rejected that idea because the stratagem was obvious, and they were probably watching her friend's mail for just such an eventuality.

The friend would be punished and Fawn's father would beat her again, or at least he threatened to beat her if they ever had contact again.

He needed to find a way to assure her he loved her. She had to come back to her room at some point. Maybe he could glue a small unsigned card to the bottom outside of her widow saying, *I love you.* Dangerous as her mother might see it while cleaning the room. Tramping *I love you* in the snow beside the window, or framing the same message with sticks, was out for the same reason. He decided to send her a gift subscription to a romance magazine full of love stories. She was smart and would check who sent the gift subscription and know the romance was meant for her, an answer to the question in her letter as to whether he still loved her.

Justin's wait for news from Israel seemed to last forever. Several times he came close to spilling the beans to his new friends, Bienville, Peabody and Horney. They'd go ape, a Nazi in their midst. Being the only boy with such important information made him feel important, better about himself.

He hoped Hauptmann did turn out to be a war criminal. Wouldn't that be great? It'd blow the school sky-high. Might not get the woman but the Head certainly, and the school would probably close. He'd have to be sent elsewhere, a school where the woman had less sway. Yippi. No more Pomford. No more German class with Hauptmann.

His daydream came to an end three weeks later when Mr. Benson grabbed him after class and told him the Israelis weren't seeking Mulder. "I asked the nice Israeli woman helping me if there could be any mistake. She said, 'No.' They had detailed records on every living Nazi of any importance involved with the Holocaust."

Justin said, "Do you see any other way we can find out what's going on?"

"I haven't thought of anything, have you?"

"No."

Mr. Benson paused a moment as though deciding on something. "I enjoy being with you. You're a very special kid. Would you like to make Sunday tea a regular thing? Don't say yes too quickly. I know Sunday afternoons are the one free time you have."

"That would be great. Let's start the Sunday after this. You know Joe Henderson died?"

"Yes."

"I want to go down to the stable and see if I can help out. I was helping Joe."

So no pay dirt with Hauptmann. He'd follow Joe Henderson's instruction. Patience would be his watchword. He would wait. Something would happen.

He went to the stable the next Sunday, finding Daryle there and much happier. He'd hired a stable hand. "I got this guy, a real wrangler off a California ranch, and he don't want much. Don't know how he got to Western Mass from California, sure happy he did. Ma will get her profit." Daryle laughed. "I checked out the guys that applied by asking them to saddle Imperator. I can't do it myself. Nobody else in this neck of the woods can either. Poor Mr. Robinson hasn't been able to ride him for months. Most of the guys that applied took one look at Imperator and skedaddled. One asshole tried and was almost killed. This new guy, Ramos, did it as easily as Pa."

The Sunday following he went over to Mr. Benson's and was warmly greeted, sinking happily into the wing chair with a fragrant cup of tea in his hand. For a half-hour it was all small talk with Mr. Benson kidding about Dr. Watson and Sherlock Holmes. "I'll be Watson. You can be Sherlock. Means it's up to you to solve the mystery. Think you can do it?"

"Sure."

He laughed and Justin laughed with him.

Maybe it was the tea and the wing chair. A similar bright day and he was sitting in the wing chair in their library at home drinking a cup of peppermint tea with his mother. Then other thoughts about his mother raced into his mind pulling along all the other horrible memories, another black time. He sat there for what seemed like minutes, immobile, staring unseeing at his lap, then Mr. Benson's hand on his shoulder.

"What's going on? Are you all right?"

"Just one of my black times. I have them every once in awhile."

"Tell me about them."

"Well sometimes it all gets to be too much, my mother, my father, the woman, the bullying. I can't stand it anymore. The worst was when I was in the infirmary. There was nothing to do but think and it all came at me. I thought I was going crazy."

"Maybe you were crazy. I've gone through similar black times. When I was young my sister was raped and killed in front of me by a crazy man. I was terribly affected. Stopped sp-speaking. Wouldn't leave the house without holding the hand of one of my parents. As I grew older I had black times like yours when all the memories came flooding back. Over the years I went to many different psychologists to try and work it out. They said I'd been t-traumatized. With their help the black times seem behind me though I still have nightmares and the stutter you hear. The point is I know a lot about black times, and though I'm not a psychologist I'm sure you're suffering trauma just as I have, not as bad as mine, but trauma none the less. Understandable with what you've gone through. It'll grow worse if you don't do something about it.

"I feel fine."

"I'm sure you do. Many on the battlefields of the World Wars suffered trauma and didn't know it. You're a strong kid. On the surface you seem to be functioning fine. Trauma is tricky stuff. It hides itself. And it can build. I know you're skeptical. But let me try some trauma questions on you I learned from my psychologists. You don't want to continue to have these black times do you?"

"No."

Justin answered with reluctance. Mr. Benson had seemed a friend. Now here he was saying he was sick or something, maybe needed psychoanalysis. He already had enough problems.

Mr. Benson started, "Here are some of the symptoms of trauma. See if any apply? With trauma you withdraw socially, a sense of estrangement from others. Have you had a hard time making friends?"

Justin had to admit a, "Yes.".

"With trauma you have a reduced emotional capacity. How much have you been grieving for your mother r-recently? And do you feel your happiness and sadness as much as before?"

"Well, I met a girl who made me happy but I may never see her again. No other happiness anymore. My mother, well I probably don't grieve for her as before. Too much bad stuff gets in the way."

"With trauma your mind plays back the trauma over and over again. Do you spend a lot of time thinking about what happened with your mother, father, the woman, the bullying?"

"You got me there. All the time."

"With trauma your mind spends its energy defending against the trauma. That limits your ability to have gratifying life experiences. Life becomes flat and uninteresting. Are you having an interesting life? Do you find what's happening around you interesting however bad?"

"Are you kidding? About everything in my whole life is uninteresting, difficult, sad, dull. Life around me is something I try and avoid."

"With trauma you have periods of depression."

"Well, I'm certainly depressed about the school and about everything else in my life. More and more of these black times. Sometimes I feel like I should curl up in a ball in the deep snow and go to sleep and never wake up. So I guess I've been traumatized."

"Right. And just like you're fighting the bullying you've got to f-fight the effects of the trauma. Once trauma gets established it takes over the mind and it's hard to overcome. Your whole life can go to hell. You need to start fighting it right now or it will haunt you forever. You don't want to go through life with few friends do you? With what's been done you could end up hating boys. Later you could feel so uncomfortable with men you have trouble relating to them, even being with them. Or your mind could play over and over again what happened in the past as mine has, drowning out the g-good things in life.

"As I said, you're a strong kid. You should be fine. But I'll give you some things you can try. They worked for me. If they don't work we'll get you to a real psychologist. Always wanted to practice psychology and now I'm doing it." He laughed.

"First, on the social thing, what have you been doing to make friends?"

"Well, recently I made three new friends, largely by chance. Last Fall I would approach groups of boys with witty remarks or something intellectual from something I studied. I guess I was trying to impress them. It got me nowhere."

"Well at least you tried. Many traumatized people wouldn't. The problem is you never made connection with the other boys on their level. You have to give more of yourself and bring them to you. And your trauma probably prevented it. What I was taught was to march right up to a person with my hand out, introduce myself, and say, 'How are things,' or 'What's up,' something to get him talking, then the important point. You look him in the eyes with your gaze never w-wavering, focus on every word he says as though it's the most important thing you've ever heard, show the boy you care a lot about him. Do the same thing in later conversations after you've met the boy. Total focus on what he says and on the eyes. The key is the eyes. Never take your eyes off the eyes when you talk to him. Try not to even blink."

Henry continued." That was very difficult for me. It scared me to death. I didn't even want to be with other people. It may be a little difficult for you, too. You've been so t-traumatized by other boys that deep down inside you may already have deep distrust for other boys, be close to hating other boys. Try it, though."

"Okay. But at Pomford views on me have hardened so much I don't think I can break through at this point."

"Perhaps. But at least you won't repeat the Pomford experience when you get to Harvard, Yale, or wherever else your excellent grades take you.

"I found the other things harder to fight as there was no simple approach. Fighting es-estrangement, reduced emotional capacity, and inability to enjoy life requires a reorientation of the mind. What you're trying to do is to integrate your traumatic experiences into your total life experiences so the trauma doesn't h-haunt you. You want to end up feeling it was just one more part of life and unimportant because it is the past. One trick to reorienting the mind is to share. You've already shared with me. Now tell your new friends about the situation with your mother and f-father and how the bullying last Fall made you feel. If they're real friends they'll respond with sympathy. We can all be allies to help you fight the bad stuff entering your mind.

"Another thing. Whenever memories of the traumatic experiences come, push them out. Don't dwell on them. At first it'll be difficult. I imagine several times a day you have all the stuff flooding in."

Justin nodded.

"You've got to work at it to stop it. Over time you can train your mind so it sees the stuff coming and bl-blocks it. I learned various techniques to do this. It comes down to exercising a lot of mind discipline and will power. I think you have that."

"Final thing. What they say about an idle mind is true. Same for an idle body. Hard to block the mind at night. In the day I found help in keeping both mind and body doing absorbing things."

Mr. Benson relaxed and sat back. "Well that was something wasn't it? Psychology 101. I've had so much of that crap I have it memorized." He gave Justin a warm smile. "I've given you enough for today, maybe enough for a l-lifetime. Hope you don't feel what I've said is unnecessary. If you've been traumatized as I think you have I may have helped. At least I don't think I've hurt you and now you know more about me. You've got a great life ahead of you. I don't want you to screwed it up."

Justin got up, strode over to Mr. Benson and formally shook his hand while gazing intently into his eyes. "Thank you."

Pomford proceeded into March. Justin didn't see any evidence of coming Spring, a cruel time depriving everyone of the better weather they hoped for, a season when it was okay to be unhappy. Regular snow storms, and he'd noticed through the winter that the snow became almost immediately dirty. Dark streaks appeared. Patches of what looked like soot blackened the snow piled shoulder high along Main Street, sometimes higher than his head. None of that virgin snow gracing country villages you find in passages of poetry. Logic said the soot was due to a coal-burning power plant ten miles upwind. He preferred to think that the black atmosphere of Pomford was darkening the snow.

March finally gave up its hold and April brought rescue from Pomford. Aunt Gertrude and Uncle Ben had invited him to their house in Palm Beach for Spring break. How wonderful! And they imposed no strictures on him during his stay, freedom to do whatever he wanted. Without children of their own maybe they didn't realize the trouble teenagers could get into. It took him a few days after the jail of Pomford to realize he really was free. Then he exulted in the lack of restriction. Each morning he traipsed to the Palm Beach Bath & Tennis Club just down the block, the most socially prestigious club in Palm Beach. Aunt Gertrude and Uncle Ben were big muck-de-mucks there, Uncle Ben having been a past president and currently a director.

The first morning he was in Palm Springs he asked his aunt what she knew of as he phrased it, "That woman living with my father?" He didn't mention the reason he wanted the information.

His aunt's mouth turned down and she looked at him sadly. "I can understand your anger. You have reason to be angry. What's going on is terrible. It's a disgrace. I've never seen anything like it." His aunt paused for a moment. "I really don't know that much. Her father was Basil Rothworth, one of the leading bankers on Wall Street. Her husband, Peter Carlisle, is a very distinguished man, former Under Secretary of State. She's put herself at the top of the New York social pyramid through the people she has befriended and the parties she gives. I don't think she has any enemies though people thinks she's very arrogant and full of herself. No children as you probably know.

"I believe after her husband's stroke she dated John Chandler for a year or so. I don't know John well but I've a good friend that does. Would you like me to ask her what she knows?"

"That would be great. Thank you."

As the vacation days passed, increasingly happy, Justin found that the prettiest, most sought after girls readily accepted his invitations to movies and to the teenage dances the club put on for Spring break. He assumed it was because of his aunt and uncle's social status. And it didn't hurt that his uncle's limo and chauffeur were made available to drive him on dates, transport to dances, movies, shops for ice cream.

He tried to be true to Fawn, but there was one girl that grabbed him in the movies and started kissing him. What could he do but kiss her back? Then she was all over him in the back seat of the limo, something he didn't exactly discourage. He expected to hear about it from either his uncle or aunt but never did. Either they didn't care or the good guy chauffeur hadn't told. He never followed up with the girl though he could see her staring at him at the club, partly an avoidance due to Fawn, but also because she had terrible breath. At one point he thought of going over and mentioning it to her after what he'd gone through as Deeth decided that would devastate her as it had him, so didn't.

With boys he employed the approach Mr. Benson had instructed and developed a number of friendships, good for the week of Spring break. A boy from his Pomford class, Francis Ordway, appeared at the club about mid-way through Spring break and called him Justin, not Deeth. Hooray! This was a prior-year boy, a player on the JV football team who was never willing to talk with him at Pomford. Was the pestilence of Pomford limited to the Pomford Valley?

Francis went on to talk to him extensively, mostly about the girls wandering around the pool. "She looks sexy. I'd like to date her."

Justin realized that wasn't very probable. Ordway, while muscular, didn't have a very attractive face or manner about him, a bit of a lug. For the first time he judged a boy by how attractive he would be to a girl, a brand new ranking system for the boys he knew at Pomford. And he realized that the reason girls wanted to date him wasn't the Palm Beach Club connection but that he was attractive to girls, a real ego booster. Girls liked him even if boys didn't.

The day before he was to return to PomfordAunt Gertrude reported. "My friend said John Chandler had an intense affair for about a year, just as I told you. It broke off abruptly, John Chandler ending it. He told my friend that it wasn't because he didn't love her anymore. Rather it was because of a political belief she held that he couldn't abide. Must have been serious to break them up. They were going at it hot and heavy. My friend thought it was odd and so do I. She has never been politically active as far as either of us know."

Justin filed the information away to mention to Mr. Benson. Whatever repelled Mr. Chandler might be at the center of the woman's meeting with the Head and Hauptmann.

Going back to Pomford was a real wrench, particularly as the weather hadn't improved much despite moving into early April. One compensation was that two letters from Fawn awaited him, both sent from her uncle's house in North Carolina where she'd been locked away for Spring break. In the first she acknowledged his cleverness with the romance magazine subscription. The second was a letter of frustration about her life, about the waste of

Spring break and about her failure to find any way for them to get together. Also, for the first time quite a lot about her parents. She adored her mother and hated her father because of his harshness toward her but also his bad treatment of her mother. She wished her mother would divorce him.

Spring term brought the dreaded sign-up list. Baseball, track, tennis and lacrosse. He chose baseball because he knew he would fail at track and tennis, lacrosse looked dangerous with clubs at each other's heads, and he didn't know enough about baseball to know whether he would fail or not. They put him in right field, telling him he could do the least damage there. Still, in an early game he let a ball slide through his legs, allowing the winning run for the other side. Worse was hitting. Turned out he had virtually zero eye-hand coordination, at least with a baseball bat. They got him an "Easton Bat," a bat designed for boys with vision impairments. It looked like a short handled canoe paddle, sort of a cricket bat, broad on the hitting end and perfectly balanced like a standard bat. It supposedly allowed one to hit as far as with a regulation bat. Not him. Some teams they played complained about it but dropped the complaint when they saw his hitting ability. Major league baseball wasn't played in the rain. Pomford baseball was. Both football and baseball sucked.

Soon after return from Spring break his wanderings took him back down to the stable. He introduced himself to Jose Ramos and offered to help, saying he'd helped Joe and Daryle.

Jose didn't look up from currying one of the horses and said, "I don't need help. You'd just get in the way. And if you got hurt by Imperator or one of the other horses it'd be on my head. Just stay the hell away."

Despite the admonition he regularly walked to the hill above the stable and viewed it from a distance, enjoying looking at the horses when they were brought into the paddock, sometimes seeing Matilda and wishing he was on her back. One day he saw Jenkins talking with Jose. They seemed to be best friends. Jenkins clapped Jose on the back and the two of them laughed together.

When Jenkins saw him watching Jenkins stared at him very hard, an intimidating look. He walked quickly away. Jenkins was the last person he wanted to irritate.

The second Sunday after returning to Pomford he was invited back to Mr. Benson's for tea. Justin filled Mr. Benson in on what he'd learned about the woman. Then Justin said, "You look very sad. The boys in class think something has happened. You're the happiest teacher we have."

"Well, something has happened." Mr. Benson looked Justin up and down as though evaluating him, and said with a deep sigh, "You're the detective. Maybe you want to help me solve it." He gave a wry smile. "When I was in California I operated on many women to prevent them from having children. These were women whose children would be insane, criminal, diseased, or a burden on s-society if allowed to be born. Most of these operations were successful. However, occasionally a woman died. I was operating in fairly primitive conditions.

"In 1938 I started getting threatening letters from someone who alleged his s-sister had died and it was my fault. The letters promised my death and that of my wife. They got increasingly brutal in their threats. Dead animals were left on our doorstep. The police tried but couldn't find the guy. Eventually it caused my wife to have a nervous breakdown and helped cause her death.

"Now I'm receiving them here. Don't know how he found me. I thought I'd c-covered my trail. They come weekly, just as in California. He doesn't write the letters longhand but pastes down words and letters cut out from newspapers and magazines. The police here are incompetent. All they tell me is the l-letters were mailed from a variety of mailboxes in the area. Want to see one?"

"Sure."

"This is the latest."

I tracked you down. Nowhere for you to hide, no can hide anywhere in the world from what you do. When one kills one is killed in return wherever they are. I enjoy going slow with your wife. See her suffer. Watch her die. For you it will be fast. You running away delayed it too long. I am closing in to kill you. You walk down main street. I am next to you. You fish in green creek and johnson brook. I watch you never catch fish in johnson brook. You ride max from the stable to the hills. I watch you photo in the hills. You will die soon.

Justin said, "Very scary."

"I agree. He wouldn't chase me clear across the country unless he was serious. I've stopped fishing and riding alone, and even on Main Street I try to walk with others. My house is l-locked up tight."

Justin said, "From the way he writes it looks like he's a foreigner."

"Right. But from what country?"

"Maybe one of the language teachers would know."

"You *are* a detective." Mr. Benson laughed. "I think the guy may be Mexican. I operated on a lot of Mexican women. The Spanish teacher, Fernando Cuevas, is a friend of mine. I already asked him to take a look at the letters. If I find out anything I'll let you know."

With warmer weather Justin perfected night-time reconnoiters through the bathroom widow and down the trellis. Pomford had a night watchman, but lazy, easily evaded, no trouble for him. The night revealed many things. He saw a series of pretty young girls go into the house of one of the faculty who regularly gave the Sunday sermon. Tomlin, the varsity football coach, mister gruff and tough, a favorite of the Head's, had regular late night visits from another faculty member, a young bachelor. Was some of that degenerative stuff going on? And on nice nights, as soon as lights out occurred, he would hear the clop of hoofs, the Head out for his evening ride, the night rider. Seeing him in a pale moonlight moving through the dark streets, dark horse, dark carriage, dark rider, always turned him cold, particularly because he often wore a grin he'd never seen on his stone cold face in the daylight. What was the Head grinning about? Having five hundred locked down boys under his total control?

One thing he observed was at his own house. When Mr. Brown was away, Mr. Benson would come visiting and would still be there when he climbed the trellis to bed. This was great. Served Mr. Brown right after all he'd done to Fawn and him. He wanted to go up to Mr. Benson after class and congratulate him. Didn't. That was the road to trouble.

Spring brought him into contact with Andrew Cunningham, another lone wolf, nicknamed Bronco, the heir to one of the great fortunes of America. On a Spring Sunday afternoon his wanderings took him to the banks of the Pomford River. Bronco was by the river with a cage containing a fairly good-sized weasel-like animal. When Bronco opened the door to the cage the animal viciously bit into his heavily gloved hand, then scampered away and into the water. He'd seen Bronco around campus, always wearing tightly molded Western pants and rough-woven woolen jackets that looked like they'd been tailored to hunt grouse or something out West, parading around with a cowboy's wide-legged just off a horse stride. He'd never talked to Bronco. By his observation Bronco talked to few people.

Now Bronco looked at him in a friendly fashion and Justin asked,

"What you doing?"

"Trapping muskrats."

"There're muskrats here? I thought they lived in the wilderness."

"Tons of muskrats here. More than in Wyoming. Problem is I don't have a buyer here so it makes no sense to skin them to sell the skins. Made good money selling skins in Wyoming. Got a real fine trap line here. The Pomford and some of the tributaries get me five or so muskrats a day now that they're out and about. Wish I could find a way to sell the damn skins. I have to just release."

Bronco talked in a Western drawl like a movie cowboy. Real or part of a westerner act?

Bronco looked him up and down and said to him in a welcoming tone, "I set the traps as soon as I can get out through the damned locked door of the dorm. Get up at 5:00. You need to get the traps set before the little buggers become active. Can't get anybody to join me at that hour. You have any interest?"

He said, "Sure." He wasn't going to turn down an opportunity to get to know another boy.

The traps were wire mesh about thirty inches long, six inches wide and six inches high with a door on each end. Bronco said, "I bait with slices of apples. In Wyoming you can't catch any with apples. I think it's because apples don't grow there much. In Wyoming I use carrots and peanut butter."

He followed Bronco along to the rest of his trap line. Some of the traps contained muskrats. Bronco freed them wearing his heavy gloves, always a vicious attack by the muskrat. Other traps were empty and he rebaited them. Traps were positioned at the entrance to muskrat dens. They barely made it back in time for breakfast, their clothes stained with mud. Now he knew why Bronco always looked like he'd been on a dirt farm.

It became a regular routine to join Bronco on his morning rounds. He liked Bronco best of all the lone-wolf boys he'd come to know. However, he wasn't sure Bronco considered him a friend. Bronco was such a loner he didn't seem to need or want friends.

Bronco finally opened up to him one day. "From what you said your ma's in an institution and your father won't talk to you. I tell you, I got it just as bad. Both my parents are dead to me like yours are. Oh, they're kicking around all the parties on the East Coast and in Europe all right. But no time for me. Ma's had four husbands and is divorcing the fourth. Pa's had five wives. They're so busy divorcing and marrying, divorcing and marrying, I think they've forgotten about me. They shipped me off to the ranch in Wyoming when I was ten. Both of them were in the middle of bloody divorces and I guess didn't want me in the way. I never even went to school in Wyoming. They had private tutors come to the ranch. And the ranch was so big there were no neighbors close by. No other boys to play with. But some of it is great. All my best friends are cowboys. I have my own horse, Rebel. He can cut out a cow like you wouldn't believe. Sure miss him. I've done some right fancy roping off Rebel's back, and I was getting pretty good at bronc riding. That's how I got my name. When I get out of this shit hole, turn eighteen and come into my trust, I'm not going to go to college no matter what my parents say. Going back to the ranch and be a cowboy."

That explained why Bronco was so standoffish to other boys. Never having other boys in his growing up life he didn't feel the need for them as friends, or maybe felt they were vastly inferior to his cowboy buddies.

They often talked about riding, or at least Bronco did and Justin listened. Justin thought he knew something about horses from keeping a horse at Camp Passumpsic. Bronco had so much more knowledge, how to diagnose the illnesses of a horse, how to judge a good horse from a bad one from a distance, how to break a wild horse in a humane way, and much more. The western drawl, and everything about Bronco, wasn't an act. He was a cowboy transplanted to an eastern prep school, about as happy at the school as any other cowboy would be when denied his horses and the open range. Bronco and he exchanged many stories about how miserable they were.

Mr. Benson came up to him after class and said that the writer was probably Spanish speaking. However, the Spanish teacher couldn't say whether Mexican or not. They discussed it at Mr. Brown's house over Sunday tea with Mr. Benson saying, "I don't think I operated on any Spanish speakers other than Mexican. He's got to be Mexican."

Justin said, "Jose Ramos at the stable is Mexican and came here in early March when you said the letters started. He's from California."

"I know. He's my lead suspect. I asked the police to check for other Spanish speaking people who have moved into the area re-recently. They found a couple of men in Greenfield in the building trade but don't know their nationality."

Justin said, "Are they going to watch Ramos?"

"They're bumblers. But even if they weren't, I doubt they'd stake-out mail boxes to see if he's mailing letters. They'd need a lot more proof."

Here was a challenge. If he was going to be a detective he had to do detecting so down the trellis in the dead of night, flashlight in hand, and a fast-paced walk to the stable. The stable office was open. He didn't recall it ever being locked. The place was a mess, feed stacked against the walls, papers scattered around the desk.

He went to the wastebasket. No scraps of cut up newspapers or magazines. But there sure were a lot of different newspapers and magazines in the basket, all in English. Was Ramos such a rabid reader of English language publications? And some of the newspapers and magazines had pages or partial pages torn out. How was Ramos going to explain that? He went to the desk hoping to find something Ramos had written that duplicated the use of language and sentence structure of the threat letters. Most of the desk clutter was bills, order confirmations and catalogs. All he found was one partially completed order for tack where Ramos wrote, "You need to ship. I no can pick it up." A small piece of evidence but evidence none the less, Ramos was their man.

Another Sunday for tea, Justin grinning from ear to ear, bursting out his news even before they were seated. "It was Ramos." He described what he'd discovered.

"What were you doing in his office?"

"I snuck in when he was away on a ride." He didn't want to reveal his night prowls.

Mr. Benson said to him, anger in his voice, "That was stupid. Detectives are killed. And what you found can't be used. You were trespassing and probably breaking the law. All I can tell the police is I think it's Ramos. They may interview him. But no search warrant without some evidence. And even if they did serve a search warrant, any evidence would be destroyed. I've decided what I need to do is to confront him and see if I can scare him off. I'll let you know what happens."

"He looks dangerous. Do you really want to do that?"

Mr. Benson replied with a voice full of conviction, " I can take care of myself. No one's going to get me."

Justin got up to leave, paused, and turned back into the room with a question he'd been holding. "Do you know why the Head focuses so much on good breeding? My father does, too."

Mr. Benson said, "That's a long story. Sit back down. By the way, how you doing on your black times?"

"Better since you talked to me."

"Great. Keep it up." After Justin settled himself. "All this good breeding bullshit came from a fellow in England in the 1880s named Galton. He was Darwin's cousin and tried to copy him in a half-assed way. Galton had a theory that was swallowed hook, line and sinker by the British upper class, the American upper class, too. The theory was selective breeding. If they married intelligent upper class white men and women to each other, and they continued to marry intelligent upper class people to each other through the generations, over time they would produce a race of superior people, dominate society, Hitler's master race. The Head bought into Galton's nonsense just like Hitler did. Now he's trying to mange the Pomford boys and their future families on Galton's model, propagate generations of good breeding. The whole idea is ridiculous. The Head lives in the past. It's still 1900 to him. This is a dead school with dead ideas. The importance of good breeding, the notion bullying strengthens boys, Galton's beliefs, all dead ideas. I was foolish enough to believe in selective breeding myself years ago. But now studies have come along showing that racial diversity in breeding is important. It strengthens the genetic stock and enables small mutations that advance mankind. Also, no one has been able to show that with the vast human gene pool you can breed for intelligence or anything else."

Justin sat up straighter in the chair. "Maybe you remember my roommate, Gerald, a real dunce and so unattractive you wondered if he was related to his parents. He told me his family had been in the Head's program back to his grandfather. Proves your point."

"I remember Gerald. A good example. The teachings of eugenics, that's what Galton called it, eugenics, they've never made sense and even less so now."

"The real problem with this good breeding nonsense is discrimination. Anyone talking about good breeding needs a lecture on discrimination. Pomford is a school for discrimination. Teaching good breeding we're teaching discrimination. Galton's theories justified the English upper class in discriminating against the lower class. Coming to America the theories supported a nation of white superiority and discrimination against blacks. And it hasn't gone away. Look what's happening in the South. Deep down inside, out of their conscious thought, many carry the remnants of Galton, a belief that they are superior, that whites are superior, entitled to more and better, that non-whites are inferior. Why do we still discriminate against blacks? Because we continue to think we're better, Galton in spades. When the Head preaches good breeding he is saying to the boys they are better and should look down on others. Damn dangerous stuff. Dangerous for blacks. Dangerous for America."

Mr. Benson had gotten increasingly serious and intense as he talked. Now he said, "Forgive me my passion. I hate Galton. I followed his theories and it ruined my life. And Justin, I hope you paid attention to what I said about discrimination. An important part of life is to resist discrimination. If you feel prejudice, or feel you're better or more entitled, knock it out of you. Fast. You'll have a much better life if you take others as they are and yourself as you are."

Justin gave Mr. Benson a strong, "I will," and a hearty handshake, and warned him to be careful with Ramos.

Mr. Benson replied with a note of anger, "Its he who has to watch out. He helped kill my wife."

Henry picked a mid-week day when the stable wasn't busy. Ramos was sitting on a bench at the stable entrance and didn't rise when he approached. "I understand you came here from California."

"Yes." Ramos's face settled in an unfriendly look.

"Do you have a sister."

"Yes. She's dead." Ramos's face clouded with irritation. "What's it to you?"

"Someone whose sister died in California is sending me threatening letters."

"I don't write letters."

"The police are looking into it. If you write more letters, you'll go to jail."

Ramos sneered, "The police won't find anything. You're the one they should be investigating. Now get the hell out of here. I've got work to do."

Henry filled Justin in on his visit. "Now he's on notice we're on to him. And I've talked to the police. They're going to interview him."

Justin said, "When they interview him they ought to get the name of the dead sister and find out how she died."

"Excellent idea. I'll ask the police, though I doubt if they'll get anything after all this time. One good thing. Ramos has had a lot of time to kill me. He hasn't. The police chief in Pomona, that's where I was living in California, told me that writers of threatening letters don't kill. They're trying to scare their victims."

A week later he received another letter.

I see you and the police attacking poor Ramos. He is not the one. I am the one. I could have kill you a long time ago. It was fun playing with you. The cat plays with the mouse it will kill. The play time is over.

Henry still thought it was Ramos, a clever diversion. Ramos wasn't going to kill him with the police alerted.

Justin worked the trap line with Bronco all Spring. May gave him the opportunity to watch the building and launching of rafts. It was a long established Spring tradition at Pomford for teams of boys to build rafts to float down the Pomford River in search of distance records. He'd not expected to be asked to join one of the teams and wasn't. Some of the rafts were quite sophisticated, logs deposited by the Spring flood lashed together to form the base and planks nailed down on top. He wondered what shed or barn in the neighborhood was being torn apart and looted for the planks. The record achieved many years ago by a boy traveling at night, hiding during the day, was over twenty miles. This year the lead raft only made ten miles before the school tracked it down.

Out on the traps one morning as Spring was turning to Summer Bronco said, "It's terrible what they're doing to you. Are you coming back next year?"

"I have to. I told you what happened with my mothers diary and my father and the woman. The woman won't allow me home. And she won't let me go to any school but Pomford. She has more control over me and can punish me more if I stay at Pomford."

"That's shitty. About the shittiest thing I know. Now I'm even sorrier for you. You're like a fur trapper in the old West, stuck in a lonesome place and surrounded by wolves. These aren't ordinary wolves. They're rabid wolves and all salivating to get you. I've been thinking about it. If you come back next year we'll set up a super trapping line together. Trapping with you has been great."

Bronco was becoming his best friend.

He'd continued his down-the-trellis outings all Spring, always happy when he saw Mr. Benson entering the house in Mr. Brown's absence. One night near the end of the term it was different. Mr. Benson entered and then later Mr. Brown drove up in his car and entered. "Uh-oh." He waited for the explosion which came in about thirty seconds, Brown's voice raised loud enough so everyone on Main Street could hear it. The front door burst open and Mr. Benson appeared, putting on his shoes, Shirley in a nightgown he could see through, and Brown yelling louder if that was possible. Shirley said something and with the back of his hand Brown hit her and knocked her off the porch into the bushes. Mr. Benson roared and slugged Brown twice, knocking him to the pavement, his voice choked with rage, "If you ever touch Shirley again I'll kill you!"

What came back was scarier because it was delivered with cold certainty. "You won't kill me. You don't have the guts to hang for murder. I do. And I *am* going to kill you. I'll track you down and kill you. Very soon. I swear it. By God, by satan, by everything and everybody in the Goddamn universe. *You will die.*"

Scary. From what he knew of Brown, Mr. Benson was a dead man. Justin had no doubt. Ramos now Brown, the only positive thing he could think of it was that when they took Brown away to hang it would change things. He and Fawn might be able to get together. He waited until the police arrived. Pretty quick. They were bandaging Shirley's face when he left. He could see from a distance it'd been pretty badly cut up by the bushes.

Should he tell Mr. Benson what he saw? No. Mr. Benson might react very negatively when he learned he'd been spying on him and Shirley for months.

As the school year wound down the calls of Deeth had not diminished despite his increased belligerence. Taunting of other targets had, though, greatly diminished. It was as though once The Suit, Hippo, and Skelty had been taunted into their assigned place in the hierarch further taunting was unnecessary. Evidently, he was being denied an assigned place. Or maybe the woman was throwing fuel on the fire, trying to do what? Probably intending him to go through the whole summer miserable and dreading Pomford in the Fall.

Ever since entering Pomford he'd made a ritual of crossing out days on his calendar. He still crossed out each day as he did earlier, feeling delight in the exercise as though each day was a vicious snake he was killing off. But as the final days approached he decided it was not enough to cross off days when he returned from class. That's what he'd done in the past. To make sure the last days of the school year were totally exterminated, the horrible days could not reappear, he started crossing them off as his last joyful act of the day, after he said his prayers and just before he put his head down. And maybe this superstition paid off. The school told him he was to spend the summer with his Aunt Gertrude and Uncle Ben in Greenwich. "Vea."

Before he left school he called on Mr. Benson to say his good-byes. Shaking hands formally with Mr. Benson after the requisite eye focus he said, "You were the only good thing in the term. Thank you. I can't thank you enough, the only one helping me. Really you've been like a father. Mine died and has been buried. I don't know for sure I will be coming back next year. The woman may send me to Afghanistan or something where my punishment will be greater." He laughed. I'm sure she's upset that Pomford didn't kill me this year. If I do come back we need to crack the mystery of Hauptmann, the woman and the Head. So please don't get yourself killed over the summer. You don't seem to be worried. I am, Ramos and somebody said Mr. Brown."

Mr. Benson opened his mouth in surprise. "Don't know how you heard about Brown. Don't worry. As I said before, I can take care of myself." His face lit up in a broad smile. "It's been great for me, too. All Spring you've been getting mentally stronger, taking charge of your life. If I contributed to that, it makes me very happy. One of the best things this year.

"One further word of advice. Don't think about Pomford this summer. It'll come into your mind all the time. Force it out. Shake your head as though it were a bad dream and force it out. It's hard. I did it. You can do it. What you need to focus on is having fun. Look for the fun. You deserve it."

CHAPTER SEVENTEEN

Fun there was. Aunt Gertrude and uncle Ben were just as welcoming in Greenwich as in Palm Springs. And there was just as much freedom. They sat him down when he arrived, positively beamed at him, and said, "We know prep school is rough. We want you to have the best time this summer you can possibly have."

He took up the challenge. As Mr. Benson instructed, made a vow to himself. "No rehashing what happened at Pomford. No thinking about the woman. Just have fun." This summer he'd be Nero fiddling while his life burned or some such thing.

The summer went quickly. A magnified version of Palm Beach at Spring break. Great clubs. He learned a new sport, sailing, and turned out to be pretty good at it. Occasional use of uncle Ben's limo with chauffeur, the greatest girl bait ever. New best friends he made using Mr. Benson's approaches. There was Harry (Wild Man) Stanley, he would do anything, Bill (The Gut) Peterson, he loved his food, and Fred (Lover Boy) Jones, the only one who claimed to have gone all the way with a girl, which everybody doubted. Many escapades with them. The other three now sixteen had fancy cars, it being Greenwich, and it was discovered that by standing tall at Wagon Wheel, Hoff Brau House and other bars across the state line in New York money would buy any drink you wanted. Also, "pig parties" when they would invite unattractive, boy hungry girls who couldn't get dates to a remote parking lot where they would slow dance them to a car radio and contest among themselves who could get furthest in car back seats and behind bushes, an activity Justin only participate in to a limited extent out of loyalty to Fawn.

Then there was full moon driving. It took many beers at the Wagon Wheel and many challenges back and forth to get the contest set. Who could drive the longest without headlights on the winding, usually deserted, back roads of Greenwich before panicking and hitting the lights? Everyone had a try. The Gut had the record of eleven minutes, though it was pointed out he'd mostly been driving on a stretch where trees were less dense and there was more light. Wild Man chugged another beer and claimed a second turn saying they'd made him too careful the first time with all their yelling to slow down and watch out for things. Everyone piled into his car fearing the worst, and the worst it was. Wild Man drove much faster this time, nonchalant, one hand on the wheel, barely making the curves, not slowing down in dark patches with no visibility for long stretches, not seeming to pay attention to where he was. A cry from everyone, "Johnson's Pond." The road dead ended at a T, the pond only feet ahead. They went in with a squeal of brakes at thirty miles an hour. Water was halfway up the windows. When they staggered up to the bank a policeman was standing there, hands on his hips looking them over. He said nothing, shook his head, and got back in his squad car as though he was used to Greenwich boys getting drunk and running cars into ponds.

These ventures with Wild Man, The Gut, and Lover Boy made Justin feel fully alive for the first time since he entered Pomford and from long before. In the hilarity of Johnson's Pond, indeed the hilarity of the whole summer, he lost part of Pomford.

One happy discovery made at Palm Beach was confirmed. The pestilence of Deeth was confined to the Pomford Valley. He had five classmates in Greenwich and they all called him Justin, not Deeth, even one guy who had been a principal tormenters. The woman wouldn't have been happy.

All summer long he practiced what Mr. Benson had instructed. Whenever traumatic black thoughts about the past forced themselves into his mind he tried to block them out. His method was to turn his thoughts to Fawn and remember what she looked like on a winter night in the radiance of a bedroom light. Fawn was curing him. Also, he stayed as active as he could, not giving his mind time for negative thoughts. It seemed to be working. There'd only been one black time and that early in the summer. And he was starting to see progress toward Mr. Benson's hope, that what he'd gone through would become just a part of living his life. Still there was much to do for him to be comfortable with other boys after what they'd done to him. He remained wary of them.

The calming of his memories did not affect his desire to avenge his mother, and as his head cleared of some of the bad stuff he found himself thinking more and more about her and increasingly grieving for her. He asked Aunt Gertrude to see if he couldn't visit her at her institution. It was located in rural Pennsylvania. Aunt Gertrude came back to him the angriest he'd ever seen her. "The institution requires permission from your father for the visit and your son-of-a-bitch father won't give it. Probably the woman. Damn his hide." This was the only time he'd ever heard Aunt Gertrude swear.

Another thing he realized as the summer wound down was that his dread of returning to the school had waned. The summer had charged him up. He felt ready for battle. He was looking forward to working with Mr. Benson uncovering Pomford's secrets. That didn't mean he was going to like returning. Just felt he had the wind at his back, a phrase he'd picked up from sailing. He could deal with it.

Toward the end of August he heard what he'd been expecting. Aunt Gertrude said to him at breakfast, "We've got to get your clothes ready for Pomford. September 20th is the start date, not much time. You've grown so much you'll need a lot of new clothes."

So the woman had decided to give Pomford another chance to destroy him. He would try his best to make sure that didn't happen.

CHAPTER EIGHTEEN

After Pomford let out on June 20th Henry Benson found he had a lot of time on his hands. No Shirley. She'd filed for divorce, wonderful news, but she'd asked him to stay away for the duration. Her lawyer didn't want him to further inflame George while they were trying to work out a settlement.

One day he saw George at the market. George's face reddened and became threatening, a crazy look. Henry thought George was going to attack him then and there. George started toward him, stopped and looked around appearing surprised at where he was, said in a low voice, "I *will* kill you," and pulled his hand across his throat in a cutting motion. Was George sane?

He did do a little fishing, always with friends. He was being cautious. He was still getting letters. When riding he also tried to get someone to join him. Often, though, he had to ride alone. Riding was his favorite sport, and he wasn't going to deny himself because of Ramos. Actually when he was alone at the stable with Ramos he treated him professionally, saddling the horse and giving no indication they'd had their confrontation. That added to his surprise when in mid-July the word *MURDERER* was scrawled on his front door in what turned out to be human blood. Someone hated him so much they'd draw their own blood to deliver a message. Could Ramos hate him that much and still saddle his horse?

A week later he went over to Gerhard's house. He still thought of Hauptmann as Gerhard. Henry headed a committee evaluating the Pomford health plans and he needed to pick up some papers from Gerhard. Since Henry had received the Israeli report clearing

Gerhard their relationship had become semi-cordial, still a long way from friendship. Gerhard had to gather the papers from another room and invited Henry into the living room to wait, a cheery room with a lot of objects that Gerhard had told him he'd spirited out of his German house. In the far corner was a small picture of a mountain, and as a photographer of mountains he went over and examined it. Gerhard was in his hiking outfit standing before a mountain that he was sure was the Zugspitze, the highest mountain in Bavaria. It looked professionally taken. He could see some evidence of shading that would have been added in the darkroom to make the mountain stand out. He turned the picture over. The Zugspitze as he imagined, the name of the photographer, the date taken, and the locale, all in tidy fashion on the back as was standard in German photography. The date was May 12, 1944.

He yelled in his loudest voice, "You son of a bitch. Come out here!" All the questions flooded his mind. He stood frozen, clutching the picture, his thoughts in turmoil.

Gerhard entered the room, looked at him calmly as though he hadn't heard him, saw him with the picture, and said, "That's the Zugspitze. Brigit and I used to hike there often. Climbed it once."

"You must think I'm the stupidest man in the world. I have been."

"What do you mean?"

"This picture says you were in Bavaria in May, 1944."

Gerhard took the picture and examined the date on the back. There was the slightest look of shock on his face, visible only to someone who knew him well, and then his smooth voice said, "The date is wrong. I was in Switzerland long before 1944."

"You're a Goddamn liar. German photographers are very meticulous. If it says 1944 it was 1944."

Gerhard looked at the picture again, "This has to be Dieter. Now I recall. He sent me the photo with a bunch of other stuff knowing Brigit and I liked to hike there."

"Another lie. Nothing but lies. The photo is very clear. Dieter had a dueling scar on his chin. The man in the picture doesn't."

Gerhard's face went grim, threatening, "Let's discuss this before you jump to wrong conclusions."

"There can be no wrong conclusions. With your background you had to be involved in the Holocaust. If the Israelis knew you are alive they'd hunt you down. You're a war criminal."

Gerhard slumped, his head lowered, a pose that Henry felt was a poor attempt to register contrition, his voice pleading, "I did what I had to do to stay alive. I fought the 'Final Solution' as long as I could without jeopardizing my life and Brigit's. I saved Jews whenever I could. Sometimes it's better to fight something from within than without."

A phony act. "How many Jews went through your hands to the concentration camps?"

Gerhard looked at him with what Henry thought was disdain, certainly not contrition, and said nothing.

Henry had all he could do to stop himself from slugging Gerhard, totally betrayed by the man, made worse by the fact that his presentation in California had helped create this monster.

"I'm going to discuss this with the Head. I assume he'll want to get the authorities involved."

Gerhard said, "You don't have to inform the Head. He knows already."

"He *knows* already?"

"Yes. It was he who invited me here. He couldn't write the sponsoring letter for the visa so we worked to get you to do it."

"You bastard. Not only the lies but you saddled me with legal liability for helping sponsor you. Stay in your house until I decide what to do with you. I strongly suggest you don't try and wander off."

Henry started out the door and turned and said, "Brigit didn't die of breast cancer, did she?"

Gerhard turned his head away.

In this whole conversation Henry had not stuttered.

Henry had a sleepless night. In the middle of the night he realized how cleverly Gerhard had used him. All those friendly, informative letters were to keep a relationship going so that Gerhard could reach out to him if he needed to escape Germany. Same with all that nice guy stuff at dinner in Pomona when Gerhard described his life with Brigit as being so like his life with Helen. Total nonsense. Gerhard had been playing him since they first met. "The bastard." It infuriated him even more.

He'd not decided what to do in the morning. His feelings about the school were negative but he didn't want to destroy it outright because of his many friends among the teachers. On the other hand, if he did nothing wasn't he supporting the Holocaust? In the morning he got a call from the stable. A new horse had come in, a Tennessee Walker. He couldn't place the voice though he thought he knew it, not Ramos with his slight Mexican accent. The voice said, "Smoothest gait imaginable. The owner has just given us permission to allow other people to ride it. You really ought to come in and try her out."

He said, "Sure." Maybe a ride would help him think. When he arrived at the stable Imperator was saddled in the paddock. Odd. Imperator had become so dangerous that even the owner didn't ride him much any more, and he didn't see the Tennessee Walker, or in fact anyone around. He stuck his head in the door of the stable. The last thing he heard was a swishing sound.

CHAPTER NINETEEN

Justin's return to Pomford September 20th was in the chauffeured elegance of Uncle Ben's limousine. He was assigned to a newly constructed junior and senior dormitory. During the summer everyone in class had been required to specify who they wanted to room next to in junior year. He'd put down a number of popular boys. Where he ended up was no where near them, in fact not close to anyone. The dormitory was set up with the juniors on the second floor and the seniors on the first. But there was one junior room on the first floor, a long, narrow room tucked in behind the front stairs and away from other first-floor rooms. When he saw that room, having first hopefully wandering along the junior corridor upstairs looking at names on doors, it confirmed how much he was disliked. The isolation ward.

Before he could unpack Bronco burst into his room, a very serious expression on his face, grabbed him by the arm, and said, "Mr. Benson is dead. They say he was kicked to death by a horse. I know it's terrible news with you so close. I'm sorry to be the one having to tell you."

Justin stared at him. So many questions and emotions he could hardly speak. "Are you sure."

"Yes. It's all over campus."

Justin dashed out without speaking further to Bronco. He had to find Fred Jamison. He scoured the campus. Justin finally tracked him down, now out of breath and with tears in his eyes. "Fred, you've got to help me right away. Now. Find out what happened to

Mr. Benson. As fast as you can. He was a best friend. I need to know how he died."

Justin then walked quickly to the administration building. "Where is Mr. Benson buried?"

He'd no trouble spotting his grave when he got to the old Pomford cemetery next to the church. Some of the earth still bore the mark of a recent turning. He stood beside the grave sorrowing. Ham's curse one more time. Another trauma on top of so many. He spoke to Mr. Benson, "I never thanked you enough for what you did for me. You talked to me. You cared about me. I didn't tell you how really bad the things were building up inside me. You showed me how to fight back. You saved me. I was facing a miserable life and now I know it. Thank you. My God, how can you be gone?" He yelled out the last and burst into tears. After an hour of off and on again crying he returned to his room. It took a long time to unpack with new crying jags. He missed dinner, but who cared. A black time came marching in, a very bad black time. He wasn't surprised. Everything was going wrong in his life—the bullying, his mother, his father, Joe Henderson, Mr. Benson. He let out a scream of despair, something he'd never done before. All he wanted to do was sit there frozen in his desk chair as long as he lived with no contact with anyone or anything forever, total withdrawal from life. He thought about Fawn, trying to block it. It didn't work. After almost an hour of painful thoughts, everything over and over again with no way to escape, head in his hands rocking in his chair, he started focusing on his conversations with Dr. Benson about all the secrets, the woman, Head, Hauptmann, added to that the mystery of Dr. Benson's own death. Mr. Benson would have wanted him to continue to try and solve them, not give up. He needed to do so, do so in memory of Dr. Benson. There was no choice. Black times be damned. He shook his head, hard. Stood up and punched the wall. It hurt his hand. He would get to the bottom of things. That was his vow to Mr. Benson.

The next day Fred Jamison came up to him outside the library. "Benson was found with his head bashed in. There was a horse named Imperator standing by, saddled. I understand Imperator is vicious. The police think Benson was trying to ride Imperator and the horse kicked him. Imperator had to be put down."

"Do you know if there was an autopsy."

"No. But if there was it would have been by the Pomford police. They were in charge of the investigation."

"That's not encouraging. I've heard they're incompetent, kowtow to the Head. The Head probably dictated whether there was an autopsy or not."

Justin walked away thinking it had to be murder with all the threats. But how could it have been murder? How do you get a horse to kick a man? And how do you get a man to stand still for a horse to kick him?

Bronco had no answer when asked, saying, "All I can think of is they held him down and had the horse stamped on his head. Probably not. It would be extremely difficult to lead a horse to stamp on a man. The horse would spook, particularly a horse as uncontrollable as Imperator. And even if they did it, the wound wouldn't look like a kick."

This didn't answer anything. It made no sense for Mr. Benson to be trying to ride Imperator. There was murder there somewhere.

Still in a funk from Mr. Benson's death he went to his mailbox, three letters from Fawn, at least something good. The initial letter was written at the beginning of the summer vacation reporting that her father had hit her mother and gotten into a fight with Mr. Benson. This was the scene he'd seen at the end of the school year. Fawn said she'd known something was going on because the previous summer, her father away, she'd seen her mother in a car with Mr. Benson. The second letter was written a month later. It was filled with joy. Great news. Her mother was getting a divorce. The third letter was mostly misery. She was very close to her mother, and with Mr. Benson's death Fawn came to know how deeply her mother had loved Mr. Benson, the love of her life. Fawn now had to do many things around the house, her mother too distraught to function. She also wondered whether her father might have killed Mr. Benson, saying he was a very dangerous man. At the bottom of the letter, holding it to the end as though she was afraid of his reaction,

My mother still won't let us see each other because of the window incident. I'm working on her. She's pretty adamant. It's the worst news ever.

He agreed. It was indeed the worst news ever. Another blow on top of the blow of Mr. Benson's death. How many blows did the stupid curse require him to take?

Living in the same dorm with other boys, he'd lost the protection he'd enjoyed living apart on Main Street. The short sheeting was not unexpected as it happened to others, puerile stuff that belonged in a summer camp when one was thirteen or younger. However, the occasional piss in his room was to be challenged. He went to the house master about it.

"It's your room. Boys need keep their rooms clean," as though it was his piss. The house master seemed to be smirking. His late night revenge was to piss on the doors of the boys he thought were the culprits. The pissing of his room stopped. Then there was one boy who would stick his head out of his room and announce his coming as Justin walked down the hall, warning everyone to close their doors to protect themselves. None did, and that stopped, too. And when a quite good crayon drawing of him was posted at the end of the hall with a bubble labelled *noxious fumes* at the mouth he tore it down in front of everyone and it wasn't replaced. Aside from these incidents and a few others, the frequency of bullying was greatly reduced, few calls of Deeth as he walked around campus. His fighting back seemed to be paying off.

Bronco came back to school with a new muskrat scheme. The buyer in Wyoming had agreed to accept pelts shipped from Massachusetts.

The problem turned out to be the damp of the Pomford Valley. The pelts didn't dry as they did in Wyoming. They got what they came to call the "Pomford Valley rot," one more malignant present from the valley. It marked the end of the scheme and back to catch and release.

Working the scheme did provide a good opportunity to chat. Justin gave Bronco everything he knew about Hauptmann, the woman, and the Head. Bronco agreed to join him in the hunt.

Bronco's conclusion was the same as his. "There has to be something they all share in common."

Justin said, "Right. But what? I'd like to find a way to get into the Head's office in the administration building, same as I did Ramos's office."

"You've crazy. The Head's office? The administration building is full of people in the day and locked tight at night, What are you going to do? Pick a lock?

"There's a way. I'll find it."

As the Fall progressed Justin acquired two new friends, Moose Brownly, star tackle on the football team, and Elton Quill, Moose's best friend and the leading ground gainer on the team. They were famous for their schemes. The previous Spring it'd been they who organized the rat races. Bronco trapped rats by the stable and behind the kitchen. Small pieces of cloth were tied to the rat's tails, soaked with kerosene, and at the start signal the tails were ignited— a mad squeaky dash down the sophomore dorm corridor with heavy betting, Moose and El cleaning up on the betting.

Justin approached them using Mr. Benson's conversation suggestions. But he rather thought they befriended him because of his strong biology background. He had knowledge valuable for their latest scheme, booze for everyone. Cider was purchased from a local farmer, a distillery set up in an abandoned shed, and a fairly sophisticated distribution system organized with sign-up sheets and runners recruited to deliver on demand. Hard cider galore, enough so that at one time or another a good part of the student body ended up kneeling before a toilet, puking their guts out. The Head must have known about it. He knew about everything. There was a rumor the Head had recruited certain boys to spy on their fellows, referred to around campus as "Head Spies," but no one knew who the recruits were. Probably he didn't shut down the distillery because drinking the foul stuff was punishment enough. Justin manned the distillery, Moose and El the purchasing of supplies, distribution, and payment collection. Justin received quite a nice share of the proceeds. They shut it down after a couple of weeks as no one would buy the rotgut any more, a final drink together, congratulations back and forth, and a vow to team on future schemes. Justin raced to the bathroom and threw up, as he always did when he drank the stuff.

As juniors, he and his classmates felt the confinement more than they had as sophomores, the prisoners were growing restless. And the juniors were more willing to react against the confinement than either the sophomores, who were still feeling their way, or the seniors, who were holding back, looking down the barrel of college admissions. Thus, it was the juniors who sparked the resistance against the hated student marches back and forth between campus and football field every Saturday afternoon. First, it was just one of his classmates chanting out sotto voce a marching song picked up from an uncle who had served in World War Two.

"I left my wife with forty-eight kids to sit around and suck on her tits, sound off, one two, sound off, three four, nothing to eat but toads and chitlin, march some more and I'll be shittin, sound off one two, sound off, three four."

A small surrounding group of juniors picked it up, also chanting quietly and breaking into uproarious laughter when it ended, the laughter bringing over mystified teachers. Then it spread, louder and louder, participation by most of the school. One part of the student body then another sounding off, staying ahead of the teachers running around to find the culprits. The Head dealt out the punishment swiftly, no dinner that night. (Exception for football players and football support troops.) Worse consequences if it happened again.

That was not to be the end of it, revenge on those who deny dinner.

In his Sunday wanderings Justin had come upon an out-of-the-way farm with a large dog in the front yard, a very large dog, well over 130 pounds, ferocious looking, some mastiff blood. The dog charged toward him. "Uh-oh." He tried to escape. The dog took a running leap knocking him down. Instead of the jaws he expected he was slobbered on every exposed part of his body, slobbered repeatedly, the dog holding him down to slobber him more. Fido from his collar. Couldn't they have come up with a more imaginative name? The friendliest dog he'd ever met, it was as though the dog had been waiting for him all his life. Thereafter he made it a point to swing by Fido's farm on his walks. Fido always greeted him with his patented charge and face licking and would follow wherever he led, sometimes all the way to his dormitory, eyes fixed on him all the time as though he were his God, looking sadly after him when he entered the dorm. He only occasionally saw the farmer, always on the far field and never with the dog who seemed a bit deserted.

The Sunday after the marching song incident Fido followed him to the dorm. Four classmates approached him. One said, "We've seen you with your dog. Mind if we borrow him for a while?"

Fido had gone up to the boys, new people to meet, and was trying to jump on one to lick his face. They had a rope they put around Fido's collar and started to lead him off.

"What the hell you doing? He belongs to a farmer. The guy loves him like a child. He'll come after you in a big way."

"Shut up Deeth. It's for a good cause. The farmer will get his dog back. We won't hurt him."

The next Saturday was the biggest game of the year, Andover. The march to the stadium proceeded quietly and sorrowfully, remembrance of how much fun it'd been last Saturday. Fido appeared at the top of a rise, obviously delighted with all these new people to meet. He wasn't slowed down in his charge by the explosion of foam coming out of his mouth, Justin later learned the product of lacing gray meat with soap flakes. Boys in the know started hopping around excitedly trying to get a good view, doubling over with laughter at what they saw. They'd apparently been told about the appearance of a "mad dog" but had no idea what Fido was like or the impact he would make. Those boys not in the know scattered across the landscape in panic, much climbing of trees, some trees clogged with boys struggling to hold on, yelling at Fido when he approached, trying to scare him away. Maybe Fido liked the yelling. He seemed to find tree people particularly desirable and would stand under the terrified boys and leap as high as he could toward them.

The scattering of the faculty was even more extensive, none of them being in the know. Fido tried to chase each one down to make friends. Justin was later told that Fido jumped on the mild-mannered history teacher, gave him a big lick on the face, and the man peed himself. The Head's exit was the fastest. It seemed to Justin only a matter of seconds before the Head had his horse in a full gallop, remarkable as Justin had never seen the Head go faster than a slow trot, and maybe he never had. He bounced up and down on the carriage seat, an airborne black sack of rotten potatoes, hanging on for dear life, steel rim glasses fallen to his nose over a mouth open in panic, a fine example for the boys—-the brave leader standing firm to inspire his troops.

The one teacher who stood firm was Hauptmann. He calmly lit a cigarette despite the Pomford prohibition against smoking on campus, inhaling deeply. Then he looked around with what Justin took to be a sneer of contempt for the cowardice of his fellow teachers. From the way he was acting human terror was old hat for him.

Justin watched as Fido came running up to Hauptmann and backed off. Unusual.

The bumbling Pomford police force arrived after what seemed a long time, Fido still on the people chase. They fired shots at Fido from up close, missed him completely, just as much bumblers in shooting as everything else. Fido, not dumb, took off. Justin hoped he would hide under the farm porch until the coast cleared.

The Head put the ringleaders on kitchen duty not only for the rest of their junior year but also their entire senior year ahead. With that prospect Justin doubted any would stay around.

Already November. He hadn't received a letter from Fawn since the beginning of the semester. Each day he went to the post office with diminishing hope, doubting that he would ever see Fawn again. That day though something different, an envelope propped dull white against the back of the box, a small envelope like a lady might use for a thank you note. Fawn's writing. He was so excited he could hardly open the box, and even more excited when he saw what Fawn wrote.

Please forgive the shortness of this letter. I'm dashing it off to make the next mail with some very good news. I couldn't write sooner. Mother got a little strange and made me promise not to write to you any more. A little while ago it all changed. She was talking about how much she loved Mr. Benson. She stopped and looked at me like she hadn't seen me in awhile. Then she said you're a woman now. I don't want you to lose someone you care about like I lost Henry. If you want to see Justin I won't stand in your way any longer. We're going to be in Pomford over Thanksgiving. I hope more than anything in my life that you're there. I can't wait to see you. Please say that you'll be there. I'm going to say prayers we'll be together. All my love. Fawn.

Hallelujah! He'd just been told that Aunt Gertrude and Uncle Ben couldn't host him over Thanksgiving. He would see Fawn.

Tears came to his eyes, the happiest moment of his life. It took him fifteen minutes to draft and post a reply.

Yes.Yes.Yes. I can hardly wait to see you, to hold you, to kiss you. You are my beloved. Every part of my heart, every shade of my soul is yours. There's no one else. There'll never be anyone else. The minutes until we're together will be the longest minutes of my life. With love forever, Justin.

As Thanksgiving approached doubts and worries set in at every level. He hadn't seen her in a year, gone through a lot. Had he changed? Would she still like him? And what about her. Was she still the same girl he loved? The day before Thanksgiving was cold, light snow flurries drifting out of a slate sky. He stood stamping his feet, waiting for hours. Why wasn't she here? Stoneleigh Prospect wasn't that far away.

Finally her mother's car rolled up and out she came. A shock of joy on seeing her. She gave an enthusiastic wave and practically ran over to him, looked him slowly up and down, happiness suffusing her face. Then with the little toss of her head he loved,

"You look great."

"You look great, too."

The same bright sparkling blue eyes, shining blond hair now down to her shoulders, a little more voluptuous, which he didn't mind. Before he could say anything further her mother smiled warmly at him and said, "Come to Thanksgiving dinner tomorrow, 1:30."

He replied, trying to pretend it wasn't the most important thing in the world, "Sure. Happy to be there."

A sleepless night thinking of Fawn. He was at their door precisely at 1:30, in fact had been standing behind a tree waiting for some time. The door was opened by Fawn. He could hear her sister practicing a rather squeaky violin somewhere.

Fawn whisked him into the parlor, gave him a quick kiss, and said. "Mother's cooking. I need to go in and help her but want to say something first." Her voice grew very serious. "I'm still terribly embarrassed about showing myself to you like that. From what somebody told me, whores display themselves like that in windows. That's not the kind of person I am. I think I was a little crazy being cooped up at Stoneleigh Prospect. And my father not letting me see boys. It was a little bit to get back at him but mostly for you. An older girl, sort of a bad girl, told me about it. I was too young and naive to know better. I hope you realize that in doing it I wasn't saying all I have to offer is looks. Or insulting you by saying I thought all you wanted from me was my looks. I know from your letters and your poetry it's more. It's much more for me, too. I don't want you to forget what you saw. I wanted you to see what I looked like. I love you." Tears were running down her cheeks. She wiped them away with the back of her hand and bowed her head, a gesture of apology.

"My God, don't apologize. I took it as a gift of love, a marvelous gift of love, the best gift I've ever had, the most beautiful girl in the world. I didn't know until later how intelligent you are. Beautiful and intelligent, being here with you is an absolute miracle." Tears of joy formed in his eyes to match Fawn's tears.

She gave him a very happy smile and the saucy toss of her head. "See you in a few minutes," and she dashed out.

Dinner was a happy affair, though Fawn's mother had circles under her eyes, he assumed still suffering from the death of Mr. Benson. He made up for the fact he hadn't been allowed to talk much the preceding Thanksgiving, relating stories of New York, Palm Beach, and Greenwich, the consummate raconteur, showing off a little bit to Fawn who smiled fetchingly at him through dinner. Fawn had dishwashing duty so he scooted off, a date for the movies set for the next day.

After the movie they walked to a nearby ice cream parlor, he with an arm around her shoulders. How great was that! The normally depressing gray clouds of Pomford became a cloud-flock of magic. Even the somber colonial buildings became lighter with Fawn at his side. They grabbed a booth at the back of the ice cream parlor. For some reason few people were around, maybe too stuffed with turkey.

He said, "I never thought I'd be allowed to see you again after what happened. I don't know what I would have done. I was miserable."

"Same for me. Eventually Mother became very understanding as I said in my letter. She'd heard from father that you spied on me. I don't know what she would have done if I'd told her the truth. Let's not tell her." She laughed and he laughed happily along with her.

Justin took Fawn's hands in his and focused his entire attention on her face, trying not to show the fear he felt, fear about how she'd react when he told her what was going on. He couldn't avoid it any longer. She might reject him completely when she found out how much other boys disliked him, the subject of so much derision. But he couldn't have her finding out from someone else, couldn't have her think he'd been trying to hide it from her all along.

"I want to tell you some things I never wrote in my letters, how I ended up at Pomford and the terrible things that have happened to me at Pomford. You're my love. You should know."

He spent more than an hour laying it all out, his father and mother, the woman, the death of Joe Henderson, the death of Mr. Benson, the bullying, even the near suicide, her asking questions along the way. By the finish she was crying steadily and he got teary seeing her crying. She came over and sat next to him, gave him the longest kiss he'd ever received, and hugged him for what seemed like ten minutes, occasionally, "My God. My God."

She straightened up, wiped the tears from her eyes, and said, "We've got to do something. Are you sure your father won't help?"

"I dislike him so much I don't want his help. Anyway the woman wouldn't let him help."

"Well isn't there someone else who'd help. What about the police? Isn't there some illegal stuff going on in the way they're treating you?"

"Perhaps. But the Head controls the police. The police are paid by the town and the Head runs the town. There are only three of them anyway. And everyone says they're dumb and slow. They're certainly fat enough.

"I shouldn't have told you my story. Now I've gotten you all upset. I was looking forward to a happy time with you. I'll be all right. So far I've survived everything they've done to me. I can't see what worse they could do. In another year and a half I'll be out of here. I'm counting the days, literally counting the days. I have a calendar on the wall and cross out each day as it passes. One saving grace, I have some of the best grades in the class. Whatever they do I should be able to go to any Ivy League College I want, probably Yale. I can't wait to have you down to a Yale football weekend. You'll be the most beautiful girl there."

She gave him a coquettish smile, "Your views are suspect. All you've got to compare me to is a lot of horrible boys. But I accept. It will mean you're out of this ghastly place."

"Look, I don't want you to think I'm not fighting back. When someone bullies me I challenge them. And I'm trying to fight back against the woman. The woman is behind the bullying. I'm positive of it. She's in cahoots with the Head and a teacher here named Hauptmann, terrible guy, an ex-Nazi. Mr. Benson contacted the Israelis so I have some information on him. What I don't have is much on the woman. I should because she's my father's girlfriend, but I don't."

"Maybe I can help. My Uncle Paul, he's my Mother's brother, works in the circulation department of the New York Times. He's my favorite uncle. I don't know what's possible but I'll ask him to check the archives of the Times."

"That would be great. Her maiden name is Rothworth, her father's name was Basil Rothworth, a prominent banker. She's married to Peter Carlisle, the former Under Secretary of State."

The rest of the Thanksgiving weekend they walked and talked a lot, stopping occasional on snowy benches to kiss and hug. Justin didn't try to push her to anything more. It was perfect as it was, just being with her was perfect. They both steered away from further talk about Pomford and his situation. Instead it was what they hoped to study and have as a career, what they liked and didn't like, food, movies, people, and toward the end of the weekend, plans for a future together for life, where they might like to live, what kind of house, even how many children.

The goodbye was as much happy as sorrowful, happy because Justin felt he had truly found the love his life. This was a world apart from the bleak surroundings of Pomford. A better world with Fawn in it. None of the bullies had anything like Fawn.

School back in session the Christmas concert was scheduled for December 10th. Everyone was looking forward to it, many of them, Justin was sure, remembering his humiliation at last year's concert and hoping for a repeat. Wouldn't happen. He'd make sure the concert didn't take place.

He was out his ground floor dorm window early on the 10th, boys just getting up. Striding up to the administrations building, he gave a fierce pull to the fire alarm lever on the outside wall. He would have liked to have done it later, just before the concert, but too many people around. This would do. One of the happiest things he'd done at Pomford. He walked back to his dorm whistling and with his head held high.

The result didn't disappoint. Hilarious. Apparently Pomford hadn't had an all-out fire drill in a long time and nobody much knew what to do. The alarm he pulled was a general alarm for the entire school. The bumbling police, and what turned out to be an equally bumbling fire department, rousted boys nilly-willy from their dorms. The news was they thought there might be an electrical fire in one of the sub-basements but didn't know where. Some of the boys came out virtually bare-assed into the December cold, caught in the process of dressing. Others were forced outside for their morning crap. One freshman, badly constipated, was surrounded by cheering boys. "Push harder Smith. You can do it!" All this didn't make the constipated crap come out easier and Smith eventually waddled away, pants down around his knees, baby steps, holding his legs tightly together.

Teachers dashed around creating confusion. "Assemble here. Assemble there." The Head had been out on his morning ride, evidently some distance away and came charging up consternation on his face, his precious school was burning. Standing up in the carriage the Head's only questions were to the firemen. "Where's the fire? What's burning?" No question about the boys, whether everyone was all right. Then learning it was a false alarm he turned to the assembled boys. "Nobody leaves until the boy who did this confesses." And a half hour later, boys still standing in the cold, "Whoever did this show your breeding. Step forward and confess. Do you want other boys to suffer out here in the cold for what you did?"

Yes. He did want to see other boys suffer. How great it was to get back at those who mocked him at last year's concert!

After three quarters of an hour or more, some of the half-naked younger boys sniffling in the cold, the Head relented. Not good to tell father's their sons froze to death. The Head's penalty was no Christmas concert, just what he'd hoped.

Christmas vacation hadn't begun well, he in Greenwich and Fawn in New York visiting her Uncle Paul. How he wished he was with her to show her New York! He did get a chance to catch up with The Gut, Wild Man Harry and Lover Boy Jones, an evening of remembrance at Hoff Brau house. The Gut had shot up and lost much of his belly. They debated changing his name but voted to keep it for old times sake. Lover Boy Jones claimed to have screwed Ann the Ugly, an unattractive and notoriously promiscuous girl always seeking boys. Nobody doubted Lover Boy this time though they all questioned why he wanted to. For Justin the evening was good for the memories, though with everything happening at Pomford he felt apart from the group. He did enjoy seeing Aunt Gertrude and Uncle Ben, telling them about Fawn. They seemed delighted.

He'd given Fawn aunt Gertrude's telephone number in Greenwich. They'd already had two lengthy calls. The day before he was to return to Pomford he received an excited third call from

Fawn. " My uncle found a lot of newspaper articles about the woman's father. Mostly they were about banking or finance. But there was one clipping that might tie into Hauptmann being a Nazi. I'll send you a copy. It shows her father standing on the podium at Madison Square Garden in front of 20,000 members of a group called the Silver Shirts. I did some research. Silver Shirts was a racist, anti-Jewish organization with about 150,000 members that operated largely in secrecy. A man named William Pelley headed it. Apparently he was very charismatic and a follower of Hitler. He wanted to be the Hitler of the US. The thing is her father was standing next to Pelley on the podium. There's another clipping of her father with Charles Lindberg. My uncle said Lindberg hated Jews. In my research I looked to see what happened to the Silver Shirts. It sort of disappeared as World War II started. Maybe went underground. Do you think the woman is involved in it? It's hard to believe she would do that after the Holocaust."

"Could be. It would explain a lot about what's going on." After they hung up, and they talked for another hour, he thought further about what Fawn had discovered. If that were all there was to it he was disappointed. He'd hoped the woman was engaged in something much more major, maybe a crime he could expose. Being a Silver Shirt wasn't it. Sure, if it came out she might suffer some ridicule, but probably nothing serious from her New York friends. He'd heard anti-Jewish remarks from just about everyone who moved in his father's social circle.

Uncle Ben's chauffeur drove him back to Pomford a few days early because Aunt Gertrude and Uncle Ben were off to Palm Beach. Getting back to Pomford didn't seem so bad. God help him, was Pomford making him comfortable with confinement? Was he getting like a zoo animal that when offered an opened door stays in its cage?

January classes started in the best way possible, no classes. The day before students were to return it started snowing strongly, heavy and wet at first, coming straight down, then colder snow blowing fiercely through the campus, finding every hidden place that man thought sheltered. The wind howled around his room, window panes rattling him from his sleep, a break for half a day to tempt one to hope, then once again the same cycle, then again and again. Four and one half feet of new snow piled on top of a good foot and a half already there. Wind-gathered drifts were well over seven feet deep and snow in frozen waves was massed against the buildings as though trying to gain entrance and destroy everything inside. The savagery of it, that's what impressed him, a week long blizzard. The storm started playing tricks with his mind. Moaning that made him think of his mother and almost brought on one of his dark times. But mostly the storm's roaring voice was anger. Anger at him? Might as well be. Everyone else was angry at him. Or maybe it was anger at the Head. Maybe the intent of the storm was to keep the boys out of the evil hands of the Head, to punish the Head. He needed any allies he could get, even storms.

Not only could boys not get back to school, teachers, even those living close by, were trapped in their houses. The Head was immobilized, no carriage or golf cart. The Polish cook women, indomitable as they were, made it in a couple of days then couldn't get in to feed him anymore. Abandoned him, no attempt by anyone else to get to him. "It's only Justin. Let him starve." He remembered some snowshoes mounted as decoration on a wall of the dining hall. The struggle to get there involved plowing through drifts taller than he was, swimming in snow. The snowshoes gave him the ability to travel anywhere on the campus. The place was his. Whoopee!

The administration building was locked but not the classrooms and the teacher's offices next to the classrooms. In the desk of Mr. Brown's office were some of his letters to Fawn. Now he knew why there were breaks in the correspondence. There was also what appeared to be a surveillance document on Mr. Benson, handwritten.

Market possibility—Tuesdays and Thursdays. 5:00 PM. Far parking lot. Then marks Justin took to be a count of how many times people were about as Mr. Benson walked back and forth to his car. *Main Street possibility—-Walks at 6 good nights only. Still light. Bushes*

at corner of Main and French. Stable possibility—-Rides Sat. Sun. after.
Sometimes saddles own horse Sun. Alone.

Horrible. A prime candidate for being a murderer if the murder he suspected happened. He still couldn't get over the hurdle of figuring out how a horse could be made to kick a man and the man to allow it. If there was a way, Mr. Brown probably found it.

Next to Mr. Brown's office was Hauptmann's office, two shitty people grouped together. Hauptmann's office and desk were clean of everything except some teaching notes and a letter. The letter was lying on the desk and looked like it'd just been opened. Postmarked Washington, D.C., it described secret Silver Shirt meetings in the Washington area. So Fawn was right about the Silver Shirts.

Each night he ate steak. A cache of steaks was displayed upfront and proud in the refrigerator. What for? The boys were never served steak. Did the Head and select teachers feast apart from the lousy Pomford food?

When classes finally resumed it wasn't long before he discovered Moose and El had a new scheme, the craziest yet. Mid-terms were coming up and both boys were close to failing. They had a solution. Their solution was that they were going to break into the admissions building, find the office where exams were kept and steal the questions for all the upcoming junior exams. They claimed it would be easy—unlike most buildings the back door to the admissions building was hinged on the outside, leaving the hinges open to attack. All they had to do was pull the back door off its hinges. They'd be in. He was needed because his was the lone ground floor junior room. The going out and coming in had to be through his window as the dormitory was locked up tight at night.

Justin had no hesitation about joining them. If he got caught he might be expelled, which would be good news. And it offered what Bronco had said he'd never have, a crack at the Head's office.

Moose and El kept set up surveillance on the admission's building. They reported that three days before the first exams were scheduled, they'd seen a printer's truck pull up to the administrations building and unload. Had to be the exams. The caper was on.

Moose and El came prepared, much better than for classes, hammers clothed in sound-deadening cloth to knock out the hinge bolts, powerful flashlights girdled with black cloth to keep the beams from spreading, dark clothes for everyone, notebooks and pens to record questions. No taking of actual exams as they might be missed. They said they stole the flashlights and gloves from the police, lured out the three dumb policemen on a ruse, dashed in and took whatever they wanted.

Their break-in went like clockwork. Had Moose and El committed burglaries before? How did they know the significance of the outside hinges? The hinges were off in three minutes and they were inside, the door propped back up so no one would be the wiser. Moose said, "See I told you. In like Flynn." Moose led them directly to the room with the exams. Moose in a Humphrey Bogart voice, "Went in the other day and cased the joint. Gave them the old 'I'm here to meet a teacher' line. Scouted the whole building. Piece of cake."

El laughed and gave him a slap on the back.

When they got to the room containing the exams the door was unlocked, just as Moose's scouting said it would be. Exams were piled high on tables. Copying all the questions would be a time consuming process even with Moose and El splitting it up. Justin's interest was elsewhere. Plenty of time to explore Ahab's lair. He decided to stop in some other offices along the way. Edmund Cranch's office had a large, not very good, picture of his father covering most of one wall. What would cause a son, under his father's thumb all day, want to be dominated by him in his office? Or maybe his father had put it up. Control. He went through a number of other offices and then turned into the accounting office, interesting to look over what supplies the dining room was ordering. There was a lot of pork. Now he knew that gray meat was pork. Also, he saw an entry for saltpeter. It may have been ordered because recipes called for it. On the other hand, there was a rumor saltpeter was added to food when the boys got restive to dampen the libido.

Finally he moved on to the Head's office, entering with some trepidation. The Head's presence dominated the room even in his absence. Flashing his light on the walls he studied the paintings, mostly early American landscapes, probably quite valuable. The desk was as intimidating as he remembered, at least as large as a gigantic antique English desk he'd admired in the Metropolitan, that one with lions carved on its legs.

A thorough rifling of the Head's desk and the built-in wall cabinets behind produced nothing. A big disappointment. He was in the process of leaving when his flashlight beam hit a fairly large metal file cabinet in the corner, odd because such a formal, antique furnished office wouldn't ordinarily harbor a metal file cabinet. Why wasn't it in the other rooms where he'd seen a lot of file cabinets stored? But what grabbed his attention was that the door to the cabinet was bolted closed with a heavy padlock. The cabinet already had a built-in lock. What was so important that you'd weld on a padlock for added security? He got very curious and started looking for the key. A rifling of the desk produced nothing. If there was a secret drawer he was out of luck. It probably wouldn't be hidden under a corner of the rug or elsewhere low down. The Head wouldn't want to crawl around on the floor. And behind the pictures would have been too much of a stretch for him. The book cases? Right height. A hollowed out book? He noticed something else on one of the book shelves, a dead house plant in what he took to be a Spode china pot. Why a single house plant in this room? And why retain a dead plant? He took it down. The saucer was elevated and under it a key. He was surprised. This was the kind of place an unimaginative housewife would choose to hide a spare house key. He thought the Head was smarter. When he opened the padlock another stupidity. The lock to the cabinet itself was unlocked.

The cabinet contained a number of separate files arranged by date, very orderly. He started with the oldest dates, a lot of historical materials including yellowed newspaper articles about the Head's family. Justin read some of them and they verified the things Joe had told him about the Head and his family. Next in date were files about Pomford and pictures of the Head accepting various degrees. Coming into the mid thirties most of the files related to Germany.

One file contained a raft of newspaper and magazine articles about the Jews (Jude), the strictures placed on them, how they were undermining German society and polluting Aryan bloodlines by marrying true Germans. He couldn't read it all with his limited German, but enough. Why would anyone want to collect this terrible stuff? Another file contained pre-World War II correspondence. Holy Christ. Gerhard Mulder. The letters reported on planned openings of concentration camps, intended movement of Jews and others to the camps, and number of racial hygiene surgeries, whatever those were. And Gerhard seemed to be in charge. Mr. Benson's suspicions were right.

The letters were filled with references to Hitler and to Hitler's policies on Jews, policies that in his letters Gerhard strongly approved, and Gerhard's writings about Jews treated them as subhumans, scum, leeches on society, a species that shouldn't exist. Justin was reminded of a movie he saw where the good guys were trying to exterminate some pretty ugly aliens, only the aliens had some good qualities and Gerhard found none in Jews. Moving through later letters, he found an announcement of inauguration of something called Action 41 which was going to do mass exterminations of the unfit and undesirable. Again Gerhard in charge. His last letter before the War talked of additional plans for concentration camps and that Gerhard expected a much larger effort against Jews. He didn't give details.

Gerhard should have been tried at Nuremberg. He was an organizer and prime participant in the Holocaust.

There were no copies of letters from the Head back to Gerhard. But one of Gerhard's letters thanked the Head for his visit and the opportunity to show him what was going on.

I think I can assure you that what we discuss for the Jews when you visited us will ultimately come to pass.

In another,

I think we see eye-to-eye on all of this.

These pre-war files contained a number of pictures of Hauptmann in Nazi uniform, two with Hitler.

It was one thing for the Head to be angry at the Jew who bank-rupted his father and contributed to his suicide. This was anti-Jew-ish hatred on an entirely different level.

The first post-war file was dated 1945/1946. He read the top letter three times, a mixture of shock and exhilaration. It was type-written with the signature also typed.

Dear Jeremiah,

This letter is written in the hope that you and your school are prospering and you are realizing success in your goal to improve the genetic quality of mankind, a goal I share.

As you can see I am now living in Switzerland under the name of Dieter Hauptmann. Dieter was a distinguished professor at Heidelberg specializing in eugenics and my best friend. He died in 1945 of kidney failure. I believe you met him in one of your visits to Germany to give support to the Nazi efforts against Jews. He insisted I use his passport so that I could avoid the misguided after-war investigations of what we accomplished. Recently Swiss friends who support the cause obtained a Swiss passport for me in Dieter's name.

The war prevented me from giving you adequate thanks for all the contributions you made. Your information about the hatred of Jews by many Americans, and your views on the need to solve the Jewish question in America, as well as Germany, were of impor-tance to us, as was the fact that an educator of your stature would come to Germany three times to urge elimination of Jews. Thank you for your efforts. It's unfortunate the war prevented us from totally reaching our goal.

My own life has become quite sad. I'm sorry to report that my beloved wife, Brigit, died in an air raid in 1944. She was a great admirer of yours. With her death everything changed in my life. I seek peace and tranquility, a place to think and write about eugen-ics. The profession I have chosen is teaching. As you may recall I taught classes at Heidelberg.

Imposing on our friendship, I hope you can find a place for me at the wonderful school you told us so much about, Pomford. Perhaps I could teach German. My teaching credentials are laid out on the next page.

With fond memories of the work we shared together,
Gerard

Justin stood stunned. This was a letter providing the necessary tie between Hauptmann and Mulder. It would hang Mulder for his role in the Holocaust and destroy the Head's own career. Why had the Head kept the letter? The only thing he could think of was that it was a cudgel over Mulder. If Mulder revealed the Head's Nazi support, the Head would bring the Nazi hunters to his door.

He turned to the next letter in the file. Couldn't believe it and read it more slowly. Then again, and let out a triumphal yell despite the need to keep their presence quiet. This was everything he'd hoped for and more. He'd almost expected it, deserved it with what he'd gone through, was owed it, a handwritten note dated April 1946 from the woman to the Head.

Jeremiah,

I got out the supporting letter for Gerhard and have prevailed upon some of my husband's State Department contacts to expedite his visa processing. He should be with us shortly. I very much look forward to meeting Gerhard and hearing about his accomplishments in Germany.

Gerard not Dieter. She knew Hauptmann was operating under a fake identity and probably knew he was a war criminal. *Yes!* John Chandler broke with her because he found out about it. Did his father know? He hoped not.

Justin continued to go through the files, now more recent, a lot of letters from all over the country from Silver Shirts. Undoubtedly the woman had met the Head through the Silver Shirts. He was just starting to read them when Moose burst in. "We've got to get out of here. The watchman's down the road, coming this way. We saw his flashlight. He may check the building."

Justin grabbed one of the pictures of Gerhard with Hitler.
There were so many pictures of Gerhard one probably wouldn't
be missed. He locked the cabinet, carefully replaced the key, and
dashed for the back door. It took very few minutes for the burglary
team to replace and lock the door. They were good. Hiding behind
nearby bushes they observed as the watchman came up and tried
the door. Close call.

Proceeding to the dorm, Moose and El slapped each other
repeatedly on the back and stifled laughter. Justin walked head
down, thinking. He'd had to quickly decide what to take from the
files. Had he made a mistake in not taking Gerhard's letter and the
woman's note? No. He could see the cabinet and files were in active
use. If he took anything major it'd be missed. They'd immediately
manufacture substitutes to take them off the hook. They could easily concoct a handwritten letter signed Dieter Hauptmann to replace
Gerhard's unsigned typed letter, a very innocent letter stating that
Dieter had left his professorship at Heidelberg for Switzerland during the War as he opposed the Nazis, and that he sought a teaching
position. If he later produced Gerhard's typewritten letter it would
be declared a forgery. Without a signature there would be no way to
prove this wrong. The woman's note would probably be replaced by
a new note dealing with some unrelated subject and ending with an
apology that she had mistakenly referred to Dieter Hauptmann as
Gerhard in the previous note. He could see it.

*I confused the name with that of another German I know and look for-
ward to meeting Dieter and hearing about Heidelberg.*

Gerhard's letters and the woman's note would only be effective
in proving criminal conduct if found in the files.

Next day he spent a whole study hall trying to decide what to
do. His feeling of exultation for finding their secrets was replaced
by the weigh of the responsibility thrust upon him. He had no way
to contact a Nazi hunter. Most of them were in Israel. How could he
contact someone in Israel? Could he contact his friend, Lieutenant
O'Reilly? A phone call was out. Phone calls were monitored. What
about a letter? What would happen then? Brian could well not

believe him. Who would believe the claim of a sixteen-year-old with a grudge against his school that the school was harboring a Nazi war criminal? A very far-fetched sounding story whoever delivered it, and if they did believe him they wouldn't just swoop in. He was providing no proof. There'd be an investigation first. As soon as an investigation started the Nazi files would disappear. And he suspected if they investigated Hauptmann/Mulder without the letters it would be impossible to show Hauptmann was Mulder. A strong background would have been manufactured regarding the Swiss passport.

He was stymied. He had to find a way for the letters to be discovered by the authorities in the Head's office. A major challenge on top of many other challenges. The only thing he could think of was starting a fire in the administration building and have the contents of the cabinet rescued and revealed. Little chance. Again a need to practice Joe Henderson's patience.

The real puzzle was Mulder. How could the Israelis not be hunting him? He had to be a major war criminal. His explanation to the Head in the letter didn't make sense. If he simply took Dieter's passport Nazi hunters would be searching the world for him. He had to manufacture his own death. It might have been possible to get a ministry official to fake his death certificate. But he must have realized that wouldn't stop any dedicated Nazi hunters. They would seek out a gravesite and would probably excavate to see whatever body was in the gravesite. To entirely escape pursuit Mulder needed a Gerhard Mulder gravesite in Germany with an appropriate body in it. And to accomplish that the Germans had to have buried a body in 1945 or whenever thinking the body was Mulder's.

He stewed over it. The key was the body the German's buried. He supposed Mulder could have found an unclaimed body of a man his size, there were probably a lot of bodies with the air raids, then bribed some grave diggers to bury the body in a grave bearing his Sheryl,

Then it came to him. Of course, he had it. He shook his fist in triumph in the air. There was only one explanation. Mr.

Benson had told him that Mulder and Hauptmann were identical in appearance. It had to be Hauptmann in Mulder's grave. He could picture how it might have happened. Mulder probably picked a snowy night in 1945 so nobody would be out and about. Mulder would be warmly greeted when he called on his old friend Hauptmann at his home in Heidelberg. (It had to be that Hauptmann was a bachelor or what he assumed happened wouldn't have happened.) When Hauptmann's back is turned, maybe to get them some of his best brandy, Mulder plunged a narrow surgical instrument into his back and heart, a scalpel or something similar that produced little blood. After taking his passport he dressed Hauptmann in his own SS colonel uniform, put the Mulder identification on Hauptmann, maybe rolled the body in a rug and pulled it down the snowy steps to his car, or maybe had an associate help him, a Nazi lackey. Then he transported the body to Frankfurt or another recently bombed city, dumped the body and roughed it up to make it look like the fake Mulder was an air raid casualty being careful to obscure Hauptmann's dueling scar. After alerting the authorities about the casualty without revealing himself, he skedaddled out of Germany using Hauptmann's passport, the Germans being left to bury Hauptmann as Mulder. He might have the details wrong but Justin was convinced that he had correctly pegged Mulder with the murder of Hauptmann. What was one more murder for Mulder? He already had the blood of millions of Jews on his hands. A monster of special evil among a group of monsters.

Had the woman and the Head thought through how Mulder got out of Germany? Justin was sure that if he could figure it out so could they. They knew what went on and brought him in anyway. They were monsters, too.

Justin exulted in solving the mystery but went cold thinking about it. One of the worst murders in modern history on campus! What to do about it? No plan appeared immediately. He resolved to find a way somehow someway to get Mulder. Mulder could not be allowed to live.

The next week was all about mid-year exams. He'd warned Moose and El that they shouldn't answer all of the exam questions correctly, miss a good number of questions, make it look like they were improving greatly but not suddenly leading the class. El listened to him but Moose, the dumber of the two, didn't. The school knew Moose cheated, but not how, and reduced his grades to what was normal for him, barely above failing. El said they questioned him, probably knew he cheated, too, but let it pass. When Moose came back to his room after being handed his low grades he was so forlorn, defeated-looking, Justin couldn't help laughing at him. "Cheer up. All good burglars sometimes don't get what they wanted. Think of it this way. You thumbed your nose at the whole school. Nobody does that and gets away with it. You're famous and nobody knows it."

Moose gave him a small punch on the arm and a big smile. "Right. Thanks."

Exams behind them Justin decided to show the picture of Gerhard with Hitler to Bronco and fill him in on what he'd found. Bronco was the obvious choice. Last Spring when he'd told Bronco about Hauptmann being a Nazi Bronco had exploded. "My uncle Dave, my favorite uncle, was killed by the Germans. He was a pilot. They shot him down over Germany in 1944. The place where he was held was billed as a prison camp. It was more a concentration camp. He was starved and died. I don't know how you can take Hauptmann's class."

That reprimand from Bronco was one of the reasons why for his junior year Justin was taking French rather than second-year German from Hauptmann.

When Bronco found out Hauptmann was really Gerhard Mulder, a Nazi war criminal, he went sort of crazy. "He's a murderer. He needs to die. I'm going to send out to the ranch for some dynamite and my gun. I'll blow the bastard's house up with him in it. If that doesn't work, I'm a good shot. They'll applaud me for killing a war criminal." Justin finally calmed him down and persuaded him that shooting bad guys in New England was probably a bad idea regardless of what was allowed in the old West.

Justin said, "I don't think we can get Mulder on our own. Let's get the whole school involved. We'll make life miserable for him, maybe drive out the truth."

They thought it through. What story should they tell other boys? The story with Mulder and the change of identities was too complicated. Furthermore, if the name Mulder appeared the Head would hear about it, might suspect his cabinet had been breached, and would destroy everything in the files. Better to simply tell everyone that Hauptmann was a wanted Nazi war criminal. And certainly don't show the picture around as it was a sure give-away the files had been raided.

Justin told the agreed-upon story to his few friends. Bronco did the same with his many friends. In a matter of days the whole school was in on it, the most exciting thing that ever happened at Pomford, a Nazi war criminal. Yellow cloth was found, Star of David cutouts produced, and started appearing on lapels. "Sieg Heil" became the campus greeting followed by a Nazi salute. Swastikas appeared on Hauptmann's house and some other buildings. After a week of this, a chalked swastika was on the blackboard of Hauptmann's class when he entered, and when his back was turned, mutters of "Sieg Heil" were heard from a number of boys. Hauptmann gave the entire class multiple demerits.

Justin could see no visible effect on Mulder. In the past he was always arrogant as he walked around campus, often a sneer on his lips as he glanced at groups of boys. Now he walked even more arrogantly, ramrod straight with the stride of someone who thought they owned the place, maybe a Nazi stride, and the sneer had gotten more pronounced. Justin took the sneer to say, "We Nazis aren't effected by the criticism of those beneath us." Mulder evidently thought himself untouchable for his past and showed it.

The Head had probably gotten calls from parents saying their sons had told them of rumors a Nazi war criminal was teaching at Pomford. A special assembly was called. The Head's usually white face was red with fury, his eyes menacing. "You boys have been lied to. The man you are attacking, Professor Hauptmann, was a distinguished professor at Heidelberg in Germany. He was not a Nazi but opposed the Nazis. He escaped to Switzerland to avoid being killed by the Nazis. He's a hero. To be praised, not attacked. What you heard was a vicious rumor. Anyone who shows disrespect for Professor Hauptmann will get kitchen duty the rest of the year. We will be watching. Everyone stand and face Professor Hauptmann. Now say in unison, 'We apologize Professor Hauptmann.'"

Feeble words of apology were heard.

"Louder."

The words of apology progressed to an halfhearted attempt.

The Head looked slowly around the room, his eyes boring into the eyes of each boy. "Louder."

This time a chorus of apology.

The good news for Justin was that the Head didn't realize it had to do with the picture he'd taken. The Head must have thought they were after Hauptmann because he was disliked. The other good news was that the boys took the Head's lecture as a piece of crap. Partly that was because they wanted to believe they had a war criminal on their hands. Partly it was because Hauptmann was hated and behaved in his arrogance like you'd expect a war criminal to behave. But mostly it was how the Head reacted, or overreacted. The special assembly, threatening lecture, public apology, all to quash a rumor? No way. The boys decided as a group that the Head wouldn't have done so much if the rumor wasn't true.

So the focus on Hauptmann continued. To Justin's surprise, one result was that no one was taunting him anymore. Concentration was on Hauptmann. Hauptmann had become the new Piggy of Pomford. This had to make the woman crazy unhappy. Everybody mocking her favorite Nazi rather than him. Great.

For fear of demerits the boys couldn't attack Hauptmann as openly as before. However, "Seig Heil" and the Nazi salute was still the preferred greeting in less public spaces and swastikas regularly appeared on buildings.

With the desolation of winter the pressure cooker of trapped boys built up steam, one gray day after another, gray snow, gray sleet, gray everything. The Pomford valley was where winter put all the weather too miserable for anywhere else. Sheets of snow perpetually renewed. Long stretches of sunless days.

The explosion when it came was a beaut, the Great Snowball Riot of 1955.

Moose and El started it with an innocent challenge to some seniors one Sunday afternoon. "Pick five of your best and we'll have a snowball fight." As a friend Justin was included as one of the five. No one knew the Head was away, but away he was, driven by Jenkins in the Head Mobile who knows where, but a substantial distance based upon how long it took him to get back.

What started as five on a side quickly spread to the whole junior and senior classes, then the sophomores and freshman. The teachers tried to break it up. Somebody threw a snowball at a teacher and then everybody was throwing at teachers. The target became Hauptmann. He was driven into his house with his arms around his head, no sneer this time. Soon the other teachers were driven inside their houses. The boys controlled the streets. It was the French Revolution.

Some boys were starting to put stones in their snowballs. One of the windows of Hauptmann's house was broken. He came out screaming. All it did was get him pelted with snowballs once again. All attention shifted to Hauptmann's house. More stones were found on the street. A biblical barrage of snowballs hit the house. Every single window was broken including small windows in the attic. The snow around the house was sparkled with shining shards of glass.

Justin remembered reading about Crystal Night in 1938 Germany where the streets were litter with broken glass from a Nazi attack on Jewish homes and businesses. The glass around Hauptmann's house was a small response. Focus was turning to other unliked teacher's houses when down Main Street roared the Head Mobile, sliding to a stop in the middle of the boys, almost hitting a few. The Head stepped out in unhurried fashion and looked very calmly around as though facing five hundred boys armed with stone implanted snowballs was something he did every day.

In the same measured voice he used at assembly he said," Quill and Brownly to my office."

How did he know they were ringleaders?

"The rest of you no dinner tonight. And no free Sunday afternoons for a month. You seem to like snow. You will spend Sunday afternoons clearing the playing fields of snow. And if you get that done early, you will shovel the snow back on the playing fields and then clear them again." The Head looked at Justin hard as though trying to decide whether to single him out for special punishment along with Moose and El, frowned at him with seeming disgust, and got back in his car.

Moose told him the next day that the Head's penalty for him and El was kitchen duty the rest of the year and that their parents had to pay for the broken windows. Moose said with a smile, "It was worth it to get the bastard."

The *Lord of the Flies* continued, the confining atmosphere driving boys crazy. Two boys in his class decided to become Buddhist, their escape from the pressure cooker. They made formal announcement in a document distributed to their classmates.

We are putting aside our studies and the material things of this world to live a life of contemplation. Pomford is polluting the essence of our being. We must reject it and everything about it if we want to save ourselves. You should all join us and withdraw from the material world. Pomford is taking yourselves from you."

Sounded great and everyone wanted to sign up but Buddhism died as quickly as it was born when their fathers arrived on campus.

Justin laughed about it, thinking about the woman's frustration if he entered a Buddhist monastery. It would almost be worth it.

A week later three seniors were picked up at the railway station by town police. The boys had substantial funds in their possession, trust-fund babies all, tickets to Rio, passports in hand, and plans for a hedonistic life. Weeks later another boy tried escape on his own, a hitchhiking venture to Boston. He was picked up within an hour after an all- points bulletin went out. Justin had learned something. The lock down at Pomford extended to the surrounding territory, like a Russian gulag, no escape no way no how.

The crystal night didn't seem to affect Hauptmann. He marched around the winter campus as arrogant as ever. This increasingly infuriated Bronco. He approached Justin with new schemes to kill Hauptmann. Justin always advised patience but wasn't sure Bronco was listening.

Justin was in study hall when the blast occurred. It rattled the windows. He bolted out, as did everyone else. Down the street a house was on fire, and when he got closer he saw it was Hauptmann's. Medical personnel and police surrounded Hauptmann who was standing though staggering a bit. His clothing appeared to be singed and they were applying something to his face.

Fred Jamison filled him in. "It was a gas explosion. The police say the gas was left on in the kitchen and the pilot light for the gas furnace in the house had gone out. What saved Hauptmann is he's a chain smoker. With the prohibition against smoking on campus he couldn't wait to light up. He told police he lit his cigarette just as he entered the front door. Inside and he would have been killed. As it was he was blown all the way out on the street. Hauptmann claimed to the police he didn't leave the gas on, that he double checks the gas when he leaves. I don't think they believe him. They haven't investigated much. They're too lazy and incompetent to do a full investigation of anything."

Justin found Bronco checking his traps for the Spring musk-rat season. "Bronco, you did it, right?" Bronco stared at him for a moment and said, "It would have been fitting if he'd died by gas," then turned his back and walked away.

Hauptmann's old arrogance was no longer seen on campus. The sneer had been replaced by watchful glances at everybody and everything. Apprehension. Hooray. Something accomplished.

Finally Spring break and bad news on two fronts. No Palm beach because of an operation on Uncle Ben's bladder and Fawn was being whisked off to New York for the vacation. But good news, too. Fawn would be in Pomford for one day before going to New York. He almost danced to classes the next week.

A shock on seeing her, an indescribable feeling that a vital part of his soul that'd gone missing and now had reappeared. The day was sunny, unusual for Pomford. Had Fawn brought the sun? Probably. Walking around town, he told her how much he'd missed her and how much he loved her and heard the same for her. He brought their walk past what he'd come to call the "tryst shack," and explained it was a place he'd identified to meet when they were still hiding from her parents.

"I'd like to see what I missed. Can we go in?"

He said, "Certainly," Trying to be as casual as possible.

When they got inside she look around, picked the cleanest spot, and sat. "Sit down next to me." She patted the ground next to her. She gave him a long kiss. Then another. "Now, lay down."

He did not have to be told. He kissed her gently. Her lips so soft. Her breath so sweet. Beyond anything. No poems captured it. He played kiss the nose and kiss the eyes. She played back, laughing. A kiss for a kiss all over each other's faces, then fingertips. She snuggled up to him and held him, his face buried in her sweet hair. Her lips came up to meet his lips. A long kiss. Then another. She started to move against him, and deeper kisses, he didn't know whether her kisses or his. She threw her head back and laughed delightedly. Then held him ever tighter. Every kiss, every movement he made, she responded so eagerly. He'd never experienced anything like this.

She sat up abruptly. "We shouldn't do any more."

"I agree." How hard was that to say.

"I love you."

"I love you, too.

They continued their walk and he told her the whole story of what had been happening, the file cabinet, Hauptmann being a war criminal, the woman's involvement. Now there were three people who knew the story, he, Bronco, and Fawn.

She stopped him and spun him around so they were facing each other. "We've got to do something. Can't you get the police involved?

He explained why he decided against it, that with an investigation the files would be destroyed.

"What about the Israelis? You told me Mr. Benson had talked to the Israeli embassy."

"I would need proof that I don't have. Besides, they monitor the one phone here that students are allowed to use."

"Let me try. Or better, I'll ask my uncle to try. As I told you, he fought in World War II against the Nazis. The Israelis wouldn't listen to a girl, or probably you for that matter. Maybe they'll listen to my uncle."

"Okay. It's worth a try. But you've got to caution your uncle not to tell anyone else about it. If it gets out the files will be destroyed and that's the only proof we have."

They sat on a bench and talked about plans for the summer. He was sure he could get his aunt and uncle to invite Fawn to Greenwich, and Fawn said she thought her mother would let her go. He laid out all the things they'd do in Greenwich, an introduction to sailing including picnics on Captain's Island, many parties and dances.

She said, "I bet you're a good dancer."

He said, "Maybe." He'd sure been dragged to a lot of dance classes.

She grabbed him, started singing a popular song, she had a good voice, and danced him around the still snowy street, laughing all the while.

At the end of the day he held her shoulders in a serious moment, staring at her face, looking deeply into her lovely blue eyes, seeing everything about her, straining to absorb and hold fast the image of Fawn. Just as earlier when she appeared it was as though a vital part of his soul had come back now it went missing as the taxi bearing Fawn and her mother departed for the train station.

The remainder of Spring vacation was boring, boring, boring, a real bust, made worse by contrast with the one beautiful day of Fawn. No Palm Beach, one gray wintery day after another. Snow in April? T. S. Eliot described Pomford. *April is the cruelest month.*

He was almost happy when vacation was over over. Maybe he was getting the Siberian disease. He understood that many prisoners in the Russian gulags got so inured to the life that when freed they settled in Siberia near their gulag. He was spending too many vacations in the Pomford gulag.

A letter arrived from Fawn reporting on her uncle's call to the embassy. *He had trouble reaching anyone who was interested. Finally, a woman took his information and promised to forward it to Israel. She cautioned they were getting so many reports on possible Nazis from everywhere in the world, they couldn't handle them all. There were only a limited number of Nazi hunters. Not very encouraging, I'm afraid.*

They would have to do it on their own. He thought about stealing into Hauptmann's home to look for further evidence. Not so easy. At night, when he could sneak out his window, burglary would be very dangerous with Hauptmann home. During the day his classes corresponded to Hauptmann's so when he left class Hauptmann would be going home. Sunday afternoons were a possibility with free time given students. However, when he investigated, Hauptmann turned out to stay at home and read Sunday afternoons.

Bronc wanted to stir things up by confronting him. "Aren't you Gerhard Mulder, the war criminal?"

Justin spent some time urging him to be patient and convincing him one more time that if the Mulder name appeared on campus the Head would destroy the letter, the one place Hauptmann and Mulder were linked.

"Broco, just ask your friends to step up the attack, more swastikas and sieg heils. We've got him on the run. I'm confident that somehow some way were going to get the bastard."

Bronco made a face and nodded in acceptance.

With his failure in baseball the preceding year he chose track as his Spring sport. The javelin looked interesting, warriors throwing spears was sort of neat. It turned out to be a good choice. Not much practice was required and that practice was on the lower playing field near the river where his errant throws wouldn't kill anyone. It gave him spare time to check the muskrat lines so he didn't have so many early morning sessions.

Not to let the Spring pass with Ham's curse leaving him unpunished, Pomford mounted a new challenge. Theft. None of the dorm rooms were locked. Initially only a few small items disappeared, possible misplacements. Then it got more serious, cash and valuable items, even supposedly a Rolex watch from The Suit. What was The Suit doing with a Rolex watch at Pomford? One evening in the dining hall Mr. Jenkins came over, grabbed him, and hauled him very publicly out of the dining hall back to his dorm room, saying he'd gotten an anonymous tip that Justin was the thief. A cheap watch and a little money were found in his dresser drawer, not his. He protested that someone planted them there to frame him but ended up with a year of demerits. More thefts and he was again called in. This time he got Jenkins to say when the latest thefts occurred and proved he'd been at an away track meet. Jenkins didn't relent. "You could have used the other stealing as a cover for your own stealing." Demerits still there, he resolved to catch the real thief.

For credibility sake he needed someone else to join in his plan. No one would believe him if he pointed out the thief. Bronco was happy to join. Bronco had lost a valuable silver belt buckle, and when he heard the plan thought it was, "Super." Not too many days later they paraded into Jenkins's office and named Gary Calder the thief. He let Bronco explain.

"I spread it around that I'd been at the post office and had seen Justin receive a large sum from his aunt. Then we borrowed some phosphorous from the chemistry lab, coated some bills with a little phosphorus, not enough to make it obvious, and left the money on Justin's dresser. Fortunately Calder doesn't seem to be a before-meals-hand-washer. We stood outside the dining hall in the dark and looked at hands. There was a glow on Calder's hands."

Jenkins said with a tone of dismissal. "That's nonsense. He's one of the Head's best football players. You're just trying to stir up trouble. And you, Whitthorne, you shouldn't even be at Pomford."

Bronco said, "Aren't you even going to check out his room? It'll only take a few minutes."

Jenkins looked from one boy to the other, grudgingly got up, and proceeded to Calder's room with them in tow. Most of the loot from the various thefts was found under the mattress.

Jenkins turned on Justin, fuming, no doubt angry at the embarrassment of yanking the wrong boy out of the dining hall. "You're nothing but trouble, Whitthorne. All this bullying you're causing. We'd have far less bullying if you left."

Justin said, "I didn't cause the bullying. People are bullying me," getting angry in return.

"Shut up! I don't want to hear anything more. We'll be watching you carefully from here on. Every move you make we'll be there. Every moment of the day. You won't see us but we'll see you. You get the slightest bit out of line and you'll find yourself with the worst punishment Pomford can hand out."

Calder remained in the school and continued to be treated in friendly fashion by the Head. Varsity football players didn't fall out of favor for a minor thing like grand theft.

CHAPTER NINETEEN

When he thought about it later he realized the chance was a one-in-a-thousand, or maybe one- in-a-million. His whole life seemed to be governed by chance—finding his mother's diary, coming in on his father just when he was screwing on the living room rug, finding the key to the Head's file cabinet, and most important, finding Fawn.

Or maybe patience made things happen. Joe Henderson believed it did.

In late May, Justin was down by the river on a Sunday, idly watching the completion of some of the rafts. Pretty Spring day, prettiest day he could remember his whole time at Pomford. The trees were greening up in celebratory escape from the forever winter as though required to be in full summer leaf in just a few days, and a canopy of green from the elms along Main Street. He should have known something momentous was about to happen. Pretty days were not part of the calendar of Pomford Valley.

He started helping a boy he knew slightly, pulling up limbs along the river bank looking for boards for the boy's raft. The Spring floods had been the strongest in memory, scouring the river to its bottom and throwing large amounts of debris on the banks. Further along boys working on another raft had stopped to hit stones into the river with a bat of some sort. He looked more closely. Shellacked brown the bat gleamed in the sunlight. Could it be? He dashed over, his bat from last year, he recognized the dent on the end. A coach had thrown it against a fence after his third strikeout in a critical game. How'd it get in the river? And what was this? As the boy turned it over to hit he saw a horseshoe had been screwed on one side of the flat part of the bat and then wired down for good measure. He almost yell out. Gulped it back and froze. He now knew that Mr. Benson had been murdered and he knew who did it. Thank you Lord! And when he thought about it he knew where to find the motive.

There were three boys playing with the bat, a contest to see who could hit the furthest. With as much calm as he could muster he said, "That's my bat. I'd appreciate it if you'd give it to me."

"Who says it's your bat?"

"I played baseball last Spring and my hitting was so bad they gave me this special bat. It's for players that can't see very well. I'd like to keep it as a memento."

"What's the horseshoe about?"

"I don't know. I'm going to take it off."

One of the boys, the ringleader, said, "We found it in the brush by the river. Had to dig it out. Hard work. Finders keepers Deeth."

"How about I buy it from you. It'd be good to have."

The boys conferred and the ringleader came back, "Twenty dollars each," grinning as he said it.

"That's highway robbery! That bat didn't cost ten dollars new. I'll give you five dollars each and that's way too much."

"From anyone else we'd accept that. But for you, Deeth, it's twenty each. Maybe there's a market for a Deeth bat if we can get rid of the smell." They all laughed, looking disdainfully at him.

Justin said, "Alright. Twenty each in the dining hall tonight." He didn't have time to fool around. The bat had to be spirited away and hidden before anyone else saw it.

The boy handed over the bat joking among themselves, their eyes following him as he walked casually away trying to avoid attention, the bat held tight to his leg as disguised as he could make it. Where to hide it? The shed where Horney stored his girly magazines was too obvious. He went off campus to the farm where Fido was kept, no farmer there as usual. He hadn't been there in awhile and had to endure the knock down and face licking of a dog deprived of a beloved human's companionship. Fido was now chained to the front porch, probably the result of the mad dog incident. He picked a place well within Fido's reach on his chain, crawled under the porch, very low and muddy, shoved the bat into the furthest corner, and emerged covered with mud and feeling the bat was safe protected by dog and porch.

The next day he walked to the farm to check on the bat, again stealing away from track practice. No Fido. Fear in the pit of his stomach, he looked under the porch, The earth had been disturbed, looking as though somebody large had crawled in. Whomever he was he'd taken the bat. Jenkins had said in their theft confrontation he'd be watched. Why didn't he pay more attention to that? Why hadn't he checked around to see if anyone was looking? Mr. Benson said he was a detective. A good detective would have cased his surroundings. How stupid can you be? Now he was a target. As soon as he hid the bat he'd became a target. There was no reason for him to hide it unless he knew about the murder. He might as well have put up a sign. *Justin knows Mr. Benson was murdered.*

His fear increased the longer he thought about it. Whoever murdered Mr. Benson would come after him.

That night he had kitchen duty. He was taking the trash can to the pick-up point, still a little Spring light. A man dashed out from behind some fir trees, running at full speed to intercept him. He was a little bit on his guard because he was expecting something, pushed the garbage can in front of the man, and ran faster than he'd ever run back for the kitchen door, yelling as he ran. He made it inside by only a few feet, badly shaken. Had the man waited until he dumped the garbage he wouldn't have had a chance. The man wore dark clothes and a black hood. Justin only got a small glimpse of the man's face. It could have been Ramos. But it could have been any other slim, medium-sized fellow of sallow complexion. And as for his own yelling, all he got was a warning from one of the Polish women not to stir up such a ruckus.

That night he slept fitfully. It was well he did. At about 1:00 AM he sensed something and saw a shadow at the window and worse, his window being silently raised. He sprinted out his door and went to Moose's room, who was too sleepy to object when he asked to sleep on his floor. The next morning he checked his window and found it had been greased or something to open silently. They were probably intended to chloroform him, take him to the river, weigh his body with stones like Horace Randall, and claim a suicide. It continued. After class there was a very formal, unsigned note on his door instructing him to immediately report to the admissions office. He ignored it. All day he stayed close to other boys, and he told Bronco what was going on and asked him to watch out for him.

He had to get away. They'd kill him here. The train station and hitchhiking were out as demonstrated by failed attempts earlier that year. The monitoring of the phone prevented a telephone call for help. Before dinner he emptied his book bag and crunched into it a warm, waterproof jacket along with the flashlight he acquired in the great mid-year exam raid. He wasn't on kitchen duty that night. Instead he was a waiter. Nobody questioned it when he brought the book bag to the table, probably assumed he was going to study later. In one of his waiter runs he managed to casually and inconspicuously deposit the bag in a corner near the back outside kitchen doors. He stuffed himself at dinner, gray meat again, not sure when he'd have his next meal. When the clean up of tables was complete, the boys on waiting duty focused on leaving the hall, he moseyed into the kitchen and over to his book bag. The Polish women were gabbing and paid no attention to him. They never paid much attention to any of the boys except to yell at them when they got in the way. The refrigerators were out of sight from the women doing dishes. He helped himself— bread, cheese, salamis, milk, as much as he could fit in, then slipped out the back door and proceeded cautiously, peering at the woods for anyone hidden, ready to run back. Nothing. They must have known he was on waiter duty, not kitchen duty. Probably waiting to pounce at the front door of the dining hall. On the riverbank he found the board he was looking for, one that could serve as a paddle. After considering all the rafts, he chose a smaller one, one constructed entirely of dark wood, easy to conceal as he made his way.

His plan was to float the rivers far enough so that he was safe walking into a riverside town and making some telephone calls. An all points bulletin would be out for him, surely all over Massachusetts. Connecticut too? It was a very long shot. In recent years no boy had gotten more than ten miles on a raft before being picked up. He'd no alternative.

There was some light, the moon glimmering through the usual Pomford clouds. The river shone sinuous into the distance like an immense letter S of beaten silver, coiling away, inviting. Off he went.

The river was flowing at one-and-one-half to two knots an hour. That should get him past Greenfield in the middle of the night when it was safest, then onto the Connecticut River where the Pomford merged with the Connecticut. He intended to come ashore each morning before first light to avoid discovery by early rising fishermen. He would hide the raft, sleep the day in a concealed place, and head off the next evening after dusk when fishermen would have left the bank.

The first night went fine. Out from the Pomford Valley the clouds dissipated. For the first time in a long time he saw the full night sky. The stars seemed friendlier, welcoming his escape, not as cold as those at Pomford. He moved through the night under a panoply of dark trees that simultaneously darkened the sky and floated in the water beside him, feeling happy despite the danger.

The next morning he found soft grass under bushes hiding him from sight, put the jacket over his eyes to block light, and slept well. And the following night went fine, too, though now on the Connecticut the flow wasn't as fast as the on the Pomford, so progress was slowed. The moon reflected across still water, tranquil and beautiful. He started feeling optimistic though he new his chances were slim. This was one of the neatest things he'd ever done if he didn't get caught, an opportunity to recover all he'd lost at Pomford, to get back at the woman for putting him there. Just before midnight a fisherman in a skiff spotted him, night fishing on a moonlit night. No challenge. Instead a thumbs up, the fisherman perhaps being impressed at a boy going down the Connecticut on a raft in the middle of the night, or perhaps reacting to how much he'd had to drink to stay warm on the river. The shadows of the dawn light stretched across the river and he holed up for the day. A short time later he thought his goose was cooked. A farm dog found him in his sleeping lair and barked an alert. A generous gift of salami made the dog his friend.

The third night was mild. Now that he was out of the Pomford Valley the nights were much warmer. Once on the river he watched the sky gradually darken, lovely in the changed shading, the irresistibly slow work of night settling on all visible forms, erasing outlines, burying shapes deeper and deeper from his view. He'd found a better board to he used as a paddle and was making good progress. Several more days and he'd be out of Massachusetts and could telephone.

He thought about a favorite book growing up, *Paddle to the Sea*. A canoe carved by an Indian boy in the Upper Mid-West travels all the way to the Gulf of Mexico, overcoming many challenges, a small inspiration, a modicum of hope. He'd already rafted farther than any Pomford boy in history.

At around 11:00 PM he passed a raucous party on shore, he thought teenagers celebrating one of the first warm days of Spring, voices wonderful in their distinct clearness carrying over the water. How he would have liked to be with them! Ashore at dawn he stumbled upon a flood-damaged shack, door gone, holes in the roof, straw in one corner of the floor, a good place to sleep. As dusk was settling he was just getting up to continue his journey when again a farm dog found him, this one followed so closely by a farmer that he didn't have time to do the salami trick.

The farmer was a big tough looking guy, greasy black hair and a scowling sunburned face. "You're that boy they're looking for ain't you."

"What are you talking about?"

"I heard the description. It's you all right. And there's a big reward. Five thousand dollars."

Well. No way to buy his way out.

The farmer grabbed his arm in a powerful grip and marched him up to a somewhat dilapidated farmhouse, treating him like he was a wanted criminal. Dirty dishes filled the kitchen sink and the sofas were stained maybe from the dog or the farmer sitting with the dirt of the field, obviously no wife. The farmer let loose of his arm but watched him carefully as he called someone, maybe the local police.

When the farmer's call ended Justin asked him if he could use the phone to call someone. "Where are you calling?"

"New York."

"That's expensive. Long distance."

Justin said, "I'll give you twenty-five dollars if you'll let me make the call."

The farmer said, "Is this some of the money you stole?" Now he knew what he was wanted for.

"This is my money. I didn't steal anything."

The farmer looked at him skeptically but readily took the money. The condemned man was allowed one call, the farmer saying, "Only a few minutes. These calls cost a lot," then moseying to the other side of the kitchen to feed the dog its dinner, watching him all the time, no escape for the goose of the golden egg. It took some time for Justin to get through to Brian and some time talking in a low voice to convince Brian to accept his story. He'd spoken as fast as he could, telling Brian about the murder, who did it, and his danger. There was no time to fill him in on the rest of the story as the farmer grabbed the phone out of his hand.

Several hours later a squad car pulled up and out of it stepped Jenkins and one of the local policemen. A tremendous feeling of relief. He'd feared a pick up by Pomford personnel in the Head Mobile.

Jenkins said, "You caused us a lot of trouble. In the car and no shenanigans." Then turned to the farmer and said, "We'll send you the reward." No thanks to the farmer.

Nobody said anything on the ride back. They arrived at midnight and Jenkins sent him directly to his room. He was sure the instruction would have been different if the policeman hadn't still been standing there.

Jenkins said, "I'm having the watchman check your room. No sneaking out. I'll deal with you first thing tomorrow morning."

He thought to wake Moose because he wanted somebody to know he'd come back in case he mysteriously disappeared. Didn't. He was exhausted. He'd do it in the morning. At 5:00 AM he was awakened by Jenkins who was standing beside his bed and kicked himself for not alerting Moose. "Get dressed."

He went into the bathroom and sat on the toilet for almost fifteen minutes.

Jenkins came in. "What are you doing in there. Do I need to yank you out bare assed?"

"I'm constipated." Then he shaved, the slowest and most meticulous shave he'd ever given himself, Jenkins standing beside glowering at him. He strung out the tooth brushing another five minutes or more, putting the tooth paste on the toothbrush with surgical precision, brushing his teeth thoroughly and then brushing them again.

"What the hell you doing?" Jenkins asked.

"Maybe you heard. The other boys think I have bad breath so I have to brush a lot." Jenkins obviously had heard because he said nothing.

He dawdled back to his room as slowly as possible, drawled in taking off and neatly hanging up his pajamas, a departure from the usual throw-them-in-the-corner of the closet approach, dawdled in putting on his clothing, then looked out the window. "These aren't warm enough," and dawdle in putting on different clothing. Jenkins's glower had gone to visible anger, lips compressed, forehead furrowed, eyes half closed in a threatening gaze. "I'll give you thirty seconds. If you're not dressed I'll drag you out of here whatever you're wearing." When they exited the dorm he still hadn't seen another boy. Not good.

"Where are you taking me?"

"You'll find out."

They started out not in the direction of the nearby administration building but toward the river. It wouldn't take Jenkins long to walk him to the river. He'd be a second Pomford suicide, same situation, bullied boy commits suicide. He started pulling away and yelling, kicked as hard as he could at Jenkin's legs, even tried to punch him. The resistance didn't do much good. Jenkins was too strong.

Jenkins said, "Do it some more and I'll knock you the hell out and carry you. Maybe I should anyway. You're such a little shit, causing all this trouble." Jenkins balled his fist and Justin pulled back, but he didn't hit him.

A thin siren in the distance took Jenkin's attention. As they listened the siren got louder. A squad car roared down Main Street and screeched to a halt in front of the administration building, gravel flying. Justin yelled as loud as he could, squirming away to avoid Jenkin's fist. He did take one glancing blow.

Before Jenkins could do more Lieutenant Brian O'Reilly came up in a flat out run, hand on his holster. He must have driven full throttle through the night, siren blasting all the way.

"What do you think you're doing! Take your hands off him!"

"Trying to teach him a little discipline. It's none of your business." Jenkins released him, scowling angrily at Brian. Jenkins clenched his fists. Would he punch a cop? "Who the hell are you? What are you doing here?"

Justin moved to put Brian between him and Jenkins.

"Lieutenant of Detectives Brian O'Reilly, New York Police Department."

"New York. You've no jurisdiction here. Our problems are our problems. We don't allow outside interference. You may be a big guy in New York but here you're just a common intruder, an illegal intruder. If you know what's good for you you'll get back in your car and haul ass out of here."

Brian said with quiet assurance, "I do have jurisdiction. It's been cleared with the Massachusetts State Police and your own town police. The Massachusetts State Police should arrive shortly."

Jenkins said, "The Massachusetts police are friends. We support them. They support us. Whatever it is that you told them you're going to end up looking very stupid. They'll send you back to New York so fast it will make your head spin." Jenkins said this with a tone of arrogance, his lips curled in contempt, seemingly sure he was totally in the right or at least could not be shown to be wrong.

Brian said with the tone of one used to calming all situations. "Police in all jurisdictions cooperate to prevent murders. The Massachusetts Police were happy to have me join them to prevent Justin's murder. It took some convincing for Justin to persuade me a school of Pomford's stature was trying to kill a student. He did." He looked at Justin with a smile. "I'm here to make sure he's protected. Now, bring us to a room where we can talk." The last was said with a no-nonsense voice.

They ended up in a conference room off the lobby of the administration building, the room that Jenkins used when he was disciplining students. The Head arrived a short time later looking very annoyed, and simultaneously two Massachusetts State Police officers arrived, Sergeant Hildebrand and Patrolman Jackson, having come down Maine Street with siren blaring. Just before they were to start two fat Pomford policeman waddled in, looking like they'd been rousted from bed at an unaccustomed hour for all their yawns.

The Head, seated at the end of the table, said, "What's this about? We have a good working relationship with the Massachusetts State Police. Why didn't you contact us first? Here you come in here with your squad car disturbing the whole school. Totally unnecessary." The Head looked hard at each of the Massachusetts officers as though his irritation alone could cause them to leave. He ignored the Pomford officers and Brian.

Brian turned to Justin, giving him the floor.

Justin paused for dramatic effect looking individually at each person in the room, then said in his strongest voice, "There's been a murder. Mr. Benson was murdered last summer."

Neither the Head nor Jenkins reacted with surprise. Maybe they were expecting it, and Jenkins waved his hand dismissively. "Nonsense. Benson was kicked to death by a vicious horse. We had to put the horse down."

The Head said to Jenkins in seeming anger, "You brought me in at this hour to hear about someone kicked to death last summer, made me miss my carriage ride for this?" Either the Head didn't know about the murder or he was a very good actor. Justin assumed the latter.

Brian nodded to Justin to continue. He explained about finding the bat and how it was rigged.

Jenkins said, "Well. Do you have the bat? I don't believe the bat exists. All made up." Jenkins smirked when he said this.

"No. I don't have the bat. It was stolen."

The Head said, "The boy is delusional. You can't believe a single thing he says. We've had a lot of trouble with him. He won't join with the other boys."

Justin said, "That's because they bully me," and started to describe the bullying.

Brian cut him off saying, "We'll get to that later."

Sergeant Hildebrand of the Massachusetts State Police asked the Pomford police officers if there'd been an autopsy. The fatter of the two officers said, "No. He was kicked to death by a horse. There was no need to," causing Sergeant Hildebrand to shake his head in seeming disbelief.

Brian said, "It's not too late. He only died last summer, right. Was he cremated or buried?"

Jenkins said, "Buried."

"Then forensics should have little trouble determining whether he was killed by a horse's hoof or the bat that Justin describes. A horse's hoof would leave a semi-round indentation in the skull, a cut. A bat would crush the side of the head."

Sergeant Hildebrand nodded. For the first time Justin saw Jenkins look uncomfortable, a shadow of fear in his eyes.

Brian turned again to Justin but before Brian could ask him Justin blurted out in what he hoped was an authoritative voice, "I know who the murders are." This is the moment he'd been waiting for. He looked right at Jenkins, not flinching, "Mr. Jenkins is one killer. There is a second, Jose Ramos, the stable manager, and maybe a third. I heard Mr. Brown say he was going to kill Mr. Benson for fooling around with his wife. He definitely meant it."

Jenkins said, "Absolutely ridiculous," and glanced over at the Head as though seeking confirmation.

Justin continued, "I know it was Mr. Jenkins. Somebody had to take my bat out of the athletic equipment locker to use it to kill Mr. Benson. Mr. Jenkins has the only key."

Jenkins said, "Others have keys."

The Sergeant Hildebrand asked, "Who."

Jenkins glanced at the Head.

The Head said, "There may be a second key. I have a lot of keys. If there is, I don't remember using it."

The Sergeant said, "Please look for it as soon as possible and let us know. Where is your key, Mr. Jenkins?"

It was attached to his belt with some other keys.

The Sergeant took it from him saying, "Don't want anyone making duplicate keys at this point, do we?"

Jenkins said in a subdued voice, looking down at the table, "Somebody else could have grabbed the bat when the equipment locker was open."

Justin said, "No way. This was the middle of the summer. No one was around. Anyway, you always watch like a hawk. No one takes anything from the locker without you checking it out. Besides, nobody would have been caught dead with that ridiculous looking bat."

Brian said to Justin, "What about Ramos?"

"He had to have been in on it. Mr. Benson was found behind Imperator. Imperator was saddled. Only Ramos could have saddled Imperator. The prior stable manager, Joe, said Imperator was one of the most vicious horses he'd ever known. Ramos even saddled

Imperator for Mr. Robinson, his owner. Mr. Robinson thought it was too dangerous. I know Ramos and Mr. Jenkins are good friends as I've seen them enjoying themselves together."

The Sergeant said to Patrolman Jackson, "Pick up Ramos for questioning. Better hurry. He might have heard the squad cars coming in and be high-tailing it. And check the Imperator story with Mr. Robinson."

Jenkins had slumped in his chair to a smaller self, shoulders hunched forward over clasped hands, a supplicant or maybe trying to disappear, looking around at everyone like a trapped animal, one of Bronc's muskrats in a cage. With a high strained voice Jenkins said, "Why would I kill Benson? I liked him. We were friends. I had no motive."

Justin said, "I don't understand it all but I think the file cabinet in the Head's office has something to do with it." The Head visibly stiffened.

"The cabinet contains a lot of stuff about Nazis. One of our teachers is a Nazi, Mr. Hauptmann. I think he's wanted for war crimes. His real name is Gerhard Mulder. He was a senior guy in all that killing of Jews in Germany. Maybe he helped kill Mr. Benson, too."

The Head shook himself in seeming disbelief, his normally white skin even whiter, face going increasingly grim, mouth compressed so strongly his lips disappeared. He seemed about ready to say something but didn't, frozen motionless like a deer immobilized by fear as the hunters approached. The cops glanced round the table at each other, startled, apparently realizing this was much bigger than a simple murder.

The Sergeant said to Jackson, "On the way to grabbing Ramos call in and get somebody on Hauptmann or Mulder, whatever his name is. Bring him in for questioning."

Justin continued, "The file cabinet has a big padlock. The key is under the saucer of the pot on the bookshelf. You can't miss the pot. It has a dead plant in it."

He'd never seen such hate as he saw in the look the Head gave him. Ahab was destroyed. Joy swelled up in him. It was almost worth the bullying.

The Sargent said, "I have a judge I can go to. We'll have search warrants for Ramos's house and the file cabinet within an hour, probably sooner. Dr. Cranch, don't leave this room until your office has been searched. And one of you two Pomford officers post yourself in Dr. Cranch's office to see no one goes in. We'll check out that Brown fellow, too."

Justin said, "I wouldn't have a Pomford officer guard the Head's office. They're under the Head's thumb. That may be why there was no autopsy."

Sergeant Hildebrand stared at Justin for a moment and then said, "Okay. I'll bring in more backup and Justin, we're going to need a statement from you. Why don't you put it together in your dorm room with Lieutenant O'Reilly. The Lieutenant can get it sworn in New York and mailed to us. We're going to need your deposition and you'll probably have to testify."

"Fine. I'd like that."

Sargent Hildebrand smiled at Justin, reached over and gave him a slap on the back. "I probably won't see you again. You engineered about the best bust I've ever had. Congratulations. Really fantastic. No one on the force could have done better. You'd be a great police detective. If you ever want to give up your amateur status come see me. Okay?" He let out a laugh.

Justin said, "Okay," and laughed with him.

Wow. What an unbelievable day. Best day of his life.

Justin bounced out of the room, the happiest he could remember being, thinking about how he was finally going to get his mother some deserved retribution. Would he ever be able to tell her?

Back in his dorm room he took more than three hours to complete his statement. He wanted to capture everything in detail and particularly focused on the woman. He reported her close relationship with Hauptmann as observed through the Head's window, played up her use of Gerhard in her note indicating she knew of the switch of identities and the implication from her note that she knew of Gerhard's Holocaust activities when she supported his entry to the US. Then the breakup with John Chandler for "political reasons," they should interview him, and her involvement in the Silver Shirts. Saving the best to last, he concluded with Mulder killing Hauptmann and that she may have known about it, thus she was sheltering a murderer as well as a war criminal. It was a long list and he was pleased when he saw what he'd written.

When he finished the statement Brian said, "Get your clothes together. You didn't belong here in the first place. You certainly don't belong here now." Justin considered how he felt about it all. Exhausted, he'd had little sleep, certainly exhilarated, and yes, a little famous. How good was that? He turned to Brian and focused on his eyes as Mr. Benson had taught him, tried to project his gratitude. "I would have died but for you. They planned to drown me in the river, make it look like a suicide Thank you for believing me."

"You're a very persuasive fellow. Lieutenants of police don't leave town in the middle of an important case as I did. And they sure don't charge across two states in the middle of the night at up to ninety miles hour chasing a possibility with no proof. Just one phone call maybe five or seven minute, that's all you needed. Remarkable." He let out a loud laugh and clapped Justin on the back. "That scene in the admin building really killed me. Jenkins and the Headmaster looked like they wanted to hide under the table or maybe die on the spot. Skewered by a sixteen year old. I'll never forget it." He let out another boisterous laugh.

The destination was Aunt Gertrude's in Greenwich. Justin had given Brian her telephone number and he'd called while Justin was completing his statement. He was to stay with her and Uncle Ben as long as he wanted. Best news ever! On the way Justin filled Brian in on the bullying.

Brian shook his head, and said, visibly angry, his jaw clenched, "You're one tough kid. Most wouldn't have survived. That was terrible! Organized abuse. I thought I'd seen it all."

Justin said ruefully, "Of course, I almost didn't survive."

"Well, you did, and I hope you're proud of yourself. I've never heard of a boy your age solving a murder. On top of that, a Nazi war criminal. I don't think anyone on the entire New York police force has ever uncovered a war criminal. You've got something to brag about the rest of your life. And thinking about that bullying, you ought to add it to your statement, if you haven't done so."

"All right. I think what actually happened was that the woman wanted Pomford to be as hard on me as possible, and when the bullying developed the Head stood aside and maybe encouraged it. I haven't been thinking the woman or the Head invented death breath, but maybe she did, a clever name. I don't think I'll ever know for sure where the name came from. And I don't think I'll ever be able to prove the woman's role in the bullying."

"Put it down anyway. You were badly abused and the Head allowed it to happen."

"One other thing. The woman got my father to do some things to put my mother in a mental institution. They worked it together. It didn't involve Pomford. Should I put it down?"

"Tell me what happened. It occurred in New York so it's in our jurisdiction."

After Justin told the story, Brian said, "My God, you went through a hell of lot. It will be up to the DA. He probably won't prosecute based upon your testimony about the phone call alone, even if the diary is found. It will depend upon whether the hospital will back up your story. I'll contact them."

Brian looked at him in silence for a few moments then spoke in a thoughtful tone. "You don't know it but what you went through is going to put you in good stead the rest of your life. Life brings bad stuff. Happens to everybody. Everybody eventually has bad stuff. But with the crap you've taken you're going to be better prepared to handle it than many. I see it all the time in police work. Some people get a lot of challenges in life. When some new bad thing comes along they deal with it and march ahead. Others have had soft, orderly lives and no serious challenges. They get one and fall apart. All that bullying has given you a protective layer. Some adults never develop one. The boys of Pomford may have taken advantage of you, but you're going to have an important advantage over them in life."

Justin said, "Okay, but it sure was a hard way to get an advantage. Don't recommend it to anyone." Brian laughed, reached over and gave him a friendly punch on the shoulder.

He started thinking about the woman. He could picture her when she heard the news, probably a phone call from the Head. She would maintain her composure in front of his father, not acknowledging its devastating effect on her. She was an excellent actress. Then she'd go into her bedroom and let it all out, her pouty mouth opening in dismay and then outrage, a long rant at everybody and everything and particularly at him, hitting her table in anger, he'd seen her pound tables before, kicking her silk covered waste basket around the room. He hoped she'd tear her hair out. Later back to his father pretending what happened at Pomford was nothing of importance. "I guess we'll have to find a new school for Justin. Pomford isn't as good anymore." Then on to other subjects that she pretended were more important to her, perhaps parties, dinners, or upcoming trips.

So his father would suspect nothing when the authorities arrived, a knock on the door of the co-op, his father or the woman opening the door, New York police or perhaps the feds. Maybe she would first parade her arrogance to them. "How dare you! Intruding on our privacy like this. Don't you know who we are? When my good friend Police Chief Callahan hears about it you'll end up in the worst part of Harlem." Or maybe she would try to sweet talk them, all smiles. "Let's sit down together and discuss what brings you here. I certainly have nothing to hide. I'm a great fan of the police and will do anything I can to help your investigation. It's a hot day. Would you like a beer." Whichever way she took the conversation at a certain point she'd realize she was in serious trouble. The police would start asking her about Mulder. She'd probably deny knowing him and they would bring out her letter to the Head about helping him. Then they would ask whether she knew it was illegal to bring someone into the US under a false identity, that there were serious criminal penalties. Then they would question her on her knowledge that Mulder was a Nazi responsible for killing many Jews, that she was involved in sheltering a war criminal. Panic would set in. He wished he was there at the exact moment she realized the enormity of his revenge. He wished he was there to see his father's shock and dismay as he looked on.

Brian said, "What are you smiling about?

"Nothing."

No more secrets. No more Ham's curse.

EPILOG

Justin was enrolled by Aunt Gertrude at Andover for his senior year and twice was called from school to testify. The first time was in the trial of Jenkins and Ramos, who were tried together. Later it was in the trial of Mulder. Ramos had turned state's evidence and named Mulder as the killer, the man who wielded the bat. Justin testified that Jenkins had the only key to the equipment locker and had to be the one who took the bat. This was corroborated by several other witnesses. He also testified to the finding of the bat with horseshoe affixed, a story confirmed in depositions of the three boys who discovered the bat at the river. Jenkins was sentenced to thirty years as an accessory to murder and Ramos twenty. A German investigation used dental records to verify Hauptmann's body was in the grave previously thought to be Mulder's and concluded that Hauptmann had been murdered by Mulder. Justin received congratulatory calls both from Brian and from Sargent Hildebrand. An international wrestling match developed between Germany and Massachusetts for the right to try Mulder. Massachusetts held firm. One of its own had been killed. Mulder was given the death penalty. He died in the Massachusetts electric chair on March 15, 1959.

Unlike the book, Captain Ahab escaped. The DA charged the Head with masterminding the scheme to bring Mulder into the country. The result was an outpouring of support for the Head from leading citizens of Massachusetts and the rich and powerful across the country. The DA bowed to the pressure and withdrew the charges on the basis the Head hadn't signed any of the immigration documents. They never were able to charge him as an accessory to

Benson's murder as Jenkins and Hauptmann didn't testify against him and Ramos, who was talking, had no direct contact with the Head. As for the bullying, they couldn't prove his involvement in it.

The Head was immediately retired. His replacement was the number two at Exeter, a man of Italian Jewish ancestry, Jacob Fortini, a large departure from the Head's good breeding standard.

Much to his disappointment, Justin was not called upon to testify in the trial of the woman. The charge against her was that she had knowingly misrepresented that Mulder was Hauptmann on immigration forms. Justin followed the trial closely from Andover. Aunt Gertrude gave him daily commentary by telephone. Justin learned that while the maximum penalty for her offense was ten years, most of this type of immigration case resulted in a suspended sentence. That's why he was delighted when she was given five years.

Prosecution of the woman for what she did to his mother turned out to be a wash-out, as Brian predicted. The mental institution wouldn't acknowledge his father's abuse, probably fearing being held liable for failing to report it.

His father was ostracized from New York society, resigned his clubs, sold the co-op and retreated in disgrace to the original family home in North Carolina, an animal hiding in its hole. Good breeding meant nothing, never had.

The series of trials created a media frenzy under the banner headline *Holocaust Murders*, the New York Times and Massachusetts papers following each trial on a day-by-day basis with many articles linking Benson's murder, the murder of Hauptmann, and what they called the gang of five— the woman, the Head, Mulder, Jenkins, and Ramos. A field day for sensationalism with a leading woman in New York society, the head of one of the foremost prep schools in America, a Nazi war criminal and the Silver Shirts. He was sometimes mentioned and got a modicum on notoriety at Andover though it didn't seem to boost him much on the popularity ladder.

He visited his mother three times in the summer of 1955. Each time she cried when she saw him and cried when he left. He cried along with her. He told her what had happen and the woman's downfall, though he was not sure she understood.

Justin prospered at Andover, making many friends using Mr. Benson's methods. He matriculated to Yale. Fawn, who'd gone to Smith, was his guest for the first big football weekend. He was sure she was the most beautiful girl on campus. His Yale roommate, Bronco, agreed.